Fall Creek Books is an imprint of Cornell University Press dedicated to making available again classic books that document the history, culture, natural history, and folkways of New York State. Presented in new paperback editions that faithfully reproduce the contents of the original editions, Fall Creek Books titles will appeal to all readers interested in New York and the state's rich past. Some of the books published under this imprint reflect the sensibilities and attitudes of an earlier era; these views do not necessarily reflect those of Cornell University Press. For a complete listing of titles published under the Fall Creek Books imprint, please visit the Cornell University Press website: www.cornellpress.cornell.edu.

NO DRUMS

A Historical Novel

E. R. EASTMAN

FALL CREEK BOOKS
AN IMPRINT OF CORNELL UNIVERSITY PRESS
Ithaca and London

FOREWORD TO THE 2011
FALL CREEK BOOKS EDITION
by Carol Kammen

The marriage of imagination with fact begets historical fiction. The resulting stories often illuminate what is known, suggest what might have been and, to our delight, portray actual and imagined characters facing dilemmas of their day. In the depiction of their lives we find timeless conundrums and struggles that shed light on our own time; this is especially true for those of us who inhabit the same land and places in which the historical story unfolds. At the same time, historical fiction personalizes the past, seeing other times through constructed personalities or characters. Historical fiction calls forth archival facts, fashioning them on a stage for a larger human story to unfold.

The handmaids of historical fiction are folklore and the artifacts of material culture—houses, wagons, and guns—as well as the technical know-how of making and working. People mark trails, do laundry, tend soldiers wounded by cannon fire, and experience childbirth with little medical aid, and fiction sets these tasks into action in their historical context. The setting of historical fiction is another time—sometimes on a landscape that is familiar, often in a place less explicitly known. The motivation for historical fiction is to explain a different era. Stephen Crane commented about his 1895 novel *The Red Badge of Courage* that reading cold history was not enough because he wanted to know what it was like to be there. Historical fiction fleshes out the record to bring facts and events to life. This was also the goal of Michael Shaara in his classic Civil War novel, *The Killer Angels* (1974).

The best historical fiction illuminates the past, taking

the known record and filling it with people who live their lives amidst the conflicts and struggles of their age. These might involve political disputes, hard economic realities, divisions of social status, separations and subordinations based on race and gender, and problems posed by emerging technologies and their opposite, obsolescence.

The novels of E. R. Eastman are in keeping with what is best in historical fiction. He made his characters come alive in and through the conflicts of their times while endowing them with individual traits and predilections. Eastman's work is exemplary of the techniques and value of historical fiction. His novels are worth reading today for their fast-paced stories and their link with the regional past.

Historians are this way and that way about historical fiction. Some read it eagerly, while others disdain it. There is little middle ground for the academically trained. Those who regard historical fiction with suspicion have powerful arguments on their side. They point out that the truth is usually more interesting than any imaginative presentation of it; they complain that historical fiction twists what is known to have been into something that often couldn't have been. They charge, with some cause, that fiction too easily approaches the past from a presentist point of view—characters set in an earlier time are often shown acting with modern sensibilities and concerns. These charges are commonplace and often true.

Those who appreciate historical fiction recognize that there is much merit in writing that is a pleasure to read and accessible to a broad public. They also recognize that historical fiction becomes a way for people to understand the past, especially the local past. Fiction allows writers to give voice to individuals who are often not well represented in the archives—because they were not literate, their letters and diaries were not collected, or the roles they played in events kept them from recording history even though they were part of it. Slaves were disadvantaged by lack of literacy. Women were not considered important enough to write about in anything but a stylized manner. Native Americans did not always record their own view of past events. The poor, tenants, those who moved on—all often left scant trace of their lives. These varying viewpoints, however, give writers the opportunity to describe events from fictional characters' vantage points, and theirs can become a vivid account of being in the midst of things. Brian Hall's *I Should be Extremely Happy in Your Company* (2003), about the travels of Meriwether Lewis and William Clark to the western shore of this continent, is a wonderful example of historical fiction. Hall wrote that he "(perhaps foolishly) rushes in where historians refrain from treading for lack of information and established facts."

Cornell historian S. Cushing Strout keenly observed that the artist has no monopoly on imagination and the historian no monopoly on the past. The historical record—both in what it says about the past and where it is silent—is fertile ground for both camps, each possessing different talents that allow them to explore and explain the lives of people who once lived in the places we now inhabit.

Despite debates over the merits of historical fiction, then, much of the reading public embraces historical fiction, especially when the story is well told, the characters vivid, and the setting close to home.

Edward Roe Eastman, known all his writing life as E. R. Eastman, was born in Berkshire, Tioga County, New York, in 1885. He attended Cornell and in 1926 graduated with a degree from the College of Agriculture. He worked as a teacher and school principal in Interlaken, Richford, and Newark Valley, and he was employed as an agricultural agent in Delaware County. Eastman was one of the founders of the Dairyman's League Cooperative and editor of its newsletter from 1917 to 1922. In 1922 he became editor of *American Agriculturist*, a position he held until 1947. Along with his daily editorial work, he found time to write a popular column, "Eastman's Chestnuts," and he authored thirteen historical novels. Eastman's historical interests equaled his desire to promote rural life, both its joys and hardships. His 1956 book, *Walking the Broad Highway*, and his last book, *Growing Up in Horse and Buggy Days* (1963), extolled rural life. Beyond his work as an author and editor, Eastman served on the New York State Board of Regents, and he was a trustee of both Ithaca College and Cornell University. Eastman's papers, which exhibit all aspects of his amazingly productive life, are contained in twenty-two boxes in the Carl A. Kroch Library at Cornell University (Collection #3105).

In the foreword to his novel *Not With Dreams* (1954), Eastman wrote that he "tried to revive, dramatize and preserve memories of men and events that laid the foundations of the American republic, with the hope that at least a few readers will come to have a little better appreciation of the blood and iron that it took to build the foundations of America." He drew from many sources, but perhaps most important were the experiences of his own family. His father and several other relatives had served in the Civil War, and Eastman grew up listening to their stories and to those of his grandmothers, who remained at home with children to feed and care for but with few resources. Eastman wrote that he longed to "pay tribute to the men and women behind the lines" of the Civil War and of other armed conflicts who, without fanfare, persevered. He also noted that in his novels, especially *No Drums* (1951), the characters were fictional but the "incidents, situations, and adventures are based on true stories from the lives of people" he once knew.

Eastman was drawn to the history of New York State. He was not alone in his interest. During the middle years of the twentieth century, Samuel Hopkins Adams, a journalist, would write *Canal Town* (1944), and Walter Edmonds, author of a number of historical novels, would pen *Drums Along the Mohawk* (1936) and *In the Hands of the Senecas* (1947). All three writers centered their dramas on moments of historical change. They created stories that drew readers into the social and private lives of characters in order to understand events, the land, and the era.

The land is particularly important to these writers, who stressed that we live amidst a vivid past. Eastman, Adams, and Edmonds featured the waterways, lakes, and sloping hills of New York. The New York of their fiction is the gateway to the interior of the nation—the mighty Mohawk River flowing west, the startling Finger Lakes resting like proofreaders' marks on the land, the powerful Genesee River, and Lake Erie, portal to the western horizon. But for these writers the landscape was as forbidding as it was inviting. They drew artistic inspiration from it but also knew that it was not easily mastered. Passage to the interior was difficult. The land was fecund but also marked with swamps and lowlands that bred mosquitoes and the miasmal illnesses they carried. The land for these New York writers was a setting for human action and, at times, a significant agent as well.

The land was also a lure and goad to action. By a treaty made by the English and the Six Nations before the American Revolution, lands in central and western New York belonged to the Iroquois. The outbreak of war forced the Indians to take sides, and most allied themselves with the English. The Iroquois and their land then became a military target. In 1779, General George Washington sent an invading force under the command of General John Sullivan, aided by General James Clinton, into Iroquoia to destroy crops, take prisoners, and push the Iroquois back from frontier settlements. Eastman told this story of invasion, remembered as the Sullivan Campaign, in *The Destroyers* (1946). He revisits some of the characters from that book in *The Settlers* (1950), a story centered on Constant and Nate Williams; their old friend Joel Decker, a wilderness scout; and friends and family who migrated in 1808 into the Lakes Country. In the years between the Revolutionary War and their trek west, they lived on a rented farm in Orange County. Although they got by, they did not improve their economic standing. The family knew that, under the circumstances, they would never do more than struggle, and that only the landowner would prosper. Loaded with debt and weary with endless toil and lack of prospects, they struck out west. These imagined characters meet up with historical figures, notably James and William Wadsworth (land agents along the Genesee) and Iroquois leaders Red Jacket and Little Beard. Eastman sets the family's pioneer story in the context of historical events, thereby creating a tale of adventure and a depiction of life in central New York when this was the American frontier.

The Settlers brings alive not only a varied cast of characters but also dilemmas of ethics and politics. The book begins with the problem of tenancy on eastern lands. The solution—westward migration—results in heart-rending separations when those who set out leave family and the known world behind. The book also explores political differences, the material difficulties of creating new homes on a frontier, and the social struggles of developing new communities. The novel sympathetically depicts the situation of women in the early nineteenth century and shows that, amidst limited choices, women made clear their worth to a community. Eastman is surprising in his treatment of some of his female characters; he portrays their wisdom and autonomy while not imposing on them the characteristics of later times.

Another dilemma running through *The Settlers* concerns the fate of the Iroquois, for whom the land was the provider of sustenance and the foundation of their culture. After Sullivan's Campaign, Iroquois society was shattered. The plight of the dispersed, who witness the sale and farming of their land, is eloquently depicted, although Eastman's sympathies are clearly with the newly arrived settlers.

Eastman portrays Indians as remnants of a culture out-of-step with the new national vision. Indeed, Eastman is convinced of the fundamental correctness of the geographic and political expansion of the United States. He sometimes shows the Indians' usefulness to settlers; Tall Chief, a fictional character, observes that the newcomers would have starved if the "red man" hadn't fed them, shown them how to use fish in the ground to make crops grow, or taught them how to hunt and how to live in winter. Ultimately, however, Eastman dismisses the Indians' legitimate right to the land; the Iroquois are depicted as impediments to the progress of the white people moving in. Clearly seeing a dismal future, Tall Chief complains that the white men raised hatchets against Indians, took their land, killed their game, leveled the forests, and drove them back. "Red men have no place to go," laments Tall Chief. While this imaginary Indian has his say, there is little sympathy for his position from the white settlers in the book. And, as Eastman makes clear in the novel, the future and the land could never belong to the Indians.

In *No Drums* (1951), Eastman moves ahead in time and takes readers to what some call the "second founding" of the United States. The novel takes place during the American Civil War and, set in central New York, it is populated with people "at home" while military battles rage to the south. Eastman is concerned in this book with the "homes and hearts of the folks behind the battle lines," the men who did not go to fight and the women who had to keep farms and nurture children. For this story he draws directly on his family's experience. Foremost among the problems, though often overlooked by local historians, were the political battles between the Peace Democrats, or Copperheads, and Republicans, who supported the full prosecution of the war. Eastman also wrote of the emotional and physical toll that the war had on women as they carried on the necessary work of farm and home; coped with loneliness in households missing husbands, fathers, and sons; and faced uncertain futures. The female characters are strong, but they clearly live in a world where much is determined for them, particularly by the marriages they made. Indeed, the struggles faced by the characters in the historical novel range from the strife of political ideology to the troubles caused by personal duplicity and greed. *No Drums*—at its heart a love story between Mark and Ann, showing what draws them together and what causes a break in their relationship—is a realistic depiction of the conflicts created by the war.

Eastman reflected his own times as well as the past in his historical novels. Writing over the course of four decades (from the 1920s through the 1950s, from the Great Depression through World War II), he was an avid proponent of "the American way of life." Eastman's depiction of his characters will not live up to today's linguistic standards; in these books, we find that women and Indians occupy stereotyped roles and are spoken about rather dismissively. His language gives us a way of judging changes in attitudes about minorities and women in twentieth-century America. Eastman uses language that we reject as inappropriate today. His writing is not always graceful but is certainly heartfelt. As a stylist, he is more storyteller than artist.

What many people respond to in historical fiction, including Eastman's novels, is a sense of authenticity. Readers want to learn about the items found in a farmhouse and how they were used. They also want to learn about the action of an ox cart and the workings of a musket. These details are found aplenty in Eastman's novels, along with information on the gathering in of maple syrup, mustering for war, and the state of medical knowledge in the eighteenth and nineteenth centuries. Eastman incorporates knowledge of the political, military, and social history of a period with an understanding of the traditional ways detailed in Jared Van Wagenen's widely popular *Golden Age of Homespun* (1960).

The richness of Eastman's fiction about central New York lies in its sense of the social, psychological, and political dimensions of history. His novels bring to life our shared past, be it that of the Civil War home front portrayed in *No Drums* or the western frontier of *The Settlers*. His characters are alive, believable, and complex. At the same time, Eastman provides a complicated picture of the eighteenth-century frontier and of economic and social problems in the first decades of the twentieth century.

Reviving these novels gives readers a chance to engage in the dilemmas of people of the past, those who lived and worked and loved and fought in central New York. In E. R. Eastman's books we encounter that startling sensation of knowing the places he writes about and finding those places occupied by people of another day, yet not so different from us in their human needs and responses. These people are surprisingly similar and closely related, in so many ways, to our own current human condition. Eastman's vibrant stories keep alive our public memory and deepen our shared sense of place.

I shall never forget one Decoration Day in the long ago when, as a very small boy, I watched the parade of our local Grand Army of the Republic, the Women's Relief Corps, and most of the other residents of the small town marching to the cemetery a mile north of the village to decorate the graves of the soldier dead. At the head of the procession rode my father as Commander of the local GAR, very much the soldier who, for the day, had discarded his farm clothes to wear once again his faded blue uniform and military hat.

The mist of the years has never dimmed my memory of my boyish pride in my father, the cavalryman, who rode his horse that day as I knew he must have ridden into a hundred battles and skirmishes in the conflict between the states. I remember how I urged my mother to hurry the old farm plug that was hitched to the democrat wagon in which we were riding, so that we could get up near the head of the procession to get a closer view of Father and to hear the martial strains of the band that led the parade.

Father, three uncles, both of my grandfathers, and many of the neighbors and friends around us when I was a boy were Civil War veterans, and I grew up in the atmosphere of "fighting it over." As I listened to their stories of the battles and the Great Adventure in which they had participated, I wondered sometimes about the women on the home front who, without benefit of adventure, glory or the beat of drum, had kept the home fires burning. When my uncles and my grandfathers went to war, they left behind them Grandmother Eastman and Grandmother Roe, with a number of small children and little means of support. Hard as were the lonesomeness, the suffering and sacrifice of the soldiers, the lot of the women left behind was still harder to bear. It was up them—the millions of women in both North and South—to keep together the bodies and souls of themselves and their children as best they could. The women, children, and older men on the home front had more than their share of privation, hard work, loneliness and anxiety.

Nor need we confine this tribute to the women of anyone war. Being personal again, I am moved to mention the endless days of worry of my wife with two of her sons in the Second World War, and that of a daughter-in-law whose husband was gone for weary years with MacArthur in the Pacific.

All of my life I have wished for the opportunity to pay tribute to the men and women behind the lines, for their self-sacrificing, uncomplaining contribution to whatever it is, if anything, that we gain from war. *No Drums* is an attempt to pay that well deserved tribute to the home front in all wars. Although the story deals with life during the Civil War period, it is just as timely as now, and will be while men continue to settle their arguments with the sword. It is a story of how people worked, loved and lived under a great strain. Being a novel, most of the characters are, of course, fictional, but the theme and most of the incidents, situations and adventures are based on true stories from the lives of people whom I once knew.   E.R.E.

CHAPTER I

MARK WILSON pulled his head out of the cow's flank, stopped milking, leaned back on his stool, and gave himself up to daydreams, meantime absently rubbing the nail of his forefinger over his upper lip. He was thinking about the party he was going to that night. It was about time, he thought, that he had a little fun. Seemed as if there'd been nothing lately but work and worry. He was darn sick of the heavy work in the woods all winter, and the way he felt now he never wanted to see a cow again!

All this talk about war got a fellow down, too. What did he have to do with the niggers and States' rights? He wanted to get married, but how could he marry and then rush right off to war?

And now he had another worry. What had got into Ann lately? She was never twice the same. She didn't use to be like that. They had always got along fine without bickering as they did now all of the time. He had been sure then that Ann loved him, but now he wasn't so sure. Sometimes she was just like she used to be; then the very next time he saw her, she would be cold and distant. Maybe that was the way with females. Maybe Ann thought that was the way to keep up his interest, but it darn well wasn't. He liked his friends where he could find them and depend on them!

Mark started milking again, this time with one hand. With the other he continued to stroke his lip meditatively. Then as a thought gripped him, he stopped milking again. Come to think of it, Ann hadn't begun to be difficult until that Henry Bain started to notice her.

"That's it!" he exclaimed. "That's just it!"

"What in heaven's name are you talking about?" demanded his father, who had come from the other end of the stable with a pail of milk. Embarrassed, Mark made no answer, and George Wilson paused to say, sternly:

"You're doing a lot of mooning around here lately. I wish you'd get your mind on your work!"

Down the line of cows where they were milking, Mark could hear his two younger brothers snickering.

"I'll kill those brats!" he muttered, angrily.

The milking done and the cows fed, George Wilson and his three sons went into supper. On pegs by the kitchen door they hung their caps and coats, covered with cow hair and smelling not unpleasantly of the stable. Then the boys stood by while their father crossed the kitchen to wash at the big sink. After pouring some cold water from a pail into the wash basin, he handed the empty pail to Mark so that he might fill it at the pump in the yard. Then, warming the cold water in the basin with hot water from the iron teakettle on the back of the kitchen stove, George Wilson lowered his whiskered face close to the basin and, dipping both hands into the water, thoroughly scrubbed his neck and face, making blowing noises through his hands as he scrubbed them vigorously up and down over his mouth and nostrils.

Although Mark had seen his father go through this ritual a hundred times, it never ceased to fascinate him. After briskly drying his face on the big roller towel, George Wilson strode across the kitchen and sat down at the head of the long table. At its other end sat his wife Nancy, perched on the edge of her chair, her small figure almost obscured by the tall teapot at her right hand. Soon they were all seated, the children ranged like stairs on both sides of the table— Mark and his two brothers and three sisters. Mark was twenty; Charles, sixteen, and Tom, twelve. Ellen was ten; Elizabeth, eight, and Hattie, four.

It was April, and although the long winter evenings were past, the darkness in the kitchen was only partly conquered by a coal oil lamp at each end of the table and the bracket lamp near the sink. Tired and hungry after their long, hard day, the first order of business with everyone was to eat. The fare was plain—boiled potatoes, salt pork, milk gravy, homemade bread, butter from the dairy, and blackberries picked by the children the summer before and canned.

The first pangs of his hunger satisfied, George Wilson raised his head, glanced worriedly at his family and then addressed his wife:

"Well, Nancy, we're in for it."

She knew perfectly well what he meant, but she snapped back:

"In for what? Why don't you say what you mean, Mr. Wilson?"

The children looked at her in surprise, for they were not used to hearing her snap at their father. Apparently he took no notice, for he answered her mildly:

"I was at the post office when the stage came in from Owego tonight. They say the rebels have fired on Fort Sumter. That means war!"

Making no comment but apparently to relieve her agitation, his wife jumped up from the table and began clearing off the dishes, assisted by the two older girls. George Wilson again let his glance wander over his family and then, as if all of his fifty years weighed heavily on him, he too got up from his chair, walked slowly across the kitchen to the mantel behind the stove and began to fill his pipe from the box of tobacco he always kept there. Watching him, Mark thought:

"Even if the house was on fire, Pa would fill his pipe and get it going before he tried to put out the fire."

Then Mark went up to the bedroom under the eaves that he shared with his brothers and began to get ready for his party, thinking dejectedly that even his best Sunday-go-to-meeting suit wasn't much of an improvement over his old everyday clothes, except perhaps it didn't reek quite so much of the cow stable. Mark couldn't remember when he had had a new suit, and this one had shrunk so that his long arms and legs stuck so far out of it that it made him look like a veritable Ichabod Crane. Taking his time to change his clothes while trying to get up his courage to ask his father for the loan of the horse and buggy, he paused to look at himself in the cracked looking glass in the old bureau. He saw a tall boy, thin and hard from work and weather. Red hair, inclined to curl, matched a red face covered with freckles. His generous mouth and his intensely blue eyes now reflected his dissatisfaction and disgust with his clothes, his appearance, and everything in general.

But finally, realizing that if he was going to the party at all he would have to get along, he went downstairs into the

sitting room where his father sat smoking his pipe and reading the weekly paper that the stage had brought up that
day from Owego, the county seat. So absorbed was George
Wilson in the paper, which was filled with war news, that
Mark had to speak twice before his father looked up and
said:

"What is it?"

"I was wondering—" said Mark, hesitatingly, "if I could
have old Molly and the buggy to take Ann over to the party
at John Hover's tonight?"

Impatiently his father pushed his steel-framed spectacles
up over his brow and scowled.

" 'Tisn't over a mile to Hover's. What in the world do you
want with a horse?"

"It's muddy, Pa," explained Mark, "and I hate to ask a
girl to walk in the mud."

"Won't hurt her a bit! Young folks are getting too soft.
I didn't have a horse and buggy and I lived a good deal
farther from your mother than you are from Ann. Besides,"
he continued, "the team's tired. You know they are. They've
been working all day. They need their rest."

He pulled his spectacles down again and raised the paper.
Mark left the room, banging the door behind him, and
marched off down the road to Ann's house, anger and frustration evident in every step that he took. But the feeling
of spring in the air, a bright full moon and the fact that he
was going to see his girl soon restored his spirits. By the
time he got to his destination, he didn't even mention his
lack of conveyance, but took Ann's hand and they started
for Hover's along the side of the muddy road.

Ann talked gaily about Spring's coming and the many
different birds she had seen that day. She bubbled with
good spirits and enthusiasm, and Mark was content to listen
and to watch her animated face as she skipped along beside
him. As he always did when she was in this mood, he thought
how lucky he was to have her. Covering her brown hair was
a gay little bonnet, from under which curly tendrils escaped
to frame her face. Slender, strong and willowy, with merry
brown eyes, a wide mouth with upturned corners, and a
freckled nose which could only be described as pug, she was
an extremely attractive girl, especially so to Mark, who

loved her. Her disposition was merry but mercurial. She was easily provoked to quarrel at one moment, but was immediately sorry for any hurt that she caused to others.

Noticing Mark's silence after a while, Ann said:

"Why are you so quiet, Mark? Mad about something?"

Instead of answering her question directly, Mark said:

"Ann, you know all about this war talk. What would you think about my going to war?"

"Wouldn't like it," she answered, promptly.

"Well, I wouldn't, either," he admitted, "but things seem to be getting pretty hot. Down in the village the other night I heard some of the older men talking about it and they seemed to think that a lot of us will have to go pretty soon."

"Those old fellows ought to have to go themselves! It seems to me from what history I've studied, that's always the way. The old men get us into war, and you young fellows have to fight it—you and the women who have to stay home and keep things going while you're gone."

"Aw, now, Ann, that's not quite fair. What're you going to do when the other side forces you into war? There comes a time, I guess, when you have to fight."

"I don't believe that time's come yet," retorted Ann, tossing her head. "I don't even know what it's all about 'cept what two or three old cranks around the neighborhood like Bill Leonard say. He's always talking about freeing the slaves. I'll bet if he owned some, he wouldn't free 'em."

"I'll bet so, too," agreed Mark, laughing. "But just the same we can't have those Southerners breaking up the Union."

"Maybe they wouldn't if we'd mind our own business and leave their property alone."

"Well, whatever has caused the trouble, we can't let 'em destroy our country, and now it looks as if that means we'll have to fight."

Ann dropped his hand and stalked over to the other side of the road.

"I can just tell you this, Mark Wilson. You needn't be in a hurry to go traipsing off, and you'd better think a lot about it if you care anything about me. I'm your promised wife, but the man I'm going to marry is going to stay here with me."

Mark looked at her, half exasperated, and pleaded:

"What's the matter with you tonight, Ann? What's the use of being so ornery? I'm not enlisting yet. I was just talking it over with you like I want to talk everything over with you. No use your getting mad about it."

"Well," she said, a little mollified, "it's just like this: I've heard all this talk and argument—Dad talks of nothing else at home, especially when he's been drinking. But I think Henry Bain is right. He says there's no use having a war. If the southern folks want their negroes, let 'em have 'em, says Henry, and if they don't want to stay with these northern states, let 'em go. I knew that sooner or later you'd catch the glory and adventure idea and be talking about going, and it has worried me. I don't want you to go, Mark; I want you here with me."

Ann's quoting Bain to Mark made him furious, but by this time they had reached the Hover house and there was no more chance for talk. They entered, to find the party in full swing. Some of the older women were sitting rather gingerly on the slippery horsehair sofa and chairs, but having a good time bringing themselves up to date on the neighborhood news. Timothy Belden, the preacher, and John Crawford, storekeeper, were in a corner of the big farm kitchen, deeply engrossed in a game of checkers. Half a dozen other men stood over them offering advice on the plays to be made and making no more impression on the players than so many flies. Several of the older men were playing dominoes, but in the main the crowd consisted of young people from nearly every family up and down the valley, and they were interested in livelier games than checkers and dominoes. Dancing was frowned upon in the neighborhood, but kissing games were popular, and of these the best liked was Post Office.

As the evening went on, it became increasingly evident to Mark that Ann was deliberately trying to avoid having him as her partner. Just as plain was the fact that she was encouraging Henry Bain's attentions. By the time they started playing Post Office, Mark's anger was at the boiling point, and when it so happened—Mark thought it was deliberate—that Bain isolated himself in the big buttery and called for Ann to pay the forfeit, it was almost more than he could stand. When Ann and Bain emerged from the buttery, it was evident from the girl's rosy face that she had been soundly kissed—all in accordance with the rules of the game, of course, but not with the rules, as Mark saw them, that should govern a girl engaged to be married.

To add further fuel to Mark's smoldering anger, Ann and Henry made it a point to sit together when refreshments were served.

Tired out from the games and excitement, the girls and women drifted together after supper, and the boys and some of the men went out to the big back kitchen. A jug of hard cider was produced, and it was not long before several were shouting their arguments for or against the war.

Loudest and most obnoxious of those who argued against the war was Henry Bain.

"Won't catch me fighting for the niggers," he shouted. "Let them go as wants to. I'll stay home and make hay while they're gone."

Although Mark had said almost the same thing to himself while milking that day, Bain's remark on top of everything else that had happened this evening infuriated him beyond endurance.

"I'm going to enlist if they need me, Bain," he said. "Do you mean that I'm one of the fools?"

"Put the coat on if it fits, Wilson. Glad to have you go. Good riddance, I'd say."

"Don't talk to me like that. If you weren't an older man, I'd knock hell out of you."

Bain was not more than forty, but the remark about his age made him furious. He walked up to Mark:

"Don't let my age stop you, Junior."

Someone in the group called:

"Stop it, boys. This is no place for a fight."

But several others, excited by the cider, shouted:

"Leave them be. Let 'em settle it."

Now Mark said, quietly:

"I don't want any brawl, Bain."

"Oh, ho, so you're backing down, Junior?"

"All right, come outside and I'll show you."

"Come on, Hank," shouted one of Bain's supporters. "Mark's called your bluff!"

"Like hell he has! Come on out, Junior, and remember, you asked for it!"

They all trooped outside, quickly formed a ring with Mark and Bain on the inside, while three or four held up lanterns. Before Mark could get his hands up in proper position, Bain hit him in the face, causing him to stagger back into the group, where he would have fallen if the men hadn't caught and held him until the dizziness passed.

Mark shook his head and, feeling something trickle down over his lips, realized that his nose was shooting a stream of blood. He held the back of his hand clumsily against his nose, and before he could lower it Bain hit him again, this time in the stomach. Mark doubled up, dizzy with pain. Then stepping back out of Bain's range and watching him warily, he waited for his head to clear and for his breath to return, in the meantime striving to restrain the worst rage he had ever felt in his life, the climax of a whole bad evening. But his rage did not blind him or confuse him, and he began to get his second wind.

Watching Bain carefully now, Mark stepped in, parried a blow to his face, and let go with everything he had. The blow landed over Bain's heart, and the crowd saw him gasp and falter, but he regained his balance and rushed Mark. Mark sidestepped and, as Bain went by, Mark hit him again, this time squarely over the left eye. Bain let out a yell, turned and hit blindly at Mark with both arms. The wound above Bain's eye started to bleed and he held his eye tightly shut. Mark was conscious of pain streaking from his knuckles like a redhot iron clear up into his shoulder. He dodged Bain coming at him now like an angry bull, side-stepped again and, as Bain partially lost his balance going by, Mark clipped him on the neck back of the ear. Bain went down and for a moment every onlooker seemed to hold his breath. Then two or three men fetched basins of water and began to patch up both belligerents.

Still overwrought with anger and excitement, Mark strode into the house where the women were, walked directly to Ann, and said:

"Get your things on. We're going home!"

Ann got quickly to her feet, her brown eyes snapping.

"Who says so?"

Mark stepped toward her, placed his hands on her shoulders, and with his nose still bleeding, his shirt torn, his knuckles raw, he shook her, and said:

"I say so! Get going!"

Ann stood looking at him for a long minute, erect, shoulders back, every inch of her breathing defiance. Suddenly she smiled a little and without a word turned and went for her cloak. When she came back into the room, Mark took her by the arm and marched her out of the house and down the road. At her doorstep as he was about to turn away without a word, she said, meekly:

"Mark, aren't you going to kiss me goodnight?"

For a moment he was motionless. Then he grabbed her, picked her up half off her feet, and held her fiercely. Putting his bloody, battered face close to hers, he kissed her hard, set her down, and said, gently:

"Ann, next time you go anywhere with me, you stay with me."

To which she replied:

"All right, Mark, dear. Just as you say."

* * *

Finishing his after-supper smoke, George Wilson got up from his old rocking chair in the sitting room, knocked the ashes out of his pipe into the stove, and said to Mark:

"I'm going down to the store to get the mail and the news. Want to come along?"

Engrossed in his thoughts, the older man said nothing as they trudged down the valley road together to the little hamlet of Jenkstown. Used to his father's taciturn ways, Mark made no attempt to break the silence. If there was going to be war, he thought, he'd have to go. In fact, he'd want to go. But what about Ann? Could he stand it to be away from her so long? Would it be easier if they were married before he left? I'm not even certain she'll marry me, his thoughts rushed on.

But tonight the war seemed far away. It was a soft April night. The days were getting longer and the western sky was still colored with the soft spring light. Down across the meadows near the creek the peepers were almost bursting their throats. Spring had come again, and it was in his blood, and just then he wanted nothing of war, not even the thought of it.

Soon they reached the little country store in the hamlet. Already sitting or lounging around the big heating stove in the back end of the store were several of their friends and neighbors, more than usual, come to get the mail that had just come up on the stage from Owego and, especially, the war news. Back of the little partition filled with pigeonholes for the mail, John Crawford was sorting a small pile of mail into the different compartments, his bald head glistening in the light of the setting sun sifting through the dusty little window. It didn't take him long to distribute the five or six letters that made up the mail. But it was on the copies of the country weekly that his attention was focussed.

John Crawford, the village storekeeper and postmaster, was in his fifties, a big man, the top of his head bald as an egg, but with a little fringe of ragged gray hair around the edges. His feet, ruined by a lifetime of walking around on hard floors and carrying too much too long, were covered with corns and bunions and were always encased in a pair of dilapidated slippers, the only footgear that gave him any comfort. Even these he was apt to throw off the moment he could sit or lie down. Over his fat belly a not-too-clean apron hung from a string around his neck.

Mark wasn't thinking too much then of the storekeeper's appearance. Instead, he was thinking how much he liked the man himself. He knew that John's short, gruff manner was merely a cloak for a big heart which was manifest when he handed out sticks of striped candy to the youngsters or something more valuable to the older people when they needed help. Under that gruffness and homely face was a dry sense of humor which often kept his friends chuckling—when the joke wasn't on them.

But right now John Crawford's face was clouded with concern. With the paper in his hand he emerged from behind the partition and joined the group around the stove.

"Well, boys," he announced gravely. "It's here! Bill Sykes, the stage driver, told me that everybody was talking about it in Owego today, and now I see it's set down in this paper. It's here," he repeated. "War!"

He paused, and all waited for him to go on.

"The rebels have taken Fort Sumter. Anderson had to pull down the flag and march out."

Another silence, and then someone said:

"Anything else, John?"

"Yes," answered Crawford. "Abe Lincoln has called for seventy-five thousand volunteers."

Crawford's statement seemed to have stunned the usually talkative group. Each was busy with his own thoughts of what the war would mean to his family and himself. Then George Wilson said, quietly:

"There's nothing new about that, John. We knew it was coming."

"Yes," agreed Crawford, "but I've been hoping that the South wouldn't fight. Now that the Southern states are seceding, it means that all hope for peace is gone."

In the silence that followed, Mark wondered why in the hundred times he had been in this store he had never thought before about how good things smelled—the barrel of crackers, the mold-covered cheese standing open on the counter, the coffee and spices, mixed with the odor of coal oil and the work clothes on the other side of the store. He looked at the glass case with its few sticks of striped candy that seemed never to have changed since his boyhood. Was it because he knew in his heart that it might be a long, long time before he'd be back in these familiar surroundings that his senses seemed so alert just now?

Henry Bain broke the silence:

"Abe Lincoln'll never get seventy-five thousand men to free the niggers. And we'd never have had this war if you Republicans hadn't pushed that backwoods rail splitter over on the country. What we need now is a leader—and look what we got!"

Harry Cortright shifted his tobacco cud, missed the spittoon, and turned his face to the speaker.

"You're right, Hank. And here's one that didn't vote for him. If we'd elected a smart feller like Douglas instead of that long-legged monkey from Illinois, the Southerners would've been satisfied and we wouldn't had no war."

John Barrett, one of the younger farmers from below the village, nodded his head.

"That's right," he agreed. "And now how can we go to war and support our families at the same time?"

"Maybe it's more than a question of support," said George Wilson, quietly. "Maybe it's defending our families and our children from the loss of our liberties in this country." Then he added: "Seems like you Democrats are thinking more about politics than you are about the Nation. It's got beyond politics now."

During this talk John Crawford had stood quietly by, holding the paper in his hand and looking from one old friend to another as they spoke. But after Wilson had spoken, John said:

"George is right. We can argue all we want to over politics in an ordinary campaign—and it's healthy—but now we've got beyond words and talk in this country. It's time for action. We can't settle this argument around the cracker barrel; we've gotta fight, and we might as well make up our minds. And we aren't fighting for the Republicans or for Abe Lincoln or even for the niggers. It's just as George Wilson says, we're fighting for this country. That means that we're fighting for our families."

Henry Bain snorted with disgust. "Nice way to treat your families, I'd say. Go traipsing off to war and let the family rustle its own wood, clothes and victuals. Won't get me runnin' off and leavin' my business just because that long-legged rail splitter in the White House says so."

John Crawford pulled his steel spectacles further down on his nose and looked over them at Bain.

"No, I guess you're right, Henry," he said mildly. "There won't anybody ketch you doing anything except looking after your own selfish interests. But then," he added, "you ain't got any family yet to worry about." His eyes twinkled and he winked at Mark. "Guess by what I hear happened to you the other night when you tried to steal another feller's girl, you ain't likely to have a family for some time to come."

Bain jumped up and stormed out of the door. Some of the men started to laugh and then, noting the serious face of the storekeeper, they got up one by one and drifted out into the night.

CHAPTER II

"Boys, GET UP! Get up, I say!"

Mark heard his father calling as from a dim and distant land and for a moment thought he was dreaming. Then he started to turn over and groaned. Every muscle in his body was still sore from his fight with Henry Bain, and the pain brought him suddenly wide awake, but before he could answer, his father called again:

"Boys, are you awake? Mark! Get up, I say. The sap has run all night, and we've got to get right at it."

Mark climbed slowly out of bed and yelled at his brothers:

"Tom! Charlie! Wake up! It's chore time. Get a move on!"

Not a sound came from the other bed, but Mark, watching closely, saw Charlie slowly open one eye and then quickly close it again, as if a new day was just too much for him to contemplate. Mark yelled again:

"No foolin', Charlie. If you don't get out of there, I'll pull you out!"

Slowly Charlie stuck one not-too-clean foot out of bed, but when it touched the cold floor he hastily pulled it back under the covers again. Although Tom hadn't moved at all, Mark knew that he, too, was playing possum.

"All right," he said, "it's your funeral, not mine. Sap ran all night. Pa's in a hurry. You'll catch you-know-what if you don't get goin'."

That got them out of bed.

Outdoors, spring was in the air. A robin chirped in the lilac bush by the corner of the stoop. In the lane that led to the pasture, grass was showing a little green at the edge of the snowdrift that was mostly gone, and the morning sun just coming up promised a warm day. But Mark was too lame and sore to notice, and anyway there was too much to do. "There always is," he thought, bitterly, as he went on to the barn.

Driven by their father's impatience, the chores were soon completed and they went indoors again to a breakfast of hot buckwheat pancakes, new maple sirup, fried salt pork, and fried potatoes. Watching a little wearily as the big stack of pancakes disappeared so rapidly into her hungry tribe, Nancy Wilson thought:

"It takes more than a war—or the rumor of war—to curb farm appetites."

Breakfast over, the boys hurried out to hitch the team to the longsleigh, on which was a big wooden tub. Then they drove into the maple grove and started to gather sap. The frost was nearly out of the ground and it was the last run of the season, but a good one. Every one of the two or three wooden buckets on each tree was full or running over with the sap, and the long wooden spiles were dripping fast. The boys carried the buckets to the tub on the sleigh, and when it was full they drove to the saphouse to empty it and then returned to fill it again. In a couple of hours every receptacle in the old sugar house was filled to the brim, and there still was plenty of sap ungathered. On their first trip to the sugar house they found that their father had finished his after-breakfast pipe and built a fire under the long sap pan. Already the sap was beginning to boil.

All day they worked to keep ahead of the big run, but when evening came the storage tanks were still full and it was evident that the fires would have to be run all night. For this job they had plenty of help, or at least company, the fore part of the night, for after supper some of the neighbors came to sit on logs or the makeshift seats in front of the arch where the blazing fire took the chill off the early spring night. The flickering light and the steam from the boiling sap, which often whirled in wisps around the men, made everything seem unreal; but the men lounging around the fire Mark had known all his life.

"Sap ain't as sweet this year," stated old Harry Cortright, stroking his grizzled beard which was sprinkled with tobacco juice. Rough of language and not too clean, opinionated and argumentative, Harry was nearly everything that he shouldn't be, but withal he had native common sense, was a hard worker, and a good farmer.

"Depends on your grove and your trees," contradicted George Wilson. "This year my sap is sweeter'n ever."

"Trouble with Harry is that he chews so much terbaccer and is gettin' so old he can't tell whether anything's sweet or sour any more," said Enoch Payne, a red-headed bachelor of around forty who farmed a small place and worked for his neighbors on the side. His remark made the other men laugh, but Cortright, ignoring it for the moment, continued:

"This last run of sap won't be no good anyhow. Buds are started. 'S too late. Sirup'll be too strong to eat. Waste of time. Might better have pulled your spiles a week ago."

Enoch laughed:

"Bet you'd eat the sirup, Harry, even if it is buddy. I never saw such a hog for sirup as he is," he said to the others. "When I was workin' there the other day, Harry piled his plate with plenty of everything on the table, and then poured sirup over the whole darn mess, potatoes and all."

"Course I did," agreed Cortright. "Sirup doesn't only taste good, but it's good for ye. Best spring medicine there is. Cleans ye right out." Turning to Enoch, he said:

"Maybe somethin' like that's what *ye* need. Forty years old if ye be a day, an' not a single kid to show for a misspent life—at least not as anyone knows about."

Before Enoch could think up a suitable answer to that one, John Barrett said:

"Maybe Harry's right about sirup being good medicine. Some kind of medicine and a change of grub is sure needed this time of year. The vegetables in the cellars are pretty well played out an' I'm darn sick of eatin' nothin' but potatoes, milk gravy, an' salt pork."

"Yeah!" agreed Harry. "Sort of between hay an' grass early spring is, ain't it. Every year 'bout this time I figure that if I can just last through till dandelion greens, I'll be all right."

"That reminds me——" began Enoch Payne.

"Never mind what it reminds ye of," interrupted Harry, grinning. "We've heard all of them 'reminds me's' of yours a dozen times. Why don't ye get a new story once in a while?"

"As I was sayin' when I was so rudely interrupted—it reminds me——" persisted Enoch . . .

"What reminded ye? Nobody asked ye to tell any of them old chestnuts."

Enoch grinned with the others, but went on just the same:

"I wasn't goin' to tell a chestnut, Harry. I was goin' to ask you if you remember the time you took the load of potatoes to Owego an' comin' back early in the evening made up your mind that you didn't have whisky enough to carry you over the weekend. So you started to turn your team around and the lumber wagon with its big double box, right in the middle of the Narrows just this side of Owego. You yanked them around too short and tipped the wagon over, with you under the box. An' there you had to stay the rest of the night until somebody came along early in the mornin' and heard you hollerin'. They tipped the box back up, and there you were!"

"Dumb lie!" snorted Harry. "I tipped that box over by myself, put it back on the wagon, turned the team around, went back to 'Wego, got my whisky, and got home in time for milkin' the next mornin'."

Everybody laughed except John Barrett. He was still thinking about the scanty food supplies at the end of the winter.

"Talking about catching colds," he said now. "We don't catch colds—they catch us. I'll bet the reason so many of us are sick this time of year is because we run out of good eats."

"You could be right," spoke up DeWitt Legg, the chubby local butcher. "I'll tell ye, boy, how to fix up your vittles so you never will be sick. Me now, I've never been sick in my life. Know what I do?" Without waiting for an answer he continued: "I never kill a beef without drinkin' all of the warm blood I can hold an' savin' some to drink afterwards."

No one spoke. Everyone felt disgusted. Back in the shadows, Mark shuddered.

"All right, you can stick up your fine noses," continued the butcher, "but some of the strongest, bravest fellows that ever lived were the Mountain Men who explored the Rockies. They never had a vegetable or a green thing to eat for years. Never had a drink of milk, never had nothin' but meat an' beans, an' some poor stuff they made out of coarse flour an' meal. An' they were never sick. They could shoot straighter, run faster an' farther an' love harder than anybody. They had to, to keep alive! They kept that way by drinkin' the blood of the buffalo or the antelope every time they killed one."

Peeved by their continued silence, he said:

"What the h——'s the difference, anyway? All of you eat meat. Blood's just as clean as meat."

"Could be," said old Harry. "I eat woodchucks sometimes, an' folks stick up their noses at that."

Rising from his seat, Mark went over to the boiling sirup and began fishing around in the back end of the pan with a long-handled skimmer. After watching him for a moment, his father asked:

"What are you doing there?"

Instead of answering, Mark pulled out an egg.

"What in time are you trying to do?" his father insisted. Mark stopped his fishing for a moment to answer:

"Mother gave me a dozen eggs to boil in the sap tonight so we could have them to eat—if I can find them," he murmured as he continued his fishing around.

"Nice way to waste money," his father snapped, but Enoch said, mildly:

"Let the boy be, George. I'll bet you did the same thing years ago—only nobody gave you the eggs—you probably stole 'em!"

George Wilson grinned and said nothing more, while Mark continued to fish eggs out of the hot sap until he had found the whole dozen. Then he passed them around, with a salt cellar, and they were eaten with great gusto.

Enoch smacked his lips. "Sure makes 'em good to cook 'em in the boilin' sap," he said.

As the evening wore on the men talked on many subjects, but at first seemed to avoid the one topic that was uppermost in all their minds. Finally Barrett brought it up.

"I guess Lincoln is goin' to get his seventy-five thousand three-months' men all right," he said. "I hear the boys are rushin' like fools into the towns everywhere to enlist."

"Seventy-five thousand, my eye!" said George Wilson. "Over ninety thousand have enlisted already. All the Northern cities are decorated, fife and drum corps are parading the streets, and thousands more are rushing to enlist. Even the Northern Democrats headed by such old war horses as Steve Douglas—who used to debate with Abe Lincoln— have thrown their hats in and are just as patriotic as the Republicans. At least some of them are. Old Steve says the time for debate is past. Every man must be for the United States or against it. It's not a question of being for or against slavery. The South is seceding and it's now a question of saving the Union."

George stopped talking for a moment and then went on:

"We can argue and debate all we want to in peace time, but when they fire on the flag that's something else again! Anderson had to pull down the flag at Fort Sumter, and just a few days ago a regiment of our boys were fired on as they marched through Baltimore on their way to Washington. The North won't stand for that sort of thing—and we shouldn't."

"Well, maybe we'll *have* to stand for it," said Cortright. "Henry Bain was sayin' just today that the dang fools rushin' to enlist will soon get a belly-full. Said 'twon't take three months, either. Henry was tellin' us how the Southerners are pourin' out by the thousands to defend their home country. Most of 'em grew up with a rifle. They're dead shots. They know all about war an' fightin'. Our fellers don't know nothin' 'bout it. Henry Bain's a smart feller. Maybe he's right. Maybe it won't take three months. Prob'ly our boys—or what's left of 'em—will come draggin' back in three or four weeks with their tails between their legs."

"Not so fast, Harry," said Enoch Payne. "Not so fast. Maybe the Southern boys do know more about guns, but our fellows can learn. They've got what it takes. Did you ever see a Yankee in a fight? He just doesn't know enough to know when he's licked! When you think it's all over with him, he's just startin' to fight. Our boys won't be back in three weeks, nor for that matter in three months. This isn't goin' to be any picnic. Our fellows have got to learn and learn fast—and they'll do it."

"It'll be a struggle," agreed George Wilson, "maybe a long one. But the North'll win. We've got more men and more resources. Abe Lincoln says that no nation can exist half slave and half free. That's right—and we're going to continue to exist! Some of us may not be here to see it, but you just put that in your pipe and smoke it."

Back in the shadows by the side of the big furnace Mark had been listening and saying nothing, but Cortright's report of what Bain had said, together with his father's statement of confidence in the North, brought to a sudden head a decision that had been simmering in his mind for days. He would go to war. Judging from his father's remarks, Mark felt he wouldn't oppose his going. Abruptly he jumped to his feet, and in the silence which followed his sudden movement, said:

"This is a good chance to tell you fellows something. I haven't had any chance to talk with Pa, but I think it'll be all right with him. Anyway, I'm going to enlist."

His self-assurance suddenly evaporating, he sat down again.

Listening to his son's young voice, George suddenly thought back across the years—not so long ago, either—to the time when this stripling had been a small boy with his make-believe games around the house and farm. And now here he was a man, making a man's decisions. George's voice was a little husky:

"All right, Mark. It's your decision, and I think it's a right one. But I think you might have talked it over at home first, don't you?"

"Guess I should," the boy agreed. "But I got a little excited."

Harry Cortright broke the silence:

"Thought you were goin' to marry that Clinton girl? What's she goin' to say to your runnin' off to war? Better look out. I heerd Henry Bain was sweet on her, too."

Mark made no answer, but Cortright had put his own doubts into words. It wouldn't change his determination to enlist, but he made up his mind that he would bring matters to a head with Ann before he left by insisting that she marry him immediately.

As the hour grew late, the men gradually drifted away until only Mark and his brother Charlie were left to keep the furnace going and the sap boiling. A little later Charlie went to bed and Mark was left alone to tend the fire. The pile of 4-foot wood by the furnace door was growing low, so Mark spent some time bringing in another supply from outside. Then he opened the big iron doors of the furnace, raked down the coals, and put in a fresh supply of wood. Hot and sweaty from his work, he went to stand in the saphouse door to cool off. The night was warm, a gentle breeze cooled his face. Overhead the sky was studded with stars. Fooled by the false dawn, a rooster crowed in the henhouse over near the barn, and from somewhere in the neighborhood came the lonesome sound of a barking dog.

Shivering a little, and with a sense of loneliness and unreality, Mark turned back into the warm saphouse and sprawled in the old makeshift chair in front of the furnace.

What would it be like to be married, he wondered. His father and mother seemed to get along all right, but he couldn't remember ever seeing his father put an arm around his mother and kiss her. Had they always been like that? Or did they keep their display of affection for themselves alone? Was it only young folks who were demonstrative? If work was all there was to marriage, it seemed commonplace, unromantic, and disappointing.

But at that his family life was so much better than that of Mert Cortright, old Harry's son. Mert was always getting drunk and beating up his wife. They had a big family of children, and Mrs. Cortright worked out around the neighborhood to get enough to feed the family. Even when Mert wasn't drunk, he wouldn't work. Funny business, marriage! If that was all people could put into it, why did they bother? Might better stay free and independent.

He didn't think it would be that way with him and Ann. When he was with her, he was happier than he had ever been before in his life—that is, when she wasn't moody. If he could just keep that feeling of happiness all of his life, marriage would be just great. Then worry asserted itself again. There were times when Ann would sort of go away from him when they were together. She'd be in a tantalizing, irritating mood, finding fault with everything he did, or else she'd be unapproachable. She wasn't always the same, and he just didn't know how to take it.

Anyway, he *had* to take it, for there was no doubt at all about his love for her. He'd never felt that way about anybody else in his life. Maybe he couldn't be happy with her, but he was darn sure he couldn't be happy without her.

That brought back to his mind the decision he had just made to enlist. How could he go away from Ann——maybe for a long time? His thoughts changed again and he dreamed a little about the glory of war, the waving flags, the martial music; the shouting, noisy crowds heaping flowers in the path of soldiers on their way to war. Perhaps he would come back covered with glory, a captain maybe, or even a colonel, with the praises of his superior officers ringing in his ears; come back with the fifes and drums playing just for him, back to the eager arms of his wife, Ann.

Yes, wife. How he loved to roll that word in his tongue.

He roused himself from his dreams to stoke the fire again, dipped the sirup from the back of the pan into a can, refilled the pan with the last of the sap, and dropped tiredly into the old chair. It seemed that he had been there just about a minute when he heard his father's voice:

"Wake up, Mark! It's daylight. The fire'll be all right now. Come on down and help with the milking, get your breakfast, and then you can go to bed and sleep for a while."

CHAPTER III

AFTER STUMBLING, half awake, through the chores that Sunday morning, Mark went to bed and slept until his mother called him to dinner. Then he went down the road to call on Ann. He hadn't seen her since the night of the party and wasn't sure what kind of a reception he would get. But when Ann opened the door she kissed him eagerly and drew him into the room where her mother and father were sitting.

Ann's father, Fred Clinton, was a gentle, quiet, friendly man who, whenever he got a few dollars ahead from his small, stony, heavily mortgaged farm, would disappear on a drunk until the money was gone. Mildred Clinton, Ann's mother, was nervous and flighty, inclined to worry and nag. The family lived constantly on the ragged side of financial disaster, saved only by Ann, who taught school and helped in the work and management of the farm. No wonder the girl seemed changeable at times. When she wasn't worrying over the family finances, she was embarrassed by her father's drinking, and since her engagement to Mark she often wondered if she was being fair to him. These worries and doubts were reflected in her moods.

Seeing that he would have no chance to talk to Ann alone in the house, Mark asked her to go for a walk with him. She consented, and they started down the road together. Mark was quiet, hesitating about opening the subject on his mind, but presently he said:

"Ann, there's something I want to say to you."

"I think I can guess what it is, Mark," she replied, gently. "You're going to enlist."

"Yes, that's part of it. I feel that I must, sweetheart."

"I know how you feel, Mark. I've been hearing the talk and thinking about it, too. Most everybody seems to think it's the right thing to do."

"Henry Bain doesn't," said Mark.

Ann drew away a little.

"Why bring him into it, Mark? He's nothing to us."

"I'm sorry, Ann. But he seems to keep butting in, and it irritates me."

"Well, forget him," she said, shortly, "and think about us."

"That's just what I want to do. I want to think about us. I want you to marry me, Ann."

She walked along silently for a moment and then looked up at him.

"All right, darling. When?"

"Right away—before I go. Will you?"

Instead of answering his question directly, she asked:

"Mark, have you thought what we would do when you get back? We can't very well live with your folks or mine except for a short time."

"Why, we'd farm it," he said. "That's the only thing I know how to do. We'd make out all right."

"I like to farm, too," Ann agreed, "but it would be tough getting started without any help at all—no stock, no tools. I'll have to help my folks, too, you know, and I don't see how we can do so much."

"We could take a good farm on shares," said Mark.

"Even then," she answered, "you should have a team, tools and some stock."

"Well, let's cross that bridge when we come to it."

"All right," she agreed. "We're both healthy and we both can work."

"What'll your folks say about your getting married?"

"It'll be all right with them. They let me do pretty much what I want to anyway. They've always known you and they like you."

"I want to enlist right away, Ann. When can we be married? It'll be tough on father to get the work done without me, but if I'm going, the sooner the better." Then he stopped and drew her to him.

"Ann— Ann— it's only a little ways now to Jenkstown. Let's keep right on walking till we get to the parsonage and ask Rev. Belden to marry us."

"Now?" she gasped. "In these clothes!!"

"Why not? You look just fine. You always do. These are your good clothes, and I've got on mine, the best I own or am likely to own for some time. Even the shirt I have on is patched," he added with a wry grin.

Ann looked up at him, her eyes soft and misty and her face flushed. She leaned a little toward him and spoke so softly that he could hardly hear her:

"All right, darling. If you're sure that's what you want."

He clasped her tightly in his arms and for a long moment the world and its troubles were forgotten. Then they turned and set their steps for the little parsonage and Timothy Belden, the old pastor who had known them both since they were born. But as they neared their destination, their steps grew ever slower until Ann stopped and whispered:

"Mark, I'm scared, just plain scared."

"So am I," admitted Mark, his voice trembling a little, "but let's not stop now."

Still hesitating, Ann said:

"Maybe we ought to have talked this over with our folks. Maybe we should have taken more time to think about it."

But Ann's hesitation and timidity only increased Mark's courage.

"We've been engaged for a long time, and our folks know all about it," he said, reassuringly. "I'm going away and we haven't got much time. So, come on!"

He drew her to him again, whispering huskily:

"It's all right, sweetheart. You know how I love you, and I always will. And you love me, don't you?"

And on receiving her whispered, "Yes, yes, I do," he took a firm grasp of her arm and they walked on. Waiting on the parsonage steps, however, for the answer to Mark's knock, both again were on the point of turning and running away when Dr. Belden opened the door. He took one look at them and then said:

"Come in! Come in! I haven't had a visit with either of you in a long time."

They followed him into the shabby study. A tall combination desk and bookcase occupied part of one side of the room. The drop cover of the desk was open and so littered with papers that it was apparent no effort was ever made to close it. The walls were lined with homemade cases filled with books. On the right of the desk and extending the length of the little room was a rather ornate sofa, the leather-covered seat cracked and bulging in spots from long use. On the other side of the desk was a big chair which once had matched the old sofa.

Seating Ann in the chair, so big that she was almost lost in it, Dr. Belden waved Mark to the sofa, and taking his place in a rickety fiddle-backed chair in front of the· desk, adjusted his steel spectacles on his nose, crinkled his eyes first at Ann and then at Mark, and said:

"Well, my children, what can I do for you?"

Tall, thin, angular, always dressed in his one suit of shiny black, his long face deeply lined, Timothy Belden, Doctor of Divinity, was the best read man in the neighborhood, if not in the county, and the most cheerful. He gave his people a religious philosophy that they could live by, use and practice every day of the week. Now as the young folks looked at his homely, kindly face, some of the tension eased and Mark, swallowing a couple of times, blurted out:

"Dr. Belden, we want to get married."

"So!" said the pastor. "I can't say I'm surprised. I have expected this for some time. When do you plan to have the ceremony?"

Again Mark gulped.

"Now!"

This time Dr. Belden showed his astonishment. He raised his long bushy eyebrows.

"Now I *am* surprised. Why such a sudden decision?" Then he added gently: "But I think I understand. You're going to war, Mark?"

"That's right, Dr. Belden, and we want to be married before I leave."

The pastor looked down at the Bible on top of the litter of papers on his desk, let his hand drop gently on it as if for guidance, then again looked across at the young people and said:

"Mark and Ann, so many couples rush into marriage, especially in times of strain and stress, without realizing all or even a part of what marriage means. I know, of course, that you two aren't doing that, for you have known one another for years. But let me visit with you for a few moments about what you plan to do."

Mark shifted uneasily, thinking he was going to be told to put off the marriage.

"Young people talk about falling in love," the gentle voice went on, "and of course they always think they are in love, just like you do now. But I often wonder if any young people can really know what they are talking about when they say they are in love. There's a mysterious natural attraction between men and women which may be nothing more than Nature asserting herself through the power of physical attraction between the sexes. That's all right, too, if with it there is at the same time the spiritual love without which no marriage can truly succeed. That's just what the marriage ceremony means when it says 'for better, for worse, in sickness and in health.'

"You two are old enough to know something about life's troubles and problems. Mere physical attraction will not stand up in the face of what we all have to go through in this life. Love doesn't reach its highest level until a couple have gone through the fire, have experienced together all things sweet and sour, good and bad, trouble and joy. Then it may truly be said of a man and a woman that they truly love when, because of all their shared experiences, their souls become so close that they are almost a part of one another. Then, when the physical attraction fails, as it will, and the gray hairs and wrinkles come, they can say with the poet Thomas Moore:

'It is not while beauty and youth are thine own
And thine cheek unprofaned by a tear
That the fervor and faith of a soul can be known
To which time will but make thee more dear;
Oh, the heart that has truly loved never forgets
But as truly loves on to the close
As the sunflower turns on her god, when he sets,
The same look that she gave when he rose.' "

As the minister's words filled the little study, Ann forgot her nervousness. With inward amusement and understanding, Dr. Belden noticed the glowing look she turned on Mark, which he returned in equal measure. He laughed a little and said:

"I guess my little sermon wasn't needed. The answer as to whether you two have the right kind of love is evident in your eyes now as you look at one another. Ann's shining eyes say more about the holiness and constancy of love than I can ever say.

"But, Mark, are you sure that you are right in marrying Ann now and then going away to war?"

"It will be hard, Dr. Belden," Mark answered, "but easier for me—and I hope for Ann—to know that she is my wife, right here waiting for me when I get back."

"And that's how I feel, too," Ann said eagerly.

"By the way," Dr. Belden continued, "do your parents know that you came here today?"

Ann looked distressed, but Mark answered quickly:

"No, sir, they don't. However, they know that I'm going away, and they know that we plan to get married some time, so I don't think they'd mind."

"What do you think, Ann?"

Ann hesitated and then said:

"I guess the folks would be all right, but—" she paused, close to tears—"a girl—kind of likes—to have a real wedding." The last words came out with a rush.

"Of course, she does," said the minister, quickly. He turned to gaze out of the window into the April sunshine. Swinging back suddenly to face them, he exclaimed:

"We'll have a real wedding yet if you'll cooperate. Tell you what we'll do. Tonight is a very special occasion for me and for the church. I've been working for a long time on a sermon that I hope will help my people in this time of trouble. I won't marry you here now, but how would you like to come to the meeting tonight, sit together on the front seat, and at the close of my sermon you come forward and I'll marry you. The church will be full—because everybody is looking for comfort and I've let it be known that I'm making a special effort to give it to them—and your wedding will be a very fitting ceremony and will send them away rejoicing in their hearts, knowing that God is still on His throne and there is still love and happiness in the world. Will you do that?"

Mark hesitated:

"We'd be kind of scared, sir."

"There's nothing to be afraid of. You'll be among your

friends, and your parents will be there, of course. Everybody will love the ceremony, and they'll love you and will never forget it, and you won't either. There's your real wedding, Ann, with all the fixings. Will you do it?" he repeated.

This time Ann answered for both of them:

"We will!"

"Fine! Now let's have a word of prayer together."

When he had finished, Dr. Belden said:

"Now trot along home, tell your folks what you're going to do, that it's all arranged, and tell them to come to church tonight."

That night when the evening service began, the little church was crowded, just as Dr. Belden had said it would be. Many were there who did not ordinarily attend church. All were looking for peace and comfort, something to cling to in time of trouble. The tall iron woodburning stoves in the rear corners of the church, with stove pipes running along both sides of the church to the chimneys in the front corners, took the April chill out of the old building and made a cheerful crackling noise. The colored glass in the long windows glowed in the light of the coal oil lamps that hung in brackets along the sides. The pews were straight, high-backed, and hard, but the congregation was used to them and didn't mind.

In his pulpit chair, while the choir and congregation sang one of the old hymns, Dr. Belden looked into the grave, worn faces of his people and prayed for inspiration and words with which to help them. He had taken as his text the 27th verse of the 14th chapter of John: "Peace I leave with you, my peace I give unto you: not as the world giveth, give I unto you. Let not your heart be troubled, neither let it be afraid."

"It may sound strange," he said, "to talk of peace at this time when, as Patrick Henry said, 'We cry Peace, Peace!— but there is no peace.' But this verse doesn't refer to the peace that follows physical conflict. This peace is available to us all, at all times, no matter what conflicts may rage in the world, the peace that is beyond all understanding, the peace that comes from faith, the undying, unconquerable belief that no matter what happens, God is on His throne and that everything will some time come right, whether that some time is here or hereafter. When Jesus spoke of 'my peace,' He knew the conflict, the tragedy that lay ahead for Him. He knew that Calvary was ahead. But because of His boundless faith, a faith that is available to all of us, Jesus knew that no matter what troubles or physical suffering we undergo, we can acquire a faith that will enable us to go ahead with courage and to look forward eventually to a peace and happiness that know no bounds."

As Dr. Belden talked in a friendly, conversational tone, just like the old friend that he was and had been to most of them for years, the strained, tense look left the faces of his people and they relaxed in the hard seats, while some of the peace of which he spoke entered their souls.

Mark and Ann, huddled together for courage on the front seat, never could remember a single word of that sermon, and it seemed to them that the preacher would never stop talking. Through both their minds was running the thought, how in the world did we ever get ourselves into a situation like this? They were just plain scared.

At long last, so it seemed to them, the sermon came to an end. A closing hymn was sung, and then, to the surprise of the congregation, instead of pronouncing the benediction, the minister motioned for them to be seated again. He came forward to stand in front of the pulpit, and, calling Mark and Ann to stand before him, he started to read:

"Dearly beloved—"

An interruption came from the back of the church. Fred Ford jumped to his feet and said something. The astonished congregation and minister looked in his direction.

"What is it?" sternly demanded the minister.

Ford sank back into his seat.

"What is it, Fred?" Dr. Belden repeated his question.

Fred's face was as red as a blaze. "Nothing!" he muttered, "Sorry!"

But the minister persisted:

"What's bothering you?"

"Nothing!" Fred repeated. "I just thought—you were making an awful mistake. I thought these young folks were here to join the church and you were reading the wrong service!"

A general laugh, in which the minister joined, relieved the

tension, and somehow that absurd incident added to the joy and happiness of the whole occasion. Even Mark and Ann relaxed. As the ceremony proceeded, women—and even many of the men—remembered when they, too, had taken those vows, "before God and this congregation." Coming at this emotional time, on top of the heart-stirring sermon, many were close to happy tears, with the resolution in their hearts that come what may, they would stand up to it and give their loved ones, their friends and neighbors, and their country, the best they had.

CHAPTER IV

WITH THE FIRST dull light that crept in through the many-paned window of Ann's bedroom the next morning, Mark was awake. For a confused moment he wondered where he was. Then all of the happenings of the previous day came back in a rush, and a flood of tenderness swept over him as he turned to look at his wife's soft face on the pillow beside him.

Her cheeks were flushed with sleep and her long brown curly hair was braided like a little girl's. She was lying on her side, her head close against his shoulder and her left arm flung across his chest as though she would hold him fast even in sleep. She looked very young and vulnerable lying there, and Mark felt protective as he gazed on her. Her apparent helplessness and confidence in him brought back some of the words of the wedding ceremony of the night before, and he inwardly renewed his vow to protect and save her from all trouble.

Yet almost his first decision since they had taken their vows would hurt her immeasurably, for he had determined to enlist that very day.

His restless movement at this unhappy thought aroused Ann. With a soft sigh, she opened her eyes, remembering instantly her new status in life. Mark raised himself on his elbow and bringing his face close to hers, said, tenderly:

"I can't believe it. You're my wife, my girl for always. It's too good to be true. Such perfect happiness can't last."

"Yes, it can," she whispered. "It can last if we make it last." Then her arms came up around his neck, the sleeves of her heavy nightgown falling back to reveal her shapely arms, and she pulled his mouth down on hers. For a long moment they clung together, then Mark raised his head and looked at her gravely.

"What's the matter, Mark?" A smile curved the corners of her red mouth. "One would think it was painful."

But he continued to gaze at her sadly, and under that look she, too, grew grave and repeated:

"What is the matter, Mark?"

He hesitated, and then said:

"I was just thinking that maybe I shouldn't have married you, for now it makes it all the harder for me to go away."

"I know, Mark. But why worry about it right now? You haven't gone yet."

"Not yet." Then he blurted out:

"But I have to go today."

"Today! Oh, Mark!" she cried, stricken, pushing him away and sitting up in bed. "You mean you're going to leave me now?"

"Yes, dear," he replied. "There's a bunch from this part of the country leaving from Owego or Elmira in a few days and it would be easier to go with them than it would with strangers. And anyway we have to part sooner or later— and the sooner we all go, the quicker it'll be over and we'll be back."

Looking at his wife's white face, he took her in his arms.

"Oh, honey, don't take it so hard. I'll soon be back."

"Yes," she whispered brokenly, "but this is so terribly soon."

Then with a mighty effort she swallowed her disappointment, made a pathetic effort to smile, and murmured into his ear:

"It's all right, dear. You do what you think is best, and I'll do my part here at home."

"And that's the harder part," said Mark. "I guess that's what Father meant the other day when he said there were no drums on the home front."

They got up, dressed, and went downstairs to eat breakfast with her father and mother. The big farm kitchen was filled with the appetizing aroma of bacon sizzling in a spider on the back of the stove, coffee bubbling in the old pot, and buckwheat pancakes browning on the big griddle. Fred Clinton had just come in from his morning chores.

The years of hard work had left their mark on Mrs. Clinton, but Mark, looking at her flushed face as she bent over the fire, knew where Ann got her beauty. After the first little awkwardness among them wore off, Mrs. Clinton kept glancing from one young face to the other and finally said, with a little laugh:

"Why so solemn this morning? One would think you young folks had been to a funeral instead of to a wedding."

The quick tears sprang to Ann's eyes as she looked down at her plate. Her father stared at her in surprise and paused with a sizeable piece of pancake dripping with sirup halfway between his plate and his mouth.

"What's the matter, Toots?"

Mark answered for Ann.

"I hate to have to tell you folks, but I've just told Ann that I've got to leave today to enlist."

"So soon?" queried the mother, echoing her daughter's cry.

"Yes," said Mark, and went on to explain. "Maybe it was a mistake, but that was the reason I wanted to get married last night. I learned a few days ago that several of the young fellows I know have already enlisted and are awaiting orders to go to the front any day now. It would be a lot easier if I could go along with them. That's why I have to go so quickly."

Fred Clinton looked up from his plate.

"I can see that, son," he said, and Mark flushed with pleasure at the term of affection. "And I suppose the sooner you get away, the sooner you'll be back. He won't be gone long, Toots," he said to Ann. "We hope this'll be all over in a few weeks."

"Do your folks know you're going today?" inquired Mrs. Clinton.

"Yes, I told them yesterday when I told them we were getting married."

"How did they feel about your marriage?"

"They felt fine," he answered. "Mother said she had expected and looked forward to it for years. I hope you're pleased, too," he added, a little wistfully.

Smiling gently at him, she said:

"We are. You're a good boy, Mark, and we welcome you into the family."

They continued eating, but it was a mere pretense on Ann's part, and soon Mark said:

"If you'll excuse us now, I'll go over and get my stuff ready. Father's going to drive me to Owego." Turning to Ann, he said:

"Get your bonnet on, Ann, and come along."

"I will that," she cried, "but you'll have to wait until I change my clothes, for I'm going to Owego with you."

Halfway across the room, Mark turned and looked at her.

"Do you think you'd better, Ann? Parting down there will be harder than it is here."

She shook her head resolutely and said:

"What do you think I am—a child? I'm your wife, remember? I'm going to Owego to see you off."

Then, with a little smile, she added:

"If I can't get a wedding trip and a honeymoon one way, I'll get them another."

"As you say," he said, with a note of pride in his voice.

Fred Clinton winked at his newly acquired son.

"I hope you didn't let that word 'obey' in the marriage service fool you any," he remarked. "When a woman makes up her mind, you may just as well save your breath!"

At the Wilsons, Mark and Ann were warmly received. The chores were finished, breakfast was over, and Old Molly was harnessed to the buggy, blanketed, and tied to the hitching post by the horse block in front of the house. The whole family was gathered in the kitchen, except Mark's mother who, with her eyes unnaturally bright, was darting in and out of the kitchen and up the stairs that led to Mark's and the other boys' bedroom. At last she said, cheerfully:

"Your things are all ready, Mark."

But the rest of the family seemed subdued, even the usually noisy, obstreperous younger brothers. Traces of tears were evident on the face of ten-year-old Ellen. Elizabeth and Hattie, too young to understand much of what was wrong, sensed that something wasn't as usual and, play forgotten, sat quietly in a corner. Nancy broke the silence:

"I packed everything that I think you'll want in the old carpet bag, son."

As Mark thanked her, his father said:

"Well, if you're ready we might as well shove off. It's a long ways down there and back in a day."

Then Ann intervened:

"You don't have to go, Mr. Wilson. I'm going anyway, and if you can spare the horse until tomorrow and will trust her to me, I'll bring her back then."

George Wilson started to speak, then caught a look from his wife. Through the years he had learned to read her looks almost as well as if she had spoken, and now he realized that she was saying to him, "Let her go! It's their only chance to be alone." So he cleared his throat and, stuttering a little, said:

"W-w-well, I-I guess that will be the best way."

And now it was time to say goodby, but no one seemed to know how to start. Finally George strode across the room, and for the first time in Mark's memory his father put his arm across his shoulders, pulled him close in a great bear hug, then turned and almost ran outdoors. In turn Mark picked up Hattie, Elizabeth, and finally Ellen and kissed them, and then he looked for the boys, but apparently they had had all they could take for they were nowhere to be seen. Then Mark crossed the room to his mother. As he looked into her eyes sparkling with unshed tears, Mark was privileged to glimpse for a moment something of the unknown spiritual world that dwells in the heart and soul of a good mother.

She only said, "Be good, Son," and reached up and kissed him. Then she turned and went quickly into her bedroom and shut the door. But after Mark had helped Ann into the buggy, picked up the reins and turned to look back at the house, there they all were—George, Nancy, his brothers and sisters, on the old front stoop, waving at them, and both brothers sticking out their tongues at him.

As the old horse jogged along, Mark and Ann, subdued and saddened by the parting, had little to say for a while. But by the time they had passed through Jenkstown and were on their way down the valley road toward Newark Valley, the spring morning, their youth, and their wonderful new relationship combined to change their mood. The pasture and meadow lands had begun to show carpets of tender green, the sun warmed their knees under the buggy top, and from almost every fence rail and tree the birds sang loud praise of the spring.

Looking at the glowing face of his bride peeking up at him from under her bonnet, Mark was filled again with a surge of pride and tenderness as he thought, "She's mine!" Then he smiled at the memory of how positively that independent little creature beside him had affirmed her intention of accompanying him to Owego. "Not all mine," he thought. "She still has a mind of her own. But she's my wife just the same." Aloud he said:

"Well, Mrs. Wilson. How do you like the sound of your new name? Is it good enough to carry all the rest of your life?"

"I'm proud of it," she answered, her face lighting, "and I'm proud of you, Mark. I always have been." With a twinkle in her eyes, she added: "Even as a little girl when you and I used to play at keeping house with the other children, I used to plan that some time I'd make ours real."

"Oho!" he said. "So I never had a chance! I thought it was the man who did the proposing."

"That's what men think," she said, grinning. "But the truth is that when a girl makes up her mind—"

"The boy might just as well throw up his hands," Mark finished the sentence for her. Then added:

"But you just wait until I get back home, my dear, and I'll show you who's boss."

Bending his head he kissed the soft mouth upturned to his. Old Molly, feeling the slack on the rein and knowing herself forgotten, turned sideways, stopped, and started to crop the short grass by the roadside. Some time later, Mark, a little breathless, picked up the lines from the dashboard, pulled the horse back on to the road and said, huskily:

"Words don't count for much beside that, do they, dear?"

"They don't," she agreed, "and I hope if we ever start any arguments, we can always settle them that way."

As they ambled along down the valley the horse picked her own way while Mark held his bride close to his side. As they drove along, they played a little game to see which one could remember and name the owners of the farms they passed, and between them they could recall almost everyone along the way from their home to Owego. Among them were the Lynchs, the Royces, the Browns, the Muzzeys, the Balls, the Beebes, the Ames, the Johnsons, and the Japhets, descendants of the Yankee settlers who had transplanted New England to the whole length of the valley, as those same Yankees had carried their names and their standards to thousands of other pioneer communities across the country.

CHAPTER V

IT WAS NEARLY NOON when Mark drove into the livery stable in Owego and put up his horse. Then, rather hesitantly, he and Ann made their way to the little waiting room across the hall from the bar in the Ah-wa-ga House to wait for the call to dinner. It was an entirely new experience for both of them to be in a hotel, and they looked around curiously.

The room was furnished with a long, uncomfortable-looking, leather-covered sofa and several chairs to match, and in the center was a marble-topped stand. Over the mantel, evidently left from the last political campaign, was a life-sized poster of Abraham Lincoln. Hand in hand they stood gazing up at the homely face, and as always when Mark heard the name or saw a picture of the gangling Western giant who had been elected to the White House, it did something to him. Apparently it had the same effect on Ann, for suddenly she whispered:

"He's good, Mark! He's good! And I think he's right. I'm glad you're doing what he wants."

The dinner bell rang and they entered the dining room to find it filled with several small tables seating from four to six people, each table covered with red cloth and the inevitable revolving cruet stand, with half a dozen bottles of ketchup, horse radish, vinegar, pepper and salt. Some tables were already occupied by men, and more were coming in. Two bored-looking, rather ancient waitresses were carrying in the food—generous dishes of potatoes, roast beef, thick brown gravy, boiled cabbage and big slices of home-made bread for each table, with a choice of coffee, tea or milk.

As the only woman in the room, Ann at first felt shy and embarrassed, but it was so evident that eating was the main interest of the men, including the two at their table, that her own healthy appetite soon asserted itself, and both she and

Mark made a hearty meal of what seemed to them the most delicious food they had ever tasted.

By the time the waitresses came to take orders for the several kinds of pie with cheese, the diners had become more sociable. One of their table companions, a dapper, rather loudly dressed individual in his thirties, winked at the other man and looking meaningly at Mark, inquired:

"What's your line, friend?"

Not understanding, Mark said: "Line?"

"Yes, line. What do you travel for?"

Sizing him up quickly and not liking his attitude, Mark answered:

"For my country."

The other diner, a quietly dressed business man, laughed.

"I guess he's got you there, my friend," he remarked to his companion. Then to Mark he said:

"I take it that you have enlisted or are going to?"

"That's right," agreed Mark.

"Taking the girl along, too?" asked the salesman, with another wink.

This riled Mark.

"If it's any of your business," he snapped in a little louder tone that caused some of the other nearby men to turn around, "this is my wife."

"Aha!" said the salesman, not easily squelched. "Just married, eh?"

At this Mark started to rise, but the older man intervened.

"Take it easy, boy. This fellow doesn't mean to be rude. And as for you, I'd like to be right back in your shoes, starting all over again, with such a pretty little bride."

"No, I didn't mean nothing," said the salesman, in a more agreeable tone. "Just tryin' to be sociable. So you're going to enlist, eh? Wish I'd time to take a nice little vacation like that."

"By jiminy!" said the other, indignantly. "I wish you could, and maybe it would take some of the cockiness out of you. 'Little vacation' indeed! You may have your wish before we get through with this matter and get that kind of a 'vacation' yourself. It would do you good. And in the meantime, those of us who are staying home for one reason or another need to show a little appreciation for what these boys are doing for us. Look at our young friend here—just married and now they have to separate. 'Vacation!' indeed!"

As they all got up from the table, the salesman walked out of the dining room, but the other man came around to Mark and Ann.

"I'd like to shake hands with you and your bride," he said. He gestured to the other diners and several of them came over, introduced themselves and shook hands, wishing the young couple luck. So cordial and sincere were the greetings that, after the men left, Mark and Ann felt as if they had been among friends.

"Now we'll see about getting a room for tonight," said Mark to Ann, "and you can rest while I go over to the recruiting office, or maybe you would like to take a walk. I don't know how long it'll take, but I'll be back just as soon as I can."

A little later, Mark found his way to a couple of small rooms on the ground floor of a vacant store building which served as the recruiting office. In the front room was a hard-faced Army recruiting sergeant and a clerk. Lined up in front of the desk were a group of young men waiting their turn. When Mark's turn came, the sergeant yelled:

"Another farmer! Look at 'em!"

He wrinkled his nose in disgust and waved his hands at the line of boys and men back of Mark, most of whom were obviously off the farms. Half scared and uneasy in their ill-fitting clothes, they were an awkward-looking lot.

"How in God's name we'll ever make soldiers out of such stuff I don't know," snarled the sergeant. Suddenly he shouted:

"Stand up straight!"

Mark wasn't sure whether the order was directed at himself or at all of the boys, but he pulled himself erect. Then, as the sergeant began to fire questions at him, the clerk took down his answers. The questioning finished, the recruiting officer motioned him to an adjoining room.

"Get in there and get your clothes off!"

In the other room Mark shed his clothes and, shivering with cold and nervousness, joined the other naked men who were working up one by one to the Army surgeon at one end of the line. In spite of the chilly room it was close in there, and rank with the odor of sweat. When Mark's turn came, the doctor thumped his chest, then dropped his ear to his chest to listen to his heart. He made no comment for a time, but his keen eyes looked approvingly at Mark's finely muscled body. Then he said:

"Practice sucking in your guts, son; chest out, shoulders back. Get that plow-handle stoop out of your shoulders while you can." Then, with one last look, he added:

"You'll do. Get your clothes on and report back to the officer in the other room."

When Mark returned to stand again before the recruiting officer, the man actually smiled, giving Mark the impression that his bark was worse than his bite. He gave Mark the oath, and then remarked:

"You're in the Army now, boy, and you'll soon be moving."

"How soon?" Mark summoned up the courage to ask.

"Don't know for sure. Never know nothing in the Army. But maybe tomorrow. Anyway, you're on your own for the night. Report back here in the morning."

Outdoors Mark drew in great gulps of the spring air and almost ran back to the hotel and Ann. He found her waiting in the decrepit old Boston rocker by the window of their room. As soon as he opened the door, she ran across the room and threw her arms around his neck, clinging to him tightly.

"I was scared for fear they'd keep you and I wouldn't see you again," she cried. "How was it? Did you get in all right?"

"Yes, darling, I'm in the Army."

"Can you come back home with me?"

"No, dear, the sergeant says we'll probably go South soon, maybe tomorrow." Then, in an effort to cheer her, he added: "But you know what they all say—that it won't take long. I'll be home before you know it, and in the meantime we can think and plan what we'll do when we are together again."

He led her across the room, pulled her down on his lap in the rocker, which groaned dismally under their double weight. As he looked around the room he laughed, a little ruefully. In addition to the chair, the furniture consisted of a wash-stand, on top of which was a large white washbowl and a pitcher half filled with water which probably had been there for weeks. One or two hard-bottomed chairs and the bed completed the equipment. But the bedstead itself was large with a deep feather bed, and the brightly colored homemade quilts were attractive. Reading his thoughts, Ann said:

"Mark Wilson, don't you go to criticizing. This is our first home, all by ourselves, and wherever we are, whatever we have or don't have, we have love, and nothing else will really matter much."

First to awake again next morning, Mark found himself dreading the day. Why, he thought, had he been so foolish as to enlist and go away from his wife when she needed him and he needed her? How would he ever stand the separation? What did one man more or less in the Army mean anyway? Why did he have to go barging off when he had so much to stay home for? There were thousands just as able and duty bound to enlist as he. Why couldn't he have had sense enough at least to have waited a while?

Looking at Ann sleeping by his side, her soft lips parted, one little hand outstretched as if reaching for him, her young breasts rising and falling with her gentle breathing, a lump came into his throat. He breathed a prayer:

"Dear God, take care of her and take care of me, so that we can soon be together again and live like other folks."

Then he felt better, for it seemed that God gave him the answer as to why he had enlisted. It was the memory of that grave, homely countenance on the poster downstairs, with the deep-set, sad and burning eyes of Abraham Lincoln, the new President of the United States.

Ann stirred, opened her eyes, and smiled at him. With great tenderness he took her in his arms, his restraint and gentleness telling her of the sadness that lay on his heart.

They had breakfast in the hotel dining room, where several of their friends of the day before greeted them smilingly but refrained from breaking in upon their time together. Breakfast over, they went back to their room. They made a pretense of being very busy packing up their few things, but finally Mark turned to face her and said:

"Well, sweetheart, it's time to go."

"Yes, Mark."

Dry-eyed, she clung to him briefly, then together they carried their belongings downstairs, and went to the livery

stable, where the attendant hitched the horse for them.
Climbing up over the buggy wheel, Ann gathered up the
reins, gave Mark a crooked smile, slapped Molly gently with
reins, and drove off, not trusting herself to look back or to
wave.

As she drove up North Avenue on her way out of town,
Ann saw a column of men led by a fife and drum corps swing
out of a side street into the Avenue ahead of her. She pulled
Molly to one side to let them pass. There were seven or eight
men in the drum corps, with bass and snare drums led by
four fifers, and at first Ann heard only the loud rat-a-tat-tat
of the snares, punctuated by the deep boom, boom, boom of
the big drums. Back of the little band were twenty-five or
thirty men in civilian clothes trying to keep step and to look
as soldierly as possible. As they came abreast of the buggy,
the fifes suddenly began to shrill and the drums changed
their rhythm to keep time with the tune. Familiar as Ann
had been with that old tune all of her life, never before had
it had any particular significance for her. But now as she
mentally fitted the words to the melody they somehow expressed the loneliness and pain in her own heart:

> I'm lonesome since I crossed the hills
> And parted with my Peggy;
> I'm lonesome since I crossed the hills
> And left the girl behind me.

As she listened and watched the procession pass on down
the Avenue, she thought of the thousands of men and boys,
and especially her own Mark, marching away to that same
tune from the girls they had left behind them. Then for the
first time she gave way to tears.

When finally she picked up the lines and spoke to old
Molly, who had been dozing by the curb, she thought half
humorously that it must be nice to be a dumb animal and
care about nothing but eating and dozing in the shade.
Driving back up the valley she thought how all the joy that
she and Mark had experienced the day before had now given
way to pain, all the shining brightness that had been a part
of their happiness—the sunshine, the song of the birds, the
green of the fields—was gone.

But at last the long, lonesome journey ended and she gave
the horse over to Charlie Wilson to unhitch and went into

the house. Mark's mother looked at her white, drawn face and said, cheerfully:

"We've been waiting supper for you, my dear. You're one of the family now. Wash up at the sink. The roller towel is over on the right. And come eat."

"That's right," said George Wilson, heartily. "We've saved a place for you at the table and there it is." He pointed to Mark's vacant chair and in a further effort to distract her he blundered on:

"That's Mark's place, and I know of no better person to fill it while he's away than his wife."

But Ann smiled at him gratefully and attempted to do her part in maintaining the matter-of-fact talk around the table, though she ate little. When the meal was over, George and the two boys went to the barn, and Ann helped the girls and their mother to clear the table and wash the dishes. Ellen and Elizabeth were more than usually willing to help clear up tonight, proud to show their new sister how they could work.

CHAPTER VI

WHEN THE SUPPER WORK was done, Nancy said:

"Ann and I are going upstairs now. You girls find something to occupy yourselves with down here."

In the chamber where the boys slept, Nancy waved Ann to a chair and sat down herself on the edge of the bed.

"My dear," she said, "I want to tell you that I understand how hard this parting has been for you today. When you're older and have children of your own, you'll know how hard it is for me, too. These boys of ours—and no matter how old they are in years they're always boys to us, God bless them —don't always look at life and its problems the way we women do. In some respects we have understanding and feelings not given to men—most men, anyway—and that very fact lays us wide open to suffering."

Quick to defend Mark from even the slightest criticism, Ann said:

"Yes, Mother,"—Nancy's face lit up at the term—"but I know that Mark felt just as bad as I did today."

"Bless his heart, of course he did. That wasn't just what I meant, Ann. Maybe I'm not clear in my own mind. Let me say it another way. Of course Mark felt bad, and will continue to be lonesome. But he'll have action and adventure, new scenes and new faces that will take his mind off himself and help him a lot. Meanwhile, we women at home will have to carry on in the same old way, in the same surroundings. I can't help resenting a little the fact that men make these wars, and the women have to fight them just as much as the men. Not with guns, of course; but with all the men gone to war, who is going to raise the food to feed them? Who's going to keep these farms going? Who's going to keep the families together? Why, the women, of course! And there will be no fifes or drums playing us on, either.

"But that wasn't what I brought you up here to say. I

don't know how I got on to this subject. What I really want to do is to tell you that, being a woman, I understand how hard this is for you. I want to tell you again how pleased I am that you are in the family, that we have a new daughter, and I want to comfort you by reminding you that everybody thinks this war will be short and Mark will soon be back with us.

"In the meantime, both Mr. Wilson and I want you to feel that this is your home and that you're very welcome to live here or with your own people, just as you think best. We just want you to be as happy as you can under these hard circumstances."

Crossing swiftly to the side of the bed where Nancy sat and putting her arms around her, Ann said:

"Thank you, Mother. I've always thought you were a dear and now I'm sure of it all over again. I haven't had time to think much about it, but probably it is best for me to continue to stay with Father and Mother. But I certainly shall be over here a lot. There's something pretty nice about having two homes!"

* * *

For days Ann haunted the post office, walking the mile back and forth, rain or shine, looking for a letter from Mark. One evening as she came out of the post office, lonesome and discouraged, Henry Bain spoke to her:

"Did you walk down?"

Learning that she had, he said:

"Come on, get into the buggy. I'm going out your way and I'll drop you off at home."

When she was seated in the buggy, Henry asked if she had heard from Mark.

"Not yet," she admitted.

"Well—these young fellows, you know how they are. When they go off on an adventure like this silly war, they get so steamed up with excitement and new scenes and faces that it's easy to forget the home folks."

"You know that Mark isn't like that," said Ann, indignantly. "He'll never forget us. And I know he'll write just as soon as he can.

"Besides," she continued, emphatically, "this isn't a silly

war. Mark had to go and—" she couldn't resist adding—
"maybe the war would be over sooner if some others felt
the same way."

Henry changed the subject and soon afterwards drove up
in front of the Clinton farm, where Ann thanked him rather
coldly and bade him goodby.

The next day her regular pilgrimage to the post office was
rewarded. John Crawford beamed at her over the top of his
spectacles and handed her a letter. Then he and the usual
loungers around the stove stood by expectantly, evidently
hoping that she would stop to read the letter there and
maybe tell them something of the war news. But Ann couldn't
do that. That letter was a most precious and personal possession. She tucked it carefully into her pocket and almost
ran out of the store. As soon as she got home, not even stopping to answer the inquiring looks of her parents, she ran for
the privacy of her own room, that room almost holy now
because it was where Mark and she had spent their first
night together.

Striving to compose herself, she sat down in the window,
facing the glory of the western sunset sky. Deliberately and
slowly she opened the letter and began to read:
"My darling wife and sweetheart:

"This is the first opportunity I have had to write you.
The outfit I am with is so far mostly noted for what it has
not. Until now I haven't been able to get a scrap of paper,
a pen, or even a pencil. On top of that, they have kept us
so busy from daylight to dark that when they blow 'Taps'
we just fall down and go to sleep, so doggone tired that it
seems we never could get rested.

"Even now I haven't time to tell you much about what is
happening to us here. As you probably know, they shipped
out a big bunch of us the very night after you left. I was glad
of it, for I didn't want to spend another night in Owego
after you had gone.

"We arrived in Philadelphia the next day. If we ran our
farms the way they run this Army, we would soon starve.
I never in my life have seen so much confusion and disorder.
We got nothing to eat that first day in Philadelphia until
evening—and then not much. In fact, the whole town is full

of soldiers, and apparently there's not enough grub to go
around. Anyway, I've been hungry ever since I saw you."

That brought a lump to Ann's throat.

"That first night we slept in a big park on the ground,
with nothing but a couple of blankets. When one of my
comrades said something to the sergeant about it, he growled
that it was good for us, that we might just as well get used
to that kind of a bed, for it's all we'd ever have.

"But there's one good thing, we've got our new uniforms
and caps, and they're warm and quite nice-looking. Wish
you could see us in them. Also, they are really trying to
make soldiers out of us. That's why we're so tired. It's drill,
drill, drill—'stand up straight, darn ye'—'suck in your guts,
you're in the Army now'—all day long. But it's good for us,
I guess, for we are learning not to slouch, we are pushing
our chests out and our chins up, and in spite of everything
you'll be glad to know that I'm feeling well.

"Say, darling, you remember that old song, 'The Girl I
Left Behind Me'? The town is full of marching soldiers, and
it seems as though they have just about as many drummers
and fifers as they have soldiers, and I guess that piece and
the one about John Brown's body are the only ones they
know how to play. If I've heard them once I've heard them
three dozen times. You know how the first one goes:

" 'I'm lonesome since I crossed the hills,' etc. No matter
how many times I hear it, it brings a lump into my throat."

"I know, I know, my darling!" Ann spoke aloud. "I heard
it, too."

"But enough of war and soldiering. Let me tell you, Ann,
dear, if I can find the words, how much I love you. I miss
you so. When you drove old Molly out of that livery stable,
it seemed to me that the end of the world had come, or
might just as well. On the crowded train to Elmira and
Philadelphia, all night long it seemed to me that the car
wheels sang, 'Goodby, Sweetheart! Goodby, Sweetheart!'
I'd close my eyes and try to rest, and all I could see was
your sweet, brave face when you lifted your chin and said
goodby to me without a tear.

"Then I thought of that picture of Abe Lincoln that you
and I stood before in the hotel, and I felt a little better because it made me feel that I was doing the right thing.

"One of the hardest things to bear is the lack of news from you and from the other folks at home. Of course you couldn't write because you didn't know where to send the letter. But now you can. My temporary address is at the head of this letter. Of course we don't know when we'll move, but I'll hope your letters will be forwarded. Write often, sweetheart, and tell me all about yourself, what you are doing, what you are thinking, and above all, tell me that you love me, for that I need to be told—and often.

Your brand new and lonesome husband,
Mark."

Totally oblivious of her surroundings, Ann read the letter to the end, and then reread it again and again. At last, jumping to her feet, she ran downstairs to where her father and mother were sitting, one on each side of the little "settin'-room" table, drawn close to the sheet-iron stove in which a fire had been lit against the chill of the spring evening.

"Mother! Dad!" she cried, "I've heard from Mark! I've heard from Mark!"

Both parents smiled, and her mother said:

"That wasn't hard to guess, dear, by the way you rushed in here and ran upstairs. And by the look on your face the news is good."

"Yes, he's all right, but tired and hungry, poor boy."

"What'd he tell you about the war?" inquired her father.

"I'll read you the letter," said Ann, still excited, then smiling shyly, "at least a part of it."

After she had read it and they had talked it over, Ann got her cloak and bonnet and announced:

"I'm going to run over to the Wilsons. They'll want to know, too."

"What? Tonight?" her mother exclaimed.

"Maybe they have a letter, too," said her father.

"I don't think so," cried the girl. "Mark hasn't been able to write before and—" a little proudly, "I think he would write me first."

The father and mother laughed indulgently as the door slammed behind the hurrying girl. A few minutes later she burst into the Wilson kitchen with so much noise and excitement that the family jumped to their feet.

"What's the matter, Ann?"

"I'm sorry," laughed Ann. "Nothing but good news. I've heard from Mark. I've heard from Mark." She waved the letter at them.

Even the small children listened eagerly and intently while Ann read part of the letter with a lilt in her voice. Then impetuously she threw her arms around Nancy's neck and cried:

"I must get back home," and was out of the door on a run.

Back home she found that her father and mother had gone to bed but had left a coal oil lamp lighted for her, so she took it and climbed slowly up the stairs to her bedroom. As she began to undress, her elation began to ebb. After all, it wasn't Mark; it was just a letter. As she got into bed, she thought that all of them could say what they had a mind to about the soldiers having it easier in war than the women. It just wasn't so. After all, she had a warm, soft bed, and enough to eat—such as it was—while her Mark was sleeping on the ground and was hungry.

Unable to sleep she got up, lit the lamp again and, wrapping the quilt from the bed around her, sat down to answer Mark's letter.

"Dearest Mark:

"I cannot tell you what it meant to me to get your letter, the first one since we were married and the first love letter, I'd have you know, I have ever received! When your letter came, I read it and then I read it again and again, and then I told Father and Mother about it. After that I ran all the way to your place to let your folks know how you were. When I came back, I guess I was tired or excited or something. Anyway, it's so lonesome in my room without you that I can't sleep, and here I am trying to talk to you in the only way I have.

"Dear, we've known each other ever since we were youngsters, and for a long time we thought we were in love. I don't know how it is with you, but I didn't realize how much I cared for you until after we were married and until I had to leave you and come home alone. I wish I knew how to find the words to tell you how you fill my thoughts all of the time, and how hard I try to imagine what you are doing each hour of the day and how much I worry for fear you are getting sick or hurt. I wish I knew how to tell you how I miss you and how long the weeks stretch ahead before I can see you.

"Now as I read this over it doesn't seem to be very brave or comforting except that maybe you will get some idea of how I love you. And maybe it will be a comfort to you to be assured that you are in my thoughts constantly, and that there is somebody here at home, in addition to your own dear folks, waiting for you with open arms. Maybe it is a comfort to you also, as it is to me, to remember that we are young, that we have years ahead for which we can plan and hope for happiness together. After all, a few weeks or a few months are not really long out of a lifetime.

"The spring is really opening up now. The farmers who are left are busy with the spring work and are planting larger crops than usual, knowing that more food will be needed because of the war. All your folks and mine are well. Write as often as you can, and take good care of my husband.

"Your loving wife,
Ann."

Ann reread the letter, folded it in an envelope, addressed it, blew out the light and, comforted, crawled back into bed. The next thing she knew the early morning sun was streaming in her window.

CHAPTER VII

APRIL WAS PAST and May had come at last, with its lilacs blooming by the kitchen door and the gnarled, untrimmed old trees in the family orchard on the slope back of the Clinton house covered with pink and white blossoms. As Ann made her way up through the orchard with a jug of water for her father, who was plowing in the field near the top of the hill, she listened to the buzz of a million bees in the blossoms and to the songs of the birds, who were loud in their praise of the warm day.

Sadly Ann thought how differently she would feel about all the beauty and fragrance around her if Mark were only there to share it with her. Strange what a difference one person could make when you loved him. Love really limited one's freedom. With it went the carefree days of youth when, with the exception of the family, no person meant more than another to you. But not for all the world would she trade what she had with Mark! She'd gladly take the loneliness for what she had gained.

Her thoughts went back again to the fragrance and beauty around her, and she contrasted the peaceful scene with the excitement and turmoil of war only a few hundred miles to the south. No matter what happened, Nature went on about her business. Come peace or war, for ten thousand times ten thousand years the sun had shone, and the rains fallen, and the seasons rolled. Let little man tear up the earth with his plow or his cannon, it mattered not, for in a brief time the grass covered the scars—and the little man, too.

When her father saw her coming through the meadow beyond the orchard, he stopped his horses and came around to sit on the beam of the plow. Fred Clinton was a short, slight man with light reddish hair streaked with gray. His reddish mustache was lighter than his hair, and its corners drooped down each side of his mouth. In fact, Fred drooped all over this morning, his whole aspect that of a discouraged and ineffectual man.

When Ann handed him the jug, he expertly removed the cork, hoisted it to lie horizontally on his shoulder, and, turning his head a little sideways, he let the cool water flow down his throat. Watching him Ann forgot her own feelings to grin at the absurd sight of her dad's Adam's apple bobbing up and down in the loose skin of his throat as he swallowed.

"What's so funny?"

"You!" she said, giggling. "Why do men have so much bigger Adam's apples than women?"

"Oh, for gosh sakes! How do I know? Why don't you ask something sensible? That sounds like one of the questions you used to pester me with when you were about four."

"You always tried to answer them, too," she said. "You were always good to me, Dad—" she paused and then added, slowly, "when I was little."

"You've always been a good daughter, Ann. But I know what you mean. Guess I haven't been much of a dad or a husband, either, for that matter."

Looking at his bent head and the discouraged slump of his shoulders, Ann felt sorry for him.

"Is anything special the matter, Dad?"

He looked back along the furrow that he had just turned, at the robins who were having a picnic on the angleworms in the new moist earth, and instead of answering directly he said:

"Farming is *such* a hard game, Ann. I was thinking just now that I wish Mother and I could set you and Mark up with some housekeeping things and a team of horses and some tools. But I guess I ain't much good. I know my failing." With a gesture to the field, he continued:

"Did you ever see so many stones in your life? Every fall I pick 'em off and lay 'em in the stone wall fence, and every time I plow again there are more'n ever. No wonder the crops are poor. How can anything grow in this rock pile?" Bitterness edged his voice as he added:

"Maybe I ain't much good, but how in God's name could anyone make a living on such cussed poor land?"

"We've always had enough to eat, Dad. We'll continue to

make out somehow, I'm sure. Things are no worse than usual, are they? Why are you so low this nice morning?"

"Well, things *are* worse than usual. Up to a year ago we were able to pay the interest on the mortgage with your help. But the crops have been bad lately, that cow died, and the others aren't doing so well. The interest is due on the mortgage and I just ain't got the money to pay it."

Ann knew that her father understood that the real trouble lay in his drinking, but she felt the need to comfort him.

"Well, maybe things will be better this fall. I heard someone say the other day that farm prices are going to be higher because so many have gone into the Army, and they have to be fed as well as ourselves. We'll sell some potatoes this fall, and I'll help with some of my teaching money. We can pay the interest all right, and maybe something on the principal, too. Don't be so discouraged."

He picked up a handful of soil and let it trickle through his fingers.

"That ain't all the trouble, Ann. The bank in Owego that held the mortgage has always been a little easy on me when I couldn't make the payments on time. But they wrote me the other day that they have been refinancing, and they've sold some of their mortgages—ours among them."

"Whom to?" she demanded. "Maybe he'll be easier to do business with even than the bank. Who was it?"

A queer look passed over her father's face.

"A friend of yours—at least he was until you married Mark Wilson—Henry Bain. I most wish you'd married him; then we wouldn't have had to worry. But now I don't know how he'll be toward me. He has money. He owns a lot of mortgages around here. They say he's a hard man to do business with. In fact, just yesterday he was kind of hintin' around to me about my interest and payin' somethin' on the principal."

"Just what I thought," she said, triumphantly. "You're doing too much worrying. I know Henry, and I don't believe he's that kind of a person. I'll just bet you'll find he's all right."

"I dunno," said her father, doubtfully. "He would have been, I guess, before you married Mark, for he was certainly sweet on you. Now I don't know."

He got up rather painfully, straightened his back, went around between the plow handles, put the lines over his shoulders, and spoke to his horses. Ann stood watching him. Suddenly the point of the plow struck a cobblestone, jumped out of the furrow and was dragged along on top of the ground before Clinton could stop the horses. Painfully he yanked it back into the furrow and started them up again.

As Ann went back down through the orchard, she felt worried, not so much about what her father had told her about the mortgage as the fact that she knew from long experience that these fits of depression usually preceded several days' absence from home on a spree.

A little way up the road from the Clinton farm on that same May day, George Wilson, his two sons, Charles and Tom, and Enoch Payne, the hired man, were planting corn on the big flat by the creek. George was marking out the long rows with a horse and the three-legged marker. The boys and Enoch, each with a small bag tied around his waist filled with tarred corn, were dropping the kernels about two to three feet apart in the row and covering them with the rich alluvial soil of the creek bottom. Young Tom complained:

"Why do we have to put tar on the corn, Enoch? It's sticky and smelly, and I hate handling the darn stuff."

Enoch grinned.

"Crows don't like the tar any better'n you do, son. It's no use to plant corn if the rascals pull it all up. That's why we plant more'n we need. You know the old rhyme:

> One for the blackbird,
> One for the crow,
> One for the cutworm,
> And three left to grow."

"Look at them over on the fence now!" Charles exclaimed. "They know what we're doing."

"Sure they do," agreed Enoch. "They're just the outposts or sentinels. They'll report what we're doing here to the main body, and in about ten days when the corn begins to sprout above the ground the whole bunch of them will be here. But they'll get fooled, Tom," he concluded, "because just about one taste of this tar is all they'll want."

Stopping his work, Enoch brushed his long reddish hair back out of his eyes, leaving a brown streak of tar and dirt across his forehead. Then taking out a plug of tobacco and sinking his strong white teeth in it, he twisted his head back and forth until he had pried loose a generous bite. With that safely stowed in the side of his mouth, he remarked to the boys, who were leaning on their hoes, glad of an excuse to stop work for a little:

"Can't help but like the black devils, though. They're so darn smart."

"Yes, they're smart all right," agreed Charlie. "When a fellow has a gun, he can't get a glimpse of one; and when you have no gun, you can almost walk up to them."

"Had a pet crow once," mused Enoch. "I climbed a tall pine to a nest filled with the little black rascals way in the top of the tree. The old bird danged near made me fall, too. She had all kinds of nerve, kept rushin' and tryin' to hit me in the face with her wings. But I stowed one of the young 'uns in my pocket, took it home and raised it. Sometimes I wished I hadn't, though. Leave anything loose around the place an' the next minute it was gone! That bird would steal ye blind."

"I've heard that you can learn a crow to talk," said Tom. "Is that true, Enoch?"

"Don't know about that. Mine didn't, unless his constant yapping, 'Caw! caw! caw!' meant anything."

"I think they talk among themselves," said Charlie. "You know how two or three will act as guards on the edge of the woods, and when they think something dangerous is coming, they rush back to tell the others. Then after a terrible racket and yelling at each other, they all fly away."

"Yeah! so they do," agreed Enoch. "But the most interesting thing they do is their fall elections. They hold them about the time ours are held."

Enoch spat a long brown stream at a potato bug.

"And they probably make jest as much sense as ours. Jest like you said, Charlie, they gather from everywhere, put out guards, and then they start yelling and cawing so you can hear them for miles. Probably some politician among them who can yell the loudest and lie the most wins the election, and then they all quiet down and fly away."

Across the field a few rods away, George Wilson had stopped to mop his brow and look meaningly at the group leaning on their hoes. So they got to work again. With long practice they were able to pick up five or six kernels almost every time they reached into their bags, drop them in the row, and pull a couple of hoefuls of soil on them, repeating the operation endlessly and monotonously. Every few minutes the boys would look longingly at the climbing sun, which it seemed to them would never reach its zenith and tell them what their stomachs had told them long before— that it was dinner time.

Finally, at the end of a row, in the shade of an old butternut tree which hung partly over the creek bed, they stopped again to rest. The smell of the soil under the hot May sun, mixed with the fishy smell of the creek, welled up to them. Overlying all was a strong aroma of mint that always grew on the creek flats.

Charles looked out across the cornfield at the simmering heat waves rising from the warm ground and spoke out of his irritation and discontent:

"Enoch, I'm sick and tired of all this. Mark had the right idea. He's getting all the fun and adventure, and he's got out of all this hard work—work that's all the harder because we have to do our share and his, too. It takes a lot longer now to do the chores and milk the cows. And then we rush out into these fields to work from morning till night. No play, no fun, nothing but work!"

But Enoch was unsympathetic.

"Work's good fer ye. An' don't fool yourself about all the fun that Mark's having, either. If ye were down there being bossed around by them officers, livin' on poor grub an' sleepin' on the ground, you'd change your tune. Minds me of a story—"

But Charles was impatient.

"The best story I can hear," he growled, "would be that I could trade this blasted hoe for a gun."

"Me, too," chimed in Tom. "We hoe corn an' potatoes into the ground, and we work all summer hoeing the weeds out of them. Then we work half the fall diggin' the potatoes with a potato hook."

"That's the way it is," said Charles, bitterly. "There was a circus in Owego last summer, but could we go? No. Pa said there wasn't money enough."

"An' d'you know what?" piped up Tom again. "Last Christmas, Ma brought home just one orange. She divided it into six pieces for us kids—didn't even save a taste for herself or Pa."

Enoch grinned tolerantly at the earnest, dirt-streaked faces of the boys.

"You wouldn't believe it now, but you'll know some time, that that little bit of orange you got meant more and tasted better than a whole orange or something else bigger than that will taste when you grow up."

The boys were in no mood for philosophy.

"All I know," Charles repeated, emphatically, "is that I'm sick and tired of all this work and I'd just like to trade this darn hoe for a gun." He paused, then added, half to himself, "And maybe I will do just that."

"What time do you think it is?" inquired Tom, whose stomach was knocking.

Enoch cocked a knowing glance at the sun. " 'Bout half past eleven. Come on! By the time we get over and back again, the dinner bell will ring."

Reluctantly the boys followed him out into the hot sun to start planting again.

"If you'd listen to my story," said Enoch, "maybe it would help pass the time."

"Oh, for gosh sakes, go ahead," said Charles, grinning. "We can stand it, and you won't feel good until you get it out of your system, anyway. But I warn you, if Ma rings that dinner bell before you get through, there won't be anybody here to listen to you."

"Well," said the hired man, "it was like this." He slapped at a fly on his face, leaving another tar mark, and went on:

"This really isn't much of a story. While you were grumbling, I was just thinking 'bout what happened to me when I was a boy younger than you. I worked out many a day hoeing 'taters against men, doin' just as good a job as they did. At the end of the day, though, the boss would pay me just half what he did the others, because I was a boy."

Charles snorted:

"Half pay! We don't even get that."

"Got a home an' folks, ain't ye?" Enoch was becoming serious. "More'n I had. My folks died young. My only home was any place I could hang my hat. There's somethin' else you got that you don't know 'nough to be thankful for. It's pleasant in these fields. Things are all the way you look at 'em."

Just then the big farm bell on the stoop started to clang, and as the boys made for the house on a run, Enoch grinned and said aloud:

"Never did get a chance to tell 'em that dang story!"

CHAPTER VIII

TIRED THOUGH HE WAS that night, Charles was determined not to go to bed, for he knew that once he laid down he wouldn't wake until morning. Waiting until Tom was asleep and until he could hear no sound from downstairs, he hastily tied a few clothes in a bundle, then with the bundle in one hand and his shoes in the other, he crept down the stairs, stopping with every step to make sure that no one was waking, and putting his feet down as quietly as he could on the side of the steps because the boards squeaked in the middle.

Heart pounding, he finally reached the bottom of the stairs and raised the latch of the door that opened into the kitchen. Then he hesitated again, listening for a long time, fearing to waken his mother and father in their downstairs bedroom. Finally, reassured by the sound of his father snoring, he took two or three tentative steps into the kitchen, hit a chair in the dark, and was startled to hear his mother mutter something. But after waiting and listening he realized that she had spoken in her sleep, so he made his way at last to the outside door and stepped out into the night.

On the porch steps he sat down to put on his shoes. Then, with his bundle under his arm, he went down the path to the small gate that led to the country road in front of the house. His heart did a somersault again when Dan, their old shepherd dog, rushed barking out of the woodshed where he always slept with one eye open and an ear cocked to catch any unusual sound. The boy sank down by the side of the yard fence and threw his arms around the dog, burying his head in his deep fur and hugging him to his chest. At the same time he strained his ears for any sounds from the house, but apparently the barking had aroused no one. All was quiet, and in a few moments Charlie got to his feet, gave the dog a shove and ordered him in a low tone to "Go back!" Obedi-

ent though wistful, the dog slowly retreated to the shed and
Charlie picked up his bundle and started plodding down the
road.

A few rods away he turned to look at the old house and
barn, shadowy in the dark. With a lump in his throat he
raised a hand in farewell and turned again to trudge resolutely
down the road which led through Jenkstown to Newark
Valley and Owego. He had set his feet to war and had no
intention of turning back.

Near the end of the farm was a little cemetery where the
neighborhood dead had been laid to rest since the beginning
of the settlement. Charlie had worked in the field around the
burial ground from the time he was a small boy, and he and
his boyhood friends had played carelessly among the graves,
their bare feet in the green myrtle that mantled the whole
cemetery; but now in the dead of the night everything somehow seemed different. Strange black objects that he couldn't
distinguish loomed along the fences and in the adjoining
fields. As he passed the cemetery he was conscious of the
quiet sleepers there as he never had been before, and he was
disturbed by the thought that maybe at this time of night
they weren't so quiet. Overhead an owl on the branch of a
maple tree that bordered the cemetery suddenly let out a
mournful hoot. With chills chasing down his spine, and
feeling that a ghostly hand was reaching out to grab him
around the neck, Charlie started to run. Well down the
road and completely out of breath he stopped and sat down
on a grassy knoll, a little ashamed and amused at his own
cowardice.

"Some soldier I'll make!" he told himself, disgustedly.

When he had recovered his breath he got up and plodded
on again, but after several miles more he felt as if he couldn't
take another step. Up at dawn to help with the chores, working all day planting corn, chores again at night on top of
everything else, sleepless and emotionally upset, Charlie knew
that he had never before been so tired. But it was too cold
to stop long by the roadside.

He had to resist the temptation to turn back home. Anyway, he told himself, it was almost as far to go back as it
was to go on. So he forced his lagging legs to drag on step by
step, mile after mile, till the only thing that mattered seemed

to be to lift one foot and put it ahead of the other. Occasionally a strange dog would rush at him, barking, then slink back, tail between his legs, as Charlie spoke to him. The boy welcomed these interruptions, for they helped to break the monotony of that long walk.

The night wore on and light began to show to his left over the eastern hills. Then came the familiar, homey sound of a rooster crowing. Coming finally to The Narrows, where the hill came down to the road and a deep bank pitched off the other side into the creek, he knew that he was nearing Owego. That and the dawn gave him his second wind. A little later he reached the small park surrounding the Court House in Owego. There he almost fell on one of the park benches and, in spite of the chill air, was instantly asleep.

When he awoke, the sun was dappling the green of the park lawn and it was warm. It took him a moment to orient himself. He wondered what they had thought at home when they missed him, and then realizing how hungry he was he stood up, a little stiff at first from his walk, and looked around. In his pocket he fingered the few coins he had managed to save, and started to walk around the streets until he finally came to the little hotel where Mark and Ann had stayed. Here for two shillings he got a breakfast of buckwheat pancakes, maple sirup, sausage, fried potatoes, coffee and doughnuts. He ate until it seemed that he never again would have room for anything more.

When he paid the proprietor for his breakfast, he inquired a little diffidently where he could join the Army. The old man pushed his spectacles further down on his nose and looked at the boy with kind grey eyes for a long moment before answering:

"So you've got the idea, too. Pretty soon Uncle Abe will have all the boys. Well, the office is right on this same street. You can't miss it."

Then coming around the end of the counter, he stuck out a hairy hand and said:

"Shake, son! I wish you luck!"

Charlie left the hotel and as he walked along Front Street toward the recruiting office, he was of two minds. Lonesome and homesick, he almost turned off on North Avenue to start on the long trek back home. Irresolutely he stopped to watch the broad Susquehanna, mist covered, flowing south and into the unknown. Then, with a deep sigh that was close to tears, he lifted his chin, squared his shoulders, and set off briskly up the street to the recruiting office.

That same morning in the three-quarter bed that George and Nancy Wilson shared, George awoke with the first light of dawn streaming in through the single window of the little bedroom off the farmhouse kitchen. His first thought was of Mark. Then remembering the responsibilities of the farm, he reluctantly stuck one foot out into the chill of the early morning, and then the other. Pulling on his pants, shirt and socks, he carried his heavy shoes into the kitchen so as to let Nancy rest for a few minutes longer. With his big jackknife he whittled some pine shavings and soon had a fire started in the kitchen stove, filled the tea kettle with water from the pail in the sink and put on his hat and coat. Then he stepped to the stairway, opened the door and called:

"Charlie! Tom! Time to be up!"

Hearing no sound, after a couple of minutes he called again, more sharply, and Tom answered:

"Charlie's up. He isn't here."

Surprised and a little pleased that Charlie would show enough responsibility to get up by himself and get to the barn chores early, George said to Tom:

"Well, you come on and help, too."

Then he went out to the barn, but in the long cow stable he saw no sign of Charlie. A little disturbed feeling crept into his mind and he went around onto the big barn floor, thinking that perhaps Charlie was there pitching down the hay for the morning feeding. But here again there was no sign or sound. Somewhat alarmed now, thinking that the boy might have been hurt, George made a thorough search of the premises. Then, work forgotten, he quickly returned to the house, passed Nancy just coming out of the bedroom all ready to get breakfast, opened the stair door and ran up the steps into the chamber where the boys slept. There he found Tom hastily pulling on his pants, but no sign of Charlie.

"Did Charlie go to bed when you did last night?" he asked Tom.

"No. He was settin' in that little chair there when I went to sleep."

"Don't you remember his being in bed with you in the night?"

"No, I don't," said Tom. "Why should I? I was asleep. Why? What's the matter?"

Without answering, his father turned and ran downstairs. To Nancy's inquiring look, he said:

"Charlie isn't at the barn or upstairs. I think he's gone."

Nancy sat down abruptly in a chair.

"Gone!" she exclaimed. "What do you mean, gone?"

"He's been talking war lately. I thought it was just talk, but I'm afraid he has slipped off to Owego."

"But how could that be possible? How could he walk all that distance after working all day?"

"I don't know, but where else could he have gone?"

Nancy was recovering from the first shock. She got up and went on with getting breakfast.

"Go on and do your chores," she said. "Probably he has just gone to the neighbor's to stay all night. He likes Ann awfully well. Maybe he's gone over there."

"Don't believe it. He's been grumbling ever since Mark left. He didn't like the work."

"I know he didn't. What boy does? Nevertheless, he always did his share."

Nancy's own worry was forgotten for the moment in her sympathy for her husband. It took a lot to make his voice tremble. Sometimes he was stern with the boys, but she knew the strong affection he had for them."

"I tell you, go on and do your chores," she said, a little sharply, to cover up her feelings. "Likely before you're done, he'll be back to help finish them."

Shoulders sagging a little, George obediently went out of the kitchen and down the path to the barn, closely followed by Tom who, scared and worried, was more than willing to do Charlie's share of the chores as well as his own.

Sensing the strain, the children around the table that morning were very quiet. Nancy had told the girls that Charlie was gone, and when they asked where, she said she didn't know but maybe to enlist like Mark had. George drank his coffee, ate a pancake, and then suddenly pushed back his chair. Looking across at his wife, he exclaimed:

"I'm going after him. He's only 16. That's too young and I'm going to bring him back."

Nancy replied:

"Whatever you think best, Mr. Wilson. But remember that Charlie is no longer a child. He has grown up, and if we force him against his will that will not be good, either."

Then she smiled sadly:

"I'll bet right now he's homesick and sorry for what he has done. Maybe a little gentle reasoning will do a lot more with him than an order. If he has enlisted," she added, "maybe you'll be too late anyway. Maybe he's being sent South today."

"That's a chance I've got to take," he replied. "I'll get started just as soon as I can finish the chores."

Some time in the middle of the afternoon George found his son sitting on the bench in the little park where he had had his brief nap in the morning. At sight of his father Charlie jumped eagerly to his feet. Then realizing that perhaps he was due for a lecture, his face clouded and he sank back on to the seat again. George stood looking down at him for a moment and then sat down beside him. For the first time that Charles could remember, his father put an arm over his shoulders. That melted all the resistance in the boy's heart, his eyes misted, and a lump came into his throat.

"Do you think, son, that you did just the right thing sneaking away in the night without saying goodby to us, particularly to your mother?"

"Well—if I'd told you, you know you wouldn't have let me go."

"Maybe I won't now," smiled his father.

"I've got to go now. I've enlisted."

"Yes, but what did you tell the officer about your age?"

Charlie hesitated:

"I told him I was 18. I'm big, you know, and he didn't question it."

"I guess they don't question much anyway. They need men. But the officer would not let you go if I told him you were only 16."

Charles did not answer, and his father continued:

"But I'm not going to. When are they shipping you out?"

"I don't know," said Charlie. "He said it would be several days."

"Well, as I said, I'm not going to get you out," repeated his father, "but I am going to ask you to come back home and say goodby to your mother."

Charles's face brightened:

"Of course I will, Pa. I want to! I'll be glad to!"

"All right," George said, getting briskly to his feet. "I've got an errand or two. Old Molly is over in the livery stable. You go over there and I'll be around in a few minutes and we'll be on our way back home."

Charlie would have been surprised if he could have followed his father, for George made his way straight to the recruiting office. He found the old sergeant with his chair tipped back against the wall, his feet on the table, smoking a cigar. George introduced himself, stated that he had two sons who had enlisted, the latest no longer ago than this morning.

"What I'm here for," he said, "is to get a little information."

Remembering Charlie and his youthful appearance, the sergeant scowled, thinking that the father was going to make trouble. But his visitor's next question surprised him.

"How bad is this situation? Do you think it calls for every able-bodied man?"

"Yes, sir," was the sergeant's answer. "It's a bad job. Some think this mess is goin' to be over in three months; my guess is three years. Why?"

"Well, I got to thinking that maybe I ought to go, too."

"You a farmer?"

"Yes."

"The Army's got to eat. Somebody's got to raise the stuff. You ain't so young, either. But one thing's sure," he added, "the more men we can put down there in a hurry, the quicker they'll all be home. So I'll sign you up if you wish."

"No-o-o—" George hesitated. "Not today. I'd have to make some changes at home. But maybe later."

All the way home that afternoon, Charles, pleased at the way that events had shaped themselves and glad that he was going to see his mother again and that he had his father's approval, wanted to talk. But he got little response from his father, who seemed to be fully occupied with his own thoughts.

CHAPTER IX

IN THE DAYS THAT FOLLOWED Charlie's departure to join his company, George Clinton was more demonstrative than usual toward his wife and children. Occasionally, to Nancy's surprise and pleasure, he let his hand touch her shoulder as he passed her. But as he went about the everyday work, made doubly hard now by the absence of the older boys, he was unusually quiet even for him.

No matter how hard he worked, or how long the days, he never missed an evening at the Post Office to get the news and maybe a letter. Frequently he met Ann there and they came back together. Had Nancy been inclined to be sensitive, she might have felt a little jealous of Ann, for it was only when she came to have a meal or to spend an evening with them that George came out of his abstraction and silence and talked freely about the war and the boys.

What Nancy didn't know was that he was plagued by the thought that perhaps he was just as able to go and it was just as necessary for him to carry a gun as it was for his boys, particularly young Charlie. Once she got an inkling of how he felt when he said, suddenly:

"The boys have gone. Maybe I ought to go and help take care of them."

"Nonsense!" she snapped. "How could you look out for them? You would probably not be assigned to the same regiment, to say nothing of the same company."

He let the matter rest there for the present, but his remark planted another worry in her mind, and she thought about it constantly, except when she was too tired to think at all. Both she and George were up at dawn each day and fell into bed at night almost too exhausted to get their clothes off. With the help of Tom and some day labor from Enoch Payne, George managed to get the last crops in and the cultivating done during June. But the worst job was the milking. Tom was too young to help much with the milking, and that left a long line of cows for George to milk every night and morning. Most of the cows had freshened in the spring, and now with the lush June pastures they were in full production. His hands and arms ached all the time from the strain of milking them. Sometimes Nancy, leaving the little girls to do the best they could with breakfast and supper, came to the barn and milked two or three of the cows. But she had so much to do in the house that she couldn't do this regularly.

After the milking was finished, George carried the milk, two pails at a time, to the big cool farmhouse cellar where Nancy poured it into the pans on the long lines of shelves. When the cream was raised, she would skim it by hand from the pans, dumping the skim milk into pails and carrying it to the barn to feed the hungry calves and the four pigs. Three or four times a week the cream had to be churned into butter. The girls helped some with this, but they soon tired, and most of the work fell upon their mother.

When the butter was churned, Nancy put it into the big butter bowl and worked it back and forth with the butter ladle to free it from the buttermilk, and then she packed it in crocks ready to sell. Once a week Nancy put these crocks of butter into the back of the big democrat wagon and drove to the village, where she traded most of her butter to John Crawford for groceries. The remainder she peddled out among her regular customers in the village.

The hens, too, were Nancy's responsibility. To keep her flock replenished, she would put thirteen eggs under each of several "setting" hens, and at the end of twenty-one days the mother hen and the fluffy little chicks she had hatched would be put into a small inverted A-shaped coop. There they had to be fed and watered and guarded from rats and other vermin until the chickens could more or less take care of themselves. Eggs from the flock, except those eaten by the family, also went to John Crawford for a few cents a dozen or were traded for groceries.

There was a garden, too, which supplied the family with vegetables. Both parents believed in developing habits of responsibility in their children, so they were taught to work as soon as they were able, and it wasn't enough to work until they were tired; the principle was to stop when the job was done. Even the little girls could weed the garden and help in feeding the calves, getting meals, and washing and drying dishes.

Occasionally, as Nancy went about her countless tasks, she would straighten her back and look off across the fields, soft and blooming in the June sunlight, and think that even with the hard work it was a good life, a wholesome life, or at least it had been until war came. War changed everything, made everything worse. And always in her mind were thoughts of Mark and Charlie. Where were they? What were they doing? Were they in danger? She liked to talk with Ann about them. It helped to be able to share her love and her worries with Ann.

Mark wrote frequently, often to his wife and occasionally to his mother. The letters were cheerful, but it was apparent that as yet he had not found the adventure that had been part of his reason for volunteering. He was impatient with the waiting, and waiting seemed to be all that the Army was doing, except for the constant drilling. He wrote that all the boys were utterly tired of it.

June, usually the nicest month of the year on the farm, slowly dragged by. The crops were all good. The corn on the flats was now knee-high and seemed to grow inches every warm night. It no longer needed any attention until harvest time. The potatoes were growing well, too. They needed hoeing, but probably wouldn't get it. In former years George had taken great pride in his good crops. This year, with work crowding him and his thoughts on the war more than on the farm, the growing crops and the work they required annoyed and worried him. Especially was this the case with the haying, which was now upon him. The meadows stretched away across the farm with a heavy growth of grass; and without the boys' help, and with all the chores to do, George didn't see how in the world he could get his haying done. He could get Enoch Payne to help some with pitching the hay on the wagon and unloading it in the barn, but Enoch felt that his first duty was to the Clintons, so he could only spare a day or so a week to help George.

Resolutely George tackled the job himself. Rising at 3:30 in the morning now, earlier than ever before, he did his chores, sharpened his scythe to a razor edge, and started the formidable job of scything. When George was mowing in the meadows near the house, Nancy could occasionally hear the familiar clang, clang, clang, when he stopped to whet his scythe. It was a long time between breakfast and dinner time, so in the middle of the morning Nancy would send one of the little girls out to George with a snack and a jug of cool milk from the cellar. Once in a while, when time permitted, she would take it herself and sit with her husband in the shade while he ate. Not much talk passed between them at these times, for their understanding was such that no talk was needed.

The sun cured the grass rapidly, and Nancy, Tom and the girls came into the fields with their hand rakes. Enoch got in the habit of coming over late in the afternoon on good haying days, and he and George would spend the last few hours of daylight putting into the barn the hay which had been cut the day before.

But the haying days of July went so rapidly and the one main job so slowly that the month was two-thirds gone and the haying only half done. Now the grass had turned brown and tough, making the scything all the harder.

The group who met in John Crawford's store in the evening to get the news and an occasional letter were even more impatient than the boys at the front about the apparent hanging back of the Union forces. "Why don't they march on to Richmond and get it over with and let the boys come home?" expressed the general feeling, especially among those who didn't have boys at the front. George Wilson listened to this talk, but said little, for one reason because he was always so tired and for another because, in common with other fathers, his heart and mind were torn with fear. "On to Richmond" meant battles, and battles meant death to some, and how could he know that it might not be his own sons? It was easy enough for those to talk who had no sons to think about.

There was rejoicing when the news came through that General George B. McClellan had driven the Confederates out of western Virginia, and that that section of Virginia would now be loyal to the Union. But then the impatience increased. Why didn't Lincoln and General Scott, McClellan and the other commanders move on to Richmond and bring the war to a speedy conclusion? That's what everybody expected them to do, and why were they hanging back? When these thoughts were voiced by a member of the group, Henry Bain said one night:

"Maybe Abe and old man Scott are just plain scared. Maybe you fellows ought to be thankful that the Army isn't moving on to Richmond. There's just as good a chance that the Confederates could move on to Washington. That would end the war, too."

That seemed to be the signal for their breaking up that night. Many of them didn't like Bain, but they said nothing, knowing that he had put into words what many of them feared.

Then one night in the latter part of July, George Wilson, chores done and supper eaten, dragged himself down again to the nightly rendezvous. There he found a larger than usual crowd of neighbors, all excited and talking at once. The stage that night had brought the news that at last General Scott had responded to the demand, "On to Richmond." But he had been met by the Confederates at a place called Bull Run and defeated. "Licked" was the word Bain used to describe the rout.

In the background John Crawford listened to the excited discussion for a few moments, then got up, sat on the edge of the counter and raised his hand for quiet. Pushing his spectacles forward on his nose and looking over the top of them at his friends and neighbors, he said:

"The news is that the North is scared and the government is even thinking of moving out of Washington. I've been listening to you talk here, and I suspect the same kind of talk is going on in a thousand other neighborhoods. But let me tell you something. The Rebs have won a battle, but not the war. All that this battle proves is what some of us have thought all along—that this is not a three months' job. It may take years."

To emphasize his point, he raised his long arm, which stuck out of a too-short shirt sleeve, and pointing his finger at them, he declared:

"Whether it takes months or years," he declared, "we're going to win this war! Of course the boys from the South are Americans, and all Americans can fight. Bain said a spell ago that they are more used to guns down there than are our boys. Maybe that's so. But," he paused for emphasis, "our boys can learn and will learn. And we've got some things the South hasn't—we've got more men and we've got more resources, and we've got the right of it. If we can hold the South from coming clear through to final victory for a while, we'll wear them out, and that's what we've got to do, and every man jack of us has got to do his part!"

He turned to look directly at Henry Bain.

"As for you, Hank, and others like you, I'm tired of hearing your kind of talk. If you ain't man enough to go to war, at least you can keep your mouth shut. There's a lot at stake in this fight, and some of us ain't foolin'. And I tell you again that if there are others in this neighborhood that feel as you do, they'd better keep their ideas to themselves."

He slid down from the counter.

"G'night, boys! I'm tired and so be you. All of us are going to need all the rest we can get."

After they had gone to bed that night, George said to Nancy:

"Nancy, I've something to tell you."

Feeling sure that she knew what it was, Nancy remained silent, which made it more difficult for George to begin. At last he said:

"The Union forces were badly licked at a place called Bull Run on July 21. They've retreated back toward Washington almost in a rout. I'm sure that Lincoln will call for more volunteers. You probably think that my duty is here with you and the children, and maybe it is. But for some time I've felt, Nancy, that if we can possibly arrange it so you can get along, I have a bigger duty to follow the boys into the Army. The more of us that feel and act this way, the sooner it'll be over and we'll have our boys back."

That was a long speech for George, and when he stopped a silence hung between them, broken finally by Nancy, whose carefully controlled voice sounded unnatural:

"If that's the way you feel, that's all right with me. I don't know how we'll get along, but there must be some way, and I'll manage. But George, you've got to remember that you are no longer young. You'll ruin your health sleeping on the ground, and things like that."

"I've thought it all out," he said, eager to explain now that the first fence was down. "You and Tom and the girls can't take care of this dairy, of course, so I've decided to sell all the cows but one or two, leaving just enough for butter and milk for you and the family. The haying isn't all done, but I can finish the rest of it in the next few days. The other crops will be all right till fall, and perhaps the war will be over then. If it isn't, maybe I can get a furlough for two or three weeks to get the corn cut and the potatoes dug. I sowed a couple of acres of buckwheat the other day. That'll give us enough buckwheat flour to get us through the winter, and I'm sure you can get Enoch to cradle the buckwheat and put it in the barn. Maybe he'll help some with the other work that you or the children can't do."

"Oh, Enoch'll go, too," she said, a little bitterly. "I wonder why men never realize that there's a home front as well as a battle front in war."

"Now, Nancy," he remonstrated, "that's a little unfair. I know what this means to you, but I've thought and thought, and, as I've told you, in order to keep our families we've first got to keep a country."

"Well," she agreed, "maybe you are right. I don't know! But I've told you we'll get along somehow, and we will."

With that he had to be content, but in spite of his weariness, sleep was long in coming and, judging by the number of times that Nancy turned and twisted in bed, he knew that she was not sleeping either.

The next day George started to reduce his farm operations to a minimum. His cows were good, but when he tried to find a market for them, there was little because so many other farmers were in the same position of reducing or getting rid of their herds, their boys or their hired help having gone to war. Reluctantly, at last George talked with Henry Bain, who dealt in cattle. As he expected, he found Henry unwilling to pay what the cattle were worth. With his mind made up to do business at any price, George was a poor bargainer, and finally he sold all except two of his cows and all his young stock to Bain for a ridiculously low price. "At least," he thought, "the few hundred dollars will keep Nancy and the children going for a long time with what little cash she will need."

With sad heart and much misgiving as to the wisdom of his decision, a few days later George watched Bain drive his herd off the place and down the road, the herd which he had spent many years in building up.

CHAPTER X

ON THE FOLLOWING Sunday morning, George walked slowly with head bent and arms locked behind him along the lane through which he and the boys had driven the cattle to and from pasture for years. Then he climbed the fence to look with pride across the corn that they had planted with Enoch Payne's help. Getting down on the field side, he walked through the corn, now waist high and beginning to show signs of tasseling, and finally he came to the creek bank where the spicy fragrance of the crushed mint was wafted up with every step he took.

In a shady spot on the bank he sat down, the hot sun raising the familiar creek flat odors of growing corn, mint, and the indescribable smell of creeks and ponds in the summer. Looking off down the valley toward the South and lost in his thoughts, George imagined he could almost hear the roar of battle. He thought about his sons, wondering where they were and what they were doing. He must have dozed off to sleep, for his next awareness was of someone calling his name. He straightened up to see Ann, shoes and stockings in her hand, skirts held high, wading across the creek toward him, the water in some places coming up to her knees.

"Don't look!" she laughed. "I'll be right with you in a minute."

Obediently he lay down again and closed his eyes, and soon Ann was sitting beside him, with her shoes and stockings on.

"Mother Nancy said you were down here somewhere, Dad. I was in hopes I'd find you. I wanted to talk with you."

He smiled at her, thinking how much she had matured lately. She had always been pretty, but now she was beautiful.

As he waited for her to tell him what was bothering her, she picked up a stone, tossed it into the water and watched the widening ripples.

"Well," she finally said, "I guess Father got completely

fed up at last. He's been gone several days again, and when he didn't come back I asked John Crawford to find out if he had enlisted. He has."

The girl swallowed a lump in her throat.

"I can understand his going," she continued, "but it seems as though he might have said goodby."

"Maybe he didn't intend to enlist when he left," George said. "Your father's a good man at heart. Don't judge him too harshly. Maybe he thought enlisting was a way to redeem himself. Maybe it is," he added, thoughtfully. "But how will you make out with the farm?"

"I'm tough," replied Ann, "so I guess I can take care of the cows, raise a garden, and find enough for Mother and me to eat."

"That's better than some womenfolks left behind can do," said George, warmly.

"Yes, but that isn't all the story. We wouldn't be able to eat if we didn't have the farm, and the farm is mortgaged for about all it's worth. Anyway, I can't handle all the crops."

"Well, most farms are mortgaged. And I don't believe anybody is going to press for payment of interest or principal while this war is on. I'm told that the bank in Owego has let it be known that they'll be as fair as they can about giving soldiers' families more time to pay."

"That's just it, Dad," said Ann, looking worried. "The bank did have our mortgage, but they sold it." She stopped talking and started nervously to pick the petals off a daisy. After a moment George asked:

"Who has it now?"

"Henry Bain."

Remembering his own difficulties with Bain on the cow deal, a shade of anxiety clouded his countenance, but he tried to reassure her.

"Well, Henry has money, I understand. He knows what you're up against, and I don't believe he'll press you."

"I'm not so sure," said Ann. "I talked with him just the other night about it, and he made some remark about there was no need for this war in the first place and why wasn't Mark home where he ought to be, working the farm instead of having a good time in the Army."

Ann's cheeks reddened with resentment.

"I guess I wasn't very diplomatic," she admitted. "I told him a few things and he went away mad."

George made no comment as he watched a hen hawk sail slowly across the blue background of the sky. Finally Ann looked up at him with tears in her eyes. "It wouldn't be much better even if Father were at home. You know how he is." Then she exclaimed:

"Do you mind if I sort of lean on your shoulder a moment, so to speak? I just have got to tell somebody or it seems as if I'd burst!"

George laid his hand over hers.

"Go ahead, Ann! Talk all you want to. But remember that things are never as bad as they sometimes seem. What's the matter? Anything else besides the mortgage business? After all, nobody starves to death in this country. You and your mother wouldn't, even if you lost the farm."

"But, Dad, a girl just has to have a little pride, and it seems as if mine has been dragged in the mud ever since I can remember. Ever since I was a little girl, I've often been so ashamed that I hated to go to school or parties or anywhere because Father made such a fool of himself when he had been drinking. Once when I was ten years old, I was coming home from school with a lot of other girls and Father overtook us. He had been drinking and he made me get on his back pig-a-back, and we went staggering up the road. The kids laughed, but I've never forgotten how ashamed I was.

"Another time I was in Jenkstown with a bunch of other little girls and Dad came staggering out of the Lawson House. I tried to hurry my friends along so they wouldn't notice, but why is it that when a man has been drinking he always has to get right on to the center of the stage? He noticed me and began to call, and then said something foolish about 'My dear little friends.' You know how kids are. They're really cruel without meaning to be, so they began to laugh at Dad and to talk to him in order to draw him out. The more he said, of course, the more foolish he seemed. He could hardly stand up.

"There were some of the boys there, too—including Mark —and all of them were laughing as hard as they could. Gosh, how I wished the road would open up and take me out of sight forever! For months afterwards I avoided those girls and boys, for I thought they were either sorry for me or making fun of me. I've never really gotten over it, and I've never gotten over hating booze.

"Some people think it's funny to see a drunk; to me it's tragic and disgraceful. We've lots of good cider apples on our farm, as you know, but we don't make any cider so it can't get hard and tempt Dad. That's one thing I just won't stand for."

Then, fearing to seem disloyal, she added:

"Dad's one of the best men in the world. He'd do anything for Mother and me, but he just can't help getting drunk now and then. Whenever he could get his hands on a few dollars, he would be gone for days, and Mother and I had to do the chores and all the farm work, or get somebody like Enoch Payne to come in and help. When Mother and I have worked and saved to get a little butter made and taken it to town and sold it, time and again Father has got his hands on that little cash and drunk it up. I don't want to complain but I never had much of any Christmas or much of any fun until Mark and I started going together. Now—" she started to cry— "maybe I've lost him."

"Here! Here!" said George, patting her shoulder awkwardly. "Don't do that! You know what Mark and Charlie mean to Nancy and me, and we don't feel we've lost them, nor are we going to. We've just got to keep hoping and praying."

"Yes," said Ann, struggling to regain her composure, "and now *you're* going away. What are we going to do with all the men gone? I've had to give up the idea of teaching this winter, for I can't do that and keep the farm going. The farm is our home and I want to hang on to it."

George looked at the earnest, troubled face of the girl and after a moment answered her:

"Well, let's look on the bright side for a moment. As I said, maybe this experience will do your father good. He's a sensitive, highly nervous man. That's the kind that drink too much. They need outlets. Maybe the Army will be good for him. Why not think that he'll come back more determined to take hold of things in the right way, more resolved to let the booze alone. Instead of being ashamed of what he has done in the past—maybe he couldn't help it—why not be proud of what he is doing now, carrying a gun for his country! Instead of thinking that you're never going to see Mark or your father or any of us again, why not think that the more of us who go now, the sooner it'll be over and we'll have peace and all be home in this nice farm country again?

"While you work and help to keep things straight here at home, you can plan for the day—maybe not too long distant —when Mark will be back and you'll have a little home and farm of your own, with children. Gosh, girl, when I look at you or my sons, I wonder if you ever stop to realize what a precious possession youth is!"

George stopped, amazed at his own eloquence. It was one of the longest speeches he had ever made in his life. He smiled a little to himself, thinking that there was something about these emotional times and this daughter-in-law of his, whom he loved, that brought him right out of himself.

He was quiet, thinking he had said too much. A bullfrog croaked across the creek; a chipmunk ran down a tree and sat up inquiringly in front of them.

Ann laughed. "I wonder if bullfrogs and chipmunks have their troubles too?"

"You bet they do," George answered smiling. "Trouble is a basic law of life. Whether it be humans, animals, or plants, we all have our enemies and there must be some good reason for it or the Creator would not have it so."

"Well, I'll bet," said the girl, smiling, "that no one else has as nice a shoulder to weep on as you have given me this morning. I'm a little ashamed that I spilled all my troubles like a big baby, but anyway you have made me feel a lot better and I'm grateful. I hope you don't mind too much."

"Of course not!" he replied, embarrassed. Then he got up, reached out a hand to Ann and pulled her to her feet. "When I left the house this morning," he said, matter-of-factly, "I think I smelled chicken cooking. There's a lot of grand smells around a farm home, but chicken cooking on a Sunday morning, with prospects of dumpling, lots of chicken gravy—and, by the way," he interrupted himself, "I saw Nancy out this morning picking some of those early sour harvest apples and putting them in her apron. I'll bet you that the fried chicken and dumpling and all the other fixings this noon will be topped off by apple pie. Let's go investigate!"

The next morning George left. Both he and Nancy were determined to show no emotion, but it seemed to Nancy that a piece of her heart was packed with every one of the few articles of clothing which were put into the old carpet bag. Before closing it, she carefully shut the bedroom door and put into the bag a note saying the words she could not speak:

"Dear George:

"Take care of yourself. Give my love to the boys if you see them, and always remember that I love you."

Your wife,

Nancy"

When the moment came for George to leave, he kissed the little girls, shook hands with Tom, and told him:

"You're the man of the house for a while now, Tom. Take care of things for me, won't you?"

Throwing his shoulders back, Tom answered stoutly:

"I will, Pa. I'll do the best I can."

Suddenly George pulled Nancy into his arms and kissed her hard. Then, releasing her and brushing away unexpected tears, he quickly went out the door and down the road, for he had decided to walk the short distance to Jenkstown where he would take the stage. When he turned to look back from the road, Nancy waved at him, and he knew that their parting took far more courage for both of them than he would ever need in battle.

CHAPTER XI

THE SUMMER OF '61 dragged slowly by. Although Ann
visited the post office regularly, letters were rare. Even
Mark wrote less frequently. There was little time or opportunity for the men to write, and they were awkward at expressing themselves. Both Ann and Nancy drugged themselves with work. The work had to be done, and there was
no one to do it except the women and children, with occasional help from Enoch Payne.

Some of the work was pleasant. When not too tired, Ann
loved to go down the long lane that led to the creek pasture
and bring the cows home at night. There was something
about lanes, she thought, that made you love them. The
cowpath that zigzagged back and forth between the fences,
the woodchuck that occasionally whistled angrily at her
when she approached so quietly that he did not hear her in
time to get into his hole, the summer smells from the fields,
and the cows waddling along, their full udders swinging from
side to side, their breath pleasantly odorous from the pasture
grasses.

But after she had them fastened in their stanchions in the
barn, her legs grew tired and cramped from holding the pail,
heavy with milk, between her knees. Before the milking was
finished her hands would cramp so that it was hard for her to
carry the full pails over the stile that led across the stone
wall bordering the farmyard and into the cellar. Still it was
pleasant to see the foaming milk gradually climb toward the
top of the pail as she milked, and to squirt the milk from the
cow's teat directly into the old tomcat's mouth as he sat up
straight, back of the cow, waiting for it. It was nice also to
turn the slow moving beasts loose after milking and watch
them move down the lane.

When chores were finished after the long day in the fields,
there was still her trip to the post office, and when she got
home again, Ann was so tired that she could hardly wait to

get her clothes off and fall into bed, no matter how early in the evening it was. Some nights when Ann wasn't too weary, and after her mother had gone to bed, she loved to fill the washtub with warm water and scrub her beautiful skin free of the accumulated dust and dirt from farm work, imagining that she was making herself nice for Mark; but too often, tired as she was, after she had crawled into her bed she could not sleep, but lay there wondering and worrying where Mark was and longing intensely for the time when he would be home again. Mornings after such sleepless nights it was difficult for Ann to start the long, hard daily rounds of work. When milking the cows or doing her other chores, she would think hopelessly of the time after time that she would have to do those same chores again before she could hope to see her husband. Almost every time when she looked at her corn field or at the other growing crops, her natural joy in seeing things grow was tempered by the thought that those same crops no doubt would grow to maturity, be harvested and probably used before she could see Mark again. Thus marched the slow days of her life.

Some of the farm field work was beyond her strength and skill. Enoch Payne could be hired, but the big problem was the lack of cash with which to pay him. Realizing this, he often refused to accept pay, so Ann tried to get along without his help as much as she could, for her pride rebelled at the idea of accepting his work for nothing.

One day late in August when there seemed to be a little respite from the farm work, Ann came over and said to Nancy that the blackberries must be getting ripe, and if Nancy didn't mind she'd like to take the girls and go back on the hill where she knew there would be blackberries in an old slashing. Ellen, Elizabeth and Hattie were delighted at the prospect. Life was dull for them, too. They fixed some sandwiches, filled a quart can with milk, and then climbed the hill pasture, finally coming to a big piece of woods near the top.

Stopping to rest, Ann turned to look back at the valley below them, the familiar country where she had been born and raised. Directly below, perhaps a mile away, were the house and barn of the Wilson homestead. Down the valley a little further, nearer to the village, lay her own home, and still farther on she could see the houses of the little town

Almost obscured by the trees which overshadowed them above the trees like a sentinel rose the spire of the village church. Ann's thoughts went back to the night when she and Mark had stood in that church not so long ago when Timothy Belden had made them man and wife. With a sigh and tightening of the throat she turned to gaze at the upper end of the valley, where the winding creek showed for miles here and there through the trees. Over the whole scene lay the smoky haze of late summer.

Catching the delicate fragrance of ripening buckwheat, she turned to look over the pasture fence and saw it, the stems a golden brown and still partly in bloom. From it came the pleasant summer sound of countless bees and insects feasting on the pollen. As she stood looking at the summer scene and let her gaze wander up and down the quiet farm valley, shining in the sunlight, the feeling of frustration and the worries and sadness of the past weeks dropped away from her temporarily. It seemed to her that God was trying to tell her that in spite of all the troubles, the worries, and the war, it was still a good world and, somehow, some time, all would be well.

Rested and refreshed in spirit, Ann led the girls along an old logging road that wound around the stumps and over the mudholes in the woods, coming after a while to an opening into a big slashing. Several acres in size, the slashing was like an island surrounded by forests. It had been timbered off two or three years earlier, and the blackberry brambles had sprung up everywhere, over the brush heaps and open spaces, until it was a tangled, almost impenetrable mass. But the blackberries on the high bushes, some of them higher than Ann could reach, hung big and black on the vines. At the edge of the woods a spring of almost ice-cold water bubbled out of the earth and settled in a little depression, the overflow tinkling off down through the old leaves.

Here the girls deposited their lunch. Little Hattie was tired from the long walk and inclined to be cross, so Ann told her to lie down on the soft forest mold near the spring and to stay there while the others picked the berries. Each took a pail and began picking. Ann suggested that Ellen and Elizabeth pick all they could right on the edge and warned them to keep within calling distance of Hattie.

Ann worked a little farther around the edge and broke into the bushes where the berries seemed especially big and thick. Disturbed by her presence, a catbird alighted not far from her and began to yell, "Thief! Thief! Thief!" Ann laughed and called back, "Thief yourself!" It was intensely hot in the bushes, yet the berries ahead always seemed larger and blacker than those near her and their lure drew her in farther and farther. Intent on filling her 10-quart pail quickly, Ann failed to keep track of time until glancing at the sun she saw that it was nearly noon. With a guilty feeling she turned to retrace her steps.

But that wasn't so easy. In working into the slashing after the best berries, she had zigzagged back and forth to avoid obstacles and the thickest of the bushes as much as she could. Now she was uncertain in which direction to go to get back out. The slashing was on a level, so she didn't have the slope of a hill to guide her, and the bushes higher than her head confused her sense of direction. The sun was of no help, either, for it was directly overhead.

She started to break a path through a clump of bushes in the direction which she thought might be right, but it seemed that she was making no progress. The briars were vicious, tearing at her clothes and her stockings with almost devilish perversity, and the flies—to which she had given little thought when engrossed in her berry-picking—now buzzed about her head in swarms.

Finally, Ann managed to reach a big pile of fallen logs and brush, and in attempting to climb over it she stepped into a hole between the logs and went down, spilling her berries. Her leg hurt badly, and fearing that she had broken it or sprained her ankle, she hauled herself up on a rotten log and gingerly examined her foot and leg. Satisfied that nothing more serious than a bad twist had resulted from her fall, Ann looked ruefully at her overturned pail with only a few berries left in the bottom. For a moment she wished she were a man so that she could use language suitable to the occasion.

As she stooped to pick up her pail, Ann realized that she still didn't know which direction to follow to get out of the slashing, but could think of nothing better to do than to plow ahead through the tall bushes. Veering off to one side to avoid a particularly thick clump of brush, she found herself looking at a little clearing a few feet in diameter. She started to go into it, and then stepped back with a startled exclamation. Ambling across the open space, stopping frequently to nuzzle something out of the ground, was a mother skunk, and following her were her six little black and white kittens. Apparently hearing Ann's exclamation, the skunk turned suddenly to face her. Quicker than she would have thought possible, Ann dodged back around the bushes. Nothing could be cuter-looking than these kittens, she thought with a wry smile, but that kind of cuteness was better admired from a distance.

Retracing her steps a short distance to make sure of avoiding the skunk, she suddenly came upon the path that she had broken through the bushes in the first place, and then found her way without further difficulty back to the edge of the slashing.

Going directly to the spring, Ann was disturbed to find that Hattie was not there. However, she felt sure that she must have joined the other girls, so she started along the edge of the slashing, calling to the girls as she went, and finally heard an answer. Ellen and Elizabeth came hurrying toward her, but they were alone. To her question, "Where's Hattie?" they answered:

"By the spring."

"She isn't there," Ann said, sharply. "I told you to keep watch of her."

"Well, we thought you wanted us to pick berries. There weren't any good ones right there by the spring."

Now thoroughly alarmed, Ann started back with the girls toward the spring and started calling:

"Hattie! Hattie!"

But there was no response. Almost frantic, Ann gave emphatic orders to Elizabeth not to move away from the spring. Then she directed Ellen to walk in one direction around the edge between the woods and the clearing while she herself started around the other way. As they went, they kept calling to Hattie and to each other, but could find no trace of the child. Finally, leaving Ellen by the spring with Elizabeth, Ann circled around through the woods keeping a hundred yards or so from the slashing and calling the child's name until she was hoarse. When she had completed the round, almost in despair and deadly tired, she came back and sat down by the spring, dropped her face on her hands and tried to think what to do next. Suddenly Ellen yelled:

"There she is!"

Sure enough, crawling out from a mat of bushes and grasses not more than twenty feet away was Hattie, her hair matted with leaves and twigs, her dress torn, but she herself in good spirits. Ann rushed to pick her up, crying:

"Where have you been?"

Calmly Hattie replied:

"Went to pick berries. Went to sleep."

Too thankful to scold, Ann hugged her and then set her down suddenly, aware that her knees were trembling so that she couldn't stand. But in a few minutes she went over to the spring and bathed her hot face in the cold water, and then they ate their lunch.

Lunch over, Ann decided it was time to start home, and off they went, the children proud of the berries they had to show their mother. But the day wasn't yet over. Ann had been so intent on trying to find Hattie that she hadn't noticed that the sky was clouding over and that there was a distant rumble of thunder. In the woods now it sounded louder and she tried to hurry the children along faster.

Coming out of the woods to the pasture that overlooked the valley, Ann saw that they could not outrun the storm to the house. The thunder was now ominously near, and although accustomed to country storms, Ann couldn't remember when she had ever seen the western sky so black and angry looking.

Undecided, she halted, and as they waited a great wind came roaring down across the valley and up the hill, bending the trees before it and finally reaching them with such force that it became almost impossible to stand up against it. Following the wind over the northwestern hills they could see a gray wall of rain coming fast. Ellen exclaimed:

"Let's get under that big chestnut, Ann! It'll protect us some."

"No," said Ann, sharply. "The lightning might hit the tree. We must stay right out here in the open." Frightened, the two younger girls began to cry.

Like galloping horses in a cavalry charge, the wall of rain

swept toward them. It seemed to Ann that the very heavens had opened up to dump out a whole lake. Frequent sharp flashes of lightning were followed by the almost continuous rumbling of the thunder. Suddenly came a crash that left their arms tingling as if they had been asleep, and the big chestnut tree showed a white streak of raw wood where the bolt had stripped the bark.

Drenched to the skin and crying in terror, the children huddled as close to Ann as they could for comfort. To their right, only a few feet away, a huge old pine that had been a landmark for years, crashed to the ground, unable to stand up against the terrific wind.

Then the storm passed more quickly than it had come. The thunder rumbled and growled away over the woods and hills to the east of them until it subsided to a distant mutter. The rain let up, and as the bedraggled little party started down across the pasture lot, the sun tried tentatively to peep through the clouds a few times and finally came out to stay. Ann looked ruefully at the berries which were now almost floating in the pails, and said aloud to the girls:

"What a day!"

Then she thought to herself:

"Well, at least I haven't had much time today to worry about Mark or the farm or anything else except to get the girls safely home again."

CHAPTER XII

THE SUN SHONE, the rain fell and, as always, the crops ripened and had to be harvested. Ann saw apples to be picked, potatoes to be dug, and buckwheat to be cradled, bound, set in the golden shocks, then hauled into the barn and threshed. A couple of acres of corn also waited to be cut, shocked, and finally the grain husked out and the cornstalks stowed away in the barn to feed the cattle.

She knew she could manage to get the corn cut and set up, and the potatoes dug, but as she stood looking at the buckwheat one September day she realized that the cradling job was beyond her. As if in answer to her thought, Enoch Payne just then ambled up the road, a cradle on his arm.

"Had a day on my hands I didn't know what to do with, Ann," he announced, lying like a gentleman, "and thought I'd come over and let down this buckwheat for you."

He stood grinning amid her expostulations.

"Shucks!" he said. "There's more'n one way to fight a war. I can't get into the Army, but I can help a little bit maybe to save the stuff the soldiers and the home folks need to eat."

A few minutes later he was swinging his cradle up across the buckwheat field, laying the grain in straight even swaths. Ann followed close behind, raking and binding. When she had raked together a bundle of the grain, she picked out a handful of the straw, twisted it deftly together to make a band, passed it around the bundle, gave the ends of her buckwheat rope a tug and a twist, and the bundle was tied. Later the bundles would be stood on their butts in shocks to cure for a few days before putting into the barn.

Day after day the women, children, and old men of the village worked from dawn till dark harvesting the crops and getting them into cellars and barns before winter could close down. Day after day as she worked in the fields, Ann's mind traveled south, trying to picture what Mark was doing. Was he getting enough to eat? Did he have a comfortable place to sleep? And, above all, was he in danger? To a lesser extent she wondered and worried about her father, always ending with the hope that he was where he couldn't get anything to drink, so that he could give the best that he had to soldiering and come back home, perhaps broken of the overpowering habit that had nearly ruined his life and theirs.

As the fall drew to a close, cold and freezing nights were frequent. Ann was finishing the last harvest job of digging the potatoes and putting them into the cellar. The ease with which she could pick up and carry a 60-lb. box or sack of potatoes brought a feeling of pride in her health and strength. She looked back across the work that she had been able to accomplish almost alone in the fields during the summer and fall, and thought with satisfaction that she was a good farmer, and that when Mark returned she certainly could pull her end of the load.

That night, when the potato digging and storing were finished, and her mother had gone to bed, she set the old washtub in the middle of the floor, heated water on top of the stove, half filled the tub and put in a generous supply of homemade soft soap. As she undressed, she wrinkled her nose in disgust at the thick coating of dust from the potato field that had adhered to her all over and blackened her feet, but a little later, glowing and refreshed, from a thorough scrubbing, she caught a glimpse of herself in the big looking-glass which had been cracked down through the center ever since she could remember, and her heartbeat accelerated as she thought of Mark. It was a happy thought—happy to know that she had a strong and beautiful body, and that she was married to the man she loved. Then her longing for him changed to sadness and a lump came into her throat as she cried:

"Mark! Mark, dear! When will I ever see you again?"

* * *

The days grew shorter, the evenings lengthened, and Ann continued her daily trek to the store. Whenever there was a letter from Mark or from Charles or George Wilson, she would almost snatch it out of John Crawford's hands and hurry to the Wilson home, where she and Nancy could pour over it together. The Wilsons weren't in the same regiments, but were near enough so they could occasionally get together, and apparently they were all getting along all right except for fatigue and boredom, caused by the constant drilling.

In one of his letters, George wrote Nancy that the last time he had seen his sons they were fed up with the "adventure" of Army life, tired and sick of drilling, and wanted to see some action or else get out of it and come home. He added that while he agreed wholeheartedly with the boys, he didn't tell them so, feeling that it would only add to their discontent, and that after the disastrous experience at Bull Run it was evident that the leaders were right that it would take something other than raw recruits to put down the Rebellion—and that something was drill and discipline.

In his letters, however, George seemed much more interested in learning how things were going at home than in writing about the war, and Nancy was glad to be able to report that with Enoch Payne's and the children's help, they had harvested all the crops, and everything was snug for the winter. There was no use telling him, she thought, that she was stretching the truth considerably. It seemed as if there weren't enough hours in the day nor energy enough to get the work done, and the small amount of cash that they had had from the sale of the cows to Henry Bain was dwindling more rapidly than she cared to think about.

But then, she thought resignedly, she was no different from almost every farm woman she knew. In past years there had always been a little extra cash to buy some of the family's clothes at the store. But now, if the children had any new clothes at all, she would have to make them. Fortunately, the spring crop of wool from their little flock of sheep had not been sold. So she got it out, washed and carded it, got out the big spinning wheel and put in every minute she could spare from her other duties working the wool into crude homespun yarn and cloth. Later she dyed the cloth. Two fleeces of white wool combined with one of black produced the favorite "sheep's grey." Copperas and alum mixed with a solution made from the bark of the butternut tree gave the yarn a very attractive brown color. Purple dye came from a solution of Nicaraugua wood, but most popular of all, especially with the men-folks, was madder red. Nancy worked far into the nights making dresses and coats for herself and the girls and a homemade suit for Tom.

"Not much to look at," she commented, a little ruefully, when she thought of all the labor that had gone into the clothes, "but at least they'll keep us warm."

But, with all of her skill Nancy had no way of making boots and shoes, and to buy them ate grievously into her little store of cash. Nevertheless, she was in a better position than Ann, who had no cash on hand at all and little produce to sell from the farm to pay taxes and interest, and to buy the few clothes and groceries that she and her mother needed. Added to Ann's other troubles was the fact that her mother, always highly nervous, irritable and complaining, now seemed to be much worse. Unlike Nancy Wilson, Mrs. Clinton was more or less helpless when thrown upon her own resources. Realizing the situation, Nancy tried to help, but Ann's pride was an obstacle. Finally, however, a compromise was reached. Ann helped Nancy with the spinning and weaving, and in return Ann got some homespun cloth which, with Nancy's help, she made into warm dresses for herself and her mother.

Nearing home one winter evening after a day spent with Nancy, Ann was surprised to see a horse and cutter standing by the horse block in front of the house. The horse was tied to the hitching post and covered with a heavy blanket. From an armchair in the big warm kitchen, Henry Bain rose lazily to greet her, while her mother fluttered around excitedly.

"Henry dropped in to say hello, Ann, and I've invited him to stay for supper."

"That's fine," said Ann, wondering what they would have for a decent meal and worrying for fear Henry had stopped to say something about the interest on the mortgage, which was past due. But Henry was affability itself.

Tired from her long day of spinning, and in no mood for small talk, Ann watched quietly while her mother fussed nervously about in an obvious effort to entertain and please Henry. Listening to her mother boasting about how well they were getting along, Ann feared that Henry would get the impression that they were better off than they actually were and fully able to take care of the payments.

To her relief, her mother finally dropped the subject of the farm and its problems and began to discuss the affairs of the neighborhood. Then Ann became really annoyed as her mother, anxious to please, agreed with Henry's comment that Mrs. Clinton and the other folks at home were having a difficult time to get along, while the men were having it easy in the Army.

"They might a deal better," he said, "be here taking care of you and paying their debts instead of interfering with the rights of the citizens in the South."

Ann managed to hold her temper, feeling that because of the mortgage, she couldn't afford the luxury of quarreling with Henry.

Finally, Henry got around to stating, with some pomposity, that he just didn't know how the folks left at home would get along at all if it weren't for a few citizens, like himself, who stayed home and kept the country running. Then, noticing Ann's flushed face, and realizing that he was on dangerous ground, he turned to Mrs. Clinton again and began to praise Ann, how proud she must be to have such a good-looking daughter who was a competent worker and could keep things going while the men were gone.

This too obvious compliment made no impression at all on Ann's anger, but it did please her mother, who looked at Henry almost affectionately. When he rose to go, she told him, much to Ann's disgust, how much they had enjoyed his visit and that she hoped he'd come often.

Ann was further upset when Henry replied that he certainly had enjoyed being with them and, since they wished him to, he would come again soon.

* * *

A few days before Christmas, Nancy said to Ann:

"Of course it isn't going to be like Christmas this year with the men gone and with no money to buy anything. On the other hand, it wouldn't be fair to the children not to do something. Have you any ideas?"

"Maybe we could have quite a little fun," responded Ann, "if you'll let me help."

So for the next few days some of the regular work was

neglected. Ann and Tom waded through the snow to the woods, found a tree that just suited them, and dragged it back to the house, setting it up in the corner of the big kitchen, where its piney fragrance mingled with the appetizing cooking odors. They popped corn, and the girls spent hours threading it on strings. Then the long strands of white corn were wound over and around the tree.

Nancy found some maple sirup from the previous spring, boiled it to just the right consistency, and, when it cooled, more of the popcorn was rolled in it to make sticky but delicious popcorn balls, some of which were also hung on the tree. Apples were brought up from the cellar and polished to a high gloss, and then they joined the popcorn balls on the tree, glowing among the green branches.

The various members of the family, including Ann, spent much time in John Crawford's store deciding how to make their few pennies buy little gifts for everyone in the family. These included long gay sticks of candy with giddy stripes running around them. Nancy invested in two big sweet oranges to be carefully divided among them on Christmas morning. But most of her little store of money, and Ann's too, went for absolute necessities which would be the more appreciated if blessed with the Christmas spirit.

Although to the children these last few days had seemed endless, Christmas Eve came at length. Mrs. Wilson had invited Mrs. Clinton to come with Ann, and Enoch Payne, too, joined the little group. Nancy had made an extra effort with the supper, but the children, even Tom, who considered himself almost a man now, were too excited to do it justice. The table was soon cleared, the dishes washed, and then Nancy said:

"I have a little surprise for you, but we'll have to wait a little longer."

But the waiting period wasn't too long even for the small fry, for soon there came a jingle of sleigh bells outside and the sound of laughter, followed by the opening of the door and the breezy entrance of John Crawford, with little white-haired Mrs. Crawford by his side; Pastor Belden and Mrs. Belden, and tall, spare, homely, middle-aged Mary Curtis, who had helped nurse them all through sicknesses and worked for them at other times, too. Like Enoch Payne, she always

seemed to be more interested in helping those who needed
help than in getting pay or helping herself.

Wraps were removed and piled on Nancy's bed. Each of
the guests had brought along two or three little packages,
except John Crawford, who had his arms full of bundles.
These he slid under the tree as soon as he arrived, and then
straightened up with a sigh of relief.

At last they were all seated, crowded close in a half circle
around the big tree, which glistened in the soft light of the
candles. Nancy spoke softly:

"Mr. Belden, it would be very fitting if you would conse-
crate our little Christmas get-together with prayer."

The old pastor stood, bowed his head, and talked to God
in exactly the same tone of voice and in the same way what
he would talk with any other old friend, saying:

"Father, you know our needs and our troubles, but it helps
if we can tell them to You. It may seem strange to some of
the unthinking that we should celebrate Christmas Eve and
the birth of the Prince of Peace when our land is being torn
asunder by civil war, when friends and neighbors, citizens all
of the same country, are at each other's throats. But we
know, O God, that in Thy sight a thousand years are but
as a night, and the truth which is beyond the understanding
of our finite minds is clear to Thy infinite knowledge. The
Christ child came to preach peace on earth and goodwill to
men, and we cannot understand why we have to suffer the
grievous affliction of this war.

"Help us to put our trust in Thee, knowing that some
time, somehow, right and not might will prevail. Give us
the wisdom to make right decisions in these momentous
times, comfort the widow and the orphan in the stricken
homes of both the North and the South. Come into this,
our own neighborhood, Lord, help us to lean on Thee when
our loneliness and sorrow seem more than we can bear. Bless
the absent loved ones and the friends gathered here tonight,
increase the joy of these little ones, and give us strength and
courage to go on. Amen."

"I had planned to have some music now," said Nancy,
when Mr. Belden finished, "but I guess the children can't
wait any longer, so we'll have music later. Tom, suppose
you pick up the presents one at a time, tell Hattie who is to

get which, and she'll pass them around. We'll wait until each present is opened before we go on to the next."

As the simple little gifts were handed out, those for the children were eagerly received and joyfully opened, but the pleasure of the others, especially of Ann and Nancy, was subdued, and when some hand-knitted socks and mittens were laid aside for the absent soldiers, Ann could hardly restrain her tears. Realizing this, Mr. Belden said, as soon as the presents had been distributed: "We can't have a Christmas tree without some Christmas music. I can see Enoch Payne's fiddle in the corner. Let's have some good old Christmas carols."

Watching Enoch's big, awkward-looking fingers, gnarled by hard work, sliding so easily over the strings as he led the group in song after song, Ann thought:

"How little we know of the hearts and souls of even our closest friends! There's Enoch now, who never had a music lesson in his life, never had anything but hard work, and yet he has the soul of an artist. Under different circumstances he might have been a noted violinist."

Then noticing the absorbed look with which Mary Curtis watched him play, Ann thought again:

"*There* is somebody who does understand the heart and soul of Enoch Payne. I hope he knows it."

With Enoch to play the old tunes and Timothy Belden to lead, the big kitchen resounded with music and song. Then came a pause while the women tucked the younger children, tired from all the excitement, away in their beds. When the singing began again, each person called for his favorite. The carols exhausted, they began to choose the old ballads, and Timothy Belden asked for a verse from Thomas Moore's "Believe Me, If All These Endearing Young Charms":

> "The heart that has truly loved never forgets
> But as truly loves on to the close
> As the sunflower turns to her god when he sets
> The same look that she gave when he rose."

Mrs. Belden wanted "Darling Nellie Grey," and when that was finished, Ann said:

"Mr. Belden, do you know the words to "The Girl I Left Behind Me?"

"A verse or two, I guess," he replied. "Want to sing it?"

"Yes," said Ann. "After I left Mark in Owego, a fife and drum corps came down the street. They were playing that tune, and somehow that was comforting, and it has seemed like Mark's and my song ever since. Let's sing it."

As Enoch took up the strain of the old marching song, Timothy Belden held up his hand and quoted a verse from memory. Then they sang it with feeling, and so engrossed were they that no one heard the door open. But the song came to an abrupt end when a laughing voice said:

"Who says I left my girl behind me?"

At the door stood Mark, tall, uniformed, grinning at them from ear to ear. There was a moment of astounded silence, and then Ann flew to his arms, almost yelling:

"Is it you? It can't really be you!"

Mark hugged her hard, and then, somewhat embarrassed, he stepped back a pace and everyone gathered around to shake his hand and pat his back. He kissed his mother, and to cover his self-consciousness, said:

"What's to eat, Mother? I'm starved!"

Nancy hastened to set some bread and milk on the table, and while he ate, everyone plied him with questions. Mark told them that he had been more fortunate than his father or Charles in getting a brief furlough, and that the others sent their love and were well the last time he had seen them. Looking at the shining Christmas tree, Mark said he wished he could have been there for the beginning of the evening's festivities, but he and some of the other fellows had missed the stage at Owego. Anyway, he was home for a while and that was all that mattered.

Knowing that the family wanted to be alone with Mark, the guests soon took their leave. Soon afterwards, Mark and Ann and her mother said goodnight to Nancy, and together went down the road to the Clinton house.

When Mark and Ann were alone in their room, he said, a little awkwardly:

"Ann, I heard what you said about hearing that tune, "The Girl I Left Behind Me," that day in Owego. I heard them tooting that piece, too, and I felt it was a sort of a special message. I didn't know then whether I was leaving my girl behind me for good. But here I am, thank God!"

Ann waited for Mark to make the first advance, but sud-

denly he was overpowered with shyness. Although the hour
was late, he asked question after question about the farm and
Ann's life since he had been gone. Then as he in turn told her
about his Army life, their awkwardness wore off. Getting up
suddenly from his chair, he pulled her up from the stool
where she was sitting, and said, huskily:

"Ann, my darling wife! I've missed you so. How I've
missed you!"

As his lips pressed hers, she whispered:

"And I've missed you, darling. How can I ever let you
go again?"

CHAPTER XIII

AFTER THE CHRISTMAS HOLIDAYS and Mark's return to camp, the days gradually grew a little longer, but the winter settled down harder than ever. For the home folks the biggest problem now was to get wood for the fires. There was plenty of it on every farm; the difficulty lay in getting it cut and drawn out from the deep snow in the woods and worked up into the lengths that the stoves would take.

Both Nancy and Ann finally gave up trying to heat any rooms in their houses except the kitchens. Morning after morning as young Tom Wilson stuck his feet hesitatingly out from under the bed covers, he could see the snow that had drifted in through the cracks in his bedroom window. Grabbing his clothes, he would make a break for the kitchen to dress in front of the fire, often forgetting that now with his father away there would be no fire until he built it. Shivering in his shirt tail, he would light the fire and get the kitchen warmed up before his mother and the girls appeared.

Soon after the chores were done and it was getting light, Enoch Payne would come trudging up the road through the snow, and then he and Tom, taking the lunch that Nancy had put up for them, would cross the creek and make their way with difficulty through the snow up the long hill until they came to the woodlot at the top. In the woods the trees protected them from the bitter wind.

One morning, while Tom watched, Enoch cleared the trash around a big maple. Then after an expert glance about him, he spat on his hands and soon had a deep gash in the tree on the side where he wanted it to fall. As the ringing blows of the axe echoed through the cold air, Tom envied Enoch's ability to place every blow of the axe exactly where he wished it.

After cutting the notch as deep as he thought necessary, Enoch called for the crosscut saw and the two of them, kneeling on each side of the tree, started the saw on the opposite side from the notch. Suddenly, as the saw bit in a little beyond the center, the tree began to creak and tremble. With a glance upward to judge the direction of the fall, Enoch yelled "Timber!" and, pulling the saw out, they ran as fast as they could away from the tree, which seemed to hesitate for a moment and then went over with a mighty crash.

Then followed the long tedious task of trimming off the branches, blocking up the trunk so the saw would not bind or pinch, and sawing it into logs that later could be rolled onto the bobsleigh and hauled out by the oxen to the homestead. It seemed a long time to Tom before Enoch declared that it was time to eat. They built a big bonfire, got their dinner pails, and, placing their sandwiches on long sticks, thawed them out and toasted them a bit over the hot coals.

To Tom that was the best part of the whole day, for it seemed as if he had never before been so hungry, or food tasted so good.

Enoch, on opening his dinner pail, had carefully laid his big slab of apple pie on a huge chip and set it on the snow away from the fire until he was ready for it. While they were busy toasting their sandwiches, a chickadee, attracted by the sight of the food, began circling over their heads. Enoch yelled at it and the frightened bird departed in haste, but left his calling card, of all places, on poor Enoch's piece of pie.

Angrier than Tom had ever seen him, Enoch jumped up, grabbed a stick and ran off through the woods, shouting and brandishing the stick in a vain effort to take vengeance on the bird. When he returned to the fire, looking somewhat shamefaced, Tom, half scared but bursting with mirth, doubled over in a sudden fit of coughing. Not a word was spoken between them for a while until finally Tom said:

"Enoch, Ma gave me too much pie, more'n I want or need."

Taking his jackknife he divided the pie and handed the half over to Enoch, who took it with a grin and ate it heartily.

Sitting on a log close to the warm fire, Tom thought how nice it would be to stay there for a while, or else go home. He hated the idea of going back to the hard work. But Enoch said:

"Come on, boy. These winter days are short, you know, and we might as well get something done while we're here."

In the middle of the afternoon Enoch notched an especially big maple, but one which was crooked at the top. When they had sawed it from the side opposite to the notch through the middle, the tree started to waver and groan. Enoch cast a rather anxious look upward, and said:

"Come on, we'd better get away from here. I'm not too sure where this darn thing is going to fall."

Enoch's fears were realized. Instead of falling in the exact spot he had planned, the maple struck a smaller tree and lodged there.

"Now we're in a mess," said Enoch, disgustedly. "Might have known I couldn't count on that old crooked top."

"What'll we do now?" inquired Tom.

"Cut down the other tree. But you keep away from it, boy. I'll get it down with the axe."

As Enoch chopped, Tom noticed that the big maple trembled violently every time the axe hit the small tree. He called out:

"Watch out, Enoch! It won't take much to pry that big one loose."

But Enoch paid no attention and kept on chopping. Suddenly a limb let loose with a loud crack and the huge tree started to fall. As Tom yelled, Enoch looked up, and then, apparently confused, ran the wrong way. Horrified, Tom saw a limb from the falling tree whip down on Enoch and throw him violently.

Panic-stricken, the boy rushed to the fallen tree and crowded in among the branches, yelling:

"Enoch! Enoch! Are you hurt?"

There was no answer. Frantic now, the boy grabbed the limb that lay on Enoch and pulled on it with all his strength. He found that it lifted fairly easily and, best of all, that it was not resting heavily on Enoch. He was able to get hold of Enoch by the shoulders and to drag him out from the brush to an open space. Laying him flat on his back, Tom leaned over him, vainly calling his name. Dropping on his knees, Tom put his ear to Enoch's chest and found that his heart was beating. His own heart thumping wildly, Tom debated what to do next. Obviously he had no way of getting a heavy man to the house by his own efforts, and if he went for help Enoch might die or freeze.

Rushing over to the fire, Tom stirred up the coals and then half-carried, half-dragged Enoch near enough so that he was within the radius of the fire's warmth. Next he set up a brush and log shelter back of Enoch to reflect the heat. Just as he was starting out on a run for help, he heard Enoch call his name. Hurrying back, he found him sitting up rubbing his head dazedly, but conscious and apparently not badly hurt. After a few moments Enoch said, weakly:

"What happened, Tom?"

Out of his fright and nervousness Tom spoke harshly:

"You durn fool! I thought you were a woodsman. Instead of runnin' away from the tree, you pretty nearly ran right under it. What got into you?"

"Didn't think it was goin' to fall that way," mumbled Enoch.

"Are you hurt?" Tom inquired, more gently. Enoch moved his arms and legs gingerly, then said:

"Guess not. Seem to have everything all in one piece and workin'. How about goin' home? I've had enough of these woods for one day."

"Can you make it?"

Enoch got slowly to his feet, tottered a bit as he stood up, then braced himself and said:

"Sure I can."

"Well, I'll carry everything if you can get yourself home, but sit down for a minute while I pick up the tools."

After picking up the axe and other tools, Tom returned to the fire and stood grinning down at Enoch.

"It ain't your day, Enoch. First the little bird; then the big tree!"

But Enoch was himself again and said, tartly:

"If you ever tell about that bird, I'll break your neck!"

"Won't promise! But I'll see that you get another piece of Ma's pie when we get home if there's any left."

A few days later Enoch, none the worse for his adventure, dropped into the Clinton kitchen to see how Ann and her mother were getting along. The kitchen was cold, and Enoch, getting a non-committal answer to his question about their wood supply, poked his head into the woodshed and found only a few sticks left.

"Got to do something about this wood business," he told Ann.

"I should think you'd had enough of the woods to last you all winter," said Ann, demurely.

But Enoch saw the twinkle in her eyes, and said:

"That darn Tom! Can't keep a thing to himself. I'll fix him! I'll make him help me get some logs out of your woodlot."

Thereafter for several days Enoch and Tom were busy cutting and drawing logs from the Clinton woodlot, but one morning as he rolled a big log forward on the skidway and got ready to start sawing with a crosscut saw, Enoch looked up to find Ann standing beside him.

"Enoch," she said, "Tom isn't here—nor should he be— and how are you going to work a two-man saw with only one man? I can't drive you away from our work here, and and I don't know how I'm ever going to pay you, but at least I think I can operate one end of that saw just as good as a man."

He rather surprised her by agreeing.

"I'll admit that one man can't do much with a two-man saw," he commented. "And I'm not sure that a two-man saw can be operated by one man and one woman, but let's see how it works."

For hour after hour, Ann pulled and shoved on her end of the saw until finally Enoch called a halt.

"You did all right at first," he told her, "but now you're tired, and you're not only dragging your feet but taking a free ride, too. We've sawed enough to keep me busy splitting it for quite a while. You go to the house and rest."

At last a sizable pile of wood was sawed and split, enough to last Ann and her mother for the kitchen fire for some time, and that certainly was a comfort.

Henry Bain had now become a regular caller at the Clinton home, where Mrs. Clinton always made him welcome. Even Ann grew accustomed to his visits and began to respond to his friendliness, his apparent interest in their farm problems, and his friendly advice. But always in the back of her mind was suspicion of his motives and the belief that his interest was based upon the hope that some day he would own the farm. It never occurred to Ann that he might have a personal interest in her. But so very friendly was Mrs. Clinton that one evening when he was alone with her, Henry hinted that he had always been interested in her daughter and was unhappy when she married Mark Wilson.

Noting the sympathetic look on Mrs. Clinton's face, he made bold to go a step farther and pointed out how much more he could have done for both Ann and her mother if Ann had married him.

After that talk, his visits became even more frequent, and Mrs. Clinton outdid herself in trying to make him welcome. One evening when he was there, she abruptly excused herself, saying that she had a headache, and went off to bed. Ann glanced at her retreating form suspiciously, for she knew that her mother did not have headaches frequently, and she had said nothing about it earlier in the evening. But Ann made a polite effort to carry on the conversation with Henry, hoping all the time that he would go. Instead, he continued to talk about the farm and the crops, and then said:

"For a girl, you certainly did a good job with the crops on this place this year, Ann. But of course, there are a lot of things that you can't do, and raising crops isn't all there is to it. Farmers have to have some cash."

Thinking that he was hinting about the unpaid interest on the mortgage, Ann flushed and said, defensively:

"Well, Henry, don't you think these are unusual times? Even good farmers aren't making much money now, with all the help gone to war."

To this her visitor made no direct reply. He sat silently for some moments, opening and shutting the blade of his jackknife, and then suddenly burst forth:

"Ann, you don't know how much I've wanted you, how heartbroken I was when you married Wilson!"

"Hush!" she exclaimed, startled.

"No, I won't hush. I've got to tell you," he persisted. "If you'd just given me a chance, you wouldn't have to do all of this hard work. I'd have taken care of you."

Embarrassed and uneasy, Ann got up out of her chair.

"You shouldn't talk to me like this, Henry," she said, quietly. "I'm sorry if I have hurt you, but I was in love with

Mark when I married him, and I'm more in love with him now than ever."

She stopped, then added:

"And I'm sure he loves me."

Henry closed his knife with a snap and put it back in his pocket.

"Well," he said, shortly, "I hope you don't ever regret your marriage to him."

To Ann the remark sounded like a threat. She turned to face him.

"I won't regret it," she stated positively.

An awkward silence followed her words and then Henry said, rather lamely:

"Well, I guess it's time to go."

Ann made no reply as he put on his overcoat and hat and went out the door, banging it behind him.

CHAPTER XIV

THE LONG WINTER inched along into March. The days were longer now, and sunshiny days became more frequent. The warm sun started the sap running in the trees and burned off the snow so that the higher knolls in the pastures and meadows were beginning to show. But this year the hope that usually springs eternal in springtime was mingled with dread, for spring meant the opening of military campaigns and offensives, and perhaps wounds or even death for loved ones on the fighting front. Nancy and Ann knew, too, that spring came earlier in the South and that therefore war plans and new campaigns were well developed or even under way.

But the letters from camp continued to be cheerful. George wrote that the monotony of the long winter had been greatly lessened by the fact that he and both of the boys had been designated as musicians.

"You'll remember," he wrote to Nancy, "that when you and I were first married I used to get you really provoked sometimes because you couldn't stand the shrillness of my fife—although I thought I could play one pretty good. Then I added insult to injury for you by going the fife one better in noise with the rattling of my snare drum. Well, that small accomplishment has come in handy here. One day I overheard an officer say they were having difficulty in finding musicians. I told him I could play either the fife or the drum, and also that I could teach my two boys to drum if we were permitted to do it and were appointed to the same outfit. By golly, he took me up on it, and we got the special assignment! Both Mark and Charles have shown real talent and learned quickly. We have practiced all winter in the big drum corps and we can really make the fifes and drums talk. Best of all, it has given us a lot of opportunity to be together."

When Ann got Mark's letter about this news she was over-

joyed, thinking it would keep him out of the front lines.
Nancy said nothing, but she felt sure that musicians didn't
miss much of the fighting.

Their worries about new spring campaigns were soon con-
firmed. Both newspaper reports and letters told of the great
hope throughout the North when at last the slow and hesitating General McClellan began to move toward Richmond
the Army that he had spent nearly a year whipping into
shape. This time instead of trying to cross the swampy
wilderness country and the rivers by going overland, Mc-
Clellan landed his forces at Fort Monroe and marched up the
Peninsula between the York and the James rivers toward
Richmond, the Confederate capital.

Letters from the front were rare now, and when they did
arrive it was easy for the women to read into the attempted
cheerfulness the real discouragement that lay deep in the
hearts of the men. An occasional sentence would creep in
about the poor food, the awful weather, and the floundering
of McClellan's whole army in the swamps and mud of the
Peninsula. News of a battle meant days or weeks of dread
for those back home until they were sure that none of their
men had fallen.

Early one June day Ann was cultivating a piece of corn
that she had planted. As she reached the end of a row she
pulled the old mare around with the lines and swung her
cultivator expertly into the next row. Then she climbed to
the top of the rail fence to give herself and the horse a breathing spell. Looking out across the cornfield, where the crop
was now several inches high, and thinking of the oats and
potatoes that she had managed to get planted in addition to
the regular chores of a small dairy, Ann was conscious of
some pride in her own husbandry. Enoch had plowed and
fitted the ground for her, but aside from that she had tarred
the corn, got it dropped and covered by hand, and had
planted the potatoes; and the sight of her crops in the bright
summer sunshine made her realize that they looked better
than any her father had ever had at this time of year. Again
she thrilled to the thought of how much help she could be to
Mark when he got back and they started out to make a
living together.

In spite of her hard work, she felt strong and well, and she rejoiced for Mark's sake in her strong, supple young body. But then came the disturbing fear that he might never come back. Seated on the crooked rail fence, with only the hum of insects to break the silence, it almost seemed to Ann that if she listened carefully she could hear the rumble and grumble of battle far away to the South. She shivered, but then, shaking her head resolutely, slid down from the fence, put the lines over her shoulder, took hold of the cultivator handles and started the old horse along the row. If she worked hard enough, she thought, she could drug herself with it and leave no time nor energy for thinking.

Finally, early in July, the news swept the North that after months of maneuvering and days of terrible fighting on the Peninsula, ending in victory for the Union forces at Malvern Hill on July 1, McClellan had decided to give up his Peninsula campaign and retreat toward Washington.

Disgusted with McClellan's wavering and what many believed to be his cowardly withdrawals, the North seethed with criticism which culminated in demands on Lincoln for a new leader of the Union army. Yielding to this pressure, Lincoln appointed General Pope to succeed McClellan, and Pope promised to attack the Confederates straightway. Suiting action to promise, Pope advanced to the Rappahannock. The two great armies met on the old battlefield of Bull Run, where again the Union forces met disaster and were forced to retreat.

Happy and confident over the victory at Bull Run, Robert E. Lee, commander of the Confederate forces, advanced into Maryland, with the idea that the Copperheads and other Southern sympathizers would join with the Confederates to bring the war to a close. But Lee's hopes in this respect were not realized. He met McClellan, who was in command again, at Antietam on September 17, and at the end of a bloody battle Lee gave up the contest and retreated across the Potomac into the South. Once again, in spite of Lincoln's urging, McClellan failed to follow up his victory, and again Lincoln took the command from him, this time transferring it to General Burnside.

In December, Burnside attacked Lee at Fredericksburg on the Rappahannock River. Here the Union forces met defeat,

Burnside was removed from command, and General Hooker took over.

Ann and Nancy were never able to forget that harrowing year. News of battles would come several days after they had taken place, followed by an agony of waiting for the slow letters from Mark, George and Charlie. It was a blessing that the hard work of everyday living filled their days so fully that there was not much time even for worry.

It was a high spot in Ann's day when Mark did write, but she never blamed him when he didn't, for she realized how hard it must be for him to do so, particularly when he was with McClellan in the Peninsula campaign. How she prized his letters! She saved every one, read and re-read them, and carried them next to her heart day after day until they were almost worn out. It pleased her to note how much Mark's writing had improved as time went on. It seemed that he was able to express in the written word his loneliness and his love for her as he never could have done orally.

"My darling," he wrote some time before the second Bull Run battle, "tomorrow, or maybe the next day, rumor has it that we are going into another great fight. So before I sleep tonight I want to tell you all over again how much you mean to me, and how much I love you. When I enlisted, I thought it was my duty to do so, but honestly I also thought it would be a great adventure. Well, it isn't. War is terrible. I know that now. Of course, there is some excitement and a lot of comradeship with other boys, all of which helps to pass the time and makes it easier for us than for you and Mother who have to keep things going at home. Father and Charlie and I talk about you and the family so many times, and we worry about how you can keep the farm work going so that you all have enough to eat and to wear.

"As you know, we have tried not to spend a cent of the small pay we get so that there may be a little to send home, but I know that it doesn't help much, especially when you have to worry about that old mortgage. I hope Henry Bain isn't bothering you about the interest, or anything else."

Ann paused in her reading and thought:

"Now I wonder what Mark means by that 'anything else.' Maybe he's a little jealous. And maybe he has some right to be. If I told him how much I worry about Henry Bain, not only about the interest on the mortgage but about his hanging around so much, I honestly believe he'd desert and come home. I can't do a thing about it, either, for if I send Henry packing, then he'll be mad and put Mother and me out of our home just as sure as preaching. Well," she sighed, "there's no use worrying Mark about it."

She went on with the rest of Mark's letter:

"What I really wanted to say in this letter, sweetheart, was just three little words which I didn't say often enough when I was beside you, three little words which I hope you will write on your heart. You know what they are: *I love you*!

"Ann, I don't want to be gloomy or silly, but I'd like to say to you just once that if anything should happen to me, I want you always to remember that you owe me nothing but what you have given me, your love. That's the greatest and most precious gift of all. You have all of your life ahead of you. I know that you wouldn't think of nor have any desire for marriage for a time, but I want to tell you now that if I should not come back, I hope in time that you will remarry. You can, you know. An attractive girl like you has everything, and above all, in this world and the next, I want you to be happy."

Ann shed tears over that letter.

"The big ninny," she said aloud, "to think that I could ever love anybody else."

She laid the letter down and her thoughts again came back to what Mark had said about Henry Bain's worrying her.

"I am worried," she thought, "and Mother's attitude makes the situation worse. I suppose Mother feels that if we aren't friendly with Henry, he'll dump us both out."

She got up and paced restlessly back and forth across the room.

"For all I care, he can take the old farm and I'll go back to teaching!"

Struck with the new idea, her face lighted up.

"Maybe that's the answer. I'll talk with Mother tomorrow."

Next morning Ann said:

"Mother, I want to talk with you frankly about something that has worried me for a long time. I don't like Henry Bain's coming here so much, nor the things he has said to me two or three times lately. After all, I'm a married woman, I love my husband, and I have no interest whatever in Henry Bain."

Mrs. Clinton said, quickly:

"I know, my dear, I know. But that's no reason why we shouldn't be pleasant and kind with our friends, and you're almost impolite to Henry ever time he comes."

"Well, I just don't want him coming here. I don't think it looks well, either."

"Well," said Mrs. Clinton, "if we make him mad, you know what he may do to us. He holds the mortgage, and we aren't making the payments."

"Don't think I haven't thought about that," Ann snapped back. "But now I think I know the answer. Let him take the place. I'll go back to teaching, and we'll be in better shape financially than we'll ever be trying to make a living on this old farm, especially with someone like Bain on our necks."

At this her mother started to cry.

"This is my home," she wailed. "I'd never be happy anywhere else. And besides—think of your father. What would he have to come back to?"

"Oh, all right," said Ann, hopelessly. "I might have known it would be this way . . ."

She said no more about it, and tried not to worry.

After Bull Run no more letters came, and Ann would turn away from the post office sick with fear. Sometimes she was irritated. He must know I'm worried and he could write a few lines, she told herself. I know it's hard for him, but somehow he should get word to me. Nancy, too, was worried, for she had had no word from George and Charlie, but she tried to reassure Ann.

"You know how hard it is for them to get time to write. No news is good news, you know."

Then disaster struck. Ann found a letter at the post office, not from Mark but from George to Nancy. Running most of the way back to the Wilson home, she pushed the letter into Nancy's hand and cried:

"Read it, quick. Read it and tell me."

With fingers that no effort of will could keep from trembling, Nancy tore open the letter and glanced over the contents. Her face turned white and she sank into a chair.

"What is it? What's the matter, Mother?" cried Ann, in terror.

Nancy braced herself to tell Ann the contents of the letter.

"I can't believe it," she said slowly, her voice trembling, "but George says that Mark has been court martialed!"

Stunned, Ann stared at her uncomprehendingly.

"Court martialed!" she echoed. "But why? I don't believe it! There must be some mistake."

Then with a sob, she sank to her knees and buried her face in Nancy's lap.

CHAPTER XV

"I CAN TAKE IT NOW," said Ann, quietly, a few moments later. "Please read the letter to me."

Nancy looked at the girl's dead-white face, drew a deep breath, and began to read aloud her husband's long letter:

"You'll remember, Nancy, that boy from Virginia who came to our neighborhood to visit the Royce's two years ago this summer. His name was Floyd Morton. If I remember right, he was some relation to Mrs. Royce. He was a very agreeable young chap, made friends easily, and our Mark took quite a shine to him.

"Well, when the outposts and picket lines of the armies were close together on the night before Bull Run, Mark was on picket duty. He told me what happened. He was walking slowly back and forth across his beat, waiting for the hours to pass until he could be relieved and get some sleep. Suddenly he heard a noise in a clump of brush that he had just passed. He dropped flat on the ground and bringing his musket to bear on the brush challenged: 'Who goes there?' The answer surprised him. It was, 'Someone you know.'

"Mark told the man to drop his gun and come out of the brush with his hands up to where he could be seen in the half light. The fellow obeyed, and then Mark found it was this Floyd Morton. He told Mark he was unarmed and that he wasn't in the Confederate forces—wasn't even a Rebel sympathizer. He had a convincing story about being engaged to a girl behind the Union lines. Said he hadn't heard from her in months, didn't even know if she was alive, and in desperation had started out to go to her home. Mark asked him why he hadn't been drafted, and he claimed he had been doing some kind of civilian war work back of the Confederate lines.

"The boy claimed that while hiding in the clump of brush, waiting for an opportunity to get through, he had recognized

Mark and purposely attracted his attention. His logical story, plus Mark's old liking for him and sympathy for anyone in love, won Mark's confidence. Some way or other Morton also convinced him that his civilian clothes were proof that he was just what he claimed to be, a Virginia farm boy trying to get news of his girl.

"Anyway, Mark let him through, but just then the pickets were changed and the man who relieved Mark saw him talking to Morton. He arrested Morton, marched him back to an officer, and reported that Mark had allowed the fellow to pass the picket line. Morton was recognized as a spy, courtmartialed the next day, and sentenced to be shot. For allowing Morton through, Mark was arrested and court-martialed, and is also under sentence of death.

"Fortunately, I have made friends among the officers, and through them I succeeded in getting a stay of execution, at least for a short time on a reasonable doubt of Mark's guilt. But I feel that you and Ann have a right to know the truth. The constant reverses of the Union forces, frequent desertions, and the prevalence of spies within our lines are making our officers stiffnecked in their determination to enforce discipline and to get this army of citizens on a military basis. So Mark's chances aren't too good."

Nancy paused to try to control her voice and her trembling hands, and then continued:

"S-some of his friends and mine have suggested an appeal to President Lincoln, but when I tried to get a furlough or even a few days to go to Washington, the officers refused. They didn't give me a reason for not letting me go, but it is generally known that they try to keep information about these court-martial cases away from the President because of his tendency to pardon the prisoners, which the generals feel interferes with military discipline."

In closing his letter, George added;

"Don't give up hope. There must be some way out."

But his own agony and hopelessness were very evident. When Nancy ceased reading, she glanced at Ann sitting in the chair opposite, and noticed how white were the knuckles of her hands as she gripped the arms of her chair in an effort to keep control. Suddenly Ann's face flushed and she jumped to her feet and stood over Nancy, her eyes snapping:

"All right," she cried. "They wouldn't let Father Wilson go to Washington, but they can't keep us from going."

The sheets of the letter fell from Nancy's lap as she, too, sprang to her feet and clutched Ann's arms so hard that the black and blue spots showed later.

"Of course, we'll go!" she agreed, excitedly. "We'll start tomorrow morning."

"Maybe I should go alone," said Ann. "Can you leave the children?"

"We can do anything when we have to," said Nancy. "You aren't making a trip like that alone. Mary Curtis'll come in and stay with the children, and Enoch will be glad to help out with the chores both here and at your place, and see that your mother gets along all right. We'll get off tomorrow morning at daylight, and Enoch can drive us to Owego. Better go home now and tell your mother. Don't pack too many things for the trip. Get what sleep you can, and Enoch and I will be at your place early tomorrow morning."

That trip behind the old horse to Owego next morning and then by train to Washington was an experience both women tried to forget for the rest of their lives, but never quite succeeded in doing so. Every farm passed, every foot of the dusty highway to Owego was like a knifethrust to Ann as she recalled the journey with Mark the morning after their wedding. Every rhythmic turn of the car wheels on the long rail trip to Washington seemed to be saying: "You can't do it; you can't do it."

Their eyes bloodshot from lack of sleep and the dust and cinders of the train, and their clothes dishevelled, Ann and Nancy, feeling completely exhausted, finally arrived in the great sprawling city that was the capital of the United States. They descended from the train into a welter of heat, confusion, noise and bustle, punctuated by the yells of the cab drivers just outside the station. The crowd that they finally pushed themselves through were a motley lot, most of them different from anyone the women had ever known. There were men with tall stovepipe hats, expensive clothes, immaculate linen and black bow ties, who had somehow managed to keep themselves looking well groomed in spite of the train ride; there were a few women looking as lost and

bewildered as Ann and Nancy felt, making their way hesitantly through the crowd, perhaps going to visit a wounded
soldier son or husband in the Washington hospitals. And
then there were the young men, also looking bewildered and
homesick, recruits for Abraham Lincoln's army, who were
being guided by the shouted commands of a non-commis-
sioned officer in uniform.

Outside the station, Nancy succeeded in getting a be-
whiskered, one-eyed cab driver to stop shouting long enough
to listen to her request to be driven to the White House.
His gaze showed that he wondered what two plainly dressed
country women could want at the White House. Then,
shifting a cud of tobacco to the other side of his mouth, he
drove a long stream of tobacco juice toward the wheel of his
cab, and grunted:

"Climb in! I'll take ye up there. Whether ye can get in
or not is somethin' else agin!"

Accustomed to thinking of Washington as a storybook
city, the capital of the great United States, Ann was disappointed with the reality. Her tired state added to her disillusionment. It had rained the night before, turning the inches
of dust on Pennsylvania Avenue to a soft, disgusting, sticky
mess, through which their cab driver raced his old horse.
Mud spattered from the horse's flying hoofs and from the
rapidly revolving wheels, some of it reaching the occupants
of the cab. But in spite of the mud and the hard going, everyone seemed to be in a hurry, joining in the mad rush of
vehicles of every description that raced up and down the
wide Avenue.

Ann had read about the beautiful government buildings,
and they lived up to the description, but they were surrounded by rambling, down-at-the-heel business places and
dwelling houses. Washington, Ann reflected, was certainly
no dream city. The whole aspect of the place was in keeping
with her own churning thoughts.

When their driver pulled up in front of the White House,
even that was disappointing to Ann. She had expected something of a palace to house the head of the nation. But later
she was to realize that the very simplicity of the White
House was in keeping with the President who now lived there
and with his ideas of the basic principles of democracy.

To the guard at the outer door Nancy said, simply:
"We want to see Mr. Lincoln on a matter of life and death!"

The man looked them up and down, noting their countrified appearance and their white, strained faces, and then muttered:

"Life and death! That's what they all say." Then he added, gruffly:

"Go ahead! But don't be surprised if the President can't see you. He's a busy man."

Nancy and Ann seated themselves in an anteroom to the President's office and watched the steady stream of callers pass in and out of the door behind which they knew was the man who held Mark's destiny and theirs in his hands. In the line of callers were well-dressed business men, looking hopeful as they entered, then a few minutes later hurrying out again, their faces indicative of whether or not their mission had been successful. In the passing throng, too, were dignified looking men with their tall stovepipe hats. Ann and Nancy thought they must be members of the Congress or at least holders of important administrative offices. Then there were the military men, high officers in their blue uniforms reporting to their Commander-in-Chief. After watching the hurrying crowd for a while, Ann said, despairingly:

"How can so busy a man as Mr. Lincoln, with such great responsibilities, have any time for us?"

After a long time there seemed to be a little lull in the stream of callers. The door of the inner office opened from the inside, and the tall, angular frame of Abraham Lincoln stood framed in it. Ann and Nancy jumped to their feet, and Nancy said:

"Mr. President!"

He looked at them, smiled and said:

"What can I do for you, ladies?"

"I'm Mrs. Nancy Wilson and this is Ann Wilson, my daughter-in-law. We've come all the way from New York State," said Nancy, "to talk with you about a matter of life and death."

The little smile left the homely, tired face. Slowly, with shoulders suddenly hunched, he turned around and started back into his office, saying, briefly:

"Come on in!"

The President's first remark after they were all seated surprised them:

"Did you have any breakfast?"

"Well, some, Mr. Lincoln. We put up a lunch and ate it on the train, but this morning we didn't want to take the time to eat, and we didn't know where to get anything. Also, we wanted to see you as soon as we could."

"Reminds me of when I was a boy and used to carry my dinner," said the President. Then leaning forward and smiling at Nancy, he drawled:

"Ever make a meal out of just crackers and cheese?"

"Yes, I have, Mr. Lincoln."

"I knew it! All country folks have."

Then he settled back in his chair again, with a far-away look on his face, and added:

"And so have I, many times. Maybe crackers and cheese weren't much for vittles, but I'd just like to have anything I eat now taste half so good!"

"A boy's appetite makes the difference, doesn't it, Mr. Lincoln?"

"Yes," he agreed, "—and a man's troubles. But now tell me what I can do for you. Why are you here?"

Both Nancy and Ann had expected that if they could see the President, he would be hurried and abrupt with them, and that being nervous and pressed for time they would have difficulty in telling their story. But Lincoln was just like the folks they had always known. They soon forgot his high office and found themselves opening up their hearts as they would to an old friend.

"Ann's husband—my son—Mark Wilson, enlisted the morning after they were married. Charlie Wilson, another of my boys, ran away and enlisted at 17. Then my husband, George, also went."

"Yes, I know, I know," he said, a little impatiently, they thought. "It's the same sad story of thousands of families. But how is it different from the others? Why have you come all this long way to see me?"

Then Nancy told the whole story. When she had finished, she leaned forward toward the President and her voice suddenly broke:

"M—M—Mark's a good boy, Mr. President. He's inno-cent of any wrongdoing."

Lincoln turned in his chair and sat gazing out over the White House lawn, simmering in the heat of a late September day in Washington. The women waited, reading into his silence a reluctance to tell them that he couldn't interfere. But after a while he turned back to them, and almost sub-consciously Nancy noticed how the lines of care and trouble had begun to cut themselves deep into the craggy face. Still without speaking he looked at them, then got up and shuffled across the room in his old carpet slippers to stand by the window, his clothes hanging loosely on his ungainly frame, his hands clasped behind him. Suddenly he swung around, came back to his desk and sat down, while Nancy and Ann waited, feeling as prisoners at the bar must feel when the jury is about to render a life or death verdict.

The President's first words were not encouraging:

"You know," he said, "that the fate of a whole Army and the lives of hundreds of men can depend upon the loyalty and the judgment of one man on the picket line. I must tell you, also, that things are entirely different in war than they are in peace. Most of the very principles we are fighting for have to be given up temporarily. That means among other things that discipline in an army must be rigidly maintained."

He smiled sadly and went on:

"The generals are always scolding me because they say I'm bad for the army discipline when I let go some boy whom the military courts have condemned."

Then, almost as if he were alone and talking to himself, he added:

"Maybe they're right. But there's something so absolute about death. These boys—almost all of them—are so young, so young!"

He straightened up in his chair, threw back his shoulders as if he were literally defying the army and all of its works, and looked directly at his visitors. For all the rest of her life Ann was to remember the infinite sadness in those great eyes. It seemed to her that that stooped figure was carrying the burden of all mankind on those broad shoulders. Suddenly the President leaned over his desk, pulled a sheet of paper toward him and began to write.

Just then came an interruption. A clerk opened the door and announced:

"The Secretary of War is here, Mr. President."

Without waiting for an invitation, Secretary Stanton entered and strode purposefully toward the President's desk. He was dressed in black, with an open collar, a black flowing tie, and carried his hat in his hand. Nancy and Ann stood up respectfully as he passed them.

"Goodday, Mr. President," he said, brusquely, and then glanced meaningly at the women. "I must see you immediately, and alone."

Lincoln grinned.

"Just a minute, Stanton. I have guests. By the way, I'm glad you are here. You're just the man I want to see."

Stanton looked impatient.

"But I've got to talk with you immediately—alone, "he insisted.

"In good time, in good time!" said Lincoln. "Meet my callers. This is Mrs. Nancy Wilson, and this Mrs. Ann Wilson, her daughter-in-law. They are the mother and wife respectively of one Mark Wilson, a soldier whom your officers, Mr. Stanton, have court-martialed and sentenced to be shot."

Stanton's face was red:

"You aren't going to interfere again, Mr. President," he burst forth. "You're raising havoc with our discipline."

"Maybe so," Lincoln agreed, "but we have enough bloodshed, God knows, without any that is unnecessary. I don't believe this boy was guilty of anything but a mistake that any of us might have made. Here's my signed pardon. Will you kindly act accordingly?"

He handed the paper on which he had just written to the Secretary of War, who stuffed it angrily and carelessly into a pocket. Lincoln smiled again, but there was something in that smile that the women and the Secretary both recognized as a hint that the order had better not be disobeyed.

Impulsively Ann stepped forward to shake the President's hand. He came around from behind his desk and put one arm across her shoulders, offering his other hand to Nancy.

"I never forget," he said, "that women fight these wars as well as the men, and that without you and others like you to carry on at home, we never could win through. May God go with you and with all the other home folks!"

CHAPTER XVI

As THEY CAME OUT OF President Lincoln's office after their talk with him, Nancy laid a detaining hand on Ann's arm and led her to a seat in the anteroom. With shining eyes and face flushed with happiness, Ann impulsively threw her arms around Nancy and hugged her hard, oblivious of the curious glances of other occupants of the room.

"A great man!" she cried. "But how sad and lonely he looked." Then she added:

"But what are we waiting for? Everything is all right now. We can go home."

Nancy started to speak, hesitated, and then said softly:

"We mustn't get our hopes up—but—we're so near our men now, wouldn't it be wonderful if we could see them?"

Excited, Ann jumped to her feet:

"Oh, yes, yes," she breathed. "But how? We don't know how."

Nancy pulled her back into the chair beside her.

"I have a plan," she whispered. "Maybe it won't work, but just be patient a little longer, dear."

As they sat there, the line of callers in the anteroom grew, all of them awaiting the end of the Secretary of War's interview with the President. Suddenly the door was flung open and Secretary Stanton marched out. Nancy rose, drawing Ann with her, and stood directly in front of him so that he had no alternative but to stop. He glared impatiently; then, recognizing her, said, shortly:

"Excuse me, Madam. I am in a hurry."

Then, looking more closely at Nancy's strained, terrified, but resolute face, he said, kindly:

"Don't worry about your son." With a grim smile, he added: "I have my orders."

Nancy often wondered afterwards how she had the temerity to stand up before this great man and ask of him what she did.

"Mr. Secretary," she said, "four of our menfolks are in this war. We've come a long way. Now that we are near them, couldn't we see them, if only for a few minutes?"

"No," barked Stanton. "It's impossible!"

As the women turned away with drooping shoulders, he stood staring at them briefly, and suddenly said:

"Wait!" Then dashing their rising hopes again, "No, the Army is on the move. McClellan is moving south after Antietam. You couldn't find the Army. Besides, you have no way of getting there even if you could."

Then, as the women turned away disconsolately again, he barked, impatiently:

"Wait till I finish, can't you?" A little smile lighted up his features as he added, "Now that the President has let your boy loose, I might as well go him one better. Give me the names of your men and their regiments."

As Nancy gave him the information, the Secretary wrote it down.

"Where are you staying?" was his next question.

When he heard that they had only come into the city that morning and had no lodgings, he gave them the name of a hotel.

"Go there," he ordered. "Wait and see what I can do. Perhaps I can send them to you. It may be two or three days —maybe not at all."

Then, as if ashamed of his softness, he turned and walked rapidly out of the room.

Never in their lives had time dragged as it did for Nancy and Ann in the next few days. They dared not risk leaving their hotel room together, even for food, lest there might be no one there if their men came. Occasionally from their bedroom window they watched the hurrying traffic on Pennsylvania Avenue, but with little interest because of their alternating hopes and fears. When either one of them went out to eat, she would hurry back in case someone had come in her absence.

After three days had gone by, when their cash was nearly gone and they had about given up hope, there came a knock on the bedroom door. Both rushed to open it, and there in the doorway were George and Mark and Charles in their blue uniforms.

For the first few minutes all were choked with emotion, too happy to speak. But finally they settled themselves, Ann on the edge of the bed, with Mark's arm around her. After the first exciting moments were over, George asked numberless questions about the farm and the children, and Nancy answered them as fast as she could. It was wonderful, she thought, to be able to talk to him.

"Tom took your parting words about his being the man of the family very seriously," she said. "He works every minute that he isn't in school, and never complains about anything. And what we would have done without Enoch Payne, I'm sure I don't know," she continued, "for he and Tom have made a great pair. Enoch likes Tom and tries to show him the best way of getting at a job."

Ann laughed.

"Tom's not the only one Enoch likes," she said. "I think he and Mary Curtis are sweet on each other."

"I'm sure I hope so," said Nancy. "I don't know a nicer couple, and they have a right to a little happiness."

"Tell me more about my little daughters," said George.

Nancy shot a merry look at Ann and said:

"Ask Ann to tell you about the time she took them blackberrying and Hattie got lost."

"Well, I found her again," protested Ann.

"Anyway," said Nancy, "the girls are coming along just fine. Better hurry up and get home or you won't know them when you see them. They're growing so fast."

Although the events leading up to their reunion in Washington were uppermost in everyone's mind, nothing was said about them until then. It was George who finally said:

"I guess we know what happened about Mark. You must have seen Mr. Lincoln."

"Yes, we did," answered Nancy, eagerly, "and Mr. Stanton, too. It was he who arranged it so you could come to see us. They say he's a hard man, but I for one will never believe all the stories about his being so stern and unbending."

"Maybe it makes a difference who talks to him," said Charlie, grinning.

Everyone laughed, and then they all seemed to talk at the same time, as excited questions and answers followed in quick succession.

Over and over, Ann and Nancy had to tell of their journey, their wonderful meeting with the President, how he looked and what he said; their hopes and fears, and finally of Nancy's great courage in intercepting the Secretary of War right in the White House. Then the men had to recount the details of their surprise and joy over Mark's sudden release and the mysterious order for the three of them to go at once to Washington to meet their womenfolk.

It was all so wonderful, they said; just like a story. But at last George declared:

"We haven't got much time. We've got to go back tomorrow; so Nancy, you and I had better do some planning."

While they talked, Ann sat silent, content and happy just to hold tightly to Mark, but her heart ached as she felt the thinness of his body through his clothes and as she looked at his worn, care-lined face.

The rest of the afternoon and evening passed all too quickly. Nancy, with the lilt back in her voice, talked again and again of the little girls and of Tom at home, but made light of the problems and responsibility of the farm and of making a living. Likewise, George and Charlie and Mark, in telling of their experiences and adventures, passed quickly over the hardships of Army life.

Ann wanted to know about her father, and George said he was fine. Looking significantly at Ann so that she understood the inner meaning of his remark, he added:

"Your father is a fine soldier, Ann, doing well, and exceptionally well liked."

That filled Ann's cup of joy almost to overflowing. But later when she and Mark were in a room by themselves she grew silent and shy. Made sensitive by his recent disgrace, Mark misunderstood her reticence and he, too, fell silent. In bed they lay stiffly side by side, each waiting for the other to make the first advance. Suddenly Ann forgot her own shyness in a realization of what Mark must be feeling. Crying, "Mark, Mark, I love you so," she threw her arms around him. Then all the loneliness, the heartache, the frustrations were forgotten. The past was past; the future could take care of itself; they had the present and each other.

Next morning, when they were all together, the talk was about a new government order abolishing all regimental bands in the volunteer service, except one for each brigade at headquarters.

George explained to Nancy and Ann that at the beginning of the war no regiment was thought complete unless it had a full brass band, some of them containing as many as fifty pieces. With four or five regiments in each brigade, three brigades in one division, and three divisions in each corps, that made a total of from thirty-six to forty bands in every Army corps.

"How wonderful!" exclaimed Ann, enthusiastically. "What a lot it must mean to lonesome, homesick boys to see and hear all of those bands playing together."

"Not any more," said George, "now that the government has suddenly decided that so many bands are too costly. If most of them are disbanded, the musicians will probably re-enlist as regular soldiers."

"I think it's mean to deprive the soldiers of their music," commented Nancy.

"Well," said Charlie, "that's one of your wonderful Secretary Stanton's ideas. He says the Army needs less nonsense and more discipline, and apparently to him music is just nonsense. But I don't care what Stanton or any of the other Army bosses think. When they take music out of the war, they knock out something that keeps men going when nothing else will. Let me tell you what happened just a short time ago, when we were marching to Sharpsburg to drive Lee out of Maryland."

George interrupted him.

"Won't that wait, Charlie? We haven't got much time for stories."

But Nancy said:

"Leave him be. You don't tell us much of what happens to you and the boys, and I want to know."

"Well," Charlie went on, eagerly, "you'd know what war's like if you'd seen the Army of Virginia, veterans of the Peninsula campaign, on that march. The men's hands and faces were burned almost black, thousands of them had no shoes, and they had to lug their cans, blankets, haversacks and canteens under that hot sun—except those who'd thrown 'em away because they couldn't carry 'em and themselves, too. You remember, Pa, how we stood on that knoll in the vanguard and looked back at that endless line? There they came, a brigade of infantry, then one of cavalry, then the big guns of the artillery, and last a wagon train of supplies. Often, the supply train was way behind and we didn't have anything to eat."

He paused for breath, and, held by his earnestness, no one spoke.

"Those men were worn out and desperate, and the only thing that kept 'em going was the drums—the music of our bands! Every time we struck up a tune you could see their heads lift, their steps pick up, and their shoulders straighten as they tried to march in time to the music. And now Stanton wants to throw it all out!"

Somewhat embarrassed by his own vehemence, but determined to tell the truth at last about how he felt about Army life, Charlie smiled wryly, and said:

"Adventure! Who said there was adventure in war? It's hellish! Starvation, suffering, endless waiting, and finally injury and maybe death."

Nancy sat watching her son, saying nothing, but remembering how he had run away to enlist for the adventure of it. How sadly he had been disillusioned!

Charlie's tale had diverted George's thoughts from the need of making plans. He, too, began to reminisce.

"I'll never forget that awful march, either. I can still see that long column stretching away as far as one could see, like a gigantic snake, and the hardbitten look on the faces of the veterans, and how their lagging steps picked up when we struck up the band. When we started to play "John Brown," the men began to sing and completely drowned us out with

> John Brown's body lies a-moldering
> in the grave
> But his soul goes marching on.

"Somehow as I looked at those men, barefoot and ragged, but still singing along, stepping in time to the music, I knew that they might lose many battles, and that it might take a long time yet, but still they wouldn't lose the war. The Union was safe."

"Well, if there are no more bands," said Ann, "doesn't that mean that you can all come home?"

"Not so fast, young lady, not so fast," George smiled. "But it does mean that Charlie and Mark will receive an honorable discharge before very long."

Now Nancy was excited.

"What do you mean, George Wilson? What about you?"

George looked gravely at his wife, hesitated, then said:

"Well, as I told you a moment ago, one band is being retained for each brigade, and when some of the officers asked me to lead it, I couldn't very well refuse."

"Father did his job too well," said Charles, proudly. "He was the best musician in our band, and the officers knew it."

Nancy walked to the dirty hotel window and stood gazing out for a few moments. Then she said, sadly:

"Then you won't be coming home to us?"

"No," said George, gently, "but the boys will be home as soon as their discharges come through."

Ann, sitting close to Mark, reached for his hand. He held hers for a moment, then let it go and suddenly stood up, facing all of them.

"I am going home as soon as I get my discharge," he said, quietly. "But I'm coming back. I can never live with myself, nor with you, until I have wiped out what happened by proving to President Lincoln and Secretary Stanton— whether they know of it or not—and to you, Ann, and you, my folks, that I *am* a good soldier and that I can do my duty. I shall re-enlist soon."

In spite of the ache in her heart and the lump in her throat, Ann felt a great pride swell in her breast for her young husband. Never, she thought, have I loved him so much.

"We understand, Mark," said Nancy, tenderly. Then she turned to look at Charles, realizing with a pang how rapidly war had matured him. When he had run away to enlist, it seemed to her that he was still just a little boy. But that could no longer be said. Her boy, who just yesterday was a baby, was now a man. Like his father and brother, he looked tired and careworn, and she knew that Mark's trouble and danger had left their mark on him, too. But now, as he sat there in his soldier's uniform, happy and relaxed, she was proud of him, too. Catching her glance, he grinned:

"Oh, I know what you're thinking, Ma. While we're at it,

we might as well get my fate settled, too. Yes, I'm coming home all right."

Then the grin left his face and his mouth settled into a hard line as he continued:

"Even though war is hellish, I'll be back, too. I liked being in the band fine, but now that's out, so I'm going to carry a gun." Then he qualified his statement, "Or let a horse carry it. I'm tired of walking, and if they'll take me, I'm goin' into the cavalry."

Nancy looked at her menfolks with mixed feelings. Everyone knew now that the war would be a long one, and no one could foresee the end. All one could do was to live a day at a time and try not to worry. But she couldn't help feeling that George and Mark and Charlie had made their plans without any consideration of the women's problems at home. She rose quickly from her chair and said to Ann, with spirit:

"Well, Ann, I guess that's that. Our men seem to have the decisions all made. We might as well be on our way."

Then, noting a hurt look on her husband's face she said, more gently:

"But maybe they are right."

CHAPTER XVII

ALL DURING the long but happy trip back from Washington, Ann thought how different she had felt on their way down. Then every minute had been torture. At times she had found herself pushing hard with her foot on the floor of the coach as if to make the train go faster. There had been room in her mind for only one thought, one prayer, that God would help them to see the President and be in time.

Now her prayer had been answered. They had seen the President, they had been in time, Mark was safe and, glory be, he would be coming home soon. Even though it would be for only a short time, she would be with him. Now she could look out of the window and take some interest in the strange country that slid by so rapidly. She could be interested in the raw recruits who crowded the railroad stations on their way south. She could sympathize with the veterans, clad in faded and often ragged blue uniforms, some of them on furlough or maybe discharged from their first term of enlistment. She observed their tired young eyes above their long beards.

It interested her, too, to see the country gradually change from the bright green of the Maryland and the southern Pennsylvania countryside, well supplied with rain, to the river and creek valleys and the wooded country of the Pennsylvania mountains, now showing autumn colors after the first frost of the fall. It began to look like home.

Even the stagecoach journey from Owego to Jenkstown was interesting, and, as they neared home, how good the familiar scenes looked to them! Nancy had been quiet during the trip. After all, George wasn't coming home, not in a long time. The boys would soon be coming back, but not to stay. Yes, it was good to be home, she thought, but was it really home with her husband and two of her boys still in constant danger? She looked over at Ann's happy face, alive with interest as she watched the passing scene, and Nancy breathed a silent prayer that happiness would be Ann's lot, or at least that there would be more happiness than sorrow for her. For herself she added a petition that the day would be hastened when peace would reign again.

There hadn't been time to let Enoch know they were coming, so no one met them at Jenkstown. They climbed off the stage, picked up some mail at John Crawford's store, answering briefly his eager questions, and set off on foot for home.

Nancy left Ann at her home and hastened on alone. Her depressed feeling did not leave her until she opened the kitchen door and saw the incredulous joy that shone in the faces of her little girls. They had just finished supper, and, as Nancy stepped into the kitchen, Mary Curtis at one end of the table and Enoch Payne at the other jumped to their feet. The girls dashed madly across the room, threw themselves upon her and hung on as if they could never let her go again. She dropped her carpet bag to put her arms around them, and then stood, divided between laughter and tears, as they danced around the kitchen, occasionally stopping to give her another hug and kiss. Tom, who had appeared from the barn, stood grinning, wishing just as much as his sisters to show his mother how glad he was that she had returned, but, boylike, a little reticent about too much outward demonstration.

Minutes later, when the children had quieted down a little, Mary Curtis came to Nancy, put her arm around her shoulders and, a little shyly, gave her a gentle hug, while Enoch pumped her hand so long that he apparently forgot he had hold of it.

How wonderful, Nancy thought, to receive such a welcome! How could she ever be cross again with the children or forget to count her blessings when she thought of her problems? And how could she ever get along without the help and friendship of folks like Mary and Enoch!

Later that evening, after the chores at the barn were finished and the little girls had finally quieted down in bed, Nancy, Mary, Enoch and Tom sat around the kitchen table with its gay checked tablecloth. A single flickering candle drove the shadows toward the walls and corners of the room

as Nancy told all that had happened on their trip and answered their questions. There was so much to tell that the
candle burned low before she finished.

In bed that night, her thoughts still racing, came the
memory of what she had only subconsciously noticed while
she was talking at the table—how in spite of their keen interest in her story, Mary and Enoch had looked at each
other more than they had at her. She hoped those glances
meant a growing understanding. If so, she thought, then our
trip has had one more good result.

At the Clinton home the situation was different. Bursting
with happiness and enthusiasm, Ann rushed into the house
and greeted her mother with a hug and a kiss, almost shouting:

"He's coming home! Mark's coming home!"

Mrs. Clinton drew herself from Ann's embrace, and said:
"That's good."

But there was such a lack of enthusiasm in her tone that
Ann looked sharply at her and said:

"Why, Mother, aren't you glad that Mark is out of trouble
and is coming home?"

Mrs. Clinton sniffed, hesitated, then said:

"Things won't be very pleasant for him around here after
the way he disgraced himself."

Ann was stunned.

"Disgraced! What do you mean? He made an honest mistake and the President of the United States pardoned him."

"Why did he get kicked out of the Army, then?"

"Kicked out! He didn't! He has an honorable discharge
as a musician. He's coming home for a while and then he's
going to re-enlist. How can you believe such things? Who's
been talking to you?"

Her mother was indefinite.

"Oh, I hear things," she said, vaguely.

Chilled, Ann changed the subject and asked about the
farm and the stock. The report was discouraging.

"Oh, Enoch Payne has been doing the chores," said her
mother, "but nothing else has been done."

"But, Mother, I haven't been gone long. The crops aren't
suffering, and just as soon as Mark and Charlie get here we'll
clean up the fall work on both farms."

"Well," her mother said, rather grudgingly, "that will help

out temporarily. But we're going to lose this war, and you and I are going to lose this farm, sure as preachin'. Then what'll we do?"

Struck by a sudden thought, Ann cried:

"Mother, that kind of talk sounds like Henry Bain. Has he been here since I've been gone?"

"Yes, he has," said her mother, defiantly, "and I don't know what I'd have done without him. One night when Enoch was off carousing to Ithaca, Henry went down and did the chores. And I don't care what you say, I'm beginning to think that he's right about this war. Look at it! Almost all the war news we get is bad news; we're defeated in almost every battle. Henry says that the Confederates have better generals, and their soldiers are trained to fight better. It certainly looks that way. Henry says that we have no business fighting on southern soil. If the southern states want to be independent and to have slaves, why, let 'em. Why should we lose everything we have? He says, too, that England and other countries think the South is right and are going to interfere to stop the war."

Tired from the strain of the past several days, Ann's temper was short. She jumped to her feet and said, hotly:

"How can you talk that way? How can you listen to a coward who stays home and makes money while all of his neighbors are fighting for their country and we women are doing what we can to stand back of them? Don't talk to me about what Henry Bain says!"

A little frightened by Ann's vehemence, Mrs. Clinton tried to mollify her.

"Maybe you're right, Ann. Maybe you're right. I just don't know. But I'm so worried that we'll lose our home and have no place to go that I'm most out of my mind. And Henry has been good to me. When I've been lonesome and worried, he has talked to me, and he's certainly right that the war is going against us."

Ann stood looking at her mother for a moment, and then said, gently:

"Well, I know you're worried, Mother. We all are. Let's get something to eat and we'll both feel better."

Too tired and excited to sleep that night, Ann lay in bed watching the big round harvest moon that threw a patch of light on her bedroom floor. She kept thinking of things her mother had said and recalled her remark about Enoch carousing in Ithaca. "Now, what did Mother mean by that," she wondered. "I never knew Enoch Payne to get drunk. I'll ask him myself."

Still thinking resentfully of her mother's remarks, Ann reflected that maybe there was a reason for her father's drinking. Maybe it was a sort of escape. A little ashamed of the thought, she remembered that even when he was sober her father wasn't too good a farmer and that they were always short of money, sometimes even of the bare necessities of life. No wonder her mother felt insecure, and worried and fretted as she did.

Finally, Ann quieted her churning thoughts by remembering what Nancy had said—that we can only live one day at a time and have to let the tomorrows take care of themselves. Her thoughts turned to Mark and the realization that he would soon be home, and, playing the little girl game of pretending that he was there beside her, she fell asleep.

Next morning when Ann saw Enoch come up the road and stop off at the barn to do the chores, she went down to assure him that she could manage the chores now and to thank him for what he had done while she was gone. She resolved to ask him about what her mother had said, but it wasn't necessary. Grinning a little after greeting her, he said:

"Who d'you suppose did the chores one night?"

"I know," Ann answered, unsmilingly. "Mother told me that Henry Bain did them."

Still grinning, Enoch asked:

"Did she also tell you why I didn't get back to do 'em?"

That question was embarrassing. After all, she loved Enoch and didn't want to hurt his feelings, so her answer was vague:

"W-well—she was just repeating gossip, I expect."

"You needn't be afraid to talk, Ann. I know what Bain's tellin' around—and I know why."

"Do you want to tell me about it, Enoch?"

"Of course, I'll tell you. I have a brother over to Ithacy and I heard he was sick. So I fixed things up here an' over to the Wilson place so's there wouldn't be any heavy chores, just a little feedin' to do for the stock night an' mornin' an' a couple of cows to milk, an' arranged for young Tom to do the chores. Then I got up early in the mornin', 'fore daylight, hired a good road horse over to the liv'ry stable, an' drove to Ithacy. I put up my horse in one of the liv'ry stables there. Glad to say I found my brother gettin' along all right. He'd been pretty sick but was most well again. Had a grand visit with him an' Lena, his wife, an' stayed all night.

"By the way, this'll interest you, Ann. While we were visitin', my brother said that there had been a well-dressed feller from these parts shootin' off his mouth a lot against Lincoln an' the war, an' tellin' some of the young fellers left around there that they should organize. He couldn't remember the feller's name at first, but after scratchin' his head for a while he got out that the name was Bain an' that we'd better keep him home for he was a Copperhead an' a trouble-maker.

"Then my brother got to frettin' 'bout the war, 'specially 'bout the Copperheads. Said all the good young fellers had gone, leavin' a lot of trash behind, who did nothin' but loaf an' complain 'bout Abe Lincoln an' the war. Those who did work were busy with schemes to get rich at the expense of their neighbors an' their country. I told him to never mind, the war would be over after a while an' then we'd take care of the Copperheads."

"Yes, yes," said Ann, impatiently. "But what happened to keep you from getting back?"

Like the Wilson boys, Ann sometimes got a little annoyed at Enoch's garrulousness and his habit of stringing out a story before he got to the point.

"Just hold your horses, Ann, an' I'll tell you. Bright an' early the next mornin' I went over to the liv'ry stable to get my horse. Ever been in one of them big liv'ry stables, Ann?"

Ann admitted that she had never seen any bigger than the one in Owego.

"Well, this 'un had a little room up front where I went to settle for keepin' the horse. Even that early in the mornin' there was a gang of loafers in there. The room was hot an' filled with tobacco smoke so thick you could cut it, an' it stunk to high heaven of blankets an' harness an' horses. The gang was playin' poker. They were all young fellows, just war age. I still had in mind what my brother had been sayin' about Copperheads, an' when I heard these fellows say

somethin' about 'that dirty old backwoodsman, Abe Lincoln,
ruinin' the country', I lost my head an' called 'em danged
Copperheads an' waded into 'em. There's no question but
my brother's right, Ann. The soldiers an' the Union have got
enemies back of 'em as well as in front of 'em!"

"But what about the fight?" asked Ann, eagerly. "Did
you win? Tell me the rest of it."

"Isn't much more to tell," said Enoch, caressing a large
black and blue spot that still adorned his forehead. "As I
said, we got into a fight. Four to one makes the odds just a
leetle too much. I got licked, good and proper—and that's
why I wasn't in shape to do the chores that night, Henry
Bain's lies to the contrary."

Enoch paused, and then added with a sly chuckle:

"Yep, I got a lickin'—but them fellers knew they'd been
in a fight, too!"

CHAPTER XVIII

ON AN OCTOBER EVENING some two weeks later, Mark and Charlie Wilson walked in, bringing both joy and relief to Ann and Nancy. Now, for a while at least, they would not have the responsibility of the heavy farm work.

The first big job was to get the potatoes dug, and the day after their return found Mark and Charlie digging potatoes in the sidehill lot on the Wilson farm. Each took two rows, picking up the potatoes as they went along and throwing them into the box between them.

"Sure does seem quiet," said Charlie, "after all the excitement and hubbub in camp."

"I like it," Mark answered. As he spoke, he stopped to lean on his potato hook, letting his gaze wander off to the horizon, blue with the autumn haze. Below them he could see an oxteam, yoked to a lumber wagon and meandering slowly over the country road. On the hills across the valley the hardwoods blazed with the brilliant autumn colors, a contrast to the dark green of the white pines and hemlocks. The hum of insects seemed to emphasize the quiet of the countryside. The sun felt warm on Mark's back, and he stood there a long minute, enjoying it.

"What you thinking?" asked Charlie, pausing in his work and noticing the far-off look on Mark's face.

Mark continued to gaze silently at the landscape, and then sighed and said:

"Oh, just what millions of other people have probably thought in time of war—what a good world this would be if men could get along together without fighting. Look how nice Nature makes it when men leave her alone."

"Like heck she does," said Charlie, scornfully. "Use your head! The whole idea of Nature is the survival of the fittest, the strong lickin' the weak."

Surprised, Mark turned to look at this younger brother of

his, realizing, as had his mother while in Washington, that Charlie was no longer a boy. But before he could say anything, Charlie continued:

"Think of the violent storms we have that tear everything to pieces. Every bug has its enemy; for that matter, so does every plant. And look how the animals fight."

"Well, anyway," Mark interrupted, "man is supposed to know better."

"He may know better, but he does worse. And to my way of thinking he always will."

"Don't you think that some time—maybe not for a good while, but some time—man will learn to follow the teachings of Jesus, and we'll really have peace on earth, goodwill to men?"

"Dunno," answered Charlie. "Maybe a long time from now. But so far, the more man learns, like inventing gunpowder or making a better rifle, the more he fights, and the better job of slaughtering he does. Look at Fair Oaks! At Malvern Hill! At second Bull Run! We were both there. We saw them mowed down; we saw the wounded fellows. Did that look like peace on earth?" he asked, bitterly. "The wars and fights in the old days in England and on the continent and with the Indians in this country were just kids' play beside the slaughter that's goin' on in this civil war, just because man has better tools to fight with." Somberly he added: "Maybe we'll go on making better and better tools till everybody's killed off!"

"What's the matter with you?" laughed Mark. "Didn't you sleep last night, or did you eat something for breakfast that you shouldn't? You've certainly got it bad this morning. But, seriously, Charlie, your way is one way of looking at it. The other way is that even though it may take a long time, the forces of good will conquer, somehow, some time, and we'll have peace on earth. I can't express it very well, but I've got the idea that the trouble is that we judge everything by what may happen while we're alive, or in the next hundred years or so. What is it the Bible says—'A thousand years are but as a day in His sight.' It may take a good many thousand years, but peace for all the world will come some time."

"Maybe so," grinned Charlie, "but it'll be too late to do

me any good. Anyway, I never thought I'd like to hoe or dig potatoes, and here I am and really liking it. I've found out there are worse things than working on these old sidehills."

"You bet," agreed Mark, beginning to dig again. "I've always liked to dig potatoes. Remember old Hank Johnson who went around the Horn in the gold rush of '49? Well, he used to say that digging potatoes is a little like prospectin' for gold—you never know just what you're goin' to find in the next hill. And it's really something of a thrill to pull out six or eight from one hill of potatoes, every one bigger than your first. Yes, —"

Suddenly he stopped talking to stand erect, a startled look in his eyes.

"Do you hear that?"

"Yes, I do," said Charlie, grinning. "It was thunder startin' to growl off there in the northwest. What'd you think it was?"

Mark looked a little shamefaced.

"Forgot where I was for a minute. Thought it was cannon."

Charlie laughed.

"Did sound like it," he admitted. "I've heard tell of an old fire horse turned out to pasture, and every time he heard a fire bell or any excitement along the road, he upped his tail and cavorted across the pasture on a dead run. That's about the way we are, I guess. And another thing, Mark," Charlie added, "even though we hate the war, the excitement of it has a kind of fascination for us."

"Maybe you're right," agreed Mark, "but I don't think so. When I get to thinkin' about the war, it's about things that keep me from sleeping. Remember little Billy Short?"

Charlie nodded, silently.

"Remember how he used to hang around our band because he loved music so and wanted to be near his Dad? Wasn't more'n fourteen. Don't know why it was permitted, except that perhaps his Dad, as a captain of artillery, had some pull. Anyway, everybody liked the little fellow and felt bad about what happened to him. Did you ever hear about it?"

"No, I never got the details," replied Charlie.

"Well, his father's battery got stuck out on a little hill ahead of the lines. Rations were short up there, so Billy got

the idea of boiling his Pa's coffee and carrying it and the
hardtack and whatever else there was to eat up the hill so
his father could have something warm. One day things got
pretty hot all the way along the line, but the boy insisted on
going up. He took the coffee and the other stuff all the way
up the hill and got through all right. His father scolded him
for taking the risk and then tried to get him to go right back.
But Billy wanted to wait and bring the coffee pan back so he
could use it another time. A shell got the kid—and I'll never
forget how sick I was when they brought back what was left
of him."

Charlie shook his head sadly:

"I remember how sick I was, too, when I saw my first
dead man," he commented. "What's more awful than the
smell of dead men bloating in the boiling sun? But then I
saw them by the hundred and got sort of used to it, like
seein' a dead calf here on the farm. The thing that gets me
is to hear the wounded cry for water when they are lying
between the lines and there's no way to get to them." He
squared his shoulders. "But I try not to think about it, and
you mustn't either, Mark. Otherwise we'd go mad."

Then they both bent to their job again.

*   *   *

After the potatoes on both farms were dug and in the
cellars came the threshing jobs. The barn floor was swept
clean, bundles of buckwheat were thrown down from the
mow, the band of each bundle cut, and the buckwheat spread
evenly on the floor in a layer five or six inches deep. Then
Mark, Charlie and Tom started to work on it with their
flails. The handles of the flails, made of white oak, were about
4 feet long and tapered toward one end. The hickory swingles
were about 3 feet long, $2\frac{1}{2}$ inches thick in the center, and
tapered toward each end. Handles and swingles were tied together with leather thongs, leaving the swingles free so that
they could be swung to strike the grain horizontally, parallel
with the floor.

A little while after the thump! thump! thunp! of the flails
had started, the boys stopped to turn the grain over, then
started in again. After one or two more turnings, the straw
was pitched off the floor, leaving the brown buckwheat

kernels. These the boys swept and shoveled into bags, later to be run through the hand fanning mill to clean them.

An hour or two after they had begun to work, Tom stopped to laugh.

"What's funny?" snapped Charlie.

"The sweat runnin'down your face. It makes streaks so even Ma wouldn't know you."

"Better look at yourself," growled Charlie. "You're a sight too!"

Toward the close of the afternoon Enoch Payne, on his way home from the village, stopped to say hello. Tired from the heavy, dirty work, all three of the boys welcomed the interruption and the opportunity to sit in the barn door with Enoch in the late afternoon sunshine and visit, even if the visit meant mostly listening to Enoch talk.

"Don't like to thresh any better'n you do," he said, "but it helps some to think how good the buckwheat pancakes are goin' to taste with sirup an' bacon an' eggs on a cold winter mornin'."

"Isn't it funny," commented Mark, "that buckwheat will make such good pancakes, but it's no good to make bread of."

"Yeah," Enoch agreed. "And that reminds me that if it wasn't for that, I might be rich now."

"I don't know which is worse," grinned Charlie, "to have to listen to Enoch's stories or fight a battle or thresh buckwheat."

"You can go back to threshin' if you want to," said Mark, leaning comfortably against the old barn door, "but as for me, I'll take the story. Go on, Enoch, tell us what buckwheat had to do with your not being rich?"

"Well—my grandpa was rich. Leastwise, he owned a lot of land. He was born up in northern New Hampshire but later moved to York State. One time he yoked up the old oxteam to a wagon, loaded it with a grist of wheat and sent my Pa, who was maybe 12 or 14 then, several miles to a mill run by an old Dutchman. When Pa got there, instead of grindin' the wheat and takin' out his share for the grindin', the Dutchman loaded up the wagon with buckwheat flour, because it was cheaper and he thought he could get away with it. When Pa got home, Grandma tried to make bread with the buckwheat flour. Where she and Grandpa had come from, up in northern New England, there was a kind of buckwheat you could make bread out of. But not this kind. And of course her bread was no good.

"It made Grandpa awful mad to think that the Dutchman had cheated him, so he loaded the rest of the flour back on the wagon and drove all the way to the mill and tried to get the Dutch miller to take back the grist. But all he succeeded in doin' was to get in a fight with the miller, and get licked. Then he got back on his wagon, headed for town and a lawyer, and sued the miller. They lawed it back and forth for years until Grandpa's property was all gone."

The boys were interested in spite of themselves in Enoch's story, and Enoch continued:

"For myself I don't care if the old gent didn't hand down any property. He left me somethin' better. He joined up in the War of 1812 and after two years came back home with one arm."

"I agree with you, Enoch," said Mark, "that's something to be proud of. But what happened to your grandmother when your grandpa went away to war?"

"She kept things goin'. Took care of four children an' ran the farm, just like your Ma and your wife have been doin'."

"That makes me think!" said Mark. "I don't know what our womenfolks would have done without you, Enoch. I—"

"Yes," interrupted Charlie. "That's right, Enoch!" Then, rather shyly but earnestly, he said:

"I hope you don't ever take me seriously when I josh about your stories. I agree with Mark. I don't know what Ma and Ann would have done without you!"

Red with embarrassment, Enoch said:

"Aw, shucks! Forget it! I can't go to war, so the least I can do is to help out here.

"I hear you two fellows are goin' back," he continued. "Hope you won't be in a hurry. There won't be much fightin' till spring."

"Can't tell about that," said Mark. "Anyway, I feel my place is down there till the trouble's over."

"Me, too," agreed Charlie. "Got to get back soon."

Enoch said nothing more, and Mark sat for a long time looking up across the fields to where the sun was going down over the woods at the top of the ridge.

CHAPTER XIX

THE THREE WILSON BOYS, with the help of Enoch Payne, were husking corn in a field on the Clinton farm. It was a late October day, and the bright sun was warm and relaxing as they sat on piles of the husked stalks. They were quietly intent on their task, and all that was heard for a long time was the rattle of the dry corn as they tipped over a standing shock, husked the bright Indian corn ears, and threw them into nearby boxes. Growing a little tired of the monotonous work, Tom began to talk.

"Say, what's the difference between corn and maize?"

A little flippantly, Charlie answered:

"All maize is corn, but all corn isn't maize!"

"What do you mean by that, smarty?"

Mark laughed.

"Charlie's right, Tom. The corn that you read about in the Bible and that they still talk about in the old countries always means any kind of grain except this Indian corn. You know from your geography and history that this corn, known as maize, wasn't known to the Europeans until they discovered America."

"Yeah," said Tom, "and I remember how the Indians showed the Pilgrims how to grow it, and how to stick a codfish into the hill with the seed corn to make it grow better."

"Corn's great stuff," declared Enoch. "When I was a boy my grandpa took great pride in growin' good corn. Each year when the corn was gettin' ripe, he'd go through and pick out the biggest, best-lookin' stalks and tie a string on 'em, so when it came time to cut the corn and husk it, he could save the best ears for seed. His father and grandfather had done that before him, an' he had such good seed that he grew better corn than any of his neighbors. He used to—"

"Oh, oh," interrupted Charlie, "Enoch's off again on a story and we're stuck so we can't get away!"

Enoch grinned, but kept right on talking:

"Grandpa used to tell how the Indians would put a few handfuls of parched corn in their pockets—"

"Didn't have pockets," broke in Charlie again, but in a low voice, and Enoch continued as if he hadn't heard him.

"Then they could travel days without anything else to eat."

"That's nothing," said the irrepressible Charlie, "you ought to see some of the hardtack that the Army lives on when we're on the march!"

"Even when I was a boy," persisted Enoch, "we lived mostly on corn. It often took the place of bread when we ground it for johnnycake. We had corn pudding, cornmeal pancakes, and Sunday nights we always had cornmeal mush and milk—when there was any milk."

"Well, old Cortright doesn't think so much of corn," said Tom. "Just the other day I heard him gruntin' and complainin' down in the store that he had so much of the danged stuff he didn't know how he was going to get it all husked with his rheumatiz. Said he got sick cuttin' and shockin' it, because two hours after he started work in the corn he'd be wet through from the dew and his wrists would turn all red and he'd itch all over."

Charlie laughed again.

"Well, handlin' corn does sometimes poison folks, but I'll bet if old Cortright would take a bath once in a while, he wouldn't itch so much. I'd be willing to bet dollars to doughnuts that the same suit of red flannels that he puts on in the fall stays on until the heat drives 'em off him in the spring!"

Mark had been unusually quiet that morning, and after a time he got up to stretch his cramped legs and stood looking at the shocks of corn standing in orderly rows like the tents of a well-organized military camp. Suddenly he turned around to Enoch and said:

"Enoch, tell me, what are the neighbors around here saying about the trouble I had in the Army?"

Taken unawares, Enoch hesitated and looked embarrassed.

"Shucks! Nothin' much. Nothin' that's important."

"Tell me the truth," Mark persisted. "I want to know."

The cornstalks fell from Enoch's lap as he also stood up, a little helpless and at a loss for words.

"That's nothin' to worry about, Mark," he said, finally. "You grew up in this neighborhood and your friends know everything is all right." Then, honestly, he added:

"Course everybody has enemies, particularly in times like these, and everybody is terribly worried about the war. There's them, too, that would like to get people off from their own necks by drawing attention to somebody else."

"I know who you mean," Mark said, bitterly. "It's Henry Bain that's doing most of the talking, isn't it?"

Enoch answered that question only indirectly:

"Hank himself is taking a lot of criticism. He's stayin' home an' gettin' rich on war prices, an' on the troubles of his neighbors. I think he's stirring up the Copperheads, too. There's them as says he ought to be tarred and feathered an' rid out of town on a rail."

Tom jumped to his feet.

"Well, then, by gosh, let's do it," he cried.

The tension was broken as everybody laughed, and one by one they resumed the job of husking. But Mark still had the subject on his mind and after a while he said:

"Enoch, you know that Charlie and I are going back, and that ought to be the answer to any of my friends about my real feeling about this war."

"Of course, it is," agreed Enoch. "When are you plannin' to leave?"

"Pretty soon. With good weather we ought to get this corn husking job done and the corn in the crib and the stalks in the barn in a day or two. Then we'll be moving on."

Again Enoch looked embarrassed.

"Well, Mark, I don't want to worry you, but there is one thing some of us are thinkin' about, and that's about this Clinton farm. We know that Bain has the mortgage an' that you and Ann and her mother can do nothin' now about meetin' the payments—and Bain's a skunk."

"I know how it is, Enoch, but there's nothing I can do about it," said Mark. "Farm or no farm, I have felt from the beginning that my first job is the war. Also, the land on this farm is poor, the buildings need repair, and I think when I get back I'd rather start anew on a better place than have anything to do with Bain.

"The more I think of it," he mused, "the more I think it would be a good idea to let Bain take the farm. It isn't much good, anyway; isn't worth much more than the mortgage. It would be just as easy to start over again."

That night at the Clinton supper table Mark at last brought up the subject of his return to the Army.

"Now that the fall work is done, Ann, and you and my mother won't have to work so hard, Charlie and I think we ought to leave soon. Charlie's going into the cavalry, and I'm going back to the regiment I enlisted with before."

Both Ann and her mother stopped eating, and Mrs. Clinton exclaimed:

"There's no need of your going now. There won't be any fighting until spring. No need of your going anyway that I can see. You might give some consideration to Ann and me. If anyone must go traipsing off, let the unmarried fellows go."

Mark caught a pleading look from Ann and choked back his rising anger.

"We all have our own ideas of duty," he answered. "I know it's hard on you folks to stay here alone; it's hard on me to be away from you, too. But you both know how I feel. As much as I love Ann, and as hard as it is to be separated, I never would be happy staying here while so many others who have just as much to lose are down there fighting."

But that didn't satisfy Mrs. Clinton.

"I should certainly think," she said, disagreeably, "that after the mess you got in, you'd have your fill of it."

Mark jumped up from the table, pushing his chair back so violently that it fell over, and went out to the barn without even stopping to put on his cap. There Ann found him a few minutes later, sitting on a box, his head in his hands. She stood close to him, looking down at the dejected figure, her hand on his shoulder.

"I'm sorry, Mark. Mother shouldn't have said what she did. But she's so worried about losing this farm."

"Well, I had a plan about the farm that I wanted to talk over with you and your mother, but I never even got a chance."

"No," she answered, gently, "but you can tell me." Pulling up another box she sat down beside him.

"The farm's not much good, Ann, you know that. I've been thinking we'd be better off to rent a different place until we could save enough money maybe to buy it. What do you say we let Bain take this farm?"

Ann didn't answer for a moment, but finally said, gently:

"That would be all right so far as we are concerned, but what about Mother and Father?"

"What do you mean?"

"Well, Pa went to war, and your father writes that he's doing well—you know what I mean, not drinking. Don't you think he needs something to come back to, if he comes back?"

"Yes, you're right," Mark agreed. "But it wouldn't take much to be just as good as this farm."

"You forget something, dear. Maybe the farm isn't much good, but to Father, and especially to Mother, it's home. Everything about it means something to them: that big lilac bush on the side of the front porch that Mother planted with her own hands; the old orchard with its blossoms in the springtime and its fruit in the fall; even the path that winds its crooked way from the house to the barn that we've all trod so many dozens of times a day. My dear, you know that's why so many farmers stay on these poor farms. There are some values not measured in dollars. Ever since I can remember, we've all sat on that front porch in spring, summer and fall and looked down beyond the cow lane that leads between the two stony meadows to the pasture on the other side of the brook. At the top of the pasture we can see, just as you can from your home, the woods—blossoming out in a million shades of green in the spring, turning so many brilliant colors in the fall. Mother and Father are getting old; no other place would seem like home to them now. It would break Mother's heart to have to leave it. I'm sure that's why she's so nervous and upset and says things she doesn't mean."

But Mark was not to be diverted from his own idea.

"I like all those things about the place just as well as you and your folks do. You know that. But you know that you and I have to make a living. We can't eat fine views and beautiful woods. We've got to be practical.

"And while we're talking, Ann, there's something else that bothers me. Two or three times lately your mother has said something about Henry Bain, what a kind, fine man he is, and so forth. Well, he isn't. He's a rascal, and some of the things he is saying around the neighborhood are almost treasonable. Moreover, he's the one that has had most to say about the trouble I had in the Army. I can't think how your mother can be talking about him so much unless she sees him often. And that means that he must be coming to the house when I'm not here."

"He is," admitted Ann. "But I don't like it and I've told Mother so. She's nice to him for the very reason I just told you, that she can't bear to think of losing this farm, and she thinks that if she's kind to Henry and treats him well, he won't foreclose the mortgage."

Mark stood up.

"Stuff and nonsense!" he exclaimed, angrily. "Bain's got just two ideas in life: one is to make money—and it doesn't matter how he does it—and the other's you. That's why he never misses an opportunity to lie about me. That's why he comes here when I'm gone."

Ann stood up to face him.

"Well," she cried, "all that you say about Henry Bain may be true, but what can I do? I don't like his coming here, and I certainly have given him no encouragement. I've tried to get Mother to discourage him, but I'm caught, Mark, I'm caught. Mother's right. If we make Henry Bain mad, we'll lose our home. Maybe you and I could make out better somewhere else, as you say, but you wouldn't want to have Father and Mother live with us, and what would they do?"

Mark stood looking at his wife. All of the months of loneliness since he had gone to war, the worry and despair over his trouble with the military authorities, the gossip and criticism of some of his neighbors were foremost in his mind as he answered her question.

"Do?" he cried. "I'm beginning to wonder how much you care for me. You know I would always do everything I could to take care of your father and mother, but did you ever stop to think that they've had their chance to live, and we haven't? I'm telling you plainly, it doesn't set well with me for you to stand there and practically tell me that Henry Bain, my bitter enemy, and our country's enemy, can come here when I am absent, when you and I know, and the whole neighborhood knows, that he is scheming all of the time, hoping against hope that something will happen to me so that he can get you."

Ann looked up at him with stricken eyes, her face white as a sheet.

"You forget something, Mark. It's you I love."

Then she turned and left the barn. For a long time Mark sat on the box, his head in his hands, his mind a chaos of conflicting and bitter thoughts. Then, forgetting the chores, he got up slowly like an old man and went down the road to his old home without a backward glance. The next morning the stage coach carried him to Owego on his way back to the Army.

CHAPTER XX

BOTH MARK AND CHARLIE WILSON rejoined the Army at Fredericksburg on the north side of the Rappahannock after its return from the long trip to Maryland where it had checked and defeated Lee at Sharpsburg or Antietam in his attempt to invade the North. But now the boys were separated. Charlie had enlisted in the cavalry and Mark had rejoined the infantry.

It was late November, cold, with occasional flurries of snow, and the veterans, tired from their long march to Maryland and back, were in a dark, complaining mood. Their uniforms were worn and inadequate. Some of the men were almost barefoot. The field hospitals were full of the sick, and, worst of all, the men were hungry all of the time because of the poor rations. The hardtack, the poor coffee, and the salt pork seemed all the worse to Mark in comparison with the food that he had just had at home.

On the long journey back to the Army, Mark had had plenty of time to realize that far worse than any physical inconvenience or suffering was mental anguish, and that the worst kind of mental suffering lies in the ashes of regret. Time and again bitterly did he curse the pride and jealousy that had caused him to leave his wife without even saying goodby. Having once made the decision and re-enlisted, there could be no turning back. He was in the Army, and there was a war on, and he would have no opportunity, perhaps for years, and maybe never, to put his arms around his girl and tell her how sorry he was.

As he dozed on the train trying to sleep, his wife's last words rang repeatedly in his ears: "It's you I love!" she had said. "It's you I love!" He tormented himself with the bitter thought that he had flouted the most precious possession a man can ever have when he walked away from his wife and back into the Army.

To be sure, he could write letters, but how could he make Ann know with mere inadequate words how sorry he was, and what a fool he knew he had been? Nevertheless, he must try to write, for now it was his only way to straighten out the mess he had made of his married life and to ease the heartache of his girl, whom he had hurt so terribly. Soon after boarding the train he had begun his letter to Ann. Using the stub of an old lead pencil, he started to pour out his heart on paper. Again and again he tried, but each time he tore up what he had written because he just couldn't say what he felt. When he did get a few words that seemed at least partly right, the jiggling and jarring of the train made them so illegible that he doubted if Ann could make them out.

Finally, in the boarding house in Washington where Mark had got a cheap room for the night he managed to finish his letter, and out of the travail of his heart he wrote better than he knew:

"My darling Ann:

"This is to ask you to forgive me, though I wouldn't blame you if you didn't. How I could ever have acted the way I did and left you without saying goodby is more than I am able to figure out, though I have thought of nothing else since I left you. This is not an excuse, but maybe you can find it in your heart to forgive me because I was so worried and troubled about you and saving your home, so torn between my desire to protect and care for you and the feeling that it was my duty to rejoin the Army that I couldn't think straight. I never was so mixed up in my entire life. Now in all my loneliness, confusion, and despair there is just one thing I am sure of—I love you, dear, and come what may, I always shall.

"On the way down here I thought of all the other boys who have left their homes, their fathers and mothers, maybe their wives, to do their part in this war, and I kept thinking that if all those others could stand it, I surely ought to be able to do so. Then would come the despairing thought that they had left their homes and loved ones with no quarrels or misunderstandings, while I had left you, the person dearest to me in all the world, without even a goodby.

"If you can find it in your heart to forgive me, I think I have had my lesson, and if God gives me the privilege of coming back to you some time I'll try to make up for all the trouble I've caused you. The only way I can get to sleep is to offer a little prayer for us both and to say over and over to myself, 'Goodnight, Ann, darling, I love you.'

"Please write to me, dearest. I can't bear to go on living unless I know you have forgiven me.

"With all my love,

Mark."

*   *   *

When Ann had gone back to the house after leaving Mark at the barn, she found her mother washing the dishes. Ann got a towel and dried them, glancing out of the window each time she passed it on her trips to and from the cupboard with the dishes, expecting to see Mark coming back toward the house. But when he did come out of the barn, instead of taking the winding path to the house, Mark walked with bent head and determined steps down the road toward the Wilson homestead. With an aching heart, Ann saw him go without even a backward glance.

The long hours of the late fall evening dragged slowly by while Ann, unable to concentrate on any reading or sewing, listened to every noise outdoors, hoping to hear Mark's step on the stoop. Once her mother said:

"What's happened to Mark?"

To which Ann answered, shortly:

"He had something to do at his house."

Realizing that something was wrong, Mrs. Clinton said nothing more. When bedtime came, she retired, but Ann sat up, still expecting Mark to come. Then she took to pacing back and forth between the kitchen and the living room in an effort to control her agitation, but quietly so as not to disturb her mother. At midnight she finally went to bed, only to say over and over to herself: Mark is going to war; he's going to war. We only have a few days. He's mad at me and we're losing the time that we might have together.

Finally, emotionally and physically exhausted, she fell asleep, only to wake and sit straight up in bed every time the wind stirred a shutter or there was some other noise that might be her husband's footsteps on the stairs.

The next morning her mother looked at Ann's tired,

strained face and for once had enough wisdom to keep silent.
They got breakfast together, Ann setting a third place in
case Mark came. But still he didn't arrive. After they had
cleared the table and washed the dishes, Ann, now a little
angry, went to the barn to do the chores. It was downright
inconsiderate, even mean, she thought, for Mark to give her
such a bad night. It didn't help her feelings, either, to have
to do the chores. She certainly would tell him what she
thought of him when he showed up!

She went back to the house and tried to occupy herself
with some of the household work, but her heart wasn't in it,
and she spent most of her time watching the road. Then
toward the end of the morning, unable to stand it any longer,
she almost ran over to the Wilsons, and when she found
that Mark had gone back to the Army without even saying
goodby her cup of bitterness overflowed. It had been hard
enough to part with her young husband the first time, which
now seemed so long ago; it had been a dreadful thing to
learn from George Wilson's letter that Mark had been condemned to death as a spy; she had thought she had come
to the ultimate in trouble when the wheels of the train carrying her and Nancy to Washington had kept singing: "You're
too late! You're too late!" But then, with all the worry and
unhappiness, she had at least been secure in her knowledge
that her husband loved her. Now she wasn't, for how
could anyone who really loved you do what Mark had done
to her?

Utterly crushed, she returned to her own home, her steps
dragging. How could two human beings, she wondered over
and over, be as close as she and Mark had been, and yet
seem so like utter strangers as they were now?

Gradually she grew calmer, but more bitter and disillusioned. Marriage, she thought, is supposed to be the closest
relationship in the world, but when it came right down to it,
what did one individual know about another, no matter how
close they seemed to be at times? And love—her lips curled
into a sneer as she thought of that word; love is just something to fool people into getting married. And when they
get married, what happens? Her father and mother were
kind, good people and must have some affection for each
other, but when did they ever show it? It was the same with

the Wilson family. They didn't quarrel, but what romance was there? And with her and Mark! Married only one day, and then he had rushed off to war. He thought more of his country than he did of her.

Back in her bedroom she looked at the grim white face in the milky old looking-glass on her bureau.

"Well," she said aloud, "those are the facts of life and the sooner I make up my mind to them, the better!"

Then suddenly the grim lines disappeared from her face and her mouth twisted in pain. Crying, "Oh, Mark! Mark!" she threw herself face downward on her bed and broke into uncontrollable sobs.

Endless days followed while she waited for a letter from Mark. The evenings were the hardest, for now it was dark by five o'clock and the evenings were longer. It had always been hard to have Mark away and to worry about the danger he might be in, but she had been able to fill up the long hours with the farm work and with reading and knitting. Now with despair in her heart, she found it impossible to settle down or concentrate on any of the homey tasks of everyday living. Naturally healthy and strong, she ordinarily had a good appetite. She could scarcely remember when she had skipped a meal, except when she had had some childhood disease, but now she had lost all desire to eat and had to force herself to choke down the food in order to keep going.

Several days after Mark's departure she saw Henry Bain drive up, hitch and blanket his horse, and stride rapidly toward the house. He greeted Mrs. Clinton cordially, and when he shook hands with Ann he gave her hand an extra pressure, his face radiating kindness and sympathy.

"Too bad," he said, "that the boys had to go back."

He stayed all evening, responded pleasantly to Mrs. Clinton's efforts to keep the conversation going, and was the soul of courtesy and consideration to Ann. In her present mood of loneliness and disillusionment, Ann found herself wondering if Henry was as bad as he had been painted. Certainly he had never been anything but kind to her mother and, in fact, to herself, in spite of the rebuffs she had given him. After all, she reflected, you couldn't hate a man for liking you and maybe, too, he was right about this war business—that the men ought to stay home and look after their families. Anyway, his visit helped her get through one evening, and she was grateful.

The morning brought Mark's letter, and all thoughts of Henry Bain were forgotten. Whatever that letter contained, she couldn't share it even with Nancy. She took it to her room to read and re-read, and as she poured over its lines most of the bitterness passed out of her heart, leaving only a great sadness.

"Poor Mark," she thought, "he feels just as bad as I do. Maybe I haven't thought enough about all the troubles and worries he has been through. Maybe I was wrong not to give more consideration to his suggestion that we let Henry Bain take the farm and start a home elsewhere. Oh, if he were only here we could let bygones be bygones, but we need to be together to get rid of all the bitterness." Then she said aloud, with vehemence:

"It's this awful war that's making all the trouble!"

Then she voiced the cry of millions of women before her:

"Why, O God, why is war necessary? Why do men tear themselves to pieces while we women work and wait and sacrifice, eating our hearts out in loneliness and worry?"

Before she could sleep, Ann answered the letter, taking much of the night to do it. Like Mark, she found it difficult to put her feelings on paper in such a way that he would surely understand that in spite of all the frustrations and misunderstandings, he was still her husband and she was still his wife, and they loved each other.

Mark's next letter to Ann was the longest she had ever received from him. It went into considerable detail about the life in camp as the two armies lay opposite each other on the north and south shores of the Rappahannock River. His somber mood was reflected in his descriptions of the cold, wet weather, the scanty rations, the muddy almost impassable roads, and the poorly clad, sometimes barefoot men.

"There are many sick in the hospital," he wrote, "with little or no accommodations."

Ann shivered as she read, thinking again of the hideousness of war, and wondering why men could not learn to live in peace.

"You probably read in the papers," Mark continued,

"that McClellan didn't chase the Confederates back from Maryland fast enough after he had defeated them at Antietam to suit Lincoln and the War Department, so they put Burnside in command. But now the men are wondering if he is any better than McClellan. We lie here in camp on the north side of the Rappahannock, cold and hungry, day after day and night after night, doing nothing. And every morning when we get up we can see that the Confederates have built more breastworks and moved in more men to defend them if we attack.

"Across the river from us and not far from the bank is the town of Fredericksburg, and then a little farther to the south there is a small hill on which the enemy is building up his breastworks every night. Located on this hill are several batteries. We are so close that we can almost see the mouths of the cannon pointed toward us. It's queer—we fight to kill each other, and yet I feel no hatred toward the boys on the other side, nor do any of the others. I think the Johnnies feel the same way, because for a long time now we have been actually visiting with the men in gray on the other side, and we frequently trade our coffee with them and other stuff for their tobacco and some of the other supplies which they have more of than we do.

"One night our brigade band started to play *John Brown.* Then it stopped and, by gracious, a band on the other side played *Dixie.* Both sides started yelling and hurrahing and when they quieted down again, our band struck up *The Girl I Left Behind Me.* It was answered with *Maryland, my Maryland* by the bands on the other side. Then, led by the bands, first one side would roar out a rollicking tune, and then thousands of men on the other side would answer with another tune. Finally, our band started to play *Home, Sweet Home.* Our men began to sing it, and the first thing we knew the other side was singing and playing the same tune. No one was thinking of fighting. All of us were just a lot of homesick boys. I had such a lump in my throat that I had to stop singing. War is a strange business!

"Most of us have concluded that we are going to stay right here all winter and aren't going to move across the river to attack the Confederates until spring."

The rest of the letter, apparently written a few days later, was dated "On the Rappahannock, December 9, 1862.

"I haven't had a chance to finish this letter until now," Mark wrote. "Everybody's excited. We haven't had any orders yet, but there is activity at headquarters and we think we are going to move after all. How we'll get across that river with the Rebel sharpshooters in the Fredericksburg houses picking us off, I don't know. Neither do I know how we'll ever take those strong fortifications on that hill.

"Anyway, I'm not supposed to know, though sometimes the soldiers seem to know better what to do than do some of the Generals.

"I don't want to seem too depressed or to make you feel that way, but we are on the eve of a battle. Should anything happen to me before I see you again, I want you always to remember that I love you, and that I ask your forgiveness for any trouble I have ever caused you. You are young, you have most of your life before you, so just in case anything happens, remember it is my wish and hope that you will get more happiness out of life than you have had in the past. If that eventually means marriage to another man, that will be all right with me."

Blinded by tears and her throat aching, Ann crumpled the letter and threw it on the floor, exclaiming:

"Just as if I didn't feel badly enough without his having to write something like that."

Then she picked up the letter again, carefully smoothed out the pages, and said aloud:

"Oh, Mark! Mark! Are you just sad because we are separated, or is this a premonition of disaster?"

CHAPTER XXI

EARLIER in December several of the men in Charlie Wilson's company were gathered around a campfire eating their noonday rations, all grumbling because, as one cavalryman said, "the grub ain't fit to feed a hog." Therefore, when Ed Winchell, after looking around to see that there were no officers within hearing, said that he knew of a plantation that probably still had food supplies, everyone was instantly alert to the possibilities, and immediately they began to plan a foraging expedition.

But there was need to be careful because of the strict orders against foraging and taking anything from the farms or plantations in Confederate territory without full pay. There was tremendous dissatisfaction with these orders, and even at the risk of punishment they were constantly violated, especially when the rations were particularly poor and insufficient.

It seemed worse to the men to have their horses go hungry even than it was for themselves, and many of the cavalrymen took chances in violating orders to forage for grain and hay for their mounts. As he listened to Winchell's plans, Charlie couldn't help remembering with a shiver what had happened just a few days before, when two cavalrymen had gone to a haystack to get some feed for their horses. The captain of the guard had shot one of the men dead and wounded the other. Mad with rage, their comrades took after the captain, chased him into some woods, and finally overtaking him, had pounded him to death. Court martials were impending, but it was the consensus of opinion that the leaders involved in the killing of the captain would be freed because there was much provocation for their act.

Charlie knew that the other men in his squad must be thinking about this tragic affair even as they planned to go on a foraging expedition, but nevertheless they were going just the same.

"It'll take some doing," said Ed Winchell, "but we can slip out of here quietly one by one, and in an hour or two make that plantation and be back without being missed or anyone raising a row. It lies way back from the road, pretty much out of the way of stragglers or foragers from either Army. I'll bet dollars to doughnuts that there's good smoked hams and other vittles hidden there. Let's go get 'em!"

Promises to share their plunder with the half-starved guards would get them by the picket lines easily, and later that afternoon, with a light snow falling, one by one the members of the group drifted by the pickets. Guided by Winchell, they rode for an hour or so, jumping the fences, keeping well away from the roads, alert every moment for fear of running unexpectedly into a band of guerillas or even a patrol of their own men.

They came without incident to the plantation that Winchell had described. The great mansion with its high pillars stood well back from the distant road, screened by a small patch of woods. It was evident that before the war the place had been large and prosperous. It was easy to picture it resounding with the laughter and songs of the slaves whose cabins were still there at the rear of the big house. A wide lawn, now untended, sloped down to meet the woods and a road winding through the woods to the highway a mile or so distant. The lawn was covered with matted, dried grass and even briars had started to grow. The once proud mansion seemed deserted, and from the house and its round white pillars that had once added dignity and beauty to it, the paint was peeling off in strips. A general air of decay wrought a note of sadness and loneliness. No smoke came from the chimneys, nor was there any evidence of life either in the cabins or in the big house itself.

Still the Union cavalrymen were cautious. Appearances were often deceiving and they were taking no chances. So they waited quietly at the edge of the woods at the foot of the lawn for some time, listening carefully and watching for some movement. Finally, feeling sure that all was well, they rode out into the open and around the house to the back. Here they dismounted, and Charlie Wilson was left to hold the horses while the others separated to see what they could find in the way of food. They were fortunate. Partly concealed back of the slave quarters in a little clump of trees and bushes, John Foster discovered a small cabin-like structure with a cupola-like top out of which was streaming the faintest thread of smoke. But the door was secured with a huge padlock. Not daring to shout to the others, John ran back to the other side of the slave quarters and waved to two of the other boys who were in sight. They came running, and the three of them soon managed to break the padlock. The sight they saw when they got the door open left them almost speechless. Hung from a pole that ran down the center of the long low building were at least a dozen hams, swinging in the lazy smoke from a bed of smoldering corncobs below them.

Caution forgotten, the boys set up a shout for the other members of the party and for Charlie to bring the horses. Grabbing their sabers, they cut the hams down and tied them in pairs swung across their saddles, two to a horse. But their forgetfulness of caution was unfortunate, for the excited shouting brought disaster. Before the hams were completely fastened on to the horses, Charlie saw a squad of cavalrymen rush out of the road that led into the woods on the lower side of the big lawn. A second startled look showed that the new group wore gray uniforms. Charlie yelled at his companions and they started to mount their now excited, plunging horses.

To make matters worse, it became evident that the old mansion had not been deserted after all, for the boys could hear women on the front side of the house, crying in shrill voices:

"They're right around the other side, boys! They're right around the back!"

By this time the Union boys were mounted and on their way. Which direction to take? Cut off by the Confederates from the road they had come in on, there was no alternative but to ride directly across the fields, with no time to think of anything but to get away. Bringing up the rear, Charlie even in his fright had time to laugh at the way the hams bounced up and down on the galloping horses of his comrades ahead of him. Finally, realizing that the hams were handicapping them and that it might be either the hams or their lives, the boys began to cut them loose. One of them said afterwards that deciding to cut those hams loose was one of the hardest decisions he had ever had to make.

Released from the weight of the hams and with apparently better horses than the Johnny Rebs, all but Charlie began to pull away from the pursuit, but he, the last to join up with the regiment, had the poorest horse in the group. Before the race had gone on five minutes it was all too clear that his friends were pulling away and that the boys in gray were coming nearer. Scared, he finally came to a long cattle lane leading off at right angles toward a ridge of hills. Yanking his old plug savagely to the right, Charlie spurted through the lane as fast as he could go. Seconds later the Confederates reached it and paused briefly to decide whether to pursue the one man in the lane or take their chances on making a bigger haul by getting all of the larger group ahead. Glancing despairingly over his shoulder, Charlie sighed with relief when he saw that his pursuers had chosen to continue to chase the others.

But his relief was short-lived. Coming to a high gate across the lane, and still too scared to risk time to open the gate, Charlie put the horse to the jump. But the old plug, not much good to start with and now winded and blown, had made his last run. He tried valiantly, struck his feet on the top of the gate, and man and horse went down in a heap on the other side.

Some moments passed before Charlie, dazed by the fall, stood up and realized what had happened. His first glance across the fields showed no sign of his pursuers, and not a sound broke the stillness of the chilly December countryside. With a feeling of relief and hoping that his comrades had got away, he began to take stock of his own situation. If the Confederates had lost the larger group, they might return to look for him.

He got painfully to his feet and looked at his mount. The horse was up, too, snorting with pain and standing on three legs. His right foreleg dangled in an unnatural way. One look at it and Charlie, the farm boy, knew what had happened. The leg was broken. The horse was useless to himself or anyone else. There was only one thing to do and that was to put the old fellow out of his misery. Glancing over the countryside again carefully to see that no living thing was in sight or within hearing, Charlie reached for his cavalry colts and, putting it into the ear of the horse, pulled the trigger. The old mount wavered, then pitched forward, and Charlie was relieved to see that he was out of his suffering.

Removing the saddle and blanket from the horse's back, Charlie sat down to ponder his plight. He was alone, on foot, miles from camp, in enemy country, in cold weather, without rations. Fortunately he had his canteen with some water left in it, his saddle blanket, and his gun and ammunition. Sitting idly for the moment, his eyes happened to stray to the corner of the lane between the gate and the fence where there seemed to be a sort of unusual mound covered with straw. Curious, he went over and gently thrust his saber down through the straw, which was matted with snow and ice. He was surprised and intrigued to hear the point of the saber strike a solid object.

Raking off the snow and ice, he was astonished to see a small keg. Using the point of his saber, he pried out the bung and kneeled down to take a good, long smell. Inexperienced with liquor, Charlie wasn't too sure what it was that filled the keg right up to the bunghole, but he thought it was brandy. Anyway, scared, tired and hungry, he thought a drink of the stuff would do him good, and he wondered how he could get it out of the keg. Then remembering boyhood experiences of sucking sweet cider from a barrel with a straw, he sorted the straw until he found a couple that had not been broken. Sticking them into the keg he took a long pull. Wow! It was something all right! It burned all the way down, but almost immediately he began to feel warm and relaxed.

He thought some of taking another pull, but decided against it. This was no time nor place to go to sleep. So he put the bung carefully back into its hole, covered the keg with the straw, and looked around for landmarks by which to recognize the place again. Then after searching the landscape carefully, he picked up his gun and blanket. He thought some of emptying the water out of his canteen and refilling it from the brandy keg, but decided that the water was more precious. Shouldering his burdens, he started off up the ridge where he could find some security in the woods that covered the top of the long low hills.

Walking close to the zigzag trail fence that bordered the lane, in order to be as inconspicuous as possible, he reached the foot of the ridge, where pasture lands spread out into the woods. Knowing how conspicuous he would be on this hillside pasture, Charlie almost ran up the hill and was thankful when he reached the shelter of the woods. From there, he looked out across the broad valley below and was relieved to see no sign of life. To his left and to the north, he could just make out the plantation where they had been caught stealing the hams; to the south somewhere—exactly where, Charlie didn't know—lay the Union camp and safety.

Well, he thought resignedly, at least so far so good.

He sat down to rest for a little, then got up and continued his journey. Beginning to feel somewhat recovered from the fall from his horse, he continued to climb through the woods toward the top of the ridge. After a little while the hill leveled off into a heavily wooded plateau. Trying to retain his sense of direction, but still anxious to keep as far away from the valley as possible in order to avoid capture, Charlie kept on through the woods until the land began to dip the other way. A little farther on, a light shining through the trees indicated the end of the woods, or at least a clearing.

Proceeding more cautiously now, he soon reached the edge of the clearing, and what he saw there made him catch his breath in surprise. He found himself looking into a huge basin or clearing hemmed in by hills which sloped down to it on every side. Milling around in a big corral at the bottom were at least fifty horses and mules.

After his first surprise Charlie realized that he had stumbled on a spot chosen by the plantation owners to save their stock from confiscation by both armies, and he realized that they could have searched for a long while before finding a safer place. Charlie's spirits immediately soared. Now he knew that if he could once get back to camp and report this find, the event would loom so big in the minds of the officers that they would conveniently forget all about why he had been absent or why he had been so far from camp.

But he was still faced with the problem of getting back on foot through enemy country. He considered briefly the possibility of capturing one of the horses below, but gave up the idea. He had neither saddle nor bridle, and without doubt there were guards around somewhere who might make it hot for him.

Well, he concluded, nothing was to be gained by standing there idly, so he made his way back up the ridge to the plateau and then headed south in the general direction of camp. Two or three miles of rough but rapid walking through the brush again brought him near to the edge of the woods. This worried him, because while it might be slower and harder going through the woods, it was far safer than in the open fields.

At the woods' edge he paused to check his bearings and found that the ridge sloped off toward the south in the direction in which he had to go. Perhaps half a mile below him, and directly in line with where he thought the Union camp was, he could see another set of plantation buildings, undoubtedly the homestead of one of the owners of the surrounding fields. Standing there he became aware of a sound which he had no difficulty in recognizing as the clop, clop, clop of galloping horses. Dropping to the ground, he inched along on his belly into a clump of bushes, and gently pushing down a few dead weeds and shrubs that screened his view, he saw that he had been dangerously close to a road. Disappearing down it toward the north were five or six cavalrymen. For a moment his heart lifted as he looked for the familiar blue uniforms, but sank again as he saw that the horsemen wore Confederate gray. For all he knew, they might be the same group that had just chased him and his comrades from the plantation. How fortunate it was, he thought, that they were going in the opposite direction from where he wanted to go.

Waiting to make sure that there were no more groups or stragglers on the road, Charlie crawled out of the bushes and followed the line of the woods away from the road for some distance. Then he struck out across the fields toward the south, trusting for concealment to his nearness to another rail fence and to the gradual darkening of the afternoon. When he was parallel with the house he had observed from the woods, but perhaps a quarter of a mile from it, he stopped by a tree to look the situation over.

CHAPTER XXII

As CHARLIE STOOD WATCHING, he saw a man armed with a musket come out from the edge of the woods at almost exactly the same point where he himself had been a short time before. Fearing that he was being pursued, Charlie remained motionless, hardly daring to breathe, but after looking around for a few moments, the man turned back into the woods and disappeared. Charlie felt sure, then, that he had not been seen in the half light, and that probably the man had been doing picket duty in guarding the herd of horses and mules. He was certain that he himself would not have noticed the man if he had not been watching so intently for any movement.

By this time the short winter day had gone and it was nearly dark, a black night with no moon. It had started to rain, too, and Charlie thought hopelessly that he couldn't go half a mile in that strange country in the darkness without either losing his direction or stumbling into the hands of enemy pickets or patrols. Nor did he have any heart for spending the night in the open on an empty stomach, and with only a saddle blanket. In desperation, he began to consider the possibility of seeking shelter at the house he had seen nearby. The chances were that if there were any people there at all, they would be women and children, or perhaps old men, all non-combatants; probably hostile, of course, but maybe not too mean to share a little warmth with him and a bite to eat. Better be darned careful, though, he thought. All these Johnnies racing around—maybe some of them are in there right now.

So, with great caution, Charlie drew nearer and nearer to the house. There was someone there all right. Lights showed around the crack of curtains at the back of the house.

"No sign of horses around here," he thought. "Can't see

myself sneaking up to peak through the windows. I've just got to take a chance."

With one part of his mind holding back with all of its might and the other urging him on, Charlie went around the house and knocked on a door near the room with the light. After a moment's silence he heard a movement within. Suddenly the door was thrown open and he found himself looking into the muzzle of a musket held by an old man with white hair and a long, carefully trimmed beard.

"What do you want?" he snarled.

Carefully holding his own gun at a harmless angle, Charlie smiled and said:

"Something to eat and a chance to rest."

"You're a Yank," said the old man, grimly. "Go away while you can."

But Charlie persisted.

"Yes, I'm a Yank," he admitted, "a cavalryman. I've lost my horse, and now I've lost my way. I mean no harm. Can't I at least come in and get warm?"

The steely blue eyes of the old man softened not at all.

"Keep moving!" he said. "Go away!"

The impasse was broken by the rustling of a woman's skirt in the hallway, and a girl perhaps eighteen or nineteen years of age looked around the gaunt, tall old form. Even in the dim light of the few candles flickering in the wind from the open door, Charlie could see that she was pretty. Like the old man, she was tall; her young face was framed in a riot of auburn curls, and even the gray hoop skirt that swung around her could not hide her slender grace. As she peeked around the old man's shoulder, she smiled at Charlie and gently took the gun from the old hands.

"He's harmless, Grandpa," she said to the old man. "He's just a hungry boy—like brother Jim. Let him come in and get warm."

The mention of her brother's name seemed to take the fight out of the old man. As he turned to look at his granddaughter, his face softened, his shoulders sagged a little, and he went back to the wooden armchair in front of the small fire in the big fireplace. Still holding the gun, the girl said:

"Come on in."

After motioning Charlie to sit by the fire, she walked

across the room and hung the gun back on pegs on the kitchen wall. As Charlie sat down, he shivered, as much from nervousness as from the chill of the night air. The old man sat looking into the fire, and then, moved either by a lifetime habit of hospitality or by the youth of the boy, he said, kindly:

"Glad to share the fire with you, and our food—such as it is."

Charlie thanked him, and answered:

"I'm sorry to intrude, but I was so cold and hungry."

"What are you doing here?" asked the old man, abruptly. "Trying to desert?"

"No, sir," said Charlie, his face flushing. He didn't wish to anger the old man by mentioning the foraging expedition, so he said, finally:

"I got separated from my comrades by accident."

"Humph!" said the old man, not in the least fooled. "Probably foraging. Taking what little food we non-combatants have left to live on." Then, noticing the look of shame and distress on Charlie's face, he added:

"But at that I don't believe I can really blame you too much." He smiled a little. "I was always hungry when I was your age." And after another pause he added:

"I'm hungry all the time now, too."

Charlie made no reply, and after a while the old man continued, half to himself:

"I've got to admit that the Yanks have left our property alone better than our own folks have."

At this the girl, who had been busy placing some food on the table, joined in the talk for the first time:

"Own folks, indeed," she repeated, bitterly. "Don't call these dirty robbers who are too cowardly to join the Army our own folks. They're the ones—not the boys like our Jim in the forces—who are riding up and down this country taking every last bit of food we have and scaring the wits out of us by their dastardly acts."

The old man nodded his head.

"You're right, honey." Then, turning to Charlie again, he asked:

"What's your name?"

"Charlie Wilson."

"A good old American name. Mine's Morgan—David

Morgan. Jennie is my granddaughter. My folks have been here ever since the early settlements. Gave a good account of themselves in the Revolution."

Beginning to feel a little better acquainted, Charlie made bold to say:

"Yes, I know from my history books that you southern folks did more than your share in the Revolution toward winning American independence."

Then, with growing confidence, he added:

"Some of us wonder why you want to break up this country now."

Morgan jumped to his feet and stood in front of the fireplace, his arm resting on the mantel. Charlie thought he was going to explode with wrath, but when he finally spoke it was in a mild tone:

"Maybe, son, you haven't studied your history as much as you should, or you have listened to the wrong kind of teaching. We didn't want to break up the Union, you know. You Yanks forced us to secede. For fifty years we have debated and argued and quarreled about our right to have and to own our own property, the slaves. We didn't bring slavery to America—your New England Yanks did that. As long as they were making money out of it, it was all right. After you had sold your slaves to us, after we had become dependent upon them to cultivate our lands and for our prosperity, and when you Yanks found you could no longer make money by shipping in and selling the slaves to us, the abolitionists began to shout about the evils of slavery. When our slaves ran away into Yankee country, instead of helping us to get our valuable property back, you hid the slaves and helped them to get away."

The old man stopped talking, and after a while Charlie said, quietly:

"Well, Mr. Morgan, I know that I don't know all the history, and maybe I haven't heard both sides of the story. I only know that I am sure it is wrong to try to break up the Union that your folks and mine, both North and South, fought so hard to create. This state of Virginia and the other southern states left the Union. I don't know about slavery; I think it's wrong, though maybe I don't understand all

about it. But I do know that secession is wrong, and that's
the reason why I am fighting."

"Well, you don't know all about that, either," said Morgan, emphatically. "I don't believe—the South doesn't believe—that the Federal government can or should force a
state to stay in the Union if it doesn't want to. We fought
the Revolution to get away from a king and a government
that had too much power. We'll lose the very rights and
liberties that we fought for in the Revolution if we permit a
central government so much power that they can dictate to
the states and to the people, as the United States government has been trying to dictate to the South for the last
fifty years. After we lost all the arguments, we had no re-
course except to resort to our right as a state to secede.

"And then what did you Yanks do?" continued Morgan,
shaking an admonishing finger at Charlie. "You raised
armies and marched on to the sacred soil of our states, destroying our property and killing our boys."

"Grandpa!" expostulated the girl, gently.

He glanced at her a little shamefacedly and sat down
again.

"I'm sorry," he said, courteously. Then, sadly to himself:

"I'm sorry that I ever lived to see these awful times. If
anyone had told me when I was young that Virginia would
come to days like these, I would have thought he was crazy."

For some moments the girl had been waiting for an opportunity to break into the talk, and now she said, laughingly:

"If you and Grandpa can stop talking long enough, Mr.
Wilson, maybe you would like to eat. There's corn bread
and milk on the table. I'm sorry we can't offer you more."

Charlie had risen as the girl spoke to him, and now he
bowed a little awkwardly and said:

"Thank you, Miss Morgan. You are very kind—and I am
very hungry! Whatever you have will be just right."

Crossing to the table he sat down, and Jennie took a seat
opposite him, but the old man remained by the fire, leaning
his head on his hand, his elbow on the arm of his chair, lost
in his memories.

In spite of his hunger it was hard for Charlie to keep his
eyes from the girl who sat across from him. The hard times
that seemed to weigh so heavily on the grandfather had not

dimmed her sparkle. It was easy to see that she was naturally lively and full of fun.

Nor was she above showing her interest and curiosity in this young man of her own age, one of those strange creatures from the far-away North customarily referred to by her family and friends as Damyankees. Well, she thought, if this boy is a specimen, maybe the Yankees aren't as bad as they have been painted. She had listened carefully and noticed that Charlie had been respectful to her grandfather. She'd bet that rest him and feed him, and get him out of that hated blue uniform, he'd be quite nice.

Shy and uneasy under her frank scrutiny, Charlie kept his head bent over his bowl of milk and the corn bread. Then, as his hunger passed, and he began to feel warm and comfortable, he responded to her chatter. "She's kind and natural," he thought, "and by jiminy, goodlooking, too. Funny about folks. Some you could be around for ever and never get very well acquainted with, and with others even in an hour you feel as if you'd known them always." That was the way with Jennie.

Her grandfather had been kind, too. Then he reminded himself to be careful. After all, they were Rebels. There was a war on, and he was on the other side.

His supper finished, Charlie went back to join the old man by the fire. After clearing off the table, Jennie joined them, and soon the three of them were talking about farming in the North and the South. Charlie was interested in finding out all about how farming was done on a southern plantation and on the smaller farms before the war, and, in turn, Jennie and her grandfather asked many questions about farm life in the North. Finally Mr. Morgan said:

"You're welcome to stay the night with us, son, but I warn you that it's not very safe. Our friends, the guerillas, pay us frequent visits, hunting for and stealing the last smoked ham, the last cow, the few miserable vegetables we have left. They might come—and if they found you—" he left the sentence unfinished.

Charlie thought for a moment and then said:

"Frankly, sir, it's cold and dark outside, I'd have to keep moving, and I'd be even more likely to walk into trouble than if I stayed here. I don't want to make any trouble for you, though. I could sit right here by the fire until it begins to get light in the morning."

"All right, Wilson, but you don't have to stay up. Jennie will get you a blanket and there's a couch over there. But again I tell you, you'd better sleep with one eye open."

He rose heavily from his chair, and as Jennie and Charlie also started to rise, the girl suddenly raised her hand in a warning gesture, her face turning white.

"Horses coming," she said, tensely.

Then Charlie heard them. Grabbing his Army coat and cap, his musket, knapsack and canteen, he started for the back door of the kitchen.

"Wait!" cried Morgan. "You'll likely walk right into their arms. They've probably surrounded the house."

"If I'm caught here, it'll be bad for you two," Charlie protested.

"Too late to think about that now. Curse these old bones of mine! Jennie," he said, "hide him—and hide him good."

With a swift stride across the room Jennie blew out the two candles on the table with one breath, and, snatching Charlie's hand, almost yanked him out of the room into a passageway. Simultaneously, there came a heavy knock on the outer door and the hoarse shouting of men.

CHAPTER XXIII

UNUSED TO THE STRANGE SURROUNDINGS, Charlie stumbled. "Pick up your feet!" came in a fierce whisper from the girl, and she emphasized her words by a pull that almost dragged him off his feet.

"Stairway," she whispered, and he found himself mounting the stairs, her hand like a small vise gripping his wrist. In the upper hall she opened a door quietly, pushed him ahead of her and followed him in. Leading him across the room, she whispered:

"Here's a big bed. Get under the feather bed fast, and pull it over you."

He started to object:

"My muddy boots in the bed? What'll I do with my gun?"

"Take them all with you," she said, "and be sure that everything is covered." Then, as he still hesitated:

"Move, you idiot, or you'll get us all killed."

"But a bed's the first place they'll look."

"Not this one," Jennie said.

"Why not?"

She gave him a push:

"Because it's mine—and I'll be right on top of the feather bed!"

By this time they could hear loud talking and the clatter of several men downstairs. There was no more time for arguing, so Charlie climbed in, pulled the thick feather bed over him, making sure that his accoutrements were all covered and leaving just a place for his nose to stick out from under the feathers at the back of the bed so he could breathe. A moment later he felt a sizable weight plunk down on top of him, and he could feel Jennie wriggle around to pull the bedclothes well up over herself.

Then came the sound of feet clumping up the stairs and a

knock on the door. Receiving no answer, Charlie could hear the door open.

"Anyone here?" inquired a gruff voice.

He got his answer all right.

"Shut that door and clear out of here," Jennie snapped.

Charlie could picture the man's hesitation by the movement of his feet on the floor, and then he learned that while Southerners are courteous and hospitable to a degree, beyond that point, male or female, they fight like wildcats.

"Haven't you any sense of decency?" said Jennie, angrily. "I'm Jennie Morgan, this is my bedroom, and I'm in bed. Now you git!"

"But——" the man persisted.

"Don't but me," she snapped. "You shut that door—from the outside!"

Charlie could catch a glimmer of light, apparently from a candle, as if the man had raised it high to glance around the room. The lumpy bed would not excite suspicion, thought Charlie. Feather beds were always lumpy. Slowly, reluctantly, the intruder retreated and closed the door. For an endless time they could hear the men searching other parts of the house.

Sweltering under the feathers in his full uniform, Charlie lay thinking of the girl above him. By her initiative and courage she had saved a stranger—and a Yank—from probable death. Fearing to bring down her wrath upon him or to make a move before the guerillas got out of the house, he lay perfectly still, awaiting orders from his hostess.

Gradually the noises below subsided. He heard a door shut with a bang, and the sound of moving horses. Then it seemed like a long time before he felt Jennie move above him and climb out on to the floor. Pulling the feather bed off Charlie, she said, in a low voice:

"Get up now, but keep still. I think they've gone. Maybe they'll be back. You stay here and I'll go talk to Grandpa."

After what seemed like an eternity he heard her light footsteps on the stairs and she came back into the room.

"What do we do now?" he inquired.

"I don't know. We thought they were looking for food, as usual, but Grandpa says no. It seems that somebody saw you this afternoon, and they were searching for you here.

Grandfather thinks he succeeded in putting them off your trail, but he isn't sure. You've got to be careful."

"Well, it's certain that I can't stay here."

"You'll have to make your own decision. You can go down and sit by the fire or lie on the couch, or you can leave." She laughed a little, and continued:

"My idea is that it's safer for you to stay, for if they come back I can hide you again. We don't want them to get you now. Come along," she added, taking him by the hand. "We mustn't show any lights. I'll lead you downstairs."

Charlie liked that little hand holding his. The kitchen was empty when they got down there.

"Grandpa sleeps in there," she said, pointing to a door opening off the kitchen. "Now get some rest. I can find something for you to eat before you start out in the morning."

Unconsciously she was still clinging to his hand in the dark. Impulsively, the boy turned toward her and taking her other hand in his, said:

"Jennie, why did you do this for me? I'll never, never forget it."

Gently she released her hands.

"Because of Jim," she said, quietly.

"Jim?" he inquired. "Who is Jim?"

"My brother," she said, simply. "He's with our Army, and if he got into difficulty like you, I hope someone would be kind to him."

Turning, she started toward the hall; then looking back at him over her shoulder, she added:

"Well, maybe I didn't do it entirely for Jim!"

With a light laugh she ran upstairs.

Tired as he was, Charlie was too excited and too fearful of a return visit from the guerillas to sleep. So he took the blanket from the couch, wrapped it around him, and sat watching the flickering flames of the slowly dying fire and dreaming dreams. When his waking dreams finally merged into sleep, he didn't know, but it seemed only a few moments later that he awoke with a start to find Jennie's hand on his shoulder, shaking him gently:

"It'll soon be light, Charlie," she said, "and you should be away from here before daylight. Come drink this glass of milk and eat this corn bread. It will help."

When he had finished eating, Jennie gave him some directions, how to get around the barn and the out-buildings and into the nearby woods without being seen, and the right direction she thought he ought to take to reach the Union lines. As he stood up, he said:

"Jennie, don't get mad at me, but I have never met a girl like you before, and even though I have been here only since last night you seem like an old friend. Some time, maybe when all this fighting is over, I'd like to come back and see you again. May I?"

"I'd like you to, Charlie," Jennie answered. "We don't know what will happen to us, but if you can, please do come back."

Taking her hand, he drew her close to him and kissed her. For a moment her slender body pressed against his, then she drew away and said:

"Now go, and God go with you."

Following Jennie's directions, Charlie reached the cover of the woods safely and turned southward, hoping that he had not been seen. By keeping away from the highway and buildings and using the cover of the brush and woods, he could, with luck, make camp all right, he thought, but even then his troubles would not be over. How was he going to escape trouble with his officers? Then his thoughts went back to Jennie. Whatever happens, he thought, just knowing her was worth it. Still thinking of her as he half walked, half ran along, he said aloud:

"I'll never forget her, and if I can, some day I'll come back!"

His worries soon returned to plague him, however. Through his mind ran the remembrance of what Mark had gone through with the military. "I'll certainly catch it!" he thought, ruefully, but he clung to the memory of those horses he had discovered. "If the officers get those horses, they'll forget all about me," he reassured himself, "—unless old Burnside is so strict about Confederate property that he won't take the horses." That possibility made him feel more depressed than ever, but his face brightened again as he thought: "But that applies to food and personal possessions. Horses are something else again. They're military supplies, and therefore contraband of war."

Late in the afternoon Charlie dragged into camp and immediately asked for an interview with his captain. Omitting only the account of his stay at the Morgan home, he told the captain the whole story of his adventures. When Charlie finished, the captain sat looking at him, drumming absent-mindedly with his fingers on the small paper-littered table behind which he sat. Finally, the captain grinned a little, and said:

"Lucky for you, boy, that I'm a volunteer and not an old regular Army man with ironclad ideas about discipline. Absent without leave, foraging contrary to strict orders, then losing your horse on top of everything else!"

Charlie couldn't resist saying:

"The horse wasn't any good, sir. If it had been, I could have kept up with the other boys and got back here all right."

"Well, maybe we can get you another mount." Then his face grew grave as he said, sternly:

"But those horses you told me about had better be there, for we're going after them tonight, and you're going to show us the way!"

CHAPTER XXIV

WHILE THE FEDERAL ARMY under General Burnside lay facing Lee on the other side of the Rappahannock during the last days of November and the first of December, 1862, George Wilson and his Army band were kept busy every day playing for the officers at headquarters and for the soldiers. As a band leader, George had more opportunity than the other soldiers to know personally some of the officers and to learn more of what was going on. Many of the men, including George, had concluded that the fighting was all over for the year and that they could relax and improve their winter quarters; but suddenly on the morning of December 10, things began to happen.

That morning there was a heavy fog on the river, and the Union engineers used it as a cover while they started to build a pontoon bridge of rafts on which the Army could cross the Rappahannock. Unfortunately, the fog soon lifted. The houses across the river in Fredericksburg were filled with sharpshooters, and as fast as the engineers could get out on the pontoon rafts, the sharpshooters in the nearby houses riddled the planks and the men on them. Many of the men pitched off into the river and were drowned, if the bullets had not already killed them.

But the Union batteries soon stopped the slaughter. They opened up on the houses in Fredericksburg, and, as George watched, he saw house after house hit by the Union shells go up in the air like small volcanoes, with pieces of lumber and heavy timbers flying in every direction. George even thought that once between the roar of the cannon he heard a man scream in agony, and he was sure that those clouds of dust and debris were filled with pieces of what had once been human beings.

Driven out of the houses, the Confederate riflemen re-treated toward the hill to the south of the village, where they continued to pour a hail of fire into the Union engineers. Finally, Union volunteers jumped into boats, rowed across the river, charged the rifle pits and drove the Confederates back, so that the pontoon bridges were finally completed, enabling the Union Army to cross in force.

Then followed a nightmare, with almost constant, bloody fighting such as George never wanted to recall. Again and again the Union forces charged the Confederate works on the hill south of the town, only to be thrown back. Near the foot of this hill was an old sunken road and on the hill just above it a stone wall. Six times the men in blue charged into that road and against the wall, only to meet with such deadly fire from the Confederate infantry that the Union columns were broken, and those who were left ran for their lives back to Fredericksburg. Hundreds who charged into that sunken road never got out. It was a hell beyond description. The Union forces lost over 12,000 men, and all in vain, for they were thoroughly licked.

George expressed the sentiment of all of the men around him when he said: "I hope old Burnside is satisfied!"

His own part in the battle, and that of the other members of his band, was to help the surgeons with the wounded—in many respects a worse job than the actual fighting. During the battle the stretcher-bearers were busy bringing the wounded to the tents of the surgeons. No matter how fast the doctors worked, many of the wounded died before they could have aid. In writing Nancy about his experiences afterwards, George said:

"There was mutilation of every kind—head wounds, arms and legs dangling in shreds. Our limited supply of ether was soon gone, so the surgeons had to saw off the limbs while we held the poor victims. I saw just one of the piles of legs and arms where they had been thrown outside the tents. It was higher than the tables on which the surgeons worked. At the time I wondered if I ever could sleep again without the cries of those poor boys ringing in my ears."

George worried about his own sons, too. He had seen Charlie a few days before the battle and found him happy and cheerful. He had told his father that he had just had a big adventure, discovered a hidden band of horses and mules, and led his captain and a detachment to bring them in. But where either Charlie or Mark were now during this battle, George didn't know.

He was further worried because Mark had seemed so despondent lately. His father knew that he had had some kind of a foolish misunderstanding with Ann, his wife.

Working in that madhouse during the battle, George Wilson thought:

"May the Good Lord forgive me if the boys and I ever get back to our peaceful farm home again and I ever complain about anything!"

At the end of the last day of fighting at Fredericksburg, George Wilson walked a short distance from the surgeons' tent, and, finding a little brush that gave him some scanty protection from the bitter wind, wrapped himself in his blanket and lay down. Emotionally and physically exhausted, he fell into a deep sleep without intending to do so. The next thing he knew a man was standing over him and shouting at him in a harsh voice. When George got the daze of sleep out of his eyes, he became aware that the man yelling at him was a Confederate officer.

"Get up!" he was saying.

George scrambled to his feet, but he was so lame and still so full of sleep that he could hardly stand erect.

"What are you doing here?"

George grinned a little and answered:

"That isn't the question, Mister. The real question is, what are *you* doing here?"

What George didn't know was that during the night the Union Army had retreated back across the river. They must have passed right around him while he was so dead to the world that he had heard nothing. So when he awoke he was within the Confederate lines and became a prisoner of war. The man who had found him marched him over to a captain who was standing with some other officers. They were all in high spirits, laughing and making sarcastic remarks about licking the Union forces.

After questioning George at some length, the captain ordered him placed with the other Union prisoners, and from them he learned that their destination was Libby Prison in the Confederate stronghold of Richmond.

The news of the defeat of Burnside and the Federal forces

at Fredericksburg brought gloom and discouragement throughout the North. To thousands of women like Ann and Nancy, the news of any battle brought an agony of waiting and dread until they could be sure that their men had come through safely.

The short, dark, dreary December days increased Ann's feeling of depression and anxiety. Finally, the blow fell one evening. It happened that she had not made her usual trip for the mail that day, and she and her mother were seated at the supper table when they heard a knock at the door. Without waiting for an answer, John Crawford opened it and walked in. One look at his face brought both women to their feet. Ann knew instantly the kind of tidings he had brought.

"I hate to be the one to tell you this, Ann," he said, gravely, "but a message has just come through from the War Department that Mark was killed in action at Fredericksburg."

"Oh, my God," said Mrs. Clinton, sinking into a chair. But Ann took the blow standing. Her eyes met John Crawford's unflinchingly, though her voice shook as she said:

"Thank you for bringing the message over."

Feeling that he could be of no help to the stricken girl, John turned and went out of the door. Slowly Ann turned back to the table, gripping the back of her chair until the knuckles of her hands shone white in the candle light, and said to her mother:

"Are you all right? I must go and tell Nancy."

As she made her way up the road to the Wilson home, she wondered why she was not suffering more, not realizing that an emotional shock, like a physical wound, deadens the nerves for a time beyond pain.

The Wilsons were still at the supper table as Ann walked in, and both Enoch Payne and Mary Curtis were there. To offset her own worries, Nancy was slyly promoting the lagging courtship of Enoch and Mary. She was always glad afterwards that those two good friends were there when she and Ann needed strong human support more than ever before in their lives. Numbed by the shock she had had, Ann could do nothing to soften the blow for Nancy and the others. Standing straight and tall, but with stricken face, she stepped just inside the door and said, bluntly:

"Mark is dead!"

There was a moment of stunned silence and then everyone at the table stood up.

"Dead?" said Nancy, incredulously. "Dead, did you say? How do you know?"

"Yes," said Ann, nodding her head mechanically, "he's dead!"

Realizing that the girl was near the breaking point, Enoch went quickly over to Ann, took her by the arm and led her to a chair, while Mary Curtis moved around the table to put an arm across Nancy's shoulders.

"Sit down, Nancy," she said, giving her a gentle push toward a chair. Tom stood leaning on the table, his eyes round, staring at Ann. The little girls, scared, started to cry. That, somehow, broke the tension.

"Where? How can you be sure?" Nancy said again, groping for hope.

"It happened at Fredericksburg. I don't know how. John Crawford brought the news."

The days that followed were days of horror for Ann. As the first shock wore off, her suffering increased, and cynically she thought that like most of the old platitudes there was no truth in the one about time making grief easier to bear. With bitter regret and remorse, she kept thinking that if she had done this or that, Mark might still be alive. Why, oh why had she not been more cooperative and understanding when he suggested that they let Henry Bain foreclose his mortgage and that they set up a new home? Ann felt bitter toward her mother, feeling that she was the cause of a lot of the trouble between her and Mark. It was for her sake that Ann had insisted on keeping the farm.

Thus blaming herself and her mother, Ann's grief seemed beyond her ability to bear. It was all so hopeless. There was something so irrevocable about death. When death comes, she thought, there's never, never another chance for either the living or the dead to make up for past mistakes. And then sometimes she was comforted by the thought that maybe the dead did have a chance. Maybe they were given infinite power to know and understand what was truly in their loved ones' hearts. If Mark knew, he would forgive all mistakes, remembering only her love.

As she had done before when Mark first left for the war,

Ann turned to work as a relief, a surcease from grief. She did all of her own chores; and after Enoch Payne and Tom Wilson had filled a big skidway of logs at her back door, she helped Enoch, sawing and splitting wood until she was so tired that she fell asleep at night too exhausted to think. Protesting at first, Enoch finally realized that work, even to exhaustion, was better for her than her brooding thoughts.

Under different circumstances Ann would have spent much time with Nancy, but now she avoided the Wilson home because there was so much there—particularly Nancy herself—to remind her of her loss. Listening to Enoch's stories and casual talk about practical, everyday matters of the farm and the neighborhood helped a lot. She had a great affection for this old friend.

As time went by, Ann resolved that she must force herself to resume her old close relationship with Nancy, for after all, Mark was Nancy's son as well as Ann's husband, and it was her loss, too. Furthermore, Nancy now had further worries, for she had had word that her husband was a prisoner of war in a Confederate military prison.

During those first weeks of sorrow, Henry Bain was a frequent caller at the Clinton home, talking soothingly to Mrs. Clinton and assuring her and Ann that as far as finances were concerned they had nothing to worry about. His presence occasionally helped to take Ann's mind off her grief, and in fact he showed himself so kind and thoughtful and such a true friend in every way that she felt she must change her mind about him. His enemies may be wrong about Henry, she thought.

One winter day he drove up in front of the Clinton house with a brand-new Portland cutter, to which was hitched a beautiful brown gelding. After tying and blanketing his horse, he came into the house and said to Ann:

"The sleighing is good, my horse hasn't had enough exercise, and I've got to go over to the Caroline hills on a business trip. Why don't you come along?"

"Oh," said Ann, instantly, "I couldn't."

But her mother intervened.

"Why not, dear? You need a change. It's time you quit moping around."

If Henry had pressed the matter at all, Ann would have

continued to refuse, but he just looked disappointed and said something about it's being a long, lonesome trip without company. Her mother kept urging her to go, and finally Ann said, resignedly:

"Oh, all right."

She allowed Henry to tuck the big red-brown buffalo robe around her. Then he climbed in himself, spoke to the lively young horse, which needed no urging, and off they went. It was one of those rare days in a north country winter when the snow sparkled in the sun like millions of diamonds. The glare was almost too much for the naked eye to stand. The air was like wine, and after a while Ann could not help but feel some of the gloom fall away as the runners of the bright new cutter glided easily over the hard packed snow, and the hooves of the horse beat a rhythmic tattoo to the tune of the sleigh bells encircling his body.

For a long time Henry said nothing, respecting Ann's mood and letting the day and the ride have their way with her. After a while they came to the top of a long ridge of hills that separated the two valleys. Henry stopped to give the horse a rest, and they sat gazing over the vast expanse of valley and hills that stretched away below them, sparkling in the sunshine. Ann relaxed with a long sigh, and Henry said:

"Beautiful, isn't it?"

Ann nodded, with a feeling of surprise, wondering what folks would think if they could have heard his remark. Neither she nor any of the others had ever credited him with having any appreciation of beauty. After a brief silence, Henry spoke again:

"Always when I get out like this where I can see the country, it looks to me as if there were more woods than there really are. Look up and down that ridge and the valley below," he said, waving his hand in a wide arc. "Doesn't it look as if there were only a few clearings?"

"Well, there *are* a lot of woods," said Ann.

"Yes," he agreed, "but nothing like there used to be. When I think of how people used to cut this beautiful virgin timber and burn it just to get it out of the way, it makes me shudder. Lumber is going to get scarcer and scarcer and be worth more. I don't mind telling you that that's why I'm taking this trip today. It's to look at some timberland I want to buy."

He added, smugly:

"These fools are anxious to sell their woodland. And I'm getting quite a lot of it without paying much for it."

Then, realizing that perhaps he had said too much, Henry hastily changed the subject, laughed a little, and said:

"Well, leastwise to look at a piece of timber was *one* reason why I came. Another was the hope that you'd come along, too."

When Ann made no reply to this remark, Henry continued after a moment:

"You know, Ann, I haven't changed my feelings about you in a long, long time—not since I began to realize how nice you are—and I never will," he added, emphatically.

Ann looked at him and said, kindly:

"That's too bad, Henry, when there are so many nice girls. You've been so very kind to Mother and me that I never will forget it. But, please, Henry, I just don't want to talk about such things."

Henry said no more on that subject, knowing better than to press his advantage. For the rest of the ride, he was tactful and kind, and Ann returned home feeling much the better for her outing.

CHAPTER XXV

AFTER GEORGE WILSON'S CAPTURE by the victorious Confederates at Fredericksburg, it was several days before he and the other Union prisoners could be moved to Libby Prison. Because transportation facilities were limited, the Confederates had to move their own and the Union wounded before they could move the prisoners. But finally George and his fellow prisoners were packed in cattle cars like sardines, so close that they couldn't even sit down.

On that horrible ride to Libby Prison, George and his comrades fell to discussing why there seemed to be so much difference in the treatment they received from the Confederate soldiers and the civilians. The soldiers were courteous, even kindly; but whenever the prison guards got their hands on the men, or when they were being marched through the streets of Richmond, they were constantly insulted. One woman, after reviling the group that George was in, ran out into the street and spat on the prisoner marcning next to George. When several of the prisoners objected, the southern guards laughed. In many cases these were the men who were too cowardly to take their places in the Confederate front lines, but through pull and political influence had got soft jobs behind the lines.

George hoped that none of the home folks were ever guilty of such conduct toward unfortunate southern boys who were in the northern military prisons, but he was forced to conclude sadly that prison guards in either the South or the North were the same type of men, and he thought of what Nancy had written him several times about the suspected activities of Henry Bain.

At Libby Prison the men got a small cup of thin bean soup twice a day and a small piece of stale bread. "How I'd hate Nancy to know how hungry I am," George thought. Mornings, dirty peddlers came to the windows on the main floor of the prison and offered the prisoners small pieces of pie, not over an inch and a half across in the widest place, for twenty-five cents. But before they reached Libby, most of the prisoners had been relieved of their money and any small personal possessions they had, so were unable to buy any pie. George concluded that he couldn't have eaten the dirty stuff anyway even if he had had the money to buy it.

The whole prison stank, and the prisoners could look down through the cracks in the floor to a basement where there were always a dozen or more who had died during the night. The guards stripped every article of clothing from the dead men and buried them naked. Because of the lack of food, the constant exposure, and worry, many of the prisoners were sick. Smallpox and black measles raged.

Worst of all to bear was the mental agony of homesickness and not knowing whether they would ever see their loved ones again. Christmas Day was particularly hard. The prisoners knew that if their folks at home found out where they were, they would send packages of food and clothing. But nothing ever reached George. Packages never got by the guards. George had written to Nancy soon after his arrival at the prison, but he had no way of knowing whether she had received his letter. It was likely, he thought, that any letter she had written had been intercepted by the thieving guards in the hope that it might contain a little money.

In writing, George was careful not to upset Nancy by describing the prison conditions in detail nor how he felt. Privately, he wondered if there was anything worse in life than hope deferred. Twice a flag-of-truce boat had arrived down at City Point, below Richmond, and twice all the prisoners had become excited, hoping that at last they were going to be exchanged and get out of the Libby Prison hell-hole. Each time, however, the guards had come in and taken out some of the sick and wounded, leaving the others.

"Of course that's right," George thought. "The sick and wounded should go first. But a little more of this pestilence, starvation, and ill treatment by the guards, and we'll all be sick."

The worst of the guards was the head one, a veritable devil by the name of Ross. Nothing was too mean for him to do, and he never punished the other guards for ill treatment of the prisoners. One day he came into the prison cell fully armed and ordered a sick prisoner to his feet. When the boy was unable to get up, the ruffian kicked him brutally in the ribs. When George remonstrated, Ross knocked him down, pulled his revolver and threatened to shoot him for interfering. After he left, George wondered what decent men like Robert Lee and the soldiers in the Confederate Army would think if they could know what was going on in their prisons.

For George, January 16, 1863, was a great day indeed, for the guards finally herded a bunch of the prisoners, including him, out of Libby and marched them down to City Point and on to a United States gunboat. One of George's first acts was to write to Nancy, and among other things he said:

"No American of the past or the future will ever feel more strongly than I did when I looked up and saw Old Glory flying at the masthead on that United States gunboat. And I hope someone will kick me if I ever grumble again about your cooking, or even about the good, substantial Army rations. Unless a man has been really hungry and has eaten the slop and hogwash that we prisoners had for weeks, he can have no idea of how good the Army rations tasted when we got on that transport and set sail for Annapolis."

George and the other prisoners were taken to Camp Parole near Annapolis. There they were not permitted to do anything at all until an exchange of prisoners could be made, so strict were the officials about honoring the conditions of the parole. Camp Parole was located on dry ground, the quarters were comfortable and the rations excellent. The only difficulty, so far as George was concerned, was a lack of any news either from home or from Mark and Charlie. George just couldn't understand why he had heard from neither Nancy nor Ann, and he concluded that his own letters home must have miscarried or been delayed, so that they didn't know where he was.

He tried to get a furlough to go home until he could be exchanged. This, however, was against the strict policy of the military authorities, for they believed that if the men were once released, it would be hard to get hold of them again to exchange them for Confederate prisoners and thus free them for military service.

Finally, after days of hopefully watching the distribution

of the camp mail, George got a letter from Nancy. When he read it, it seemed to him as if the world had finally crashed about his head and that all he had suffered was as nothing compared to this final blow. The letter consisted of only a few lines, Nancy apparently being unable to pen more. She said that Ann, as next of kin, had received a message that Mark had been killed at the Battle of Fredericksburg.

The date and address on the envelope showed that Nancy's letter had gone first to Libby, and had finally caught up with him. She said that she had just received his first letter written from Libby and was hoping and praying that he would soon be paroled and could come home, and then added just three words which to George said more than a volume: "We need you."

After George had recovered from the first shock of the news, he went, with the letter in his hand, directly to Colonel Sangster, in command of Camp Parole, and asked again for a furlough. The Colonel, a kindly man, shook his head.

"It's out of my hands," he said. "I'm powerless to grant you a furlough. We have strict orders to make no exceptions."

Then he smiled a little, winked, and said:

"Strictly between us, if you should disappear some night, we wouldn't look for you very hard. But I warn you the provost guards are watching all the roads to capture and bring back parolees."

George thanked him, returned to his quarters and immediately began to consider ways and means of getting home. The paymaster had visited camp that day and paid off the men. This was fortunate, in that George now had funds with which to get home, but it was unfortunate also because the provost guards were likely to redouble their vigilance, knowing that the time immediately following payday would be when most men would try to "skedaddle."

George decided that his best chance was to walk by night to Baltimore, keeping away from the main traveled roads and the bridges, and from Baltimore he might catch a train for the North. After he had gone several miles in the dark, he came to the Severn River. Now he was in trouble. It was too cold to swim, and the river was too swift and deep to wade. Locating a hut with a dim light shining through the window, he found a negro who agreed to take him across the river. But no amount of persuasion, not even the offer of a considerable sum of money, could persuade the man to take him across in the dark. There was nothing to do but to wait for daylight.

The hospitable negro and his family made him comfortable on the kitchen floor before a little fireplace. For his bed, a big armful of clean straw was brought in from the little barn across the yard. The morning was just beginning to show a gray light through a heavy fog when there came a great pounding at the door and the demand to "Open up!"

Fearful as he was, George found amusement in the figure of the old negro rushing out from the little bedroom adjoining the kitchen, clad in nothing but his short shirt and shivering with cold and nervousness.

"The barn," he whispered to George, and pointing to the back door. "Hide there!"

Picking up his coat, George quietly opened the door, to meet an almost solid wall of fog. But underneath he could make out a path which he thought probably led to the barn. Following it, he reached the barn, got the clumsy door open, went in and pulled the door shut behind him. It was still pitch dark in there, but rich with the smell of hay, animals and manure.

Feeling sure it would only be a matter of time before the officers would come to the barn unless the negro could get them off his track, George began to edge slowly around the walls, feeling carefully with his hands and getting some homey comfort when he touched the warm body of a cow. Keeping going, he came upon a little ladder, and, climbing it, found himself in a loft filled with straw, the roof so low that he couldn't stand erect. Crawling over the top of the straw to the farthest corner, George started to pull out the straw and burrow toward its center. Working himself in backwards into the hole he had made, he pulled some of the straw over the opening, leaving just enough room so that there was air for him to breathe. For the first time, he took a long breath and tried to relax. It was probably just a routine search, he thought, and wouldn't be very thorough. It would be a good opportunity to sleep, for he had not had any rest during the night, haunted by memories of Mark and of how Nancy and Ann must be feeling. But it was a long time before he fell into a troubled sleep. He had just dropped off when he heard a movement below him as the searchers entered the barn. He heard one of them climb the ladder and for a moment saw a dim light as the man swung his lantern around to see if anyone was there. Then all was quiet again.

A short time later he heard the soft voice of the old negro calling:

"Mistah suh, where's you at? Dey's gone."

George crawled out of the straw to the opening and climbed stiffly down the ladder to the lower floor of the barn. There the old man pressed upon him some indescribable garments, insisting that he never "could git nowhere" if the guards caught him in uniform. So, with considerable reluctance, George exchanged his fairly good uniform for the ragged, ill-fitting clothes. Then the negro stepped in beside the cow, pulled a cup out of his pocket, filled it with milk and handed it to George with a sizable chunk of cornpone. He stood grinning while George choked it down, and when he had finished, said cheerfully:

"Now I'll take you across 'fore the fog lifts."

Following closely behind the old man, George soon came to a spot on the river's edge where the negro had a rickety rowboat cleverly hidden under the willows that overhung the edge of the river. Warning George to be very quiet, the old man, apparently an expert oarsman, soon landed him on the other side of the river, and seemed more grateful for George's warm expression of gratitude than for the money he gave him.

Fortunately, the heavy fog hung on all the forenoon, and by following the directions that he had received from the old negro, thereby keeping away from the places where the provost guards were most likely to be watching, George was able to make his way to Baltimore. There he boarded a train for Elmira, and from there got another train to Owego, where he caught the stage for home.

That evening after supper, Ann made one of her rare visits to Nancy. It was getting dark when she opened the door and stepped into the Wilson kitchen, and in the dusk she was surprised at first glance to see a stranger turn toward her, with the family all gathered around him. Then she recognized her father-in-law, and rushing forward she threw her arms around him. Standing back to look at him after her embrace, she exclaimed:

"No wonder I didn't know you!"

Since Nancy and she had seen George in Washington he had lost twenty pounds. His thin face was covered with a scraggly beard, and he still wore the nondescript clothes that the negro on the River Severn in Maryland had given him.

After the first excitement of greeting him was over, they gathered around to hear his tale of sad experiences, but he touched upon them only briefly and lightly. Then followed the inevitable silence as they all thought of their loss. Since the news of Mark's death, Ann had received a brief letter from the Captain of his company, expressing his great regret to have to be the conveyor of such sad news. He added that he could give no particulars except to say that a comrade of Mark's had seen him fall in one of the charges at Fredericksburg.

"Apparently," the Captain's letter concluded, "no one was able to identify your husband, so the Adjutant General's office will not be able to forward any of his personal belongings."

"I haven't seen much of you lately, Ann," said Nancy. "I know why, and I understand. But I've wanted to talk something over with you. Now that George is home—" she stopped because her voice was trembling so much —"and we have all the news we'll ever have of Mark, I think that we should have a memorial service for him."

George stood up and put his arm over his wife's shoulder: "Yes, my dear," he said, "we will. We'll talk with Mr. Belden about it tomorrow."

A week later the church at Jenkstown was packed with the friends and neighbors who came to do honor to the memory of Mark Wilson and, through him, to the living and the dead who fought to save the Union. Flags draped the pulpit as Timothy Belden rose to ask them to bow their heads in prayer. Gritting her teeth for self-control during the preliminary part of the service, Ann kept thinking of the time, not so long ago, when she and Mark had sat together almost in this same front pew and endured the hymns and the sermon until they could stand up together and be married.

What was life all about anyway? What was the use of living, she asked herself now.

Then she became conscious of the old man in the pulpit talking, and it seemed somehow that he was talking directly to her and to all the other tortured and worried hearts within the sound of his voice. Almost unconsciously she began to listen, and as the soothing, kindly voice of her old friend went on, she began to relax and to get some measure of comfort.

"We don't know why it is," the pastor said, "but mankind has always been afflicted with sorrow, and no doubt always will be as long as time shall last. We do know—and that is our comfort—that God is always on His throne and that He in His infinite wisdom has a plan; and if we can just have faith, some day we will have the answer. It will be the right one, and we will know that His plan, even though it brought us sorrow and suffering, was right. Don't forget that we here are not the only ones who suffer. Today, North and South, this is a stricken land. Thousands of families are having this cross to bear; thousands more will before the war is done. It seems an awful thing that men have to settle these great issues by the sword, but perhaps, just as the surgeon uses his knife, so God may use the awful instrument of war to bring about His purposes in the shortest time and with the least permanent cost.

"To me, God's purpose in permitting this awful war does seem plain. Our fathers believed that they had found something in this American democracy that was infinitely precious, far beyond the value of life itself. And they fought for it, just as Mark Wilson and his comrades fought and gave up their lives for it. What is this thing we call democracy? What is it our fathers thought they had? Is it just a meaningless high-sounding word?

"To answer it, take a look at the Old World before the landing of the Pilgrims. Slavery was world-wide; in most countries women were not much better than slaves; the home as we know it today did not exist; education was confined to monasteries and to a few in the upper classes; freedom of worship did not exist. Those who tried to worship according to their conscience were persecuted; there was little or no political freedom, government was based on 'the divine right of kings', which meant that the individual existed solely for the state, not the state for the individual. Might always made right, oppression and taxation stalked the land, privation and suffering were the common lot.

"Those were the conditions that the Pilgrims, the Puritans and the other New World emigrants left behind them. Do you wonder that they gloried in their new-found freedom, in the opportunity in the new air of a new world for the individual soul to flower? These first American settlers knew from actual bitter experience what they had escaped from in the Old World. They never forgot it, nor permitted their children to forget the blessing of liberty. That bitter experience and the glory of new-found freedom were common talk in every American household for generations. To our fathers, this America which we fought to preserve was a synonym for true religion founded on the fatherhood of God and the brotherhood of man. It was a synonym for political freedom, the right to elect or appoint their own leaders—and to put them out when they failed.

"That, my friends, is our heritage. That is what we are trying to preserve in driving slavery from the land and making this country truly free, one country undivided, with liberty and justice for all. With all of our suffering and tears, let us keep our faith in our cause and in God's wisdom shining here like the stars of a summer night."

The intensity went out of the earnest old voice. He paused, and then, speaking in the gentle tones that Ann knew so well, the minister continued:

"It is not my purpose to prolong the misery of those closest and dearest to Mark Wilson by eulogizing him. Sufficient to say that he was your friend and my friend, fine in every way, and he gave his life for our country. No man can do more."

CHAPTER XXVI

AFTER THE MEMORIAL SERVICE for Mark, Nancy brought up the question of her husband's going back to camp.

"It would seem," she said, with some asperity, "that this family has done and is doing enough without your making any more sacrifices."

George stared at his wife in some surprise.

"Have you forgotten, Nancy, that I am on parole? I'm supposed to be in the camp for parolees right this moment. When I told you about my escape, maybe I didn't make it plain that the commanding officer at Camp Parole suggested indirectly that I could try it, but he certainly didn't mean that I had any right to stay here. I must return to Camp Parole and wait until I am exchanged. And then I still have the rest of my term of enlistment to serve."

Nancy turned away, her shoulders drooping, and started to wash the dishes at the sink. But in a moment she turned around again, looking a little defiant, and said:

"Well, I suppose that means that you'll be leaving in a day or two?"

"Not quite so soon," he said, patiently. "But I certainly must within a week."

It seemed to Nancy in the next few days before George left that everything in the world had gone wrong. Mark's death, instead of drawing George and her closer, had created a situation where neither could ease the pain in their hearts by talking with the other. That George was suffering she had no doubt. She often heard him walking the kitchen floor at night after she and the rest of the family had gone to bed.

Going to the barn after something one day, she heard one of the most distressing sounds in the world, a strong man sobbing his heart out. When she found him, flat on his face on a pile of straw, she sat down beside him and lifted his head into her lap. As she gently stroked his head, George gradually grew calm, and at last the barriers were down and they again reached that closeness which is achieved all too rarely in a perfect union of two human souls. When they returned to the house, they both had a feeling of peace and renewed courage with which to withstand anything that might come.

That very night Ann came over, seeming a little more like her old self, and long after Nancy and the children had gone to bed she could hear the murmur of Ann and George's voices as they sat in the kitchen. Nancy finally fell asleep with the hope that Ann was unburdening her heavy heart to George, and that he could find the words to comfort her.

The next day, clothed in one of his old well-worn suits, but looking much better than when he had arrived, George went away again, and this time it seemed easier to Nancy to let him go because of the understanding between them and her feeling of faith that somehow God would bring him back to her.

George had little trouble in getting back to Camp Parole, and it amused him to think how much easier it was to get back into a camp or a jail than to get out of it. He reported immediately to Colonel Sangster who, to George's surprise, seemed more than ordinarily glad to see him. The reason was soon evident.

"Wilson," he said, "I think I have the toughest job in this whole Army. There are ten thousand parolees in this camp with absolutely nothing to do. If we permit them to do anything at all, even as much as clean up the camp, then the government feels they have broken their parole. The result is that the prolonged idleness makes for all sorts of trouble. The men are getting out of hand, and I'm almost at my wits' end."

He stopped speaking, and George waited to hear what this had to do with him.

"I know you were a band leader," continued the Colonel, "before you were captured."

George nodded.

"It may be some time before you are finally exchanged, and I'm going to set up a band here. I have already got the instruments, and my officers have found some musicians.

I want you to organize the band and see if plenty of music won't be of some disciplinary value with this unruly rabble I have on my hands."

Two days later, George found himself whipping a new band into shape, and one of the first concerts they gave was in front of Colonel Sangster's headquarters. When they marched up with a considerable flourish, playing "John Brown," Mrs. Sangster was sitting by her husband's side in front of the tent. She was the author of a song called "Marching Along," and as the band had just rehearsed it, George led them into the piece. They were rewarded by the shining eyes and flushed face of the lady, and by her enthusiastic compliments at the end of the concert. On George's suggestion, Mrs. Sangster then recited some of the words of the song, while the band accompanied her quietly in the background.

The Colonel's hope that the band would be helpful in entertaining the men was well justified. The band was kept playing a good part of the time; so much so, in fact, that they were often tired out at the end of a long day and evening. Often the whole camp of thousands of men would sing with the band as they played "John Brown's Body" or "Marching Along," or "Hell on the Rappahannock." Sometimes the band would play some of the old hymns and ballads that had been part of the home life of the soldiers in happier times. After they had sung a few of these, the men had less inclination for getting into mischief.

George himself never failed to be emotionally affected by the tremendous volume of so many men singing, and by all the music, particularly when it was followed at the end of the day by the trumpets in the band and the buglers blowing "Retreat" or "Lights Out."

* * *

At last spring came again, the spring of the fateful year of 1863, and again the armies were on the march. George and the members of his band had been exchanged and were back with the Army of the Potomac.

Dissatisfied with Burnside's defeat and failure at Fredericksburg, the President had replaced him with General Joe Hooker, and in the bright and beautiful days of early May, "Fighting Joe," as he was affectionately known to his soldiers, moved across the Rappahannock and up the river to meet Lee and his legions at Chancellorsville, only a short distance from Fredericksburg, that other fateful battlefield. But again the Confederate forces were victorious.

"Unless one has actually seen it," George wrote to Nancy, "he can never know the fear and panic engendered by seeing hundreds of men on the run. I saw the Eleventh Corps, who were surprised by Stonewall Jackson's men while they were cooking their rations or playing cards, come running down the road and over the fields like panicky sheep with dogs chasing them. Nothing could stop them! The cavalry—including Charlie's regiment—drew their swords and threatened the men, but they were deaf to any pleas, and dodged right between the horses and kept on running.

"It is being said that the officers, not the men, were to blame, and that the camp was not properly picketed. There's a lot of complaints and grumbling among the men. They think they are being sacrificed to inefficiency and mismanagement. And it looks that way when we lose battle after battle. But I feel sorry for that man in the White House. He must be pretty discouraged, for he keeps changing the generals, and the new ones seem to be no better than the old."

To the same letter, George added:

"Since writing the above, I have had an opportunity to visit Charlie. You would be proud of your young cavalryman, could you see him. His outfit takes pride in their martial appearance, and Charlie looked very fine indeed in his shining cavalry boots, his nicely fitting uniform, and with his erect, soldierly bearing.

"There's no love lost between the infantry and the cavalry. Some of the boys in the infantry claim that the cavalry are always picking fights with the Johnnies and then retreating to let the infantry fight it out. But when I remember these cavalrymen astride their horses, trying to stem the rout that I told you about in the first part of this letter, I conclude that the cavalry have their share of courage all right.

"You chided me a bit, Nancy, about my not writing much about my Army life. Well, I guess I'm not much of a letter-writer, and, anyway, a lot of the time Army life is pretty dull, just waiting. But I was thinking this morning that it's kind of interesting to see a great Army come awake in the morning. If you happen to be half awake, suddenly you hear the corps bugler, maybe quite a ways off, blowing 'Reveille.' Then, nearer at hand, the division bugler takes it up, followed by the bugler for the brigade, and then right near you the regimental bugler responds. Sometimes the drum and fife corps start up the noise, and once in a while they rout out the band in the early morning, and, in less time than it takes to tell it, the sleeping camp springs to life. In a well-disciplined Army there is something for every man to do—fires to start, breakfast to get ready, blankets to be aired and piled, and if you don't do it in a hurry the next bugle call will get you.

" 'Reveille' is soon followed by the 'doctor's call', which some boys have nicknamed 'quinine call.' How I hate the bitter stuff! But once in a while there's a malingerer who, even though he is perfectly well, apparently would rather take the quinine if it will release him from his duties or from going into a battle.

"After the bugler blows the 'doctor's call,' come the 'Guard Mount' and 'Drill Call.' And so it goes all day. We live by the drums and the bugle."

As Nancy read the letter days later, she thought, "Maybe it would be easier if there were some drums on the home front, too, or at least some music."

In another letter George spoke of the bitterness of the old veterans about the bounty jumpers:

"There are new men in the service who have enlisted for only one year and received as much as $650, while some of us veterans get little or nothing beyond our regular small monthly pay. Moreover, men are deserting, returning to some other northern community under different names and re-enlisting so they can get another bounty. It's a great evil, but fortunately the officers and the War Department are catching up with them. Yesterday I had a sad but necessary duty to perform. Our band led a sad procession to the place where seven men, who had been condemned by military court for jumping the bounty, were to be executed. Seven rude wooden coffins were placed in open Army wagons, and on each coffin rode one of the condemned men. At the head of the column we marched very slowly, playing the 'Dead March.' When the procession stopped, the coffins were removed from the wagons and each placed at the edge of an open grave, and the poor wretches again seated on them, facing a firing squad. The whole scene was framed in a hollow square of soldiers. An Army chaplain stepped forward and said a word of prayer. Then there was a dramatic silence while we all held our breath, our hearts in our throats. Suddenly came a single tap of a drum and with it the blast of the guns of the detail assigned for the task. The prisoners fell over, most of them right into their own coffins. Then we turned and marched away, playing a lively tune.

"I couldn't get the horrible scene out of my mind. It is necessary, but the trouble is it didn't happen where it would do the most good. What we need, Nancy, is some way to put the fear of God in the hearts of some of the Copperheads and even some of the indifferent citizens back home who are not taking this war seriously enough. Believe me, there's no doubt about its seriousness with us in the Army, nor with the officers, nor in the heart of our President. Abraham Lincoln is going through with this thing to the bitter end and the soldiers are with him. Traitors had better watch out!"

George had underscored this last part of his letter three times. Nancy laughed a little when she read it, and exclaimed:

"A body might think that George meant me. Just as if we home folks weren't worrying and working ourselves to death to win the war, too." But she knew that George fully realized that she and most of the home folks agreed with him, and when she answered his letter she said:

"Of course you're right, my dear. I feel just as strongly as you do about this traitor talk and resistance to the war effort on the part of some of the people here at home. Just last Sunday after church I heard Cora Cortright say they weren't going to get her Mert—or if they did, they'd pay plenty of bounty. Old man Cortright nodded his head in agreement. First time I've seen him at church in a dog's age. He mumbled something—I couldn't hear it all—but, apparently agreeing with Cora, said something like we should have let the South go in the first place; that if they wanted to have slaves, it was none of our business.

"Well, you'll be interested to know that the old fool got shut up mighty fast for once in his life. I wasn't the only one that heard what he said. Enoch Payne was there. Seems as though he's always around when he's needed. He just hopped all over Cortright, and most everybody else there nodded their heads. Enoch told him off all right. Said Mert was a coward or he would have been in the service long ago, and Enoch ended up by saying, 'I'd advise you to keep your mouth shut if you and your son both don't want to be run out of this town straddling a rail and wearing a coat of tar and feathers!'

"There are Copperheads around, too, only they're learning to keep quiet and work underneath. And there are a lot of others, not really Copperheads but like you said, they haven't woke up to know that Abe Lincoln and a lot of the rest of us mean business."

CHAPTER XXVII

IN THE WEEKS that followed Charlie Wilson's escape from the guerillas in the Morgan home, Charlie's memory of Jennie Morgan and her kindness never dimmed. So when "Uncle Joe" Hooker and the Army of the Potomac moved toward Chancellorsville, encompassing the Morgan home within the Union lines, Charlie's excitement knew no bounds, and he longed and constantly watched for the opportunity to renew his acquaintance with the Morgans. That opportunity came when Charlie's regiment was finally bivouacked in a field across the road from the Morgan homestead.

One warm evening late in April, just before the Battle of Chancellorsville, an explanation to his captain that the folks in the Morgan home had saved him from capture by the guerillas secured a pass for Charlie. With some hesitation he walked through the camp and across the road to the yard, where he was challenged by a blue-coated guard. Showing his pass, Charlie stopped to chat with the guard for a minute, asking why he was there. The man laughed.

"When I jined up," he said, "I never thought I'd be protectin' Johnny Reb property. But that's jest what I'm doin'. Have my orders to let no one bother these folks or take their belongin's." He turned to spit a long, yellow stream over the yard fence, and then added:

"Not that there's much prop'ty left to guard. The Johnny Rebs' own soldiers, 'specially the guerillas, have already taken 'bout everythin', I guess."

Charlie left him and continued along the path bordered by weeds. On reaching the steps that led to the big porch, he thought how different the surroundings looked in the daytime. The door was opened promptly to his knock and Jennie stood smiling before him.

"I thought you'd come," she said, offering him both hands, "and I knew it was you when you stopped to talk with the guard by the gate. Come in."

In the kitchen David Morgan looked up from his favorite
chair to say, rather gruffly:

"You here again?"

But by the twinkle in the blue eyes shining under the
shaggy white eyebrows, Charlie knew that the old man
wasn't really displeased.

"Yes, sir," he said, "we're bivouacked just across the
road, and I thought I'd come and pay my respects."

Still with a sly twinkle in his eyes, the grandfather said:

"How'd you get by the guard? Colonel Preston told me
we wouldn't be bothered by any Yanks."

"Now, Grandpa," remonstrated Jennie, "that's not very
nice." Then, turning to Charlie, she explained:

"Colonel Preston and some of his officers stayed overnight
here."

The wave of resentment that came over him at her mention
of the officers staying there surprised Charlie—or was it
jealousy, he wondered.

"Yes," said David Morgan, "I must say we've had better
treatment from the Yanks than we had from some of our own
folks. Your men have been careful to take nothing—except
what was left of our fences for their campfires. But the
Confederate guerillas," he added bitterly, "have robbed us
of everything."

Charlie said, impulsively:

"Gee! I hope you have enough to eat."

"Didn't till your men came," said the old man.

"That's right," said Jennie. "Your folks gave us a supply
of flour and beans and—"

Her grandfather interrupted:

"And coffee! The only decent coffee I've had in a year.
Sit down, young man!"

"Thank you," said Charlie, "but I can't stay. I've got to
get back to camp soon."

Without any comment Morgan pushed himself slowly and
painfully up from his chair, and, mumbling something about
work to do, left the kitchen. After his departure there was a
brief silence, and then Charlie said, dolefully:

"I wish I could stay longer."

Jennie came over and pulled a chair up beside his.

"Are you going to be around here long, Charlie?"

"We never know," he answered. "And, of course, I couldn't tell if I did know." Then, after a moment, he added:

"Maybe your General Lee can answer that question better than I can, or even our officers. But, Jennie, let's forget the war for a few minutes. I came over to tell you how many, many times I have thought about you and of how kind you were to me. You really saved my life, you know."

"Oh, no," she protested. "It was night anyway. You could probably have got away."

"Not after I came in here," he said, firmly. "If you hadn't hid me—"

She held up a hand, her face flushing:

"Please! Let's not talk about that!"

He laid his hand over hers, and said, earnestly:

"Time is short, Jennie, and I have to say quickly what maybe I'd take a long time in saying were conditions different. But, Jennie, I can't get you out of my mind—nor my heart," he added, simply and humbly.

"I've thought of you, too," Jennie said, softly. "But, Charlie, you know we shouldn't. What hope or chance have we of continuing our friendship?"

"This war isn't going to last for ever," he said, stoutly.

"Maybe not," she answered, sadly, "but the feelings it has started will last a long time. I'm a Southerner. I wouldn't be welcomed by northern folks. And, anyway, we live a long, long way apart."

Charlie pulled his chair around to face her, and, leaning over, took both of her hands in his. She made no effort to free them. For a long moment they looked earnestly into each other's eyes, and it almost seemed as if each was looking into the other's soul. Jennie's soft, lovely lips trembled a little.

"Jennie," said Charlie, finally, "I've always wondered what love was. Now I know. I love you."

"And I do you," she cried, releasing her hand to lay it against his face. "But you'll go away; you'll have to go away; and I'll never see you again."

"No," he said, "if you'll wait, I'll come back. Nothing can stop me from coming. We are meant for each other and nothing can keep us apart. For a time, yes," he amended, "but there's nothing in the world so strong as my love for you."

He stood up, pulling her gently to her feet and holding her close to him. As their lips met, war, hate and all the troubles of mankind dissolved for them, leaving nothing but love.

Charlie was able to see Jennie but once more, and that was only for a few moments after Hooker's disastrous defeat at Chancellorsville. He and the rest of the cavalry were kept busy scouting to see what Lee was going to do next. They found that Lee's whole Army was moving North again, and on June 11 the bugles sounded "Pack Up" through the camp, and the Army of the Potomac started back toward the North after Lee, always making sure to stay between him and the city of Washington.

Day after day during most of that hot month of June, the Army plodded after Lee. Never in his life had Charlie been so tired. At the end of each long day, he almost fell out of his saddle, took care of his horse, ate his rations and fell instantly asleep in his blanket, only to be aroused at daybreak the next morning by the bugles and drums, climb in his saddle, and ride wearily on. The foot soldiers complained bitterly of thirst and the heat, and the road was lined with baggage which the men had refused to carry farther.

The infantry complained that the cavalry could ride while they had to walk, but it seemed to Charlie that the complaints should be the other way around. For every mile that the infantry advanced, the cavalry had to go two, for theirs was the reconnaissance job, to ride this way and that, in order that Hooker might have some information as to where Lee was going and what he was up to.

On June 18 the Army camped on the old Bull Run battlefield. It was late in the evening and dark when Charlie, numb with exhaustion, threw his blanket down, and, using his saddle for a pillow, lay down to sleep. But tired as he was, somehow he couldn't get comfortable. His blanket felt lumpier than usual, and finally, sitting up in the dark, he rolled part of the blanket over to get at the stick that he thought was bothering him. Then suddenly he jumped to his feet, realizing that he held in his hand a human bone. He shivered, started to throw it, and then, recovering himself, laid it down carefully and with respect, thinking of the strangeness of life. Only a short time before, he reflected, that bone had been part of a man, a young man, probably; a man who had lived and loved and walked the earth with the same feelings, the same sensations as himself.

"No wonder I couldn't sleep," he thought. "But I ought to be used to this sort of thing by now."

Then shaking himself and with a shrug of his shoulders he rolled up his blanket, picked up his saddle, and moved to another spot.

Both the infantry and cavalry grumbled at what seemed to be unnecessarily long and forced marches, but some of the grumbling let up as it became generally known that the reasons for the haste were to keep the Army between Washington and the Confederates, so that the old fox Lee could not suddenly turn and descend on the capitol, and to thwart his apparent determination to invade the North. When the cavalrymen finally discovered that Lee had moved westward over the Blue Mountain Ridge, and that therefore his objective was not Washington, Hooker's job became a little easier.

On June 25, after a long march, the Army halted in the vicinity of several large plantations. Immediately the bands struck up a lively tune, and then, to the delight of the soldiers, hundreds of negroes—men, women and children—came pouring out of their cabins, jumping up and down, yelling and shouting with joy. The music delighted them, and perhaps, too, they were beginning to absorb the fact that Abe Lincoln's Proclamation of Emancipation had made them free. As Charlie sat on his horse, one leg thrown over the cantle, and watched the negroes, he thought about the future of these black folks, though not very clearly. What happens, he asked himself, when a people who have been completely dependent on others are suddenly given complete responsibility for their own acts?

Days later, riding with his unit on the flanks of the Union Army near Frederick in Maryland, Charlie saw something swinging in the wind from a tree. Curious, he spurred his horse nearer and then wished he hadn't. It was the body of a man, his face horribly contorted by his awful death. Awed, chilled, and yet fascinated by the sight, Charlie continued to gaze until Sergeant Miller drew up alongside him:

"Not a pleasant sight, Charlie," he said, "but necessary. He was a spy. There was no doubt about it, and the officers weren't long in tryin' him and stringin' him up."

As they turned their horses and left the grizzly scene, Charlie, remembering Mark's experience, said:

"Sergeant, how can you be so sure that sometimes a mistake isn't made, particularly when a man is tried and hanged so fast?"

"No mistake!" replied Miller. "The Captain told me that this fellow was caught red-handed, and that the evidence at the court-martial showed that he was an old offender."

Charlie shivered.

"I still don't quite see it," he said. "He was a young man. The war will be over some time, we hope. Why couldn't he have been sentenced to prison just as well?"

The sergeant pulled his horse to a stop and turned a sharp eye on Charlie. Taking off his cavalry cap, he ran his fingers through his heavy, unkempt hair, matted with sweat and dust.

"You're pretty young yourself, Wilson, but it seems as if you've been around this Army long enough to know better than to say a thing like that. Don't you know enough to realize that one spy can be responsible for the death of hundreds and even thousands of us, or even the defeat of our Army? This is war. It's his life against ours, and he knew that when he took the chance."

Miller clapped his cap back on his head, kicked his horse, and they rode on. Then, realizing that he had been somewhat rough, Miller added:

"Know how you feel. Didn't like that sight myself. But that's the way war is."

Charlie nodded, and Miller changed the subject.

"Old Foxy Lee certainly got fooled by his reception here in Maryland. He thought the folks were all goin' to rise up and call him blessed; even issued a proclamation."

"Yeah!" agreed Charlie. "I heard about it. He told the Marylanders that he was going to 'deliver them from the Yankee yoke' and appealed to the young men to join up with him."

"But they didn't take him up on it!" laughed Miller.
"And, by golly, it does me good to hear these folks cheer
as we ride along. Remember yesterday when we stopped for
that breather? How the women came running out with
water and cookies when our band struck up 'John Brown.'
One of them actually handed me a bouquet—" he straightened up in his saddle and pounded his chest— "me, Hank
Miller, a bouquet of posies! Maybe she'd even have kissed
me if I'd leaned down a little!"

Charlie grinned but said nothing. He was thinking that
all of them had certainly got enough of the other sort of
thing, and it seemed good to be among friendly civilians.

Around the campfires that night the news ran through the
camp that Joe Hooker was out and General George G.
Meade had been appointed to succeed him. Charlie Wilson
listened to the grumbling of his comrades, and he, too, was
disturbed by the apparent confusion and lack of confidence
in the leadership, and was inclined to agree with the general
sentiment. The men vigorously criticized the constant changing of their generals, and the fact that they had to follow
and fight under generals in whom the War Department
seemed to have no continued confidence.

However, the old veterans were somewhat reassured later
when General Meade addressed the Army and said in part:
"The country looks to this Army to relieve it from the
devastation and disgrace of a hostile invasion."

Listening to him, Charlie couldn't help remembering that
old David Morgan, Jennie's grandfather, had expressed the
same sentiments about the Yankee invasion of Virginia.

In concluding his brief statement, Meade said:
"It is with just diffidence that I relieve in command of this
Army an eminent and accomplished soldier (Joe Hooker)
whose name must ever appear conspicuous in the history of
its achievements; but I rely on the hearty support of my
companions in arms to assist me in the discharge of the duties
of the important trust which has been confided to me."

On June 30, Charlie camped with the cavalry near the
little Pennsylvania town of Emmitsburg and was overjoyed
to have a visit from his father. After exchanging greetings
and whatever information each had from home, George
laughed ruefully about the demoralized condition of his band

after the long, punishing march from Virginia to Pennsylvania in pursuit of Lee.

"Our big drum is gone," he said. "Both heads are busted. So is the snare drum, and you can't blow a note through half of our smaller instruments.

"I don't know what you've heard, Charlie," he continued, in a lower tone, "but I'm violating no confidence when I tell you that something big is afoot. They say that Lee has turned on us and we'll soon be in a fight which may be the most important of the whole war. If he defeats us then, he'll be free to continue his invasion of the North, to capture Harrisburg and Philadelphia, and maybe bring the war to an end."

On that momentous note father and son shook hands, George to return to his band, and Charlie to sleep, if he could.

CHAPTER XXVIII

NEXT MORNING, Charlie woke soaked to the skin. It had poured all night, and now was coming down harder than ever. Fires built to boil their coffee smoked and sputtered in the rain and mostly refused to do anything but smolder.

Tired, sullen, and depressed, the men finally found themselves in the saddle and on the move again. With heads down and shoulders hunched against the driving rain, opening their mouths only to growl at one another, the long columns of men on horseback moved slowly North again. Suddenly every cavalryman straightened up as one man. Without orders, they pulled their horses to a stop to listen, every sense alert. Yes, there was no mistake. They had heard right. From the North came a distant, steady, ominous rumbling. No, it wasn't thunder; these veterans had heard it too many times to be mistaken; it was cannon. Charlie shivered and thought of his father's words: "Something big is afoot."

Still without spoken orders but as if by common consent, the troop pushed on at a trot toward that fearful rumble constantly growing louder. Sergeant Miller, moving up the column a little faster than the rest, pulled his horse alongside Charlie's. Drawing his arm across his face to clear it of water, he grunted out of the side of his mouth:

"Guess this is it, Wilson. General Reynolds up there got his cavalry too close to Lee's tail for the old fox's comfort, so he's had to change his mind about goin' on to Harrisburg and is tryin' to drive Reynolds back. Leastwise, that's the word that's comin' down the line."

"Where we at?" asked Charlie.

"A little town called Gettisville or Gettysburg, or somethin' like that. Never heard of it before."

The sergeant pulled a plug of greasy, wet tobacco out of a hip pocket, put it between his teeth and worried it back

and forth until he had pried loose a good-sized chunk. After
getting the cud stowed in one side of his mouth, he grumbled
around it:

" 'Tain't so good for our boys, neither. 'Cordin' to what
I hear, Reynolds has been killed, an' our men are bein'
chased back through the village."

Suddenly the sergeant pointed:

"Look there!"

Charlie turned to look and saw through the rain, inching
down the Emmitsburg Road, a strange, motley procession of
civilians, some with a horse hitched to a buggy, some with
teams on farm wagons, many afoot, women, children and old
men. In the vehicles, piled helter-skelter, was every manner
of household furniture, cooking utensils, and even farm tools.
One old man was leading a cow, or trying to, for just as they
got close to the Sergeant and Charlie, the cow laid down.
The men laughed to see the old man push and pull frantically
to get the animal on her feet again. Finally, a kindly cavalryman swung his horse around ahead of the cow and fastened
the lead rope to his saddle. Then, with the old man pushing
and yelling behind and the horse pulling ahead, the mulish
animal was forced to her feet, while every nearby soldier
stopped to watch, cheer and laugh. Cannon and death just
over the horizon were momentarily forgotten.

Though inclined to find scared civilians amusing at first,
the soldiers soon grew grave. Here were their own country-
men, women, children and old men, forced from their homes
into the storm because of an enemy invader. As he thought
of this, Charlie thought that that must be exactly the way
the Southerners felt when the "damyanks," as they called
them, were overrunning their beloved home country. Maybe,
thought Charlie, that's one reason why the Confederates
are fighting so hard; they feel they're fighting to preserve
their homes and their way of life. "There's nothing like
having the same experience to make you know how the
other fellow feels," he thought.

Watching the panic-stricken refugees, Charlie pondered on
the lack of reason and judgment when people are scared.
Then in all honesty he reminded himself how frightened he
had been, and how unreliable was his own judgment at the
beginning of a battle. Probably all of the men felt the same

way, he reflected, and maybe the only thing that saved them from the disgrace of bolting was their greater fear of what the other men would think if they failed in a crisis. Now as he looked at his comrades to see what effect the sad procession was having on them, he saw them straighten in their saddles, and urge on their horses; and he realized that the men had a renewed sense of patriotism, and a better realization of why they were there and why they were fighting. Patriotism became something visible for them, something for which men, if need be, fought and died.

It still rained. Every time Charlie moved, more water ran down his back. Forced off the road by the fleeing refugees and their vehicles, the cavalrymen rode through the roadside ditches and adjoining fields. The whole countryside was soon trampled by the Army into a vast sea of mud, horses' hooves often making a loud plop as they pulled their feet up out of the engulfing mess.

At dusk on July 1, Charlie's regiment came within sight of the village of Gettysburg. The fighting was over for the day. All knew that it had been a bad one for the Federals. The Confederate troops had driven them through the village to a long slope or low ridge to the south and east of the village known as Cemetery Ridge. Across the wide valley on a smaller, partly-wooded ridge were the Southerners.

As Charlie's regiment rode forward, they could see on their left, not a hundred yards distant, a hundred twinkling campfires of the Southerners, over which they were cooking and eating their suppers and paying not the slightest attention to the Union troops riding within easy range of their guns. Turning off from the Emmitsburg Road, the troops rode in back of Cemetery Ridge, dismounted, picketed the horses, rubbed them down, fed them the meagre supply of grain, and then, with great effort, built their own fires to make a pan of hot coffee to wash down their hardtack.

A little later, standing on the rocky escarpment known as Round Top that rises above Cemetery Ridge, Charlie looked across the wide valley to the campfires of the enemy still twinkling on the other side, and then back toward Gettysburg at the long line of Union campfires, now dying down to beds of coals, and around which lay thousands of Federal troops waiting for the morrow. It was quiet. On that July night, even the Confederates knew that while they had been successful in the first day's fighting, it was only the beginning, and only God knew what the final answer would be.

Someone laid a hand on Charlie's shoulder. Startled, he swung around with an exclamation.

"Take it easy, boy. Don't be so jumpy," said his friend, Sergeant Miller. "I jest came up here to look, too. Prob'ly we're thinkin' 'bout the same thing. Notice them Johnnies at their supper as we came in?"

"Yes, I did."

"Know what I thought?"

Charlie made no answer, knowing that none was expected. The sergeant went on:

"I sort of wondered what it's all about. Them boys over there are jest like us. They've got mothers an' sisters an' sweethearts back home, prob'ly."

Charlie's mind leaped to Jennie and he thought how surprised Miller would be if he knew that he was in love with a Southerner.

But Miller was paying little attention to whether Charlie answered him or not.

"Yeah!" he continued. "They eat an' they drink an' they sleep. Some of 'em are stinkers, jest like some of our boys are, but by an' large they're just the same as us. So how did we ever get into this hellish mess where we're shootin' at each other? I don't hate 'em—do you?"

Charlie shook his head.

"Look down there now. Remember that peach orchard we saw when we were coming in? There was a piece of wheat, too, just ready to be cut before we marched through it. There was pastures with cattle grazin'. I even saw where a farmer had got some hay cocked up in the field 'fore he left in a hurry."

Miller stopped, running out of words.

"Why the hell don't you say somethin'?" he growled.

"What is there to say?" Charlie replied, quietly. "I agree with you. I don't know what it's all about. That's not quite right, though. I do know, but now that we're in this mess we've got to fight our way out. What bothers me is why the big boys got us into war in the first place. Why couldn't they have settled things some way without our having to kill each other?''

"Yeah!" said Miller, "that's what I was tryin' to say."

He stopped to spit, and in the half light Charlie could see his jaw going vigorously on his cud of tobacco.

"I'll tell you one thing, bub. You think you've seen some fightin'. From what I hear, an' from the way these armies are lined up, it looks like we're all here, the whole kit and caboodle! Over there's the whole Army of Virginia, an' over here's the whole Army of the Potomac. Tomorrow's goin' to be quite a day! An' for some of us there ain't goin' to be any more tomorrows!''

Charlie could hear him mumbling to himself as he left abruptly and went off down the slope to find his blankets and a place to sleep.

* * *

The sun always pops up early over the horizon on a clear July day in Gettysburg, and July 2, 1863, was no exception. But the 85,000 men under General George G. Meade—who had succeeded Joe Hooker as Commander of the Army of the Potomac—and Robert E. Lee's 80,000 Confederates were up even before the sun. From the start of that second day's battle at Gettysburg, it seemed that every man on both sides fought as if he somehow knew that on the result of this one battle depended the success of the whole bloody war.

It was a part of Lee's strategy, while keeping his front lines busy, to get his cavalry around the flanks of the Union Army and come at the Federals from the back as well as the front, thus catching them in a gigantic trap. But it didn't work out that way, for one reason because the Union cavalry, including Charlie Wilson's regiment, were able to check the Confederate horsemen and drive them back. So busy were Charlie and his comrades with their own fighting that day that they knew nothing of the deadly conflict raging in the long, gently sloping farm valley that lay between Cemetery and Seminary ridges. But at last, when the long twilight of the summer day had faded, Charlie got some small idea of what had happened on that day of horror as he wandered from one group to another and listened as the men clung together, whispering or talking in low tones as if afraid to face their thoughts alone. Some sat saying nothing, stunned by what they had seen and heard.

Knowing that the bandsmen were working with the field hospitals, Charlie searched for his father and came after a while to Rock Creek, where some of the field hospitals had been set up near a supply of water. Here they had brought all of the wounded from this section of the battle where much of the fighting had occurred during the day. Like the stacks of wood that Charlie had helped to split and pile back home, the dead were corded in piles. They had been dead when the ambulances brought them to the tents where the surgeons worked, or had died there under the surgeons' knives. All through the meadow that bordered this little creek, other dead lay where they had fallen, so thick that it was hard to walk without stepping on them.

In the tents the surgeons had put up tables, and, with shirts off and bare arms covered with blood to the shoulders, they were still hard at work, throwing amputated arms and legs into constantly growing piles just outside the tent doors. Paralyzed with horror, Charlie stood watching and saw one of the doctors suddenly throw up his arms and sit down.

"In God's name!" he muttered, "what can doctors do when men kill and maim each other like this!" Exhausted, he sat down with slack mouth open, hands dangling at his side, fingers dripping blood.

Another doctor spoke gently to a boy on the operating table who was yelling with pain.

"Breathe deep, son. This will help."

It was chloroform, and as the boy grew quiet, the surgeon muttered:

"Thank God for this, anyway."

Already the awful stench of flesh decaying in the hot weather was sickening and overpowering, like a rotting dead horse or cow at home, only worse, much worse, Charlie thought. He kept moving. At last he found his father. He, too, was shirtless and covered with blood. By the smoky lanterns Charlie saw how pale and tired he looked. He was busy moving the wounded to and from the surgeons' tables, and had little time to talk.

"Thank God you're safe, son," he said. "Maybe the worst is over."

"Not yet," said Charlie. "Neither side's won. The boys all say this is to be a fight to a finish. Tomorrow will be another day."

"Yes," said George, wiping the sweat from his forehead and leaving bloody streaks, "tomorrow will be another day, but the officers say that the issue was really decided today."

He turned to help another worker carry a moaning boy into the tent, and Charlie started back to his own company to get what sleep he could.

The next morning, the hot July sun again climbed over the eastern horizon to find the great armies already astir. All that morning Charlie watched the galloping horses of the cannoneers—urged to ever greater speed by the kicking, yelling riders on each team—haul the rolling, rumbling, rocking cannon, each with its attached caisson and clinging men, dashing to get into position on Cemetery Ridge. When approximately located, the horses were unhitched and rushed away to haul up another big gun, while the cannoneers cut the caisson loose and placed the gun in exact position. Across the death valley, the Confederates lined up 150 cannon on Seminary Ridge, as against the Federals' eighty heavy guns (all that Meade could find room for). The Union guns were located a little back of the front lines, ranging from Cemetery Hill to Little Round Top.

Anticipating what was to come, the Union infantry worked frantically to build stone walls and entrenchments. Suddenly it seemed to Charlie that all the noise in all the world was centered in that one spot as the batteries of both armies opened fire. The very ground shivered and shook as in an earthquake. Looking around, he noticed that the men stood with their mouths open. He opened his and knew why. It helped to ease the strain on his eardrums.

Added to the din and roar of the cannon was the noise of the bursting shells and the screams of the wounded when occasionally a shell from a Confederate gun landed squarely on a Union battery, throwing metal and human debris into the air. Sergeant Miller, who stood beside Charlie, said something to him, but the only way that Charlie knew that he was talking was because he could see his lips moving. Then Miller moved closer and leaned over to shout in the boy's ear:

"This is only the beginning," he yelled. "The hellions hope to paralyze us. But we'll show 'em. When this stops, watch out!"

It did stop, but not until after two hours of the mightiest artillery dual in history. The firing suddenly stopped. There was time for the men to eat—but no one was hungry. The men said little, and when they did speak it was almost in a whisper. It was so quiet that Charlie found himself walking on tiptoe.

"It's like waiting for the end of the world, for doomsday," he thought, and he knew that for thousands of them it *was* doomsday.

Then down the long Union line, men began to stir, rolling out of the depressions and standing up back of the breastworks. They scanned the other ridge, and, sure enough, there was soon something to see. Across the valley in the woods and brush on Seminary Ridge there was movement. Out from the brush came a long line, so far away that the men looked like pygmies. Down the gentle slope the line moved briskly. Back of the first line was another, and back of that still another, the lines merging into one oncoming mass—eighteen thousand veterans of Lee's best, the flower of the Confederacy, under General George E. Pickett. Miller spoke in an undertone:

"This is it, Charlie! This is it!"

Charlie shivered. Paralyzed with fear, he wanted to run backwards, get on his horse, and ride away from there. Instead, he stood watching that army in gray coming toward them. Its advance seemed as relentless as time itself. Nothing could stop them, nothing. This was indeed the end—doomsday.

Then the tumult and noise broke loose again with the boom of Union artillery. It took but a moment for the gunners to shorten the range and guide the guns on those advancing lines, and soon the shells began to fall among the men. They left gaps, but the men in gray never faltered. The gaps were closed again and again, and on and on they came, now so close that Charlie could see their grim faces.

Up and down the Union line sounded the constant crackle and roar of rifles, merged with the artillery in one tremendous roar. There were more gaps in the Rebel lines now, and they were perceptibly shorter. After all, thought Charlie, there must be limits to what those men can take. Watching them through the eddying smoke, he saw that the line formation was gone. They were merged into an unorganized crowd. Still they kept coming on, now at the double. Then the men in gray were over the walls and on them.

Charlie was in there with the rest, swinging his saber, fighting hand to hand, all fear forgotten, mad with battle lust to kill and kill and kill. Suddenly, a smoke-blackened graycoat appeared in front of Charlie, his pistol aimed directly at him. The next moment the man in gray didn't seem to have any head. He reeled backwards and was gone. Glancing sideways, Charlie saw Sergeant Miller, his saber dripping, turn to meet another antagonist.

Then as suddenly as the men in gray had come over the wall, they were gone, killed or literally thrown back over the breastworks. What was left of them could be seen drifting in little groups of two or three down across the valley strewn with the dead and back up the slope of Seminary Ridge. Pickett's Charge was over, and also the Battle of Gettysburg.

That night, as if Heaven would wash out the horrid stains made by fighting men, it rained so hard that Rock Creek became a flood and overflowed its banks. Hundreds of the wounded, before they could be moved, were drowned. That night, also, Robert E. Lee gathered his broken forces and began the sad trek back to his own Virginia, while the Union forces lay still and licked their own wounds, too shattered themselves to follow Lee and finish the war.

CHAPTER XXIX

PERHAPS BECAUSE NANCY had grown more used to the war, or because she was driven so hard by the necessity of keeping her family fed and clothed, the summer and fall of 1863 somehow got by without her worrying as much as she had in the first years of the war. When she realized this, she thought of Mark and wondered if she were getting hardened to grief.

"Maybe there's a limit," she thought, "to what a woman can stand. After that limit is reached, nothing much matters."

It helped that Tom was a little older and able to take more of the responsibility for the outdoor work. Enoch Payne was just as helpful as ever, although it was getting more and more difficult for Nancy to get him to accept any pay for his services.

The crops weren't so good. Nancy knew that it doesn't take long for a farm to go backwards when the hand of the master is absent. But still the family had managed to get in some of the most necessary crops, and the two cows had calved. They were raising a nice heifer, and she planned to butcher the bull calf in the fall for meat for the family.

Hardest of all for Nancy to take was Ann's behavior. She no longer seemed to care about anything. Once in a while she got the mail and brought a letter from George or Charlie home to Nancy. Sometimes she would stay to listen while Nancy read the letter aloud, but as often as not, before Nancy was halfway through it, she would slip quietly out of the door and they wouldn't see her again for some time.

This happened when she brought Nancy a letter from George in which he described in some detail the Battle of Gettysburg. When Nancy got the letter, in spite of her horror as she read of the awful carnage, she was happy that her husband and Charlie had come through safely. She was filled with a feeling of optimism as a result of the victory of the Union forces. After all, Lee had failed in his great invasion, the enthusiasm of the North had been revived, and maybe this *was* the beginning of the end.

But this time, also, before Nancy had finished reading the letter, Ann turned from her and dashed away. What did one battle more or less mean to her? Her husband was dead.

To Ann it seemed that the farm this year was just about in the same "don't-care" mood that she was. She had managed to plant the crops, but they had not done well, not only because of the poor season but because she had not planted or cared for them with the same care and enthusiasm that she had at first. Even her mother's constant worrying and nagging about the farm and the likelihood of their losing it made little impression on her. When she thought at all, she just felt numb. Why struggle and worry? Nothing could happen worse than what had happened.

Even when her mother began to hint that maybe the answer to their problem, the way to get a little security, was for Ann to be kinder to Henry Bain, Ann didn't argue. Maybe that *was* the way to save the farm, she thought. What difference did it make now?

As for Henry, he played his cards well. He was a frequent caller, always kind and thoughtful, and careful not to be too personal or to annoy Ann in any way. Occasionally he took her for a ride, and she went in the same apathetic mood in which she did everything else, and as much to please her mother and get a little peace at home as for any other reason.

Gradually, almost without realizing it, Ann began to depend on Henry's kindness. She no longer felt close to Nancy, because Nancy and all of her old friends reminded her so poignantly of her grief that she preferred to avoid them. Two or three times in her despair she thought of going to Pastor Belden for help. But there again she felt that he couldn't help, because she would be thinking all the time that it was he who had married her to Mark.

Quick to note that Ann seemed to be a little easier, a little more like herself when Henry was there, her mother stepped up her sly campaign to break down Ann's resistance. She even let Henry know that she quite approved of his attentions to her daughter.

On one of Ann's rides with Henry in the middle of October,

he took her to the top of a ridge. After tying his horse, they walked a short distance from the road and stopped to admire the view and the fall coloring of the maples and the other hardwoods. The sun was warm. As she listened to Henry's talk, looked across the countryside blazing with color and heard the drowsy undertone of insect life, Ann felt more relaxed and more at peace than she had been in a long, long time. She sat down, and Henry sank down beside her. Taking her hand, he said, tenderly:

"Ann, my dear, I just can't bear to see you and your mother so worried about security, about your farm. This afternoon I brought you up here not only to see these beautiful woods, but to tell you that, look in any direction you wish, all these woods and lands belong to me. I know that you don't love me, but I love you. I have for a long, long time. Mark is gone. Marry me. Maybe in time you'll learn to love me. In the meantime, I'm sure I can make things easy for you, for your mother, and for your father when he comes back."

As he talked, Ann withdrew her hand and drew a little apart from him. Inside her a little voice seemed to be saying: "The devil taketh him up into an exceeding high mountain and sheweth him all the kingdoms of the world and the glory of them. And sayeth unto him, 'All these things will I give thee if thou wilt fall down and worship me'."

Then, ashamed of such an unkind thought, Ann forgot all the things to Henry's discredit, remembering only how kind he had been to her and her mother. She drew closer to him again, reached for his hand, and said:

"Henry, don't think I am ungrateful. I have come to depend on you more and more, but it's true that I don't love you. I never can love another man."

"Never is a long time," he interrupted.

"Maybe so, but that will be true for me."

Turning to look directly into his eyes, she continued:

"Henry, I just don't care what happens to me. But I do care about Mother and Dad. If you are sure you know just how I feel, I will marry you and try to be a good wife to you."

Exultantly he jumped to his feet, pulling her up with him, and took her in his arms, pressing his mouth to hers. But even in his ardor he felt the coldness of the lips that met his, the lack of response. After standing it as long as she could, Ann stepped back, cold shivers running up and down her spine. She felt more alive than she had since the news of Mark's death had come, not in response to Henry's caresses, but because of a complete physical aversion to them. Then, her indifference returning, she thought:

"I can stand even that. Maybe I'll get used to it. Anyway, Mother'll be pleased."

Sensing her mood, Henry took her hand and led her back to the buggy. That night Ann told her mother. Mrs. Clinton couldn't restrain her satisfaction.

"Oh, I'm so glad!" she said. "Now we'll all be taken care of."

Then she made a mistake.

"Even if Mark had come back—" she began, but got no further, for her daughter jumped to her feet and, in a low voice, said:

"Never say a thing like that to me again!" Brutally frank, she continued:

"You might as well know that I don't love Henry Bain. I'll never love him. I'm marrying him for your sake and to save this damned farm—and you know it!"

Almost frightened by Ann's vehemence, her mother was wise enough to hold her peace. All she said was:

"When?"

"Tomorrow," snapped Ann. "The sooner the better. Let's get it over with. Another thing," she continued, "I want no fuss. You're not to tell anyone until we get back. We're going to Ithaca and find a Justice of the Peace."

Mrs. Clinton said no more. On the surface she was quiet and a little subdued; inwardly she was jubilant.

The next day in Ithaca, Ann and Henry Bain stood before a shirt-sleeved stranger and were married. Only the Justice's wife and another stranger were present for witnesses. As Ann repeated the vows, they seemed to choke her, and she had a desperate and fearful longing to turn and run away from there, away from everybody.

They ate supper that day in Ithaca, and then took a room in the local hotel. Henry excused himself and was gone for a long time. Ann was glad to be alone, dreading his return, but couldn't help thinking that his absence was strange. Now she remembered Enoch Payne's story of his experience in Ithaca with the Copperheads, and the gossip that she had almost forgotten that Henry Bain—her husband—had for a long time now made frequent trips to Ithaca and was a leader of the Copperheads.

Awaiting and dreading his return, Ann's feeling of indifference and apathy gave way to fear that she had made a terrible mistake. Had she in trying to settle some of her problems not added the worst one of all? Then she shrugged her shoulders, lapsed back into indifference, and muttered aloud:

"What do I care? What's done is done. Nothing, not even this, matters. Nothing can ever really touch me again."

Sinking into the old hotel chair, worn threadbare by the guests of a quarter century, Ann closed her eyes and waited with neither anticipation nor fear for her husband's return.

* * *

As if to justify Mrs. Clinton's hopes in Ann's marriage to Henry, the Clinton farm now took on a new life and activity. The crops were harvested. New stock and enough hay to feed them were moved from one of Henry Bain's other farms to the Clinton barns. Henry, after moving to the Clinton home, had immediately taken over the full management of the farm along with his many other activities.

Since her marriage, Ann had gotten completely out of touch with Nancy and the other Wilsons and their activities. In fact, she no longer went to the post office or store, and avoided former friends and neighbors, quick to sense their coldness and antagonism.

Nancy had been profoundly shocked when she heard that Ann had married Henry Bain, the most hated man in the entire community. What Nancy didn't realize at first was that Ann had been so stunned by Mark's death and the whole impact of the war, plus her mother's constant nagging and worrying about the farm, that she had married Henry Bain as an escape. When Nancy's insight finally made her reach this conclusion, she sighed deeply, knowing full well that it was no escape, and that Ann, still young, would before long recover from the shock she had had, and would then realize that in marrying Bain she had made a dreadful mistake that would eventually bring her a greater sorrow.

Although it hurt Nancy deeply that Ann never came to see her any more, she understood why. She knew that Ann felt that none of the Wilsons would ever understand why she had married Bain. But Nancy did understand. What was hard to do was to write George and tell him that their beloved Ann was now lost to them because she had married the man they knew to be a stinker. While neither Enoch Payne nor Mary Curtis, frequent visitors at the Wilson home, dealt in gossip, yet both of them well knew what was thought and talked about in that part of the county, and it was natural for them to pass this on to Nancy. So from them and from other friends she knew how much Henry Bain was hated and despised, not only because he had continued to profit at other people's expense during the war and had failed to take any part in or give any support to the war, but especially because they now knew that he was actually giving aid and comfort to the enemy. Nancy wondered how much Ann knew of this, and hoped, for Ann's sake, that she knew nothing of it.

As for Ann, she was unaware of Henry's activities, for he was very close-mouthed at home. In the months that followed their marriage late in the fall of 1863, he was frequently absent on business, sometimes overnight, but never offered any explanation to his wife or to anyone else. The neighbors now knew with certainty that he was not only a Copperhead but an active leader, and that during his absences from home he was in Ithaca, planning and leading traitorous activities. At one time during the winter he was gone an entire week to New York City, that hotbed of anti-Lincoln, anti-Union sentiment and Copperhead activity.

When, after a mild question or two as to where he had been, he had told Ann it was none of her business where he went, she shrugged it off, as she did everything else, and told herself that she didn't want to know. What he did was a matter of utter indifference to her. What she couldn't ignore, however, was his attitude around home. Here his true nature was beginning to show itself. Ann could stand Henry's arrogant bossing of everything about the farm outdoors. After all, she was glad to be rid of that responsibility. What she resented most was his changed attitude toward her mother. He no longer made any attempt to be considerate or even polite to her. Often when Mrs. Clinton was speaking, he would interrupt her, and once he had told her to stop talking so much. Ann couldn't help thinking that she had married Henry mainly to give her mother some peace and security and to make it easier for her, and now she began to wonder what would happen when her Dad got home.

Harder still to take was Henry's attitude toward herself. It was easy enough to think that nothing mattered, that she had known when she married him that she didn't love him and so what could she expect, but it rankled just the same. He had been so kind before they were married and now he was neither kind nor considerate. Maybe she was to blame. In her most honest moments, she admitted that she was no true wife to Henry. Fight herself as she constantly did, tell herself that he had certain rights, she could not help her whole being rebelling against their relationship, nor prevent cold chills from chasing up and down her spine every time Henry laid even a possessive finger on her.

As they got to know each other better in the intimacy of home and of marriage, she grew more and more annoyed by little habits and idiosyncrasies which, had she loved him, would have gone unnoticed or been completely discounted. She began to do considerable worrying as to whether her forced toleration wasn't rapidly curdling into an intense hatred.

Henry wasn't long in realizing his wife's coldness, but in his complete egotism he felt sure that what she or any woman needed was to be made to realize that a husband was the boss. Sure, Ann had told him when she consented to marry him that she didn't love him, but it mattered not at all to him how she felt. It was a man's feelings and needs that mattered, he said to himself. Any man, and particularly a man of his ability and means, needed a wife, and that was that. In time he would drive the foolishness out of her or he would know the reason why. As for her mother, she was going to be put in her place, too. No more of that whining and complaining around him.

Ann had never forgotten the homely, sad, but striking face of Abraham Lincoln in the picture that she and Mark had stood before in the Owego Hotel. Nor had she forgotten the kindness in that face, and particularly in the deep-set eyes under the shaggy brows when she and Nancy sat before the President of the United States in the White House and pleaded for Mark's life. Those memories, together with the patriotism inherent in every good American, were now coming back to plague Ann's thoughts as she began to realize that the man to whom she was married was almost if not quite a traitor, opposed to everything for which Mark Wilson and so many other boys had fought and died, and for which so many more of her friends were fighting.

As Ann began to think about the war again, she felt more and more unhappy and helpless to do anything. She had made her choice and her bed; now she had to abide by her decision. But she was awake at last to the situation she had created. In marrying Henry Bain she realized that she had made a bad situation even worse for her mother and father, and most of all for herself.

She finally reached the conclusion that being the wife of Henry Bain—or of any other man—did not mean that she was his slave. He could possess her body, but never her soul, nor her love and affection, until he had earned that right. It was hopeless for her to try to influence Henry's actions, especially his anti-Union activities, but she did have the right to assert her own attitude and loyalty to the Union.

The differences between Ann and Henry finally flared into the open when Ann announced her intention of taking a more active part with the other women of the neighborhood in making and sending various articles, chiefly clothing, to the United States Sanitary Commission, for the comfort of the Union soldiers. She returned home from Jenkstown one night about supper time to find Henry waiting for her in a towering rage.

"Where've you been?" he demanded.

Turning in the center of the kitchen floor to face him, she answered:

"You told me once, Henry Bain, when I asked you where you had been that it was none of my business. I don't think that's the way a husband and wife should be, so I'll tell you where I have been. I spent the afternoon—as I intend to spend many other days—making things for the Union soldiers."

He started to shout at her, but was so enraged that his voice cracked, and he had to start again:

"I don't want to hear of your doing it again, do you hear? No wife of mine will have any part in prolonging this war."

He was trembling all over. Ann spoke quietly:

"Henry, if you want me to continue to be your wife, we might just as well understand each other right now. No soldier on the battlefield, no person back here at home, can feel more intensely about our winning the war than I do. I can't do much, but whatever I can do, I shall. And you can't stop me!"

She was standing close to him, gazing directly at him with white face and blazing eyes. He stood for a moment staring at her almost in awe, and then turned and without a word went out of the house.

CHAPTER XXX

IN THE DAYS that followed Ann's defiance of Henry and her announcement that she intended to serve the Union cause in every way within her means and power, they went about their respective tasks with little said between them. But Ann thought she noticed an attitude of increased respect on the part of her husband, even to the point of his showing a little more consideration for her mother.

"Maybe that's all he needs," she thought, hopefully. "He's always had his own way, and it may be good for him to find out that other people have their rights, too. Maybe he'll show more respect for those rights."

So gradually Ann relaxed her formal manner with Henry and was more friendly. Then something strange happened. One night after they were asleep, they were startled by a loud knocking on the front door. Henry got up hurriedly, lit the light, pulled on his pants, and went downstairs. Listening intently Ann could hear voices apparently raised in angry argument, but couldn't make out what was said. After a while Henry came back, blew out the light, climbed into bed and started to shiver violently. Feeling sorry for him, Ann broke her rule of not interfering, turned to put a comforting arm over him and asked him what was the matter.

"Those men," he muttered. "Ruffians! They had masks on."

"Robbers?"

"No."

"What were they, then?"

"I don't know," he temporized.

"But what did they want?" she insisted.

"Said for me to get out of the county—or else."

Ann's instinct for fair play was roused. She laid a hand on her husband's hot face.

"Don't worry," she said. "Men who come that way *are*

ruffians, as you said. They are cowards. They won't dare do anything. Now let's try to go to sleep."

It was perhaps a week later that Ann, uneasy and unhappy, bundled herself against the cold and went for a walk across lots on the Clinton farm toward the woods. Her work with the other women for the Sanitary Commission was not going well. She could sense their antagonism—even from many of the women whom she had always known and liked. Now she was torn between her desire to help and her independent feeling that she had no wish to go where she was not wanted.

Although the wind was cold, there was bright sunshine. She stopped to listen to the pleasant, familiar sound of the loud cawing of crows. Apparently something beyond the hill where Henry owned another farm with a large tract of heavily timbered land was responsible for their raucous cries. Gazing in this direction now, Ann perceived a haze, and, watching intently, she was sure she could see smoke from a fire which seemed to extend a considerable distance in both directions.

There had been a long dry spell, and Ann realized that a fire might mean serious trouble. As if to confirm her suspicions, the church bell in Jenkstown began to ring in the urgent, jerky way that people had learned to associate with trouble, in contrast to its usual calm ring on a Sunday morning. Ann knew then that others had also seen the fire and realized its danger. If it should spread, it might even endanger the buildings on Henry's farm, including the house where Jameson, his tenant farmer, lived. She wondered where Henry was. As usual, he had told her nothing when he had left that morning, so she didn't know whether he had gone on a trip or only to one of his other farms.

Hurrying down across the hillside to her home, Ann stopped just long enough to tell her mother about the fire and then started for the village as fast as she could go. Hearing the rumbling of a buggy on the frozen road back of her, she turned and saw that it was occupied by Enoch Payne and Tom Wilson. They stopped and Enoch said, shortly, "Get in!," as he pulled the horse and cramped the wheels to one side so that she could climb up beside them. Then he urged the horse to a gallop. By the time they reached the village, most of the male population had gathered, armed with shovels or brooms. Everyone knew what a fire could mean in that heavily wooded country in a dry time. The church bell was still clanging, adding to the excitement and confusion.

As Ann looked at the crowd, she thought of what it means to a community when calamity strikes and all the active young men are gone. In the group now rapidly moving up the road ahead of them in the direction of the fire, she counted her old friends and acquaintances, Pastor Timothy Belden, John Crawford, the storekeeper; old Harry Cortright, and DeWitt Legg, all middle-aged or older. In fact, Enoch Payne was the youngest and most active man among them, with the exception of young boys like Tom Wilson. But if they lacked youth and agility, they were certainly not lacking in their determination to get to the scene of the trouble and conquer it. When Enoch had driven as near to the fire as he thought it was safe to take the horses, he jumped out of the buggy with Tom, telling Ann to watch the horses.

"I'm just as able to help as some of these old men," she objected. "I'm going with you."

A few moments later Ann could feel the heat from the burning pines and hemlocks. Fanned by the wind, the line of fire was at least a mile and a half in length and coming rapidly. She wondered what a few old men and boys could do to stop that glittering, flaming line of destruction.

But under Enoch Payne's directions the men were soon making an organized defense. With shovels and brooms they beat out small blazes set off by sparks in the clearing in advance of the oncoming main line of fire. Even in the midst of their work and worry, they found time to laugh at the scurrying rabbits, so scared by the fire that they had lost all fear of man. Ann watched a fox trot rapidly out of the woods and stop near her. He sat down facing the fire, barked indignantly at it, then trotted away.

In a long open space considerably in advance of the fire the men started to dig a trench for a fire break, but they soon saw that they were making slow progress with hand work. One man rushed down the hill to the tenant buildings below them on the Bain farm to get a team and a plow with the hope that they could quickly plow a strip that would be too wide for the fire to jump over it.

As Ann watched, the fire reached the foot of a majestic pine tree near the edge of the clearing. Almost before she could draw a breath, the flame swept into the lower limbs of the tree and quickly leaped to the top, making it a gigantic crackling torch of wondrous and awesome splendor.

Whipped and driven by the wind, eddies of choking smoke blackened the faces of the struggling men, reddened their eyes, and set them to coughing and gagging. Farther away, Ann could feel the hot breath of the inferno almost scorching her face. Suddenly, the fire reached the first uncompleted line of defense and crossed it, crackling and roaring as if in glee at the futility of man's puny efforts.

As soon as the team and plow arrived, the smoke-blackened men started another line, but the horses, made frantic by the noise and the flames, reared and plunged. When only halfway across the clearing with the first furrow, and in spite of everything the driver could do, the team turned and dashed madly down the slope away from the fire, with the driver yelling and cursing and pulling on the lines. Enoch Payne, who was holding the plow handles, finally was thrown free by the bumping of the plow over the rough ground. Then one of the lines broke, the driver let loose of the other, and the horses, galloping wildly now, with the plow jumping and plunging behind them, continued their breakneck dash down across the clearing, to bring up finally against the side of the barn, trembling and with the sweat rolling off their sides.

After failing to make any kind of a fire break, Enoch and some of the other men gave brief consideration to starting a back fire, but relinquished the idea, realizing that it would be utterly impossible to get a fire burning backwards with the wind blowing directly toward them.

The fire was now across the clearing and in the scattered trees on the lower side of the slope, the roar of the flames drowning out the shouts of the men. Staring at it, Ann found herself yelling, hardly knowing that she did so, as it came to her that all of the buildings and the farmhouse where the Jamesons lived were doomed. The men had now turned their efforts to turning the stock in the barn loose and driving it to safety. Then with pails, blankets and quilts they tried to save the buildings. Soaking the blankets with water from the well, they laid them across the roof of the house. When the wet blankets ran short, the rest of the shingles were soaked down with water. The tenant farmer, Jameson, who had been working with the others on the fire break, ran to his wife where she stood with small children clinging to her skirts. She was whitefaced from the strain and was wringing her hands in despair. Neighbors picked up the children and pulled her farther down the hill to where a democrat wagon was parked. Loading the family in, one of the men drove them back to the village and safety.

Now the crowd began to carry out the furniture from the house, piece by piece. Soon all that was left in the house was the heavy stove. Finally the group, faces streaked with sweat and blackened almost beyond recognition, stood helpless and resigned, watching the fire come closer and moving back only as the heat and smoke became too intense to bear. Within a few minutes, trees close to the house sprang into flame, and almost at the same time, despite the soaked quilts and blankets, the roof of the house began to sputter and smoke. Here and there little forks of flame started in the shingles. Then the small individual flames swept into a sheet of flame streaming high above the roof, until the whole house, which only a few moments before had been a home where folks lived and worked and loved, was nothing but a huge bonfire.

Driven back by the heat, yet fascinated by the horror of the fire, the small crowd moved slowly away from the house to watch the scene repeat itself in the barn, only with greater intensity as the flames reached the big mows filled to overflowing with hay to feed the herd until spring.

"Well," DeWitt Legg growled resignedly, "it can't go much farther. There's nothing left to burn."

It was a downcast, silent group who walked and rode back to their homes in the village and the valley. In the buggy with Enoch and Tom, Ann had nothing to say. Enoch, too was silent until they neared the Clinton home. Then he said, simply:

"I'm sorry, Ann. This means a big loss to you and Henry."

"Well, it couldn't be helped," she replied. "Everybody did what they could to stop it."

But her own feelings surprised her. She realized that she was thinking more about the loss and trouble Jameson and his family had suffered than of any financial loss to Henry and her. In fact, she had never thought of herself as being a part owner in Henry's property. He was too possessive. So far as his loss was concerned, she felt no more regret than if the property had belonged to a stranger.

Mrs. Clinton had supper ready when Ann got back, and after Ann had washed up, she told her mother briefly what had happened.

"Oh, I am sorry it was our property," exclaimed Mrs. Clinton. "What a terrible loss!"

Ann didn't answer, thinking of her mother's use of the word "our." Obviously her own feeling of having no part in Henry's property was not shared by her mother.

Before the meal was finished, Bain came home. One glance at his face was sufficient to tell the women that he knew what had happened. Without a word of greeting he hung up his hat and coat, washed at the kitchen sink, and sat down at the table, while Mrs. Clinton hurried to put before him the food that she had kept warm on the back of the stove. They were accustomed to his irregularity at meal times.

In silence he ate a few mouthfuls, then pushing his plate away and shoving back a little from the table, he growled:

"Well," he said, addressing Ann coldly, "you were there. What happened?"

Still very much stirred by the drama of the scene, Ann almost forgot his personal connection with the property as she vividly described the fire to her husband. Then, looking at his cold, set face, she suddenly realized what the fire meant to him, a man who set such store by property.

"Well," he said, sarcastically, "at least it made a picnic for you and the town folks. Seems as though they might have done something about it."

"Henry Bain, how can you make a remark like that?" Ann exclaimed. "Those men fought that fire for hours. They did everything they could. Every one of them was completely exhausted."

"Yeah!" he sneered. "A lot of smart workers. Just a lot of doddering old fools. Didn't even save the house and barn. If there had been a few real men around, instead of all of them gone to this fool war, maybe they could have done something."

Ann leaned forward, her elbows on the table, and her chin cupped in her hand.

"Henry," she said, deliberately and quietly, "I just don't understand you. I was at that fire all afternoon. There was a stiff wind right back of it, and, as you well know, the woods were as dry as tinder. I never dreamed that a fire could run so fast or raise so much havoc. It would reach a pine tree and, in a matter of seconds, flame clear to the top. Of course, they are old men, but they did what they could. They tried frantically to dig a fire break. Then they got a team and a plow. But with that wind back of the fire it was just too fast for them. Then they rushed down to the house and carried water by the bucketful to wet down the roofs. They got Mrs. Jameson and her children out, and took them down to the village. They rescued your stock and drove them down the hill. One of the men crowded his own stock to take in your cows and young stock and your horses. They even carried out the Jameson furniture and put it in their rigs, piece by piece. What more could have been done, even by young men, I don't know. And yet you sit there and criticize them!"

He started to speak, but Ann stopped him.

"You wait until I'm through. It's no wonder you've been warned to move out of the county. What do you expect from people when you talk about them and treat them the way you do? Besides," she added, looking him straight in the eye, "you blow about the young men being away to war, not here to save *your* property; where were *you* today? I heard that question asked time and again today, and asked with some emphasis. Unless you change your ways, you're riding for a fall just as sure as the sun rises in the morning!"

Henry stared back at his wife. In the dim light of the candles on the table his face was white.

"You've given me an idea," he gritted through his teeth. "You're right. They did warn me the other night to move out."

He straightened up and threw back his shoulders.

"And I told them where they could go. Now this is their first move."

"What do you mean?"

"That fire didn't just happen. It was set."

"No, oh, no," she cried.

"Yes, oh yes," he retorted. "And if that's the way they want it, that's all right by me! They'll find that I can play their game, too."

CHAPTER XXXI

CHRISTMAS WAS ANYTHING but a joyous occasion in war-torn America in the winter of 1863. But although Nancy's heart wasn't in it, she felt that she owed it to the little girls to have a Christmas tree and decorate it, as they had always done, with strings of popcorn. She had found time to knit stockings and mittens and had managed to buy a few little trinkets in John Crawford's store. But funds were growing shorter all the time and it was necessary to make every cent count toward the things they had to have to live.

Then, too, how could there be any real Christmas spirit, any real enthusiasm, she asked herself, with Mark gone out of their lives forever, and her husband and Charlie far away in a dismal war camp with little hope that they would be home in a long time, if ever? Yet it might not be so long after all, she thought, more hopefully. There were some indications that the South was weakening—the great victory at Gettysburg back in July, and the other victory by that man Grant when he captured Vicksburg on the Fourth of July and cleared the Mississippi of the Rebels for its entire length. Yes, the news did actually seem to be better. Only a month back, on November 23, Hooker had defeated the Confederate leader Bragg at Lookout Mountain in "the battle above the clouds." She was thrilled when she had read how the boys in blue had charged up an almost inaccessible mountainside to throw the enemy out.

Anyway, sad or glad, life must go on. There was Tom. What a fine boy he had become! And Ellen, Elizabeth and Hattie tried so hard to be helpful. Yes, no matter what happened, it was her job to take care of them, and as she thought how meager their Christmas would be, and how hard it was to provide enough clothes and shoes for all of them, her heart filled and she chided herself for not doing a better job. All summer long, until the frost lay on the ground, the girls had gone barefoot in order to save shoes, and now, in the winter when they were not in school, they removed their shoes the moment they got into the house.

Thank God for the children, she thought. How lonesome it was on week days when Tom and Ellen and Elizabeth went down the road to attend the nearby district school, leaving only Hattie at home out of her whole brood. "How lonely it must be," she reflected, "for mothers of large families when the children grow up almost overnight and go away to live their own lives! How they must wish again for those years of being busy and happy, and even for the times when they were nervous and irritated by all the work and worry and noise that the children made."

Then she laughed aloud as she thought of some of the scrapes the children were constantly getting into, frightening and irritating when they happened but funny in retrospect. Just the other day Ellen had climbed up into the hayloft and somehow or other managed to fall through an opening in the floor onto one of the old cows in the stall below. Difficult, indeed, was it to tell which made the loudest noise or which was the more scared—Ellen or the bawling cow. When Enoch, busy at his chores nearby, heard the rumpus and came running, there was Ellen astraddle the cow and hanging on for dear life, while the cow was doing her utmost to buck her off.

Nancy chuckled to herself as she recalled Ellen's injured dignity, and then her thoughts went back to the time last summer when the girls got to quarreling down near the brook. Ellen got Hattie's head under water and probably would have drowned her if Elizabeth hadn't knocked her off.

Well, maybe there was some purpose after all in fixing up the Christmas tree, and trying one's best to be happy and to make others happy no matter what came. Someone said that it was always darkest just before dawn. Maybe it would be that way now.

Then Nancy's thoughts turned to Mary Curtis and Enoch Payne. On her urgent invitation, these two had come to live with her some weeks before. Welcoming the opportunity to be near one another, they had needed no second invitation. In addition to all the work they both did in the barn and in the house, what a blessing they were to the children and to herself with their cheerful, kindly dispositions.

Pondering over them, Nancy was puzzled as to why they didn't marry, for if she was any judge they certainly were in love. She laughed as she thought how shy and awkward either was when the other one came around. That was the reason, probably, Enoch just couldn't get up courage to pop the question.

But the day before Christmas, when the children were out playing in the snow, Enoch and Mary came and stood awkwardly before Nancy to tell her their glad news. Evidently the Christmas spirit had given Enoch the courage to ask her to marry him.

"I knew it! I knew it!" Nancy laughed. "I think I knew it before either of you. And I'm so glad."

Indeed, Nancy was happier than she had been in many a day.

"And now, we must plan the wedding!" she said gaily.

Enoch ran his fingers through his hair, shifted from one foot to the other, and finally said:

"Well, Nancy, this is the nearest to home either of us have. We've talked it over. We've waited a long time for marriage, and now we'd sorta like to be married right here in this house."

"That's wonderful," said Nancy, "and it makes me very happy. I've been worrying about Christmas, for as you know, the happiest occasions in the past can be the saddest when the anniversaries roll around again and loved ones are absent. Why don't we make Christmas Day your wedding day, right here tomorrow?"

Mary looked a little startled, but Enoch nodded vigorous approval, and then Mary, glancing up at him, her shyness forgotten, stepped closer and slipped her arm through his and said:

"Nancy, I think that would just top off our happiness."

"Well, now, we've certainly got something," Nancy agreed, her eyes shining. Then, becoming practical, she said, crisply: "There's work to be done."

On the afternoon of Christmas Day the walls of the sitting-room in the Wilson home were almost covered with the green boughs of evergreens brought fresh from the woods,

and the room was rich with their fragrance. Chunks burned
in the big box stove. There had been no time to send out
formal invitations, but word had got around, and a good
many friends of Mary and Enoch—who had spent most of
their lives working for others—now filled the room to give
them a real send-off down their own road to happiness.

When Enoch and Mary stood with Pastor Belden in front
of the mantel where the old clock, flanked by a little stone
dog on each side, ticked away the hours, it seemed to Nancy
that everyone crowded into that room was holding his
breath; and when this middle-aged man and woman, their
faces strained with deep emotion, gave their promises one
to the other, there wasn't a dry eye among the women in
the room, and even the men were conscious of lumps in their
throats. These were strange, confused, uncertain times. No
one knew what lay ahead, but as they watched Mary and
Enoch, all realized that somehow, no matter what happened,
love and life are eternal.

Not the least of the joys of the occasion to Nancy and to
the bride and groom was the fact that Ann came to the
wedding. But some of Nancy's happiness in having Ann
present was offset by her feeling that the other guests drew
away from her. Maybe she only imagined it, thought Nancy,
but she took care to go over and stand by Ann, and she
reached for her hand during the ceremony. Ann responded
with a little squeeze of her hand, but after the ceremony
had ended and she had warmly congratulated Mary and
Enoch, she immediately slipped away.

* * *

Though the weather grew colder after Christmas, it was
easier to be cheerful and optimistic because the days were
soon noticeably longer. It was still winter, but when they
could eat supper and breakfast by daylight, it gave Nancy
the feeling that another spring and summer were not too far
away. Many, many times she thought how lucky she was to
have Mary and Enoch make their home with her. Even
though she knew that eventually they would want to have
a home of their own, there was a feeling of security in just
having the solid, substantial couple around, and Nancy came
closer to being happy than she had been since George and

her boys had gone away and the news of Mark's death had come.

The war news was better, too. Although there was no fighting in the winter, the North had been cheered by Lincoln's appointment of Ulysses S. Grant, the victorious general in the West, as commander now of all the Union forces. At last maybe they had found a general who would stand and fight. The people were in agreement with their President when he said, "Wherever Grant is, things move."

Ann's attendance at the wedding had broken the ice and given Nancy an opportunity to renew their friendship. Several times during the winter Nancy visited her, and Ann again formed the habit of dropping in occasionally on Nancy.

But Nancy's relatively good winter wasn't destined to remain uninterrupted. For weeks, Enoch and Tom had been busy between chores getting out wood and working it up for the big stove in the living room which during the winter was kept going day and night and which, the men agreed, ate wood like an elephant eats peanuts. One day in early March as Enoch and Tom were skidding out a log from a tree they had felled and cut in log lengths, the team, excited by struggling around in the deep snow, gave an unexpected jump, rolling the log and catching Tom, before he could spring out of the way, between the log and a tree. As he went down, Tom felt an excruciating pain shoot through his leg.

Working nearby, Enoch saw what had happened and, dropping his axe, he caught and stopped the struggling horses, and then rushed with a canthook to roll the log off the boy. Tom's face was white and he was moaning with the pain. Enoch felt sure that the leg was crushed or broken. Working as fast as he could, Enoch hitched the horses back on to the bobsleigh and secured the boy, now almost unconscious from pain, onto the rear bob. Then he drove the horses carefully along the woods road and back to the house. When he finally got Tom on to Nancy's bed in the downstairs bedroom off the kitchen, Enoch rushed out, threw the harness off the horses, leaving only the bridle on the mare, and, straddling her bareback, he galloped off to Jenkstown to bring back Dr. Barr.

When Dr. Barr arrived, Nancy went into the bedroom

with him while he made his examination and did what he could to relieve Tom's pain. In the kitchen Enoch and Mary and the scared little girls waited forlornly, but when the doctor and Nancy finally came out of the bedroom, both of them were smiling.

"Not as bad as it might have been," said the doctor, cheerfully. "A sprained knee, but nothing that two or three weeks' rest won't put in shape again."

"But it's bad enough," thought Nancy, "Tom not only has to suffer, but Enoch will have to do all the chores alone and finish the wood-chopping, and sap might start to run any day."

When she said something about this to Enoch, he pooh-poohed the idea.

"I'll miss my partner, of course," he said, "but like as not when the time comes to tap the trees, Tom'll be all right—at least able to hobble around and feed the furnace even if he can't do very much work."

A few days later Nancy sat by Tom's bed knitting. It seemed to her that even though she knitted during every spare moment she had, she could never get enough socks, stockings and mittens ahead to keep her family supplied. But, anyway, she could get a little rest that way, and she enjoyed knitting. There was something about it that eased one's worries and relieved the tension. The spring sun was shining through the window, and the grass was showing a little green outside. Tom had been asleep, but she suddenly realized that he had been looking at her for some moments. When he noticed her looking at him, he grinned and said:

"Always hated the darn hens, Mom. Seems as though they're always full of lice in the summer time, and nothing but a lot of care and eatin' their heads off in the winter. But, do you know, right now when I heard them clucking around outside that window, an' the old rooster calling them, I got to thinkin' that, after all, I'd kinda miss the critters if they weren't around."

His mother smiled.

"More than either of the other boys, Tom, you're a natural farmer. Or is it because your father's away and you've just taken hold of things here? Anyway," she leaned forward to lay her hand on his head, "I'm so glad that you weren't hurt badly. I don't know what I'd do without you."

"Aw, shucks, Ma!" Tom laughed, embarrassed. "I wasn't talking about me. I was talking about those old biddies out there."

He pulled himself up in bed.

"Not goin' to stay here much longer," he announced. "In fact, if you'll get out of that chair and help me a little, I'll crawl into it."

Although she objected a little, Nancy couldn't see what harm it would do if he didn't put any weight on his foot, so she helped him into the chair, and that night they pulled Tom in the chair out to the supper table. That was a real event.

A few days later, with the help of a cane in one hand and Enoch on his other side, Tom hobbled up to the saphouse. Enoch heaped a big pile of long sticks of wood in front of the furnace, so that by sitting on a bench by the wood pile Tom could keep the fire going and the sap boiling while Enoch managed to gather the sap, haul it to the sap house, and do the chores on the farm.

One night when the tubs of sap were all full, Mary and Enoch spent most of the night in the warm, steamy, fragrant sugar house boiling the sap. During the evening, as they sat before the glowing fire in the furnace, Nancy and Ann walked in. At first the four of them sat in the quiet companionship of long-time friends, gazing at the fire and listening to the boiling sap. To Nancy it seemed so good to be on friendly terms again with Ann, but it was soon evident that Ann herself was not relaxed, and that she had something disquieting on her mind. After a while she said:

"I'm worried, terribly worried. I haven't anyone to talk to except you three, for no one else would understand."

She fell silent, and Nancy said:

"Of course, you can talk to us, dear. What's the matter?"

"Well—," Ann hesitated, trying to find words. "It's Henry! I know I oughtn't to say this even to you, but maybe you can tell me what to do."

Nancy thought:

"Poor girl! She's only a child yet, and doesn't know that there are some situations we get ourselves into for which there just isn't anything to do, except to endure them."

Ann was talking in such a low tone that all three of them had to listen intently to catch her voice above the crackling of the fire.

"That time when we had the big woods fire, Henry wasn't here. I don't know where he was. I don't know where he goes. But when he came back he was terribly excited about the loss of all the buildings and so much fine timber."

"That was natural," said Enoch. "It was a big loss. We all hated to see those good trees and the buildings go."

"But, listen," she begged. "Henry thought that fire was set purposely."

"Oh, no!" Nancy exclaimed.

"Yes, that's what he thought. It didn't seem possible at first to me that anyone would do such a thing, but I've been thinking about it since, and now I wonder."

"Does Henry have any evidence?" Enoch asked.

Ann hesitated as if afraid of saying anything further, then added:

"Yes, he has this: Only a few nights before the fire, some masked men came to the door. When he came back upstairs after talking with them, he was shaking all over, and he said the men had warned him to get out of the county or else they'd put him out."

The girl stopped speaking, and the others sat quietly, knowing how much Henry Bain was hated by most of his neighbors. Then Ann spoke again:

"We all know how dry it was at the time of the fire, but as I think about it, I remember that the line of fire extended at least a mile and a half. So it couldn't have started from some careless woodchopper's one fire. It must have been set in several places!"

Enoch nodded his head, and said:

"Yes, I thought of that, too. And I'll say this: If one or more persons did set a fire like that, even though they hated your husband, they ought to be shot for destroying good property and endangering the lives of innocent people."

Ann gave him a grateful smile.

"There's more that I've got to get off my heart," she said. "You know how anxious I am about this war, and I've tried to help. I've been trying to work with the other women to make things for the soldiers." Her voice faltered.

"But it's so hard. They—don't like me. Even some of my old friends won't speak to me."

Nancy put out a hand to clasp Ann's.

"Don't you fret, dear," she cried. "Your real friends love you. Everybody is upset and unreasonable in these times. They'll get over it."

"But maybe they're right," Ann protested, now almost in tears. "Henry does say the awfullest things about Mr. Lincoln and our soldiers, and he does go away and I don't know where he goes, and—" she added, "I *am* his wife."

Enoch stood up, threw some more wood on the fire, and went around the side to test the sirup boiling in the pan. Then he came back to stand in front of the little group, his hands in his pockets and his shoulders thrown back. As he stood there, Nancy thought him the embodiment of masculinity, courage and gentleness.

"Ann," he said, "don't worry too much. As Nancy says, people are upset now. This war is going to be over before too long, and things will quiet down. No matter how much anyone is for the Union and against Henry Bain, no good citizen is going to stand for any more criminal acts like burning woods and buildings."

He refrained from voicing his own belief that if Henry Bain didn't watch his step, just the strength of public opinion would force him to leave the county. Nor did he know how to give Ann any real comfort for the mistake she had made in marrying a man like that. So he reached down, took her hands and pulled her to her feet, saying:

"Come on, Ann. I'll take you home, while Mary and Nancy watch the fire."

CHAPTER XXXII

OFTEN WHEN SHE SAW THE WARM, tender glances that passed between Enoch and Mary and the way both seemed years younger since their marriage, Nancy felt lonesome and longed for the return of her own husband and Charlie. But on the whole Enoch and Mary were so happy that they shed happiness around them. At times they acted like a pair of happy kids. On the first of April Nancy got just about as much fun as Mary did out of helping her to bake a string pancake for Enoch. They wound the string around and around in the batter when it was first put on the griddle, making sure that it was carefully hidden. Then, taking Tom and the girls into their confidence so that all could share the joke, they fixed it so that Enoch would surely get that particular pancake. When Enoch got a great big piece of the pancake, dripping with maple sirup, in his mouth, it was fun to see the surprised, incredulous expression that came over his face as he chewed and chewed, and finally pulled out a long piece of string as everybody yelled, "April Fool!"

But now spring was in full swing and there was little time either for jokes or for being lonesome. The sitting room stove had to be taken down and moved out into a corner of the woodshed and covered with an old blanket. Then the tacks were taken out of the carpet and it was carried out and hung on the clothesline, where the girls whipped the dust out of it. On another line, Nancy and Mary hung out blankets and quilts for a thorough airing and brushing in the bright spring sunshine. It was house-cleaning time, and Enoch and Tom, hating it, managed to find excuses to stay in the fields or in the barn, coming into the house only to eat and sleep.

Springtime also brought new life to the old farm. There were two brand-new calves, with their soft, deer-like eyes looking deceptively gentle and innocent. But when Enoch came to the house one morning after having tried to teach one of the calves to drink out of a pail, both Nancy and Mary couldn't help laughing at the spectacle he presented. He was completely splattered with milk from head to foot, and still mad because when he had straddled the calf's neck and pushed her head down into the pail of milk, she had reared her head up, in spite of him, catching the bail of the pail and dumping all of the milk onto Enoch. What Enoch said to the calf would not bear repeating in the house.

One day, as Nancy lifted an old setting hen off her thirteen eggs to find twelve little downy chicks, she thought that no matter how many times she watched chicks hatch out, she never would get over wondering about the miracle of birth. She picked up the little bundles of down in her apron, and with Elizabeth fetching the mother hen, carried them carefully to the A-coop which would be their home for some weeks. Straightening up after depositing the chicks, she stood looking across the countryside, and thought how much she loved it, even with all of the work and the problems. There were so many interesting things to do.

To Elizabeth she said:

"This afternoon we'll all go down in the swamp pasture and get a mess of dandelion greens. They'll taste good."

"Don't like 'em," said Elizabeth, making a face. "Bitter old stuff!"

Nancy looked at her daughter. "Some day you won't be so positive about everything," she remarked. Then she said, half to herself: "The horse-radish roots must be big enough by now. We'll let Mary grate them, though," she added, with a grin. "They make me weep."

On the limb of an old apple tree, a robin sang his cheery song.

"It's so good to have the robins back," said Nancy, "and last night the peepers were singing in the swamp. They've been carrying on for several nights like all get out. Wonder if your father can hear them where he is?"

There was a faraway look in her eyes as she went on to say:

"Look at those maples down there on the edge of the yard, the woods at the end of the pasture, and the brown fields. They look dead, but they aren't. They're just asleep. It won't be long till all of this country will bloom again with life. Somebody was saying after church Sunday that they wished we could have miracles now like they had in Bible times. Well, we do have miracles if we just know enough to see them. What more do we want in the way of a miracle than the way the leaves come out on the trees? No matter how many times I've seen it, every spring I think about the millions of leaves, all alike yet all different. And the grass, too. It's unconquerable. Plow it under; freeze it; but just give it time and it's back again as green as ever."

Elizabeth stood looking at her mother in some wonder, causing Nancy to laugh and say gaily:

"Don't mind me, Elizabeth! I guess I just have a little attack of spring fever."

Then the happiness faded out of Nancy's face and the lines of care became more pronounced again as she thought of Mark and wondered if the grass was growing green over his grave. Elizabeth turned back to the house, but Nancy stood there alone for a long time, thinking sadly of her lost son, her first-born, and of the strangeness of life. Then her face lighted with hope again as she thought:

"Just as it is with the leaves and the grass, so it is with us. We shall not really die, but just fall asleep to wait and rest until the resurrection of the Great Spring. That's what Jesus meant, I'm sure," she thought, "when He said: 'I am the resurrection and the life; he that believeth in me though he were dead yet shall he live. And whosoever liveth and believeth in me shall never die.'"

Refreshed and with renewed courage, Nancy went back to the house to find Ann there waiting for her. She had slipped across the fields and come in the back way. There was color in the girl's cheeks, and it seemed to Nancy that she looked better than she had in a long time.

"Got spring fever, I guess, Nancy," she said, smiling at her. "You and I used to go fishing. How about it? There must be some poles, lines, and hooks around somewhere. Let's find them, dig some worms and try our luck."

Nancy hesitated. She did have a lot to do. But here was a further opportunity to cement their renewed friendship and not for the world would she refuse.

"Well," she said, finally, "it's almost dinner time. You help me get something on the table for the family and have some dinner with us. I'm sure Mary won't mind doing up the work, and as soon as we finish eating we'll go down to the old swimming hole and see what we can do."

An hour or so later, the two women were seated on the bank of the creek where they had often had good luck before. The quiet of the warm spring afternoon was broken only by the soft murmur of the stream, the distant calling of a crow and the fault-finding of a catbird who was objecting strenuously to their presence. The sight of a hawk floating effortlessly high in the sky made Nancy think of her chickens and hope that they would know enough to keep within the protection of their coop. But mainly she was at peace, and so was Ann, the kind of peace that Nature gives to those who love and understand her, the peace and relaxation that drive a true fisherman back to the water every opportunity that he gets.

Both women were having good luck and had landed several sizable perch and a couple of suckers. Suddenly Nancy felt a great tug on her line. Excited, she jumped up, too close to the edge of the bank, which had been softened by the spring rains. The bank, which was three or four feet above the water, gave way and Nancy went with it, rolling unhurt, but with clothes awry, into the shallow water at the edge of the creek.

Startled by Nancy's cry, Ann jumped to her feet. Then, as she realized that nothing but Nancy's dignity had been injured, she sat down again and burst into peals of laughter, the loudest and heartiest in months.

Half indignant at her mishap and Ann's laughter, Nancy struggled in vain to get herself up until Ann, still giggling, slithered down through the mud and dirt and helped her to her feet. When they had regained the top of the bank, they both sat down and laughed until they were weak, then gathered up the fish, which they had strung on a forked twig, and walked back across the pasture. At the Wilson house, Nancy went in to get on dry clothing, and Ann continued on to her own home.

When she had invited Nancy to go fishing, it had been in Ann's mind to talk with her about some of her problems with Henry, but the accident had made it difficult to bring up the subject. Now she was rather glad that she had said nothing. She had already unburdened herself to Nancy, Enoch and Mary in the saphouse the other night, and besides, she thought, "Nancy has plenty of troubles of her own without my adding to them."

Branching off from the direct road home, Ann found a sheltered spot back of a clump of bushes, out of the spring wind, and there she sat in the sunshine for a long time, thinking over her relationship with her husband, their relations with their neighbors, and wondering what, if anything, she could do to ease things. "Maybe," she thought, hopefully, "Henry is on the way to solving our problems himself." For several weeks now—in fact, since he had received that warning from those masked men—he had been absent from home very little, only once or twice, and then, so far as she knew, his trips have been confined to visiting and managing his many pieces of property in the other end of the county.

Only a week or so ago he had surprised Ann by bringing up the subject of her doing war work with the other women of the neighborhood, remarking that he had noticed she hadn't been attending the meetings lately.

"Why is that?" he asked.

He had seemed sincere, too, when he added:

"Don't let me stop you. Maybe you *should* help."

There had been several times lately, also, when Henry had gone out of his way to speak more kindly about Lincoln and to express satisfaction at the recent Union victories. Nancy had mentioned to Ann, too, that Enoch Payne had reported the surprise of some of the men in John Crawford's store when Henry had expressed favorable sentiments toward the Union cause. Nancy had passed this information on to Ann with the hope that it would comfort her.

Now, adding it all up, Ann, with a guilty feeling of disloyalty to her husband, still could not help wondering if Henry's changed attitude was not due entirely to his being just plain scared. Well she knew that at heart he was easily frightened, and that nothing could frighten him more than the prospect of losing his property which meant so much to him.

Turning her thoughts to her own status in the community, she remembered Enoch and Nancy's comforting words— that emotions are always more powerful than reason in wartime, and that hatreds flare even more fiercely back of the lines than on the battlefront. It looked now as if the war might end before long, and if Henry continued to change his attitude, it could be, as Nancy and Enoch had said, that the bitter feelings of the neighbors would in time die out, and she could live a more peaceful life, if not a happy one, with Henry.

Of her personal relations with Henry, Ann thought:

"Maybe he would be a better husband if I were a more understanding, sympathetic, and loving wife."

And with that thought in mind, she knelt on the ground, with her arms on the big boulder on which she had been sitting, bowed her head and asked God for help to meet her problems with courage, to do her duty and to be a true wife to the man she had married.

CHAPTER XXXIII

AFTER GRANT'S APPOINTMENT in March, 1864, things did begin to move, but not always as the North desired. Early in May, Grant crossed the Rapidan River and entered the tangled, gloom-filled region known as the Wilderness, only a short distance from where the Union forces had met disaster at Fredericksburg and Chancellorsville. Here at his headquarters in a little place called Culpepper, Grant planned his "hammering campaign" to take Richmond, wired Sherman to advance against the Confederate forces under Johnson, and declared he would "fight it out on this line if it takes all summer."

Among the 118,000 men with whom Grant proposed to do this job was Charlie Wilson. Like all of his comrades, exhausted and almost ill from his terrible experiences at Gettysburg the summer before, Charlie had made the long trek back from Pennsylvania to Virginia with the Army, knowing that every step of his horse carried him farther away from his home and probably into more battles. And he'd had enough —yes, enough for two lifetimes!

Yet at times on that journey when he had pulled his horse to a halt on some knoll and watched the columns and the great wagon trains winding like a gigantic snake back toward the South again, Charlie had been comforted by two thoughts. One was that his father had survived all the fighting and apparently was reasonably well. Somewhere the officers had managed to find new instruments and George Wilson's band was playing again. Charlie's second cause for rejoicing was that with every step he was drawing nearer to Virginia and Jennie Morgan. Funny what a man will think about, he mused. Here he was, a Yankee, fighting to preserve the Union. Up to a short time ago, his interests and loyalties were all on one side—with his home and his family in the North. Then he had met Jennie and, in spite of himself, had begun to look at the war a little from her point of view and her grandfather's. So here he was, a part of his heart hundreds of miles North in his old farm home, and the other part with this girl in the strange land of Virginia.

That he was in love with Jennie Morgan, a Southern girl, there was no doubt. At times he had to restrain himself to keep from pushing his horse faster as they moved southward. He could hardly wait to get there. As a boy, Charlie had often wondered what it was like to be in love, and now he knew. Love was something to dream about, something that drew him South day after day through the heat and the choking dust that rose like a heavy fog over the marching columns, something that built up hope and made all the misery easier to endure. When hunger gnawed at his vitals, when he was dead with weariness, or was lonesome or home-sick, he could close his eyes and see in his mind a picture of that gentle, lovable, beautiful girl who had saved his life and had told him that she hoped he would come back to her.

Sometimes, though, the hopes and dreams would fade as Charlie rode along with his troop, his head bowed and shoulders drooping, oblivious to the men riding with him. Hope? What right had he to hope? He was nothing but a soldier caught in the maw of war. At the battles he had taken part in—Sharpsburg, Antietam, Fredericksburg, Chancellorsville, Gettysburg—he had just been lucky. How long can a man's luck hold? He was headed back to Jennie Morgan's country all right—but what for? More fighting! And even if he survived, he thought, what did he have to offer a girl as beautiful as Jennie, a girl who could have her choice of Southern boys once the war ended?

So General Lee's Army of Virginia went back to entrench itself again around Richmond, followed by General Meade's Army of the Potomac, with Charlie Wilson riding with the cavalry. Charlie had been promoted to a sergeancy, he stood well with his lieutenants and with the captain of the company, and several times he was fortunate in getting permission to visit Jennie's home, which was nearby and well within the Federal lines.

It tore his heart to see the privations which the Morgans were undergoing. The farm had been robbed of every animal, mostly by the Rebel guerillas. It was useless to try to grow even a pig for pork. The work would be wasted because they were sure to be robbed of the animal before it was time for butchering. Jennie did succeed in growing a small vegetable garden. She told Charlie that they had a little money, most of it in Confederate paper and rapidly becoming worthless; but so far they had been able to supplement the vegetables they raised with a few necessary groceries, and the Union officers had been as generous as the pride of the old man would permit in allowing them some flour, pork, and a little beef from time to time.

The Morgans were fortunate, too, in that Jim Morgan, Jennie's brother, had survived the fighting and was well. In visiting with the grandfather, Charlie noted with interest that while David Morgan was, of course, a loyal supporter of the Confederacy, he was not bitter, as were so many of the non-combatants. George Wilson's stories of the bitter reaction of the civilians in Richmond when he was on his way to Libby Prison had impressed Charlie a lot, and he had wondered about it, for he knew that there was none of this sentiment among the soldiers themselves, except in the lust of battle. Old David Morgan, openminded, courteous, and hospitable was a pleasant exception to what Charlie knew was the general attitude of the southerners back of the line, and, for that matter, of the northern civilians, too.

The only trouble Charlie had with Grandpa Morgan was that he wanted to visit too much, taking time that Charlie would rather have spent with Jennie. But even in this the old man was considerate. Usually after chatting for a while, he would limp off outdoors, or, if it were in the evening, retire to his bedroom.

The time came when Charlie thought he ought to tell David Morgan of his love for Jennie and that she returned it. When he and Jennie came together to stand hand in hand before the grandfather, he sat in silence for a long time. Then he finally said:

"When a man forgets that he was ever young and can't remember how it feels to be young, then he is indeed old. I've known for a long time how it is with you two. It has worried me, as I know it must have worried you. I don't need to stress the differences between you—in miles, in background, in sympathies. Nor, as a soldier, do you need to be reminded, Charlie, that we are in a bitter, bloody civil war. You are an enemy of our State, and the war isn't ended.

"Naturally I had hoped that Jennie would fall in love with one of our young men in this part of Virginia. She knew many of them before these sad times came upon us, but she was very young then, and most of the time—" he smiled a little sadly—"most of the time since then none of these young men, not even her brother, has been able to get home. But I want Jennie to be happy. I've been studying you the few times we have met." Laughing gently, he added: "I think Jennie might do much worse. But at present I don't just see what the answer is for you. Maybe you two do."

Then he addressed himself directly to Jennie:

"There's your brother to consider, my dear. As intensely Southern as he is in his sympathies, what is he going to think about your falling in love with a Northerner?"

Both were surprised when Jennie answered:

"He knows. I told him."

She released Charlie's hand to go to her grandfather and place a comforting arm around his shoulders.

"Jim surprised me," she continued. "No, he didn't, either, because Jim is that way. You know, Grandpa, we've always been very close. He was terribly upset and disappointed when I first told him, but as I told him more about Charlie, he believed me and said that if I was sure, it would be all right with him."

David Morgan seemed lost in thought for a moment or two, then spoke softly:

"I remember my own youth, and that other Jennie, your grandmother. I haven't forgotten that above all the considerations of war, of country, even of family, comes love."

Straightening up as if to bring himself back to the present, Mr. Morgan looked keenly at Charlie, and said:

"It's the individual that counts most, not where he lives, North or South, East or West. But we can't entirely forget the practical aspect of life, my son, and one of the first things is to remember your own people, your love for them and their love for you. So if I were you I'd write your mother, and talk it over with your father. If they agree, your love can, I believe, carry you through all the obstacles that stand in your way, and you have my blessing."

When Mr. Morgan finished talking, Charlie stood looking at him for a moment, thinking how much he liked and respected the old man, and then he said, rather hesitantly:

"Sir, I would like to have my father meet you and Jennie if I could be sure that you would like it."

The old man laughed:

"What's one more Yankee, more or less! I ought to be getting used to them by now." Then, more seriously, he added:

"Of course, I'd like to meet your father. Bring him along any time it can be arranged."

It wasn't hard for Charlie to tell his father about Jennie and her grandfather, for George Wilson was an understanding man, and the war experiences that he and Charlie had shared had wiped out the years between them. They both felt that they could discuss anything with each other without fear of being misunderstood.

Like David Morgan and the young couple themselves, George was worried over the situation, for the obstacles in the way of this union seemed almost insurmountable. When Charlie suggested to his father that he would like to have him meet the Morgans, George readily agreed, and passes were soon obtained from the military authorities.

When they arrived, Charlie said, simply:

" Jennie, this is my father."

George stepped forward, shook hands with Jennie, appraising her keenly and liking what he saw. Then he turned to acknowledge the introduction to David Morgan. The old man rose from his chair, extended his hand, and said courteously:

"Sir, I am glad to know you."

But Charlie noted a frosty gleam in his eyes. He seemed determined to be formally courteous, but no more than that, at least until he knew this Yankee better.

When the four of them were seated, there was a long, awkward pause, for, after all, they represented different sides of a bitter argument and it was hard to get over that hurdle. The ice was broken by David Morgan saying to George:

"Your son tells me that you are a musician."

"Yes," acknowledged George, "a musician of sorts. I lead one of the brigade bands."

Morgan smiled a little sadly and replied:

"In happier times, long since gone, I played in a country band."

That started the conversation off, and before long George found himself telling how stirred he had been when the bands of both armies, lying on each side of the Rappahannock before the Battle of Fredericksburg, had led the men in song, and how each side sang the old ballads, finally ending with playing and singing together "Home, Sweet Home."

As George talked, Mr. Morgan sat gazing out of the window with a faraway expression in his eyes, and when George finished he turned back and said:

"That's the way it ought to be. That's the way God intended it, that we should be singing and playing together instead of trying to kill one another off."

After that it was easy to talk more informally, and finally to get around to the question of most importance to them all.

"When Charlie told me that he loved my granddaughter," remarked Mr. Morgan, "I told him that though I am old I haven't forgotten my own youth and my own sweetheart. I would have missed the best part of my life altogether had anyone interfered with the happiness which we shared for many years. Frankly, I don't see how these young people are going to work out their problems—you know what these problems are. But in spite of this, and if you and Mrs. Wilson agree, I'll put no obstacles in their way."

George stood up and went over to the old man to offer his hand. "I feel exactly the same way," he said, "and I'm sure that my Nancy will agree, too. They'll have to wait a while until the war is over."

Up to this point Charlie had kept still while his and Jennie's fortunes were being discussed, but this was as long as he could keep out of it. Taking Jennie's hand, he drew her over to stand with him before the two older men while he said:

"Jennie and I have been talking. We want our chance of happiness while we can get it. I'm a soldier—there are more bloody battles ahead. We want your permission to be married now."

"Now!" ejaculated George, incredulously. "That's impossible. What do you mean?"

Grandpa Morgan surprised them by pushing himself up out of his chair and saying:

"Mr. Wilson, I can realize how shocked you are at this proposal. I'm only a little less so because I've been on the spot and have seen it coming. I've had time to think about it, and, if you consent, I think we should let these young folks do what they wish."

Jennie threw herself on her grandfather's neck and hugged him enthusiastically. When he could release himself from her embrace, Morgan continued:

"It's as the boy said. At best, life is a transient affair, and, of course, especially so in brutal war times like these. Let them have their happiness while they can."

George stood looking from one to the other, bewildered by the swift turn of events. He looked at Charlie and Jennie, a lump forming in his throat.

"Sir," he said to Morgan when he could speak, "how well I know the truth of what you say, that life is transient. I had another son in this conflict. He was married the day before he enlisted." George's voice sank to a whisper: "Now he is gone."

When he had control of his voice again, he continued in a more matter of fact tone:

"I have only one reservation. They must wait until we can write to Charlie's mother and get an answer."

Both father and son wrote to Nancy and told her as well as they could of all the events that had led up to Charlie's love for Jennie. Some of this Charlie had written before, so Nancy was not wholly unprepared for the news. George's letter giving his impressions of David Morgan, and especially of Jennie, arrived a few days after the one from Charlie. George told of his visit to the Morgan home, of his approval of an immediate marriage, and his hope that Nancy would feel the way he did about it.

Some three weeks later, a little group gathered in the Morgan home to witness the wedding of Charlie Wilson and Jennie Morgan. All was quiet on the military front, so it had not been difficult for Charlie to get a few days' furlough. He had invited to the wedding his friend Sergeant Hank

Miller and the captain of his company. Under the circumstances, Jennie and her grandfather had not considered it wise to announce her marriage, and had invited only two or three friends of long standing and the pastor of their church.

When Jennie had approached Pastor Hall with the request that he conduct the service, he had at first raised his eyebrows and tried to dissuade her. But further conversation and explanations influenced him to agree, as had Jennie's grandfather, that love is more important than anything else and can overcome all obstacles, and he consented to marry her to her Yankee.

The big living room, which was opened up for the occasion, was the setting for a strange gathering. Here were partisans of the North and the South, in a southern home in Virginia surrounded by an invading army. The civilians were dressed in their best, made shabby by the privations of war, and the military men in uniforms which showed the wear and tear of long marches and camp life. There was every reason for hatred among those present, but there was no hate in that room. Some awkwardness maybe, some reaction to the strangeness of the situation. But the awkwardness soon wore off, and finally when Charlie and Jennie stood before Pastor Hall and exchanged vows, all thoughts of war were forgotten.

After the ceremony, refreshments (most of them contributed by friends and the Union officers) were served to the guests, and congratulations, best wishes, and good fellowship prevailed. Then, one by one, the guests went their several ways. Even David Morgan, tired from emotional excitement, had given them his blessing and disappeared into his bedroom, and Jennie and Charlie were alone.

As they went upstairs that night, hand in hand, Charlie could not restrain a chuckle at the remembrance of the last time they had climbed those stairs together, when Jennie had hidden him in her bed to save him from the guerillas. Jennie read his thoughts, and they both laughed until she closed her eyes in the ecstasy of her new husband's kiss.

CHAPTER XXXIV

CHARLIE AND JENNIE WILSON'S honeymoon was short. General Grant, suiting action to words, moved on Lee and attacked him while he was entrenched in the tangled forests of the Wilderness in May of 1864. Early on the bright morning of May 6, Charlie Wilson's cavalry troop rode up to test and probe the Confederate lines, and then, having met more than they had bargained for, rode back again through the infantry lines, while the boys on foot yelled and shouted curses at the cavalry for again "starting something you can't finish!"

As he listened to the foot soldiers' particularly bitter tirade this time, Charlie wondered if the hatred among the different Union services was not even worse than that between the Union forces and the Confederates. Then, because he was essentially fair-minded, he concluded that maybe if he were slogging along on foot, knowing nothing of the facts and seeing the cavalry constantly retreating after its advances, he might feel exactly the way the infantrymen did.

What the foot soldiers didn't know, or would not admit, was that one of the duties of the cavalry was to do just what they had been doing that morning—try out the Confederate lines and forces so that the officers could know just what was the situation ahead. Usually vastly outnumbered, the cavalry were not expected to stand and fight, although there was plenty of evidence of their glorious record where a stand was needed, and of hand-to-hand saber duels. Often cavalry losses outnumbered those of the infantry.

During those early May days, Charlie had reason to revise his belief that he had seen the ultimate in horror in the fighting at Gettysburg the year before. There the dead had lain so thick on the ground that it was difficult for either man or horse not to step on them. And then had come the cloudburst on the last day of the fighting, flooding Rock

Creek and washing away and drowning many of the wounded. But in this murky Wilderness, the wounded weren't drowned; they were burned to death. Soon after the fighting started, the woods were filled with powder smoke, lighted by constant flashes of guns. Out of the murk there frequently came grey lines of Confederate troops, screeching the blood-curdling, high pitched, nasal yell which they always used in a charge. Fires soon started in the dead limbs and the leaves that littered the ground, adding to the smoke, and time and again Charlie heard the desperate cries of the wounded as the creeping ground fires reached them.

On one of those hideous Wilderness days when the cavalry were acting as a reserve for the infantry, an officer suddenly shouted "Count Fours!" Down the line came the short, staccato count: "One—Two—Three—Four!" "One—Two—Three—Four!" And then the order: "Dismount! Every number four man hold the horses; the others prepare to go forward."

Charlie was disgusted to find that he was a fourth man, for he had no desire to hold horses while the others went forward into the fighting. Knowing that Sergeant Miller was ill that day and that he had had difficulty staying in the saddle, Charlie proposed to him that he take his place.

"You hold the horses, Hank," he said. "I don't want to stay here, and you aren't fit to go forward."

It didn't take much urging, for Miller knew that he was really incapable of doing much fighting. So he remained behind, but later in the day when the troops came back to where they had left their horses, the horses were gone. So were the men. A troop of Rebel cavalry had come around the flanks of the Federals, captured the horses and made prisoners of the men who were holding them.

Realizing that had he taken the apparently easier and safer job of staying behind with the horses, he would now be a prisoner of war, Charlie Wilson thought once again of how lucky he had been. So far, in all the battles and skirmishes, he had come through without a scratch, while almost every week new faces filled up the ranks of those who rode with him. How long could his luck hold? A long time afterwards, when the war was over, he learned that his friend and comrade, Hank Miller, who had ridden the weary miles of the marches with him and stood with him so many times in the heat of battle, had died in Andersonville Prison.

Defeated in the battles of the Wilderness on the 6th and 7th of May, the indomitable Grant moved in again on May 9th and 10th against the Confederates at Spottsylvania Court House and at Cold Harbor. Again he was defeated. In a visit with his father after these fights, Charlie learned that the Federals had lost seven thousand men in one desperate charge at Cold Harbor, and that after six weeks of fighting in the Wilderness country, from May 5 to June 15, 1864, Grant lost 55,000 men, or almost as many as Lee's entire forces in the field. When these terrific losses were reported back to the northern homes from which the boys came, sadness hung like a gray pall over the North. Even with these hideous losses, Grant "the butcher" as he came to be called, seemed to be making no more progress toward the Confederate capital than had his predecessors.

But after each defeat, the short, stubby man in his unpressed uniform gritted his teeth on the cigar that was always in his mouth and moved in again, hanging on like a bulldog even when he was licked, and gradually wearing down Lee's resistance. Finally, unable to make much headway from the North toward Richmond, Grant swung his forces around to Petersburg, bordering Richmond on the south, knowing that if he could capture Petersburg, Richmond would have to fall. Here for weeks the Union forces made little progress. Someone conceived the idea of digging a great underground tunnel under the Confederate forts that defended Petersburg and laying a powder mine in the tunnel. When all was ready, the powder was exploded, causing the tunnel to erupt like a volcano. Into the crater rushed the Union forces, hoping to take Richmond. Instead, they were caught in a death trap in which thousands of them were killed or taken prisoner. Grant had failed again.

To Nancy at home it often seemed that peace would never come. It had been so long now since those distant happy days before the war that they were almost like a dream, and she sometimes lost hope that they would return again. The abnormal had become the normal.

"Maybe," she thought, "I'm getting some of the same

lack of the capacity to feel, the same indifferent attitude that Ann has had."

Even when the long letters came from George and Charlie telling her of Charlie's love for Jennie Morgan and their desire to marry, she couldn't seem to be as much concerned as she would ordinarily have been without all the other problems that the war had brought. What was to be, would be, and one might as well be resigned to it. Then, in a more cheerful mood, she would think about Charlie's wife and look forward to seeing her and welcoming her into the family —that is, if the family were ever together again.

One day Mary Payne put some of Nancy's thoughts into words when she said:

"Did you ever think, Nancy, about all the costs and casualties of war beyond the actual dollars and cents cost and the loss of the dead and the wounded?"

"I think I know what you mean, Mary," Nancy replied. "For one thing, it will take years to get over the hard, bitter feelings between former friends and neighbors right here in our own county, to say nothing about the hatreds that will last a long, long time between the North and South."

"Yes," Mary agreed, "that's a bad part of it, and I know from what little history I have read how war always affects people's morals. It seems to increase extravagance, waste, fraud, and dirty politics."

"Yes," said Nancy, "and it robs us women of our youth as well as of our husbands and sons. I was a comparatively young woman when this war started. At least I thought of myself as young, even though Mark had grown up. But now I certainly am old. Only a wife or mother can ever know the price women pay for war."

"I know," said Mary. "There are no drums for us on the home front, but maybe it's God's way of getting good things done. Maybe it's worth all the cost to us here and to the soldiers to free the negroes and to save the Union, but I do wish it could be done some other way."

During the awful Wilderness campaign, when the newspapers were filled with the news of Grant's repeated defeats and with the long lists of the war dead and the missing, Nancy would scan the lists feverishly, and, when no one else was likely to bring the mail, she trudged down the road to the post office herself, always hoping for a letter from George or Charlie assuring her of their safety. It was like living on a keg of dynamite that might explode at any moment, destroying all possibility of happiness.

With the help of Tom and Enoch Payne and the little money that George managed to send home now and then, Nancy was able to get along and find enough for them to eat, such as it was, and clothes for them to wear. She was thankful for the responsibility of taking care of the family. The immediate problems of the day helped her to forget her worries, and the hard work tired her out so that she could sleep. It was good, too, to have Ann dropping in to see her. The girl seemed to be getting on better. Though she no longer discussed her personal problems with Nancy, Nancy knew that her distrust of her husband was growing less because of Bain's apparent change of attitude toward the war.

When Nancy spoke to Enoch about this, he laughed cynically and said:

"Don't give Hank Bain too much credit. I think he's quit his Copperhead activities only because he had to. That warning he got and the fire were just what he needed. Moreover, he's making plenty of money now because of the high war prices for the stuff he sells. He knows the Johnnies are going to be licked, and so he's climbed on the band wagon of the winning side."

Nancy said no more, but she was glad for Ann's sake that whatever Bain's reasons were for changing, his attitude made things pleasanter for his wife.

Ann did frequently speak of her father, and George had mentioned Fred Clinton several times in his letters. According to reports, Fred was a good soldier and, strange to say, in spite of the hardships of Army life and the general drinking, he seemed to have reformed on that score. George and he had had several visits, and George wrote to Nancy that the man really had a lot of character and was a good fellow. What probably had ailed him at home was that he was not a good farmer, and the constant worry and irritation of trying to make a living for himself and his family on a poor farm had gotten him down.

Then one day following the Battle of Cold Harbor, Ann,

whitefaced and shaking, came in to Nancy's kitchen and held out a message for her to read. Before she took it from the girl's trembling hand, Nancy guessed what it contained, and she was right. It was the customary brief notice, addressed to Mrs. Clinton, that Fred Clinton had been killed in action.

Ann sank into a chair, and Nancy stood looking at her, wondering what she could say. What was there to say? She knew that Ann had gone through just about all that she could stand, but even in her sympathy for Ann, Nancy couldn't help thinking that maybe it was for the best. Fred Clinton had redeemed himself as a soldier and as a man, and, after all, what did he have to come back to? Henry Bain had his farm, and there was little prospect of happiness for him in the kind of life that he would have had if he had come back.

* * *

Of the early part of the Petersburg siege Charlie Wilson saw very little. During the summer of 1864 Lee sent his great cavalryman, Early, with 20,000 men on a road through the rich Shenandoah Valley for supplies, and possibly to capture Washington. Foreseeing this move, Grant had kept back enough forces to protect the city of Washington, but out of the Shenandoah Valley, most productive farm valley in America, Early brought back thousands of horses, cattle and other supplies to feed the Confederate Army. That this might not happen again, Grant sent General Philip Sheridan to destroy everything in the Valley, and Charlie was one of the 26,000 men who rode with Sheridan, Merritt, and Custer into the Valley.

As a farm boy, it distressed Charlie to see a great farm country laid waste. Sheridan rode the length of the Valley, up and down again, and slaughtered or drove off thousands of cattle and sheep, burned more than 70 grist mills, and destroyed over 2,000 farms filled with hay and grain. When he was through, it was said that a crow couldn't fly over the Valley unless he carried his provisions with him.

But Sheridan didn't get away from his raid unscathed. When Lee learned what was up, Early was ordered to return to the Valley and drive out the destructive Union cavalrymen. On the morning of October 19, 1864, Charlie was eating breakfast with his messmates around a little breakfast fire. Of late the rations both for men and horses had been especially good because they were living off the rich country. It was a foggy morning, and not dreaming that the enemy was anywhere near, the men were happy and relaxed, and there was joking and laughter as they ate. Suddenly out of the fog came the screaming yip, yip, yip of the Confederates, and the graycoats were upon them. Though surprised, the discipline and experience of the veterans helped them to rally, mount their horses, and get away, with the Confederates in hot pursuit. Gradually the Federals began to slow up and to turn and fire at their pursuers from their saddles.

When the fighting began, Sheridan was at the village of Winchester, twenty miles away, where he had stopped overnight from a trip to confer with Washington officials. Hearing the firing, he hastily mounted his famous black horse, Rienzi, and rode the twenty miles to the battle at a gallop. His presence and leadership helped, but by the time he arrived, the Federal cavalry had already turned on their pursuers and the situation had become reversed.

While the fighting was going on, Charlie saw Custer "the Dandy," whose uniform and accoutrements were always bright and shining, stand up in his stirrups at the edge of Cedar Creek, his long hair waving in the breeze and saber in air as he led his forces into and across the creek in pursuit of the now rapidly retreating Confederates. Back through the disordered and littered camp which the Federals had left so hastily in the morning, they now drove the Southerners, winning the battle and thoroughly discouraging Early from attempting to stop Sheridan's ruthless destruction of the Rebel Army's food supplies in the Valley.

In his blankets that night as he lay thinking about the fight, Charlie thought mostly of Rienzi, the General's fine horse. When Sheridan had come pounding in at Cedar Creek that morning, he had pulled up the foam-covered charger within a few feet of Charlie's company, waved his hat in the air and yelled to rally the men. "What a horse!" thought Charlie as he lay remembering the thrill he had felt on seeing the magnificent animal in the heat of battle.

Coal black except for three white feet, Rienzi stood 16 hands high. He was a purebred Morgan, nervous and high tempered, but gentle and affectionate, and he loved attention. His endurance was amazing. Though badly wounded in one battle, he had recovered and was as full of courage and energy as ever. Sheridan bragged that no matter what the test to which he put him, Rienzi was never overcome by fatigue and was always more than ready and willing to respond to anything he was asked to do.

Rienzi had been presented to Sheridan by Captain Archibald P. Campbell of the Second Michigan Cavalry, who had become a close friend of Charlie's father. Campbell did not like to ride Rienzi, but he was very fond of him and frequently visited Sheridan's headquarters just to see the horse and pet him. Charlie had often gone along on these visits, and occasionally went alone. He had always loved horses and was especially drawn to Rienzi. One day as he stood looking at the beautiful animal, he made up his mind that if he ever got back to farming again, he would have at least one Morgan horse and a good buggy, so that when he had to go somewhere it would be with something besides an old farm plug!

Sheridan was so proud of Rienzi that he liked to have him admired by others, and Charlie had an opportunity to get acquainted with the General through their mutual interest in his horse. Charlie's visits to Rienzi had also given him an opportunity to make friends with John Ashley, the regimental farrier whose special duty it was to take care of Sheridan's horse. Anyone who was fond of Rienzi immediately became John's friend for life.

After the Shenandoah Valley campaign, Sheridan's cavalry helped Grant and Meade in their campaign to take Petersburg and Richmond. Also, during that summer of '64, Sheridan, acting under Grant's orders, began his part of a gigantic squeeze with his march into Georgia and then northward, catching the Confederates between the Union Army of the West and the Army of the Potomac. On May 4, the same day on which Grant had advanced into the Wilderness, Sherman moved against Joseph E. Jackson, who was entrenched in the hills of Dalton, Georgia, with an army of 100,000 men; and then, after a series of battles, laying waste the country as he advanced, Sherman finally took Atlanta, the great manufacturing center of the South, on September 1. From there Sherman began his march to the East and then northward, finally joining Grant at Richmond early in 1865.

Riding almost constantly with the cavalry to destroy railroads and intercept supplies for the Confederates in and around Richmond, Charlie had no opportunity to visit Jennie, but always there was time to think and to long for her. Like the other men, he lived on hope that the war would soon be over.

And there were signs that this hope was justified. No matter how brave the veteran Confederate Army was, no matter how skilful Lee and his generals, there were limits to what human beings could take, and the Confederates were fast approaching those limits. The soldiers were almost starving, their uniforms were in rags, many of them were barefoot. Hundreds were sick. Lee knew that the end was approaching.

On the fourth of March, thousands of soldiers and the millions on the home front read Lincoln's second inaugural address. It was not pleasing to those who hated with bitter intensity the South and all of its works, but to the soldiers who had actually done the fighting, to George and Charlie Wilson and to Ann and Nancy, Lincoln's words struck a responsive chord in their hearts when they read:

"Fondly do we hope, fervently do we pray that the mighty scourge of war may speedily pass away. With malice toward none, with charity for all, with firmness in the right as God gives us to see the right, let us press on to finish the work we are in, to bind up the nation's wounds, to care for him who shall have borne the battle and for his widow and orphan, to do all which may achieve and cherish a just and lasting peace among ourselves and with all nations."

Yes, there were many who knew and appreciated the wisdom and the charity of those words and the great man who uttered them.

That inaugural address was given on March 4, 1865. On April 2, Grant and Meade assaulted Petersburg and captured it, forcing Lee to abandon both Petersburg and Richmond. Charlie never forgot the awesome spectacle of a city on fire when he entered the Southern capital with the Union forces, to find that the retreating Confederates had tried to burn their own city. The first job of the Union troops was to save it from destruction. Seven days later, on April 9, General Robert E. Lee surrendered his Army to Grant at a house owned by a man named McLean at Appomattox Court House. The ceremonies were simple and soon over. Lee was told that his forces must lay down their arms and pledge themselves to obey the laws of the United States. Grant allowed the men to keep their personal property and their horses "to work their little farms."

When the terms were signed, the proud Lee stood erect, his face drawn with suffering, and said:

"General Grant, I have one request. My men are starving—"

Without waiting for him to finish, Grant said:

"Sir, rations will be provided immediately"—and they were.

As the news spread and reached the waiting armies, a great cheer was started by the Federals, only to die out in complete silence almost before it was born. There was something infinitely sad about the end of such a conflict and the defeat of men who had fought so valiantly for a lost cause, a sadness that was sensed and felt even by the soldiers who had won.

CHAPTER XXXV

To Nancy and all the other mothers and wives, and to the soldiers themselves, almost the hardest part of the whole war was what seemed to them the unnecessary delay, after Lee's surrender, in mustering the men out of the Army so that they could go home again. Letters to Nancy from George and Charlie told of forced hard marches from Richmond to Arlington, near Washington, and then, after all the hurry, of sitting down to wait a long time to be released. With discipline relaxed, there were constant brawls among the men, particularly between the soldiers of the Army of the West and those in the Army of the Potomac. Each claimed all credit for winning the war, and they were willing to fight to prove their point.

One relief from the long wait was the Grand Review of all the Union forces on Pennsylvania Avenue in Washington. Proudly George Wilson led his band ahead of his brigade, proudly Charlie Wilson rode in that great parade, with thousands looking on and cheering. Even Rienzi and the other prancing, dancing horses seemed to know that the war was over. Only four years before, most of those marching men had been, like Charlie Wilson, just beardless boys, mostly farm boys. Now, after four years of the shouting and tumult of war, they had left boyhood far behind. They were veterans, many of them skin poor, eyes sunken, their tanned and weatherbeaten faces almost black from constant exposure to the southern sun and wind. But they were hard as nails, and if they remembered their comrades who no longer marched or rode with them, if any were saddened because their great President was not there to greet them, it did not show in their jaunty, springy, step or their erect soldierly bearing. The past was gone beyond recall, the war was won, and they had helped to win it. The most important thing now was that they were going home.

It was a great moment for Charlie, his greatest next to his wedding to Jennie, and the climax of all that had gone before. The glory was dimmed only by the fact that his Jennie was not there, and would not have been happy if she had been.

Soon after the Grand Review, both George and Charlie received their honorable discharges. Long before, Charlie had discussed plans with Jennie and her grandfather and they had all agreed that with the bitter feeling existing in Virginia it would be unwise and unsafe for Charlie to return there for some time after the war was over. So she met him in Washington and, with George Wilson, they rode the trains loaded with the whooping, noisy Union veterans back to Owego, and from there took the stage for Jenkstown.

Great was the rejoicing in the Wilson home when they arrived. As they all sat down to supper that night, Nancy's heart would have overflowed with joy and thankfulness, had it not been for Mark's vacant chair. The war was over at last, but Mark, her firstborn, was dead and would never come home again.

* * *

It was May, 1865. The roar of musket and cannon had ceased, and men had set about to reconstruct a nation almost destroyed. But in the factories, and particularly on the farms to which the soldiers returned, there seemed to have been little change, except for the missing faces. The sun shone, the wind blew, the rains fell, and the crops grew just as they always had. Men and women went about the accustomed ways of peace and, except for the political strife and the problems of reconstruction, particularly in the South, everything seemed to go on much the same as before the war.

But did it? Can men used to the unnatural excitement, the battle lust, the roar of musketry and cannon in a hundred fights, ever be the same men? Would they on a May morning raise their heads, maybe, to listen in imagination to the menacing rattle of musketry, the dull boom of cannon way off yonder over the horizon? Can men with the experiences of ten lifetimes packed into four years ever really settle down to the monotonous grind of everyday life? Phil Sheridan, George Custer and thousands of the veterans from both North and South answered that question in the negative. They never returned to their homes at all, or only for a short stay after the war. Instead, they re-enlisted in the Army to free the Western trails of Indians and to open the way for thousands of emigrants and their families to the settlements of the great West.

But some of the soldiers had had enough, many because they liked farming better than soldiering or pioneering. So there were plenty who returned to old Tioga County and to all the other northern and southern counties to produce the food needed by the fastest growing nation the world had ever seen.

On a bright summer morning in 1865 Ann Bain, who had been Ann Wilson, and before that Ann Clinton, stood looking from her kitchen window across the fields that led to a bend in the road toward Jenkstown. Ann often stood in that window watching the road, though why she could not have said; she didn't even realize that she had developed the habit. This morning as she stared at the road, she saw a man come around the bend of the road and into view. He was walking very slowly and with a limp. Something familiar about that solitary figure set Ann's heart to pounding. Who could it be? Surely someone she had known.

Then, suddenly, as he drew nearer, she knew. Even though the man seemed almost old, with unkempt hair, long beard and limping, slow footsteps, she knew that it was Mark. As recognition became a certainty, she pressed a hand to her heart and sank almost fainting to a chair, but never taking her eyes off that slow-moving figure which kept coming toward her.

As she watched, he crossed the yard, climbed the porch steps, and slowly, so slowly, opened the door without knocking, and called in a deep, hollow voice:

"Ann, my Ann! Where are you?"

The girl came slowly to her feet to face him, bewildered, horrified.

"But you're dead," she cried. "You're dead!"

He grinned wryly:

"No, I'm not, dear. Almost, I admit, but not quite."

Opening his arms he stepped toward her, but she threw

up her hands, palms out, and as he advanced she moved backwards.

"No, oh no!" she cried, in anguish.

He stopped.

"Don't you know me, Ann? It's Mark, your husband. What's the matter?" he asked.

"I— I thought you were dead!"

"But I'm not," he insisted. "I'm alive. I'm here."

"Where have you been?" she gasped. "You were reported dead. A memorial service was held here for you."

"I was wounded and captured, and I've been in Andersonville, where men died like flies. But I didn't die." He paused. "They couldn't kill me because I had you to come back to."

"We had no word. All these years we had no word," she moaned.

Not understanding but still patient, he said:

"There was no way of getting word to you. You have no idea of the horrors at Andersonville. No one could write, no one received any mail. We lived in holes in the ground, like hogs. But I'm here, Ann darling. I'm here. I know I look terrible, but I'll get over that."

Sympathy flooded her heart:

"Of course, you'll get over it! But what am I to do? What am I to do?"

Bewildered in turn, he said:

"Do? Why, our troubles are over, Ann, dear. I'm home again. Nothing else counts."

Again he started toward her and again she put up her hands to ward him off. Then she took him by the arm, even in her mental stress thinking how poor that arm was, nothing but skin and bone. She led him to a chair, and seated herself in one on the other side of the table, saying:

"Mark, let me explain. Listen, and tell me what to do."

More bewildered every minute, he sat staring at her with his deep-sunken eyes.

"What's happened? Tell me?"

"We had official notice from the Adjutant-General's office that you had been killed in action. Funeral services were preached here in Jenkstown for you. I thought you were dead, Mark; I thought you were dead, and I wished I was dead, too."

"But I'm not dead." He grinned a little. "Why so serious? I'm here, and we're together again."

She shook her head.

"How can I ever tell you, Mark? Pray God that you will understand. A long time after the memorial services, Mother and I were having a difficult time to get along. I couldn't continue to work the farm, and Mother was worried and fretting. Besides, I thought you were dead and nothing else mattered. I cared about nothing in the world. So—" she hesitated—"to help Mother keep her home, to have a home for father when he returned—" a sob choked her—"he's dead, you know, killed at Cold Harbor."

When she could control herself, she continued, speaking slowly and painfully:

"So—I married again!"

The man across the table from her looked at her with incredulous eyes.

"Married again? My God! You married again, Ann! Who? Who was it?"

Then he answered his own question:

"Henry Bain!"

She nodded silently.

"And I didn't know! I was so eager to get home to you that I stopped to talk to no one! I didn't even go home!" He swallowed. "Home? Home? I haven't any home."

Slowly he pulled himself to his feet, turned to take a long look at the crushed girl now weeping with her head on her arms on the table, then slowly limped out of the door and down the steps and up the road to the Wilson farm.

CHAPTER XXXVI

To NANCY the coming of Mark was almost as much of a shock as it would have been had he actually risen from the dead. He looked so ill and changed that the first thing she did was to get his clothes off and put him to bed. Her questions as to what had happened to him were answered almost in monosyllables, or not at all. Without asking, she knew that he had seen Ann.

From then on Nancy kept him perfectly quiet, but he wouldn't eat, and she knew that he didn't sleep. Finally she had Dr. Barr come to see him, and when the doctor came down from the upstairs bedroom after giving Mark a careful examination, his face was very serious.

"This young man has had an experience that few survive," he said, gravely. "On top of that, we know without discussing the matter what a shock he had in learning that his wife had remarried. I want to be honest with you. His very reason is in danger. I have given him something to make him sleep, and I'll come again tomorrow. Keep him quiet."

Henry Bain returned to the Clinton homestead that evening to learn from Ann's lips of Mark's return. He had stopped at the post office on his way home and wondered at the quick cessation of conversation when he had entered the store and tne peculiar looks he had received. But he was used to his unpopularity now and didn't think much about it, although he had hoped that the situation was improving. When Ann told him the news, he only said:

"We can fix this up. You can get a divorce from Wilson."

Mrs. Clinton, who was listening to the conversation, nodded her head.

"Yes, that's the thing to do!" she cried.

Ann turned to look at her.

"Mother," she said, coolly, "from now on you keep out

of this. I don't know how we can settle this, but whatever the decision I propose to make it myself."

With an injured air, Mrs. Clinton rose and slowly went out of the room. When she had gone, Henry continued:

"I'll move out for a while, and you can get the divorce. Surely you want nothing more to do with this ne'er-do-well who has been alive all this time and never let you have a word from him!"

Ann sat for a long moment looking steadily at him, and then she said:

"Henry, I'm neither wise nor good. If I had been good, I never would have married you without love. And it's no excuse that I did it because I thought Mark was dead and because I thought it would make my mother and father happier. I told you when I married you—God forgive me— that I didn't love you. I've tried as hard as I could to be a good wife. I thought that maybe in time we could at least live together in peace with some contentment."

She paused for a moment, and then, sitting straight in her chair and pointing her finger at him, she said, passionately:

"But no man and woman can live together in the intimacy of marriage without knowing full well the real character of the other, and I know you, Henry Bain! I'm not talking about faults such as we all have. I'm talking about the principles that you don't have, never have had, and never will have. I've tried to see some sincerity in your apparent change of heart in the past year, but I know there's no real change. You made believe that you favored the Union cause, and that you were no longer a Copperhead only because you were just plain scared. You're a coward! I've known this in my heart for a long, long time, but I was your wife, and my idea of marriage is to keep the faith even if the other fellow doesn't. Now I no longer have to. I have no hope in the world that Mark Wilson, the man whose memory I revered, the man I loved and still love, will ever look at me again, and for that I cannot blame him; but at least I don't have to go on living with you."

Jumping to his feet, Bain said, hotly:

"You've had *your* little say. Now you listen to *me*! I married you chiefly to give me some standing in this part of the county—although little good that did me. I've taken this poor old rocky farm, put stock on it, fertilized and seeded it, made something of it, and given you and your mother a home. And this is the thanks I get!

"But I'll tell you one thing, young lady. No one gets very far ahead of Henry Bain! Need I remind you that when I married you I held the mortgage on this farm? And you haven't paid a cent on the mortgage or the interest since. Don't look for any generosity from me so far as this property is concerned. You're not going to be able to turn around and give it to Wilson, who no doubt was glad to save his hide in a Confederate prison in order to keep out of the battles."

"That will be enough, Henry," Ann said, calmly. "If I had followed Mark Wilson's advice in the first place and let you take this farm, how much better off we all would have been than we are now. You're so wrong in your whole attitude toward people and toward life that I actually feel sorry for you. You'll never be a happy man. Mother and I will move out of here just as soon as we can find another place to go to. And now, Henry, I'll say goodnight and goodby."

In the way that gossip always gets around, everybody in the neighborhood soon knew that Ann had separated from Henry Bain the very day that Mark Wilson came back. But it was not until Ann learned that Mark was unconscious and so ill that he would not know her that she dared go over to the Wilson house to find out from Nancy exactly how he was, and to greet George and Charlie and meet Charlie's wife, the slender, lovable girl from Virginia.

Mark's condition had grown rapidly worse, and when Nancy, with tears in her eyes, told Ann that he wavered between life and death, Ann asked her, humbly:

"Nancy, could I see him? He won't know me, and I'll be very quiet so it won't hurt him."

"Of course, my dear," said Nancy, quickly. "Come with me."

They went up to the little bedroom that had been shared by the three boys before the war. It was hot up there, but the doctor had advised against moving Mark to the downstairs bedroom at this critical period of his illness. The grief-stricken girl stood looking down on the skeleton-like form outlined under the single sheet on the bed, and then, moved by an irresistable impulse, she suddenly went over and knelt on the floor, taking the wasted hand in both of hers. For a moment the muttering, twisting and turning ceased, and then started again.

Nancy went downstairs and left them alone. How long Ann knelt there she never knew, but when Nancy came upstairs again Ann had to be helped to her feet and into a chair until the circulation returned to her legs. Then she and Nancy tiptoed out of the room and down the stairs.

"You're going to need help, Nancy," Ann said. "As long as he's unconscious and doesn't know me, do you think I could stay?"

Too emotional to trust her voice, Nancy nodded.

Then followed days and nights with Ann almost constantly at Mark's bedside, sleeping little and eating only because she had to keep up her strength. When she was with Mark, he seemed to be easier and rested more quietly, but still his hands moved restlessly across the sheet and he muttered frequently, with only a word now and then that Ann could understand. In his delirium he always seemed to be struggling to get somewhere—probably out of prison, Ann thought, and home again. Two or three times he called her name, startling her so much that she thought he had returned to sanity.

But gradually after a time Mark became quiet, especially under the touch of her hands. The doctor was more hopeful. The crisis was passing. He was sure now that Mark would get well in spite of his greatly weakened resistance.

Finally, one afternoon as Ann sat in a chair at his bedside and gently stroked his forehead, Mark opened his eyes and looked directly into her face. She couldn't restrain a little cry, for she could see that he was completely conscious. At first he looked puzzled as if he didn't know where he was, or why, and she said, softly:

"Mark, darling!"

Suddenly he remembered everything, and after looking attentively at her for a moment, he said nothing and slowly turned his face to the wall. His rejection of her was like a knife stab in Ann's heart. Rising quickly, she went out of the room to tell Nancy that Mark had regained consciousness and that she had better go to him. Then the girl went back

down the road to her own home, feeling more alone and
forsaken and heartbroken than she had ever felt before in
her life.

During the next few days Ann continued to visit Nancy
to inquire about Mark, but she did not go upstairs again.
Nancy, understanding, did not urge her, and Mark did not
ask for her.

Mark's convalescence was painfully slow, and the first
time he was allowed to come downstairs, the family celebrated in their own special way. On the back stoop of the
Wilson farmhouse was a big farm bell which Nancy had used
for years to call the men from the field to their meals or
when they were needed for some farm emergency. But the
bell also played another important part in the lives of the
Wilsons, for it was their custom to ring it long and loud
when some big and happy event occurred in the family. The
bell had been rung when the men had come home on furlough
from the war. Nancy had rung it vigorously the day Tom
got out of bed after his accident in the woods, and when
George and Charlie and his bride had returned from the
wars it was rung as never before. It had not been rung when
Mark came home because he was so sick, but one day late
in that summer of 1865, Mark was helped downstairs for the
first time, almost carried by his father and brothers, and deposited with quilts wrapped around him in the big rocker by
the pleasant kitchen window. That was indeed an event to
be celebrated, and celebrated it was by a loud and prolonged
ringing of the old farm bell.

But the enthusiasm of the family soon passed, because
their own happiness found no response in Mark's sad eyes
and grave face. In the days that followed, he sat for long
hours gazing out across the farm fields, saying nothing. They
all knew what was the matter, and one day when Nancy
had stood it as long as she could, she went to Jenkstown to
talk it over with Timothy Belden.

"Mark isn't doing as well as he should," she told the old
minister. "We have him downstairs now, but he takes little
interest in his vittles, and he's still not sleeping well. We're
all worried. Of course, you know why he doesn't improve.
He is very much in love with his wife, and he can't reconcile
himself to the situation. He's eating his heart out because

he thinks Ann was disloyal in marrying a man whom he detested."

"Have you tried to talk to him?"

"No," she said, "I never could, and he wouldn't listen. I thought maybe you could."

For a long time the old man sat toying with a heavy watch chain that reached from one vest pocket to the other. Then he spoke:

"One has to live such a long time before we know very much—and I'm not sure how much we know even then," he added, whimsically.

Nancy looked a little puzzled.

"You're old enough, Nancy, to know what I mean. It's the heart and the spirit that count, not the body. It's hard for a young man to understand that. What a person does under the awful stress of circumstances doesn't really matter. It is easier for an older man to understand that what does matter is what the girl is at heart and how she feels now, not how she felt or what she did a year ago.

"You're an understanding woman, Nancy. You and I know the terrible strain that Ann went through. We know and understand why she yielded to Bain's importunities and married him. Like you, I've known her ever since she was born, and no finer person has ever lived in this neighborhood. I believe you when you say that her love for Mark has never changed and is even finer today after the fire she has been through than ever before. Our problem, of course, is to get our tolerance and understanding of the facts and the true situation across to Mark."

He fell silent again for a time, and then said:

"I don't know how much good it will do, but I'll talk with Mark."

Nancy stood up, her face softened with affection for the old minister.

"I don't know what the world would do without men like you," she said as she went out.

A few days later the Pastor's buggy stopped at the Wilson door, and the old minister persuaded Mark to take a ride with him. As soon as they were on their way, the minister came directly to the point:

"Perhaps you have guessed, Mark, why I asked you to ride with me today?"

"If it's about Ann," Mark answered, "then I'd rather not talk about it even with you."

"All right," Mr. Belden agreed, "you just keep still for a little while and let me talk. I think I have the right to talk to you, not as your pastor, not as the man who married you to Ann, but as a friend who has known you and Ann and all of your people a long lifetime. There is much at stake, Mark, and, frankly, even if you don't want to consider your own happiness, you do have some obligation to consider the happiness of others."

"Some of them don't seem to have had much consideration for my happiness," said Mark, bitterly.

"Well, that's just what I want to talk with you about. I think if you thoroughly understood all that has been involved, you might feel differently. Anyway, you owe it to yourself and to the rest to face the facts. Then, of course, the final decision must be yours.

"I know the circumstances under which you left for the war the last time," the pastor went on. "Not from Ann, but from the other best friend you have in the world, your mother. And, again very frankly, Mark, you weren't without fault in the cavalier way you left your young bride!"

"I know that!" Mark answered. "And I apologized for it."

"There are some things," the old man said gravely, "that cannot exactly be washed out by a few words of apology. This came pretty close to being one of them."

They rode in silence for a few minutes, then Mr. Belden went on:

"I've married a good many couples, Mark, and it's the privilege of a minister to come close to many lives. I have never known a girl to be any more in love than Ann was— and is, with you."

Mark stirred impatiently on the buggy seat, but said nothing.

The minister slowed the horse down to a walk and after a moment continued:

"Ann haunted the post office to get your letters, and she worked hard and long on her farm against the day of your return. The farm was one of the chief troubles."

"Yes, I know."

"I'm pretty sure you are feeling that Ann lacks stability and acted irresponsibly, but it's a curious fact that all the trouble resulted because she was too responsible. She wanted to keep the farm for her father and mother and to have something of her own when you came back."

Mark made no remark, and the old man gently slapped a line against the horse's hip to drive off a big horse fly.

"Then," continued Mr. Belden, "after a long time of agonizing waiting and watching, the blow fell, and Ann and the rest of us got the report that you had been killed. Perhaps if you *had* been killed, your spirit would have understood what that blow meant to your wife. Perhaps we may say that she lacked judgment in marrying Henry Bain, for some of us have long known that he is a scoundrel."

Mark started to speak, but the minister laid a restraining hand on his arm:

"Just listen, please, and try to understand. Here was a girl, so shocked that she almost lost her reason. She became utterly indifferent. Nothing really mattered. In all kindliness, let us say as little as possible about her mother. To be as charitable as possible, let us say that Mrs. Clinton has always had a hard life and is a worrier. So perhaps it was natural, with you reported dead, for her to seek security for her husband, herself and her daughter by influencing Ann to marry Bain.

"On his part, clever scoundrel that he is, Bain seemingly became everything that a friend should be, always around, always apparently kind."

Again Mark stirred impatiently.

"If you don't mind," he said, "let us leave him out of it."

"But I do mind," insisted the minister. "It's impossible to leave him out. You've got to understand. Let's put it this way. You don't care much what happens to yourself right now, do you? Well, that's exactly the way Ann felt. The very intensity of her love for you made life so hopeless that nothing mattered. So when Bain offered to marry her, in her mistaken judgment she thought how good and kind he had been during her grief and that it would be a solution to the problem of her mother and father. Bear in mind all of the time, Mark, that all of us thought you were dead and long since gone.

"As time went on, Ann realized her mistake. She found out—and her mother, too—what Bain was really like. But that girl of yours, my boy, has character. When she gives a promise, she expects to keep it. And she was determined to be a good wife even if he wasn't a good husband."

The old voice ceased. The silence became oppressive, broken only by the sound of the rolling buggy wheels and the footsteps of the horse. But Mr. Belden had not finished.

"When you came back, what happened?" he continued. "That very night Ann sent Henry Bain packing, tremendously relieved that all her obligations to him were completely cancelled, even though she realized that her relations with you might never be resumed. Then came your sickness. She took care of you night and day until you came back to consciousness and rejected her. That sort of love, my boy, is the most precious thing in God's world, too precious to be cast aside for foolish pride, jealousy, or anything else."

Turning to look at Mark, the minister was pleased to see tears rolling down the boy's face. Finally Mark said, brokenly:

"How can I go back to her thinking all the time that she, my own bride, lived with another man?"

The minister slipped an arm across the thin shoulders.

"Mark," he said, "I understand how you feel. Any man would have some of the same feeling at your age. But it really doesn't matter. Ann never loved anybody but you. When you and she stood before me in our church—it seems so long ago, but it really isn't long—she gave herself to you spiritually as well as physically, and I say to you truly, as your friend, as one man to another, as an old man speaking with some experience of human nature, that that kind of love never changes. She was your wife then, she was your wife even while you were away, and, my boy, she is your wife now."

* * *

That evening Ann heard an unsteady step on the stoop. Her heart told her who it was, and when she rushed to open the door, she found Mark standing before her. She stepped back a little, uncertain, while he came in and stood with his hands gripping the back of a chair until his knuckles showed white.

"Ann," he said, hoarsely, "a long time ago I went away from you without even saying goodby. But now I've come home to you again."

He swallowed, and added:

"If you'll have me, dearest."

Ann reached for him, pushing the chair out of the way, and drawing him to her breast and holding him tight, she whispered:

"Oh, my darling, thank God we are *both* home at last!"

FINIS

LaVergne, TN USA
04 March 2011
218933LV00001B/5/P